# NATURAL BORN ANGEL

# NATURAL BORN ANGEL

## AN IMMORTAL CITY NOVEL

## SCOTT SPEER

An Imprint of Penguin Group (USA) Inc.

Published by the Penguin Group
Penguin Group (USA) Inc., 375 Hudson Street, New York, New York 10014, USA
Penguin Group (Canada), 90 Eglinton Avenue East, Suite 700, Toronto, Ontario M4P 2Y3,
Canada (a division of Pearson Penguin Canada Inc.)
Penguin Books Ltd, 80 Strand, London WC2R 0RL, England
Penguin Ireland, 25 St Stephen's Green, Dublin 2, Ireland (a division of Penguin Books Ltd)
Penguin Group (Australia), 707 Collins St., Melbourne, Victoria 3008, Australia
(a division of Pearson Australia Group Pty Ltd)
Penguin Books India Pvt Ltd, 11 Community Centre, Panchsheel Park,
New Delhi–110 017, India
Penguin Group (NZ), 67 Apollo Drive, Rosedale, Auckland 0632, New Zealand
(a division of Pearson New Zealand Ltd)
Penguin Books, Rosebank Office Park, 181 Jan Smuts Avenue, Parktown North 2193,
South Africa
Penguin China, B7 Jiaming Center, 27 East Third Ring Road North, Chaoyang District,
Beijing 100020, China

Penguin Books Ltd, Registered Offices: 80 Strand, London WC2R 0RL, England

ISBN: 978-1-59514-513-0

Published simultaneously in Canada

Library of Congress Cataloging-in-Publication Data is available

Printed in the United States of America

10 9 8 7 6 5 4 3 2 1

This is a work of fiction. Names, characters, places, and incidents either are the product of
the author's imagination or are used fictitiously, and any resemblance to actual persons, living
or dead, businesses, companies, events, or locales is entirely coincidental.

*To my hero, my dad.*

# CHAPTER ONE

The massive blood-red disk of the sun sank into the ocean just ahead of the aircraft carrier USS *Abraham Lincoln*. The sky seemed to catch fire and burn as the sun set along the horizon; it appeared almost close enough to touch.

The tremendous nuclear-powered navy vessel was an impressive sight as it powered its way through the darkening waves deep in the middle of the Pacific. As the sun continued setting, the ship's formidable form was silhouetted against the blazing sky. On the flight deck, navy personnel wearing large white earmuffs scrambled. A pilot was maneuvering a fighter aircraft on the thick steel surface, setting it into the football-field-length, steam-powered catapult that would hurl the jet off the carrier's short runway.

The fading light radiated off the silver skin of the supersonic fighter jet, an F/A-18E Super Hornet. Inside, First Lieutenant Troy "Showtime" Jenkins began the normal course of checking his instruments and ensuring his rudder and ventral flaps were operational. Everything seemed good to go.

Behind the plane, the crew lifted the wide jet blast deflector. As soon as he saw it was safe, Lieutenant Jenkins turned on the powerful jet engine. The roar was incredible as it fired to life. Steam rose off the flight deck as the crew made last-second preparations for liftoff.

The voice in his radio crackled: *"Raider one-one-two, this is Giant Killer. You are cleared for takeoff. Ready when you are, Showtime."*

"Roger, Giant Killer, this is Raider one-one-two. Looks like a beautiful night for a Sunday drive," Troy said, looking out on the sunset. The jet engine whined as it reached full power, ready to thrust at the right moment.

Giving a thumbs-up to the catapult operators on the flight deck, the lieutenant used one hand to clutch the handle in front of him. His hands ached with the tight grip. He said a quick prayer.

The steam catapult activated like an enormous gun. The pressure was unbelievable as it slung the fighter jet forward at 165 miles per hour.

One moment, the F-18 was sitting on the flight deck. The next, Lieutenant Jenkins and the jet were flying 165 miles per hour above the dark, cresting waves of the Pacific. *Just clocking in for another boring day at work*, Lieutenant Jenkins thought to himself with a smile as the fighter screamed along the ocean.

"Giant Killer, I am outbound at one-one-four SE, ascending to one-zero ten thousand feet. Clear skies as far as I can see, over."

*"Copy Raider one-one-two, that's affirmative. Proceed to one-zero ten thousand."*

Pulling back the center stick, the pilot began making his climb toward the clouds. Suddenly a strange blip appeared on his green heads-up display screen in front of him. Something very low. And then, just as suddenly, it disappeared.

"Giant Killer, did you just see that on radar?" Lieutenant Jenkins asked.

*"Affirmative, we are checking if there are any bogies in the area."*

The pilot's concentrated gaze focused on the screen. Nothing. For a moment there was a small blip again. But then it vanished.

*"Showtime, we're showing no activity in this area, and the bogey has disappeared. Probably just a fluke. Proceed to one-zero ten thousand feet, over."*

Lieutenant Jenkins looked out over the endless horizon, where whatever he saw on the radar had been.

"Negative, Giant Killer," the pilot said. "I'm going in for visual."

Tilting the stick forward and to the left, he steered the jet closer to the ocean again, screaming toward the setting sun. The exhaust on the back of the fighter jet burned the same fiery orange as the horizon.

*"Showtime, proceed with your original flight plan. Raider one-one-two, do you copy?"*

"Roger, getting visual on unidentified bogey." Lieutenant Jenkins smiled—what were they going to do, fire him? He was one of the only guys around who knew how to do this. Well, do it this well, at least.

The lieutenant tried not to listen to the series of curses from the control tower coming over his radio.

Within moments he was nearing the position of the unidentified object on the radar. But he still didn't have visual contact. He craned his neck around, looking through the glass as the fleeting light darkened the sky. He saw nothing, not a trace.

"Where are you? Where'd you go?" Jenkins asked the unknown object.

Dropping down even further, the nimble jet roared to just barely above the rolling, deep Pacific waves. The lieutenant scanned all around. Still, he saw nothing.

Suddenly, his radar beeped. It was right in front of him. But he couldn't see it.

"Giant Killer, unidentified bogey at my twelve, within range but I do not see anything. Pretty spooky, over." There was a taste of fear in the pilot's voice this time.

"Where the hell are you?" the pilot said aloud.

*"Showtime, get out of there now. That is a direct order!"*

The pilot's eyes grew in terror and shock. He saw it: just ahead of him, emerging from the waves, was some sort of enormous, terrible, black, smoking object. It seemed to be on fire. And he was heading straight for it.

*"Showtime, you're on a vector for collision. Take evasive maneuvers. Now, now!"*

The cockpit erupted in alarms as all of the F-18's instruments suddenly began failing. With all his strength, Jenkins pulled on the stick to pull the jet up, but he was helpless: it wouldn't respond. There was no changing course. He was being drawn in.

With supreme terror, the pilot saw the giant, flaming *thing* turn toward him as it surged further up from the roiling waves. He saw its eyes. Red and unblinking.

"Dear God! MAYDAY! MAYDAY! MAYDAY!"

The giant hand of the thing reached toward the screaming F-18 and pulled the jet down to the ocean, with Lieutenant Jenkins in it, as easy as a child playing with a toy. The aircraft crumpled under the impact. Instantly igniting, the jet fuel turned the fighter into a tumbling mass of fire, human body parts, and shrapnel.

*"Raider one-one-two, do you copy? Raider one-one-two, do you copy? Jesus, Showtime, answer!"* they called from the tower. But Lieutenant Jenkins could not hear them. There was no more Lieutenant Jenkins.

The burning flotsam of the shattered and twisted remains of the jet floated atop the waves, pouring black smoke into the darkening sky.

Satisfied, the terrible thing slowly submerged again beneath the murky waves, as if it had never even been there. Slipping underwater, it somehow continued flaming and roiling hot smoke even as it dove. The fiery creature flared with menace as it slowly drifted ever deeper undersea, a bonfire burning into the ocean depths.

# CHAPTER TWO

**M**addy woke with a start, her eyelids popping open, her breath coming quick and shallow. She pushed herself up in bed and sat there gasping, letting the terror of the horrific nightmare slowly bleed out of her. A cold sheen of sickly sweat clung to her skin. *Just a dream, Maddy*, she told herself. *It was just a dream.* Lifting her head, she looked out the window. There it was, like a ghost in the misty half-light—the Angel City sign. It loomed huge and silent on the hill, perfectly framed by Maddy's bedroom window. She sighed. The final remnants of the dream faded to nothing, replaced by the reality that she was still living in Los Angeles. Still stuck in the Immortal City.

She looked out the window at the brilliant Southern California morning. The grass on the hill beyond her bedroom window was brown and dry from the hot summer, and the towering, fifty-foot letters of the Angel City sign gleamed in the sunlight above it. She let her eyes drift from the window to the walls of her bedroom, which seemed strangely naked, no longer covered with childhood posters and mementos of her youth, and then to her nearly empty closet, which had a few lonely wire hangers in it.

The nightmare had plagued Maddy more than a few times now. And it was always the same: Jackson Godspeed came into her uncle's diner, just as he did the first time they met, except in the dream he wore a casual T-shirt and faded blue jeans. The truth was, it didn't matter what he wore. He was the world's most famous Guardian Angel, and he had the perpetual look of a model who had just stepped out of a fashion magazine or off a billboard. He came in, looked at her with his pale blue eyes, and told her she was going to train to be a Guardian. Just like he had done in real life almost nine months before.

And in the dream she always hesitated.

"I . . . I don't know what to say, Jacks," she said to him. "I guess I need time to think about it."

"Maddy," he said, looking at her and yet seeing right through her, his eyes distant in a way she'd never witnessed when she was awake. "You don't have a choice. You don't seem to understand. You're already changing."

In the dream, she opened her mouth to speak, but the words died on her lips as a sharp pain erupted in her back. The muscles of her back contracted violently, twisting into excruciating knots. Maddy staggered backward across the dining room. Her hand flew out to catch herself but managed only to knock over a nearby table, sending cups and dirty plates shattering to the floor.

Jacks hadn't moved.

She convulsed again, and all at once she realized it was more than a muscle spasm in her back. Much more. Something was *moving* back there. Something inside her was alive. The skin on her back stretched tight, pulled taught like a drum. She choked back a wave of nausea as she felt the thing—no, *things*—twist inside her again, pushing eagerly against her, trying desperately to get out.

Then she heard it.

It started like the sound of tearing construction paper, followed by a tremendous *POP*. It was the sound of her skin splitting along her spine. There was the feeling of something exploding out of her back, and then with a sudden *whoosh* of air, she was pushed hard against the floor.

She had wings.

They protruded out of her back, jutting up through her shredded waitress uniform and the mangled remains of her back. She lifted her head to look at her reflection in the plate glass window. Her wings looked nothing like Jacks's wings, nothing like the beautiful, luminescent wings of the Guardians. Maddy's wings were horrific. Deformed and sickly, they thrashed uncontrollably on her back like the ill-formed appendages of something that was never meant to be.

*The wings of a monster.*

Recalling the nightmare again, Maddy shuddered and ran her hands across her back. She put one foot, then her second foot on the floor next to the bed. Pulling up the T-shirt she slept in, she quickly spun and looked at her back in the full-length mirror. She knew it had been a dream. But she wanted to make sure, nevertheless.

The wings of her nightmare were not present in the mirror. Instead, what looked to be two elegant tattoos remained on her back. These were her Immortal Marks, the mark of every Angel, indicating Maddy was not—or at least not entirely—human. They were different from Jacks's marks, or any of the other Angels', for that matter. Full-blooded Angels had marks that were elaborate and ornate. The marks that had begun forming on Maddy's back over the last several months were simpler and smaller than most, but they were also undeniable. They were a sure sign that the secrets she had learned about her past were true.

The doctors thought her Angelic traits were activating with the end of puberty, and that more changes could be on the way. By that, they meant the superhuman abilities of the Immortals, including, of course, *wings* and the ability to fly. Beyond that, she had no idea what might be lurking inside her, or how she might be changing. No one did.

Maddy sighed in relief and let the T-shirt drape back down to her waist. She wondered if the nightmares would start to taper off once she was out of Angel City. She looked at the corner of the room, where she had stacked a couple of small boxes, all ready to be taped up and sent to Northwestern University, where she was going to begin college in just a few days.

To the left of the boxes sat a suitcase. She'd packed it the night before. After cleaning and sorting through things, she was surprised by how much of her eighteen years could be condensed to a small, neat pile in a corner of her room.

She had already seen her best friend, Gwen Moore, off to school; Gwen was attending Arizona State and had left the week before. Things were changing quickly.

On the nightstand, Maddy's phone rang. She glanced at the caller ID and saw it was Jacks.

"Hey!" she said, answering.

"Hey," Jacks said on the other line. Even now, almost ten months after they'd first met, his voice still made her feel butterflies in her stomach. "What's my favorite college student up to?"

"Weelll, I just woke up," Maddy said. "And, technically, Jackson Godspeed, I'm not a student yet. Not until I register when I arrive on campus."

"Just a technicality," Jacks said, trying to remain lighthearted. Maddy knew it was hitting Jacks hard, her decision to pursue a degree halfway across the country.

"So . . . " Jacks said.

"So."

"Can I take you out for ice cream later? These days are precious. Pretty soon you'll be off in Illinois curing cancer and learning Chinese and reading philosophers and coming back smarter than everybody."

"*Jacks*, we'll see each other once a month, like planned," Maddy said. "And then summers I'll be back. As long as I can get good internships here in Angel City."

Below the surface of their conversation lay a complicated backstory. Ever since Jackson had walked into her uncle's diner and given her the Archangels' offer to become a Guardian, Maddy had known her decision was going to be one of the most difficult of her life.

Jacks had wanted her to stay in California and embrace the life of an Angel. Of course, it would probably be a dream come true for most people, to be offered the chance to become a rich and powerful Guardian Angel. But Maddy wasn't "most people," and the truth was that she had gotten into some very good schools, even getting a scholarship at her top choice, Northwestern. College had been a dream of hers ever since she could remember. Plus, if she chose to cultivate her Angelic side and explore her supernatural ability, who was to guarantee what she was capable of? Could she really save people's lives? Was there enough of her father in her?

Would she even ever get her wings?

Maddy's uncle Kevin, who had raised her from childhood, had been no aid at all in helping her decide. He stayed quiet, telling her she had to make her own decision. But she knew how he felt about Angels, whom he blamed for the death of his sister, Maddy's mom, and she could imagine what he would have chosen for her.

Maddy had waited until the final weeks of her senior year at Angel City High School (ACHS) before making her decision. But ultimately she chose to continue with her lifelong dream, her college plan. And move out of Angel City.

Which was a secret relief, as much as she was going to miss Jacks. The Angel lifestyle as she'd experienced it with Jacks was too much. The constant attention, the paparazzi camped out on the sidewalk outside her house, the never-ending hubbub wherever they went: Maddy had never asked for these things. Just by being around Jackson for nearly a year she'd gotten a good taste of what it might be like to be a Guardian.

But she and Jacks couldn't bear to break up, not when they'd gone through so much just to be together. They were going to try to do the long-distance thing and were both hopeful it could work out, though she knew Jackson was terribly disappointed she'd be leaving.

Jacks's voice continued on the phone: "You can't blame me for wanting to spend as much time as I can with you before you leave on Friday, anyway. So ice cream it is?"

"That sounds good," Maddy said, smiling. "As long as they have strawberry. Pick me up at three?"

"I have treatment until three thirty. But I can be there by four," Jacks responded.

"How are you feeling?" Maddy asked tentatively. "Is it . . . any better?"

"No," Jacks growled in sudden anger over the phone. "I had more tests yesterday. They're going to try a different procedure next month."

Jackson had almost been made mortal in a vicious attack, and his wings still hadn't recovered. Mark Godspeed, Jacks's stepfather, was paying for every treatment known to Angelkind; they'd reattached Jacks's severed wing using cutting-edge surgical technology, yet Jackson was still not making much—if any—progress toward flying again.

"Sorry for getting like this . . . I'm just frustrated is all," Jacks said.

"It's okay, Jacks. Anyone would be." Every day that passed without being able to assume Guardianship weighed on Jacks, Maddy knew. She felt a pang.

"See you at four?"

"Wouldn't miss it for the world."

Maddy put the phone down, sighing, sorry she had brought up his wings. She constantly tried to let Jackson know she loved him regardless of whether he was an acting Guardian or not. That love had deepened over the past year as she had gotten to know Jackson more and more, spending more time with him, sharing their thoughts and feelings and the private little jokes they came up with. They'd sneak away to dodge the paparazzi and have secret picnics high in the Hollywood Hills, or Jacks would have her over for dinner at his own new gorgeous house in Empyrean Canyon, and they'd stay up late cuddling and making out, streaming cheesy TV shows from when they were younger.

Even though he was *the* Jackson Godspeed, Maddy just felt comfortable with him. Like she could really be herself for once, free to express herself without shyness. And even when they talked about sex, Jacks was a true gentleman. Maddy of course *wanted* to have sex with Jacks—sometimes she was so attracted to him that she almost couldn't believe it—but she also wanted the first time to be the right time, and she wasn't quite ready to take the plunge. They'd talked without embarrassment, and they agreed that she should focus on finishing high school and starting college before they actually took things to a more physical level. "We have a lot of time," Jacks had told her. She loved him for that.

On her bedroom desk sat a framed picture of her and Jacks in front of the pond in Central Park—he'd taken her on her first trip to New York City as a graduation present that spring. The Plaza Hotel and Midtown skyscrapers rose from behind the screen of lush trees and the duck-filled pond they stood in front of. They had been so happy that week. She picked the photo up and studied their glowing faces before putting the photo on top of her suitcase. There was no way she was leaving it behind.

She walked downstairs, yawning, each step of the staircase in the old house creaking as she descended. Every step had a different creak, and at this point she knew them by heart, like notes on a scale.

Suddenly, a jolt coursed through Maddy's body. Her hand gripped the banister tightly. Her vision rapidly became blurry—everything seemed to grow gray and foggy. She could see nothing concrete, and she felt like she was going to trip forward into an empty expanse, a gray void that would expand forever, with her falling through it.

All at once, she felt heat. The worst kind of heat she could imagine. Blistering, searing, inescapable. Smoke appeared, with flames following. Maddy's pulse raced as she realized it was a fire.

From the smoky darkness suddenly emerged a small boy in a striped shirt whom she had never seen before. His hands stretched toward Maddy as he attempted to escape the flames. The child's eyes bulged terribly out of his pale skin as he began coughing. Coughing blood.

Maddy shrieked.

And just as suddenly found herself standing on the stairs in her uncle's house, gasping for air, her fingernails making marks in the wood of the banister. There was no fire.

It must have been a vision. She sometimes had seemingly random, splinter-like visions of grim violence and destruction. Similar visions to this had been one of the signs that she might be part Angel.

But what had this been a vision of?

And who was the boy? She'd never seen him before. She hoped against hope that he was going to be okay. But she had no way to know who he was, where he was, anything. Just those seconds of her vision. For all she knew, the visions weren't always even truly real, just tricks of her overactive half-human, half-Angel brain.

Step-by-step, she slowly took the final part of the staircase down to the kitchen on the ground floor. Kevin was there, dashing in for a moment with his apron from the diner still on.

"Hey, Mads! Have you seen my phone around here anywhere?" Kevin asked her.

"Did you leave it by the microwave?" Maddy suggested absently. That was where he always left it.

"Good thinking." He turned to the microwave and lifted it off the counter. "Aha."

"How's the new waitress doing?" Maddy asked, seeking the sanctuary of a familiar topic.

"Oh, she'll be fine," Kevin said, playing with a loose thread on his apron. "It's been getting pretty busy, you know. I might even bring on someone to help me with managing the kitchen."

Maddy could only shake her head and smile. Yeah, right. She couldn't imagine anyone manning the cooking besides her uncle. Yet . . . change *was* in the air.

"How is it out there today?" she said.

Kevin peered out the slats of the front blinds. "Could be worse."

They were talking, of course, about the paparazzi that had followed her from basically the first night she went out with Jacks. They were a constant part of her life now, but she was hoping they would leave her alone once she went to college. She mostly tried to avoid them, and when she couldn't, she would smile and try to be polite. Maddy realized her uncle was studying her.

"Maddy, you're pale," Kevin said. "What's wrong?"

"Nothing," she said. "I just had a . . . feeling."

Kevin led her by the arm to the kitchen table.

"Here, sit down." He pulled a chair out for her then poured her a glass of water.

"I know your decision was difficult," Kevin said tentatively. He was always a little stiff with the father-daughter stuff. "You must be having a lot of feelings about leaving Angel City."

"Well, it wasn't that, actually. It was a feeling. Like one of my visions."

A dark cloud passed across Kevin's brow.

"I just don't know what it means," she said.

Far off in the distance, sirens could be faintly heard. Maddy sat up straight in her chair. The sirens began to grow louder and louder. She jumped up from her chair and threw open the front door just as a pair of ambulances and three Angel City Police Department (ACPD) cruisers roared past on the street. Their sirens rang in her ear as they disappeared at top speed.

They were all streaming downtown. Maddy stepped out into the lawn and looked toward the tall buildings of downtown Angel City. The paparazzi began shouting questions at her, but she paid no attention. Far off, she could see a tendril of smoke rising. Her eyes popped open and she raced inside to her confused uncle.

"I need to borrow the car."

Maddy followed the spire of smoke coming from downtown, past the tall buildings and into the rough area east, where her uncle had told her never to go. Chinese stores crammed with plastic gewgaws and streets crammed with pedestrians gave way to grimy blocks peppered with the homeless, who shuffled around under the hot sun. Skid Row. The dark side of Angel City's glamour.

Soon she was able to follow the smoke and emergency vehicles to a building set on a cracked side street. She parked her uncle's old station wagon and jumped out, but was quickly stopped by bright-yellow crime scene tape and a line of ACPD officers guarding the perimeter. Smoke continued to roil out of the building as the firemen on the ladder shot water into the dying flames from their hoses. Maddy could read the remains of the name on the scorched building: ANGEL CITY MISSION FOR THE HOMELESS. A shelter.

Firemen and paramedics were placing blankets on the shoulders of soot-covered women and children, their eyes rimmed red and faces pale as they staggered away from the building. Survivors.

A news van suddenly appeared at the scene. Maddy tried to cover her face so she wouldn't be recognized. That was the last thing she needed.

Ducking away, Maddy approached a firefighter near the yellow tape who was gulping water from a sports bottle. He was sweat-drenched, dark ash smeared on his yellow fire suit.

"What happened?" Maddy asked him diffidently.

The fireman nodded toward the building. "Fire at the family shelter. It started over on the men's side. The guys were able to get out. But the fire had spread to the side with the women and their kids. Two out of three exits on their side were locked. Don't ask me why. Not all of them could get out."

His words sent a shiver along Maddy's spine.

Two emergency workers emerged from the now-smoldering entrance with a stretcher. Maddy watched them in horror. On the stretcher was the body of someone small, covered with a black tarp. With nauseating dread pouring into her stomach, Maddy realized it must be a child. The tarp briefly pulled back as the two men shifted it in their arms. For a split second, Maddy saw an arm underneath the tarp.

She couldn't be sure. But she thought she saw a striped shirt.

# CHAPTER THREE

Maddy placed Kevin's car keys absentmindedly on the counter as she walked into the house in a daze, her mind still back at the terrible scene downtown. She climbed the stairs and reached her room, sitting down on the corner of her bed as she tried to sort her confused and surging emotions.

She looked around the room—or, at least, at what was left of it. The room seemed almost strange to her now. Foreign. Bare walls, empty closet. Ghostly outlines where posters and pictures once hung. The room felt naked, stripped of its identity. It was her room, but it wasn't her room anymore.

Maddy began shivering uncontrollably as she relived the vision she'd had on the staircase. It *had* to have been a premonition of the fire at the shelter. That boy emerging from the flames and smoke. His pale face and doomed hands reaching out to Maddy as his lungs blistered and burst from the inside. Flames licking up the striped shirt.

Maddy felt like she might throw up, and she began rushing to the bathroom before she controlled the nausea. Numbed, she slowly sat back down on her bed.

She could have saved that child. She could have prevented those people's deaths. If she had only known how to focus on the frequency, as Jacks called it. They might not have had to die.

Her eyes drifted to the boxes and suitcase in the corner, the picture of her and Jacks sitting on top. Slowly, she walked over and picked up her suitcase. She hesitated only a moment before placing it on her bed. Opening both latches, she began unpacking it, putting clothes back in her drawers.

Maddy Montgomery wouldn't be going to college.

In the space of just a few moments, Maddy had felt it deep in her bones.

She needed to become a Guardian.

"Maddy?"

The voice startled her.

Uncle Kevin stood in the doorway, concern on his face. "Are you all right? You left in such a rush." He nodded to the open suitcase on the bed. "Are you still packing?"

"I—I'm unpacking," Maddy said, her face turning slightly away from her uncle. She had a feeling he was going to be upset.

"I don't understand," Kevin said. "Why?"

Maddy turned toward him and sat back down on the bed.

"I—I can't fully explain," she said, her eyes on the floor. "But what I saw today. It was a fire downtown. I could have saved them. I had part of the vision, but I didn't know what to do. If I had, I could have saved those people. That's what's inside of me, or at least a big part of me. And not having done it makes me feel like I'm somehow not complete." She looked up at her uncle. "I know this may seem like a shock, but I think it's my calling. To be a Guardian. I'd be making a huge mistake if I walked away from it." She rushed on. "I know the Angel worship and the whole Protection for Pay setup is . . . mercenary, somehow. I know how you feel about it and I agree. But just now I realized it doesn't have to be that way forever. I could have the opportunity to start changing things in the Angels, from within. And along the way, I could be *helping* people. Saving them from dying. Like I could have saved that boy today."

An unreadable look came across Kevin's face.

"Kevin, you know I've wanted your opinion this whole time, and you wouldn't give it to me. Said I had to make my own decision. But I know you've thought college was the right choice for me the whole time. I'm so sorry if you're disappointed in me, but I know now that this is what I have to do." Maddy felt her chest grow incredibly tight. Why wouldn't he say something?

"Well . . ." Kevin coughed. He hesitated, but his eyes glinted. A slight smile crossed his face. "Will you wait right here?"

After a few moments Kevin returned with a small cloth bag and a tattered-looking old leather journal. The bag held something small and heavy.

"Maddy, I've spent the last eighteen years thinking my sister made a mistake. I blamed her for it. I blamed your father. I blamed the Angels, too. It took me eighteen years to realize that it wasn't a mistake. She was called to a great destiny. Her destiny was to have you. Sometimes we don't understand why things happen, but I do believe, somehow, that there is"—he paused, searching for the right words—"a plan."

He looked her directly in the eyes.

"'The strength of a hero is not in her abilities. In her weapons. These things are important, but they are not the source of her strength. The source of her strength is in her belief in an idea—the idea that those who are strong, and those who are able, protect those who are not, and those who cannot protect themselves. The idea that the good, and the right, will triumph. She is willing to put herself in harm's way—in mortal danger—to prove her belief in this idea.'"

Kevin opened the cloth bag he held. An Immortal Ring fell from the bag into his hand. A tingling passed over Maddy's body.

"'That it is the duty of those who have within themselves the power, and the gift, to help others.'" Kevin looked at the ring in his palm. "I didn't say that. Your father did. In a speech to the Council a week before he was killed."

Kevin handed her the ring. Her *father's* ring.

The Divine Ring looked enormous in her small, delicate hands. Like Jacks's, it sparkled just as magnificently, throwing pools of amber light against her palm.

"He wanted you to have this when the time was right. He had hoped it would guide you on your way. I swore I would never give it to you, but something kept me holding on to it. I didn't know at the time, but I think I know now."

Tears were forming in Maddy's eyes. "Oh, Kevin . . ."

Now he handed her the journal. Its dark and worn leather wrapped around yellowed, battered pages, some poking out unevenly. The whole thing was held together by a thick blue rubber band. Maddy's breath caught in her throat as she slowly slid the rubber band up the edge of the smoothed and worn leather. Carefully, she opened the journal and saw an inscription on the first page:

*Jacob Godright—Guardian Training Notes*

She slowly flipped through the pages: complex formulas, long journal entries, diagrams . . . they were all from her father. His handwriting, so distinctive—she thought she recognized the shape of her own *R*'s in his—filled each page. She felt overwhelmed with emotion holding this book, which her father had spent years filling with his knowledge, in her hand.

"Everything your father ever learned on his way to becoming one of the most skilled Guardians in his day was kept in that book. He told me himself. It only makes sense that you should have it now."

As Maddy moved through the pages, something fell out from between the paper, slowly floating to the floor. Reaching down, Maddy picked it up. It was a wallet-sized photo of her mother. On the back was simply written: "With love, forever, Regina."

Maddy swiped a few tears from her eyes and looked up at her uncle.

"Thank you. For everything," she said, leaning forward and giving him a warm hug. She heard a sniffle. Her uncle was looking away. She was pretty sure he might be crying a little bit.

"Oh, I was just cutting some onions before I came up here. Must be one of those delayed-reaction things." He squeezed Maddy on the shoulder. "Now I should get back to the kitchen before things go too haywire."

Maddy nodded, smiling, and watched Kevin leave the room. Her eyes once again turned down to her father's Divine Ring in her hand. It glowed as she touched her fingers to it. She could sense its energy.

She was going to become an Angel. A Guardian Angel.

She could not wait to tell Jacks.

# CHAPTER FOUR

The world around Jacks seemed to swim, rippling with his every breath. A blue tint filtered through the room. The light turned the Angel doctor, a specially trained Immortal, indigo in his white lab coat outside the hyperbaric immersion chamber. The doctor examined numbers on his handheld instrument reader, dictating notes to his medical assistant. Their faces twisted and stretched like in a funhouse mirror. Even if he hadn't been listening to his favorite playlist piped in through his headphones, Jacks wouldn't have been able to hear them—he was fully submerged in the advanced therapeutic solution, and the glass of the chamber was too thick. Jacks's muscular limbs drifted as he floated suspended in the chamber, breathing through a mask, his sole functioning wing outstretched behind him, a series of cables and hoses connected to his body. They trailed up to the top of the tank to send readings and numbers to the team of technicians outside.

If only the blue light had come from Jacks's famous wings and not the series of screens along the back wall of the darkened room. But ever since the accident, his wings had lost their unique blue iridescence.

At his stepfather's insistence, Jacks had been submitting himself three times a week to this immersion therapy, by far the most advanced and expensive of its kind, hoping to speed the recovery of his wings, one of which had been reattached in the wake of the vicious demon attack he'd survived. And three times a week, he left disappointed. The doctors always told him to be patient, that "next time we'll see some improvement." But there never was.

He still couldn't fly. And that's all that mattered.

Inside the chamber, two incredibly complex robotic machines operated underwater where Jacks's wings met the back of his shoulders, the outline of his Immortal Marks visible and glowing. The finely tuned machines—advanced nerve reconnectors—knit tissue and cells back together inside the solution that had been specially engineered just for Jacks. The sensation wasn't unpleasant. It sometimes tickled Jacks a bit, but it wasn't too bad.

The pain would come later. It always did.

A door across the room opened, and Jacks's stepfather, Mark, entered the room. He walked up to the chamber, nodded to his stepson through the glass, and began talking to the technicians. Almost every session, Mark came to check on the progress, carving out time from his packed schedule as one of the senior Archangels. Jacks, tangled in cords and hoses, briefly lifted his hand to wave at Mark.

Jacks could see the doctor and Mark talking. Mark's face remained grave. *Great, still no good news*, Jacks thought.

The doctor looked at his handheld computer and alerted the technicians with a circular motion of his finger. Jacks knew this meant it was time to get out.

The nerve reconnectors retracted from Jacks's submerged body. Jacks happily pulled off some of the sensors and connectors as soon as he saw it was time. The always nervous assistant shook her head as she watched him roughly handle the multimillion-dollar equipment.

The top of the immersion chamber popped open and two assistants peered into the water. Reaching down, they lifted Jacks out of the solution and disconnected the rest of the hoses and monitors from his body. Jacks himself removed the breathing mask. He stepped down the narrow ladder to the floor, where a pretty female assistant put a robe on over his trunks and enthusiastically started toweling him off.

"I got this one," Jacks said, taking the towel from her.

"Let me know if you need anything else," she said, disappointment coloring her eyes as she stepped away from Jacks. "And don't forget, don't—"

"Retract my wings for at least one hour," Jacks said, finishing her sentence. "I'll remember."

Mark walked up to his stepson.

"The doctor says that progress is being made. It's slow, but—"

"It's the same thing every time, you know that," Jacks cut him off. He looked down at the floor, trying to keep his frustration in check.

Mark placed a hand on Jacks's shoulder.

"You—you just have to have faith."

"That's easy for you to say," Jacks said, hearing his voice sound snappish. "You're not the one getting poked and prodded and practically"— he waved at the now-empty chamber—"drowned every other day." He looked up at his stepfather, his gaze softening. "I'm sorry, I just—"

"There's nothing to be sorry for, Jacks," Mark said. "Your frustration is more than understandable. And if there's anyone who should be sorry . . ." Mark trailed off. His eyes drifted away, distant. Jacks could almost see them going to that terrible rooftop downtown months ago, when Jacks had nearly lost both wings.

"The doctor said they're bringing in a new specialist, from Germany,"

Mark said. "That she's been developing some very promising new treatments we haven't even seen in Angel City yet." Mark's eyes were hopeful.

"Good . . . I mean, that's great," Jacks said, trying to sound at least somewhat enthusiastic. Mark's BlackBerry buzzed. The Archangel reached for the phone, but then held back. Jacks looked at him.

"It's okay. Go ahead, go back to work, Mark. The world doesn't need to stop just because"—here Jacks swallowed his words for a moment—"Jackson Godspeed can't fly anymore." He put a self-deprecating grin on, though, to make it come across like a joke.

Mark nodded, slowly. Jacks turned to walk back to the changing room, where his street clothes were waiting.

"Jacks?"

Jackson turned back.

"No matter what happens, I'm proud of you."

The young Angel nodded, pressing his lips together.

"I'm going to fly again, Mark. I will."

Mark pressed his hand and smiled. "Of course you are," his stepfather said. "Of course you are."

Jacks turned back and began walking to the dressing room. Behind him he heard the click of the door as Mark left. The medical staff didn't even look up from their screens.

Inside his private dressing room, Jacks sat down on a chair and let out a deep sigh. He thought of the team outside, all working toward the same goal: *to fix Jacks*. And he thought of what he had just told Mark: he would fly again. But what if he could never be fixed? When would they call it a day, pack up their equipment, and head to whatever challenge awaited them next? They still got paid whether Jacks was cured or not. *What if there was no cure?*

He drove the thought from his mind.

As he slowly got dressed, leaving his wings extended, his mind wandered to what, if he was honest with himself, was the most troubling thing to him right now.

Maddy.

He had known ever since he met her that Maddy could be stubborn when she decided something. He had seen it time and again over their relationship. Ever since she insisted on confronting her uncle to find out about her parents after he had saved her outside Ethan's party. And then in the midst of her newfound celebrity, the way she insisted on turning down endorsements and photo shoots, keeping her job at the diner, finishing at Angel City High when she could've started training to be a Guardian and had five private tutors if she wanted.

And now . . . whenever Jacks thought of her turning her back on Guardian training, of leaving Angel City . . . his stomach felt hollowed out.

But she had made her decision.

Jacks knew they had promised to visit each other every chance they could get, and that Maddy would be back for holidays. But he knew something would be different. Illinois. It seemed so far away. *And I can't even fly myself to visit her*, he thought angrily. Jacks looked at the clock. Only forty more minutes until he could retract his wings and get out of there.

He reached for the remote and powered on the flat screen. One of the twenty-four-hour news stations was on.

"*. . . and polls today showing a small percentage jump for Senator Ted Linden's anti-Angel presidential campaign. The fringe candidate has growing support in certain parts of the country, but experts say his third-party campaign is more of a statement than a real contender come November.*" Linden's smiling face appeared on screen at an event as he waved to supporters. With a look of disgust, Jacks flipped the channel. He found Linden's anti-Angel posturing to be so repulsive that he couldn't even bear to follow his campaign in the newspapers.

On ANN, Tara Reeves was on screen. She never looked like she grew older by even a day. Jacks wondered if the time would come when she would age a dozen years in twenty-four hours, making up for lost time. He heard his name and snapped to attention:

*"Rumors continue swirling about Jackson Godspeed's step away from the limelight, with Immortal City tongues wagging about whether that 'break for exhaustion' following last year's traumatic events is something more than just temporary. Plus exclusive footage from this morning's thrilling save by Steven Churchson in the Santa Barbara Mountains. And more on who will be this year's hottest Protections. But first ANN catches up with it-girl Vivian Holycross to talk about her latest perfume and rumors of a romance with hottie French Angel Julien Santé."*

Vivian appeared on-screen, flanked by a group of mad paparazzi. She looked incredible, smiling coyly from behind her oversized sunglasses as she stopped and cocked her hand on her hip, posing briefly for the cameras.

Jacks turned off the TV, feeling suddenly tired. Reaching into the breast pocket of his blazer, he retrieved his iPhone. He had some missed calls and texts, but not as many as he would've had a year ago—there were only three texts, plus one voicemail from his publicist, Darcy. *Huh*, he thought. He hadn't even heard from Darcy in a week.

But there was a missed call and text that stood out from the rest, from Maddy. The text read, simply: *"Give me a call."*

A strange feeling settled into Jackson's stomach. He couldn't describe why. He noticed his heart starting to beat slightly faster with nervousness. Ignoring the voicemail from Darcy, Jacks pressed the button to call Maddy back.

"Hello?" Her familiar voice made his heart thump the way it always did.

"Hey! What's up, Mads?" Jacks tried to mask his uncertainty.

Maddy took a deep breath on the other end of the line.

"I'm so glad you called me back," she said. She paused. It sounded like she was weighing her words. "I want to tell you something."

Jacks couldn't remember his gut ever feeling so knotted. Was she breaking up with him? Had she decided long distance with a deformed Angel just wasn't worth it? "Yes?"

"Well, you know how I feel about the Angels."

Jacks blew the air out of his lungs and took another sharp breath. "How many times do I have to tell you, Maddy, *you're* an Angel."

Maddy was quiet on the line.

Jacks continued: "You're not what you think you are. You're not a freak. You're wonderful."

"I'm not so sure I'd go that far."

"Can you just trust me for once?" he said. "You *are* wonderful."

"No . . . *you* are great," she said. "Jacks, I don't know how to say this"—Jackson's stomach flipped again as he heard Maddy's voice on the other end—"but I've thought about what you've said, about being able to help make things better, to maybe change the Angels from within, despite the past. To open up the protection program to more disadvantaged people. About what a chance it is. And now I'm thinking about what my dad would have considered my duty."

"What are you telling me?" Jackson said. He unconsciously held his breath, silent. Time seemed to stop.

Maddy's voice was clear: "Jacks, I want to become a Guardian."

Phone up to his ear, Jacks felt a smile slowly begin on the very edge of his lips, then spread until his whole mouth was open with joy. He began to laugh.

"Maddy! That's so great! I mean, I thought, what about—" Jacks cut himself off. "It's just so fantastic!"

"It's a lot right now. But I think it's the right decision. And that means no long—"

"Distance relationship," Jacks finished her thought. "And I thought you were going to be all the way out in Chicago. For four years!"

"I'll be right here."

"You have so much to do!" Jacks couldn't stop smiling. His voice was shot through with excitement. "What are you going to set up first?"

Maddy laughed. "How am I supposed to know, Jacks? You're the Guardian Angel! This is all new to me."

"You're right, you're right. Well, you have at *least* two years of Guardian training, so don't be too hard on yourself, okay?" Jacks said, trying to collect his thoughts. "It's just such great news! We have some celebrating to do. Forget ice cream. My house in forty-five?"

Maddy laughed. "Okay. Just as long as there's not champagne. The bubbles give me a headache."

Jacks hung up when he heard her disconnect, and he quickly began gathering his stuff up from the dressing room. His mind was racing. After what seemed like the umpteenth discouraging session at physical therapy, he at last had some cheerful news. He thought of all the training Maddy would be getting, learning all the Guardian skills, including how to fly—if she got her wings—and joining the Guardian ranks presumably in a few years.

And as his mind drifted over these things, he was shocked to realize that a tiny, bitter part of him was the slightest bit . . . envious. Jealous of all the cool things Maddy was going to be doing. Things that he could no longer do with his wings a mangled shadow of their former selves. A phantom pang streaked across his back.

Shaking his head, Jacks chased the thought from his mind. How could he think something like that, even just for a second? Maddy was becoming a Guardian, she was staying in Angel City, and he was nothing but happy, for her and for them.

He couldn't believe any other thought had even crossed his mind.

# CHAPTER FIVE

Just minutes after giving Mark Godspeed and the National Angel Services the news that she wanted to be a Guardian, Maddy's iPhone, last year's birthday gift from Jacks, vibrated. She saw that it was an e-mail from MGodspeedAsst@NAS.ang—Mark's assistant. The e-mail detailed her schedule for the next week, day-by-day, hour-by-hour. Jacks, nuzzling her neck, looked over her shoulder. Headquartered in Angel City, the NAS, as the National Angel Services was usually called, had been formed after the Great Awakening to oversee and administer Guardians and Protection for Pay. They'd been doing it for almost 150 years. And now they'd be overseeing Maddy.

Before Maddy had even had a chance to digest a third of the email, her phone began ringing. The caller ID read "DARCY."

Maddy gulped. Darcy, Jacks's longtime publicist, was also technically working for Maddy, too, although Maddy had turned down all media and appearance requests as she finished out her final year of high school (which had never ceased to both shock and horrify Darcy). The woman was a legend in Angel City—she never took no for an answer and always managed to get her clients the best magazine covers and land them at the top of the Angel Power rankings.

"Hello . . . ?" Maddy said uncertainly into the phone.

Darcy's voice was clipped and excited. "Heard the news. So glad you've finally come to your senses. Luckily my guy at the *Today Show* is still interested, because we can do much better than cable for your first big interview. Remember this isn't public yet, but don't be too coy. Also, I've already got a call in to *American Protection*, and your fitting for the annual Angel issue of *Teen Vogue* is next week. If you're feeling a little bit bloated, I hope you follow that raw cleanse I e-mailed you over the summer. Buckle your seatbelt. We have a lot of work to do."

Maddy just stood there, stunned, not even knowing where to start. "*Raw?*" she managed to sputter into the phone.

"This is NBC. Gotta go," Darcy said, distracted. "Talk later."

"But—" Before Maddy could even get out a word of protest, Darcy had already hung up. Maddy held her iPhone out in front of her as if it were a snake about to bite, her eyes wide. She looked at Jacks.

He just laughed. "Welcome to the life of an Angel," he said.

The next few days for Maddy were a blur of nonstop phone calls and meetings with Darcy and a series of assistants to the Archangels. And now Maddy found herself riding in Jacks's Ferrari as it turned off Beverly toward the sleek and gleaming building that held the offices of the NAS and its board, the Archangels.

Maddy had never actually been to the offices before. The structure was much more impressive in person than in the photos she'd seen. It seemed futuristic and beyond modern, and she remembered reading that it had taken its Japanese architect ten years to fully complete. The dark glass monolith loomed above them.

"I can't believe we're going in *there*," Maddy said, motioning to the building nervously. She remembered that night not so long ago when Jacks had taken her to her first "event." She'd been sitting in the same seat in the same car. Now she was having that same sinking feeling as Jacks pulled off the street.

Jacks squeezed her hand.

"Don't worry, you're going to do great. Remember: no one starts out ready to be a Guardian. They'll train you for two, three years before even thinking about nominating you. Just be you and you'll do perfect. You don't need to know any right answers."

On their way in, they passed a clutch of paparazzi standing on the sidewalk: "What's going on, Maddy?! Jacks, what's going on?!" They turned their heads away from the windows and kept driving, entering the underground parking garage. Maddy peered up at the imposing glass walls of the structure as they were swallowed up and surrounded by it. She wasn't so sure about how great she was, in fact, going to do.

She knew what she *wanted* to talk to the Archangels about: the idea she had for a charity program for the disadvantaged who couldn't afford Guardians and who weren't one of the lucky few to win protection via lottery. This proposal would of course face some spirited debate, she imagined. Her idea was to get this front and center in her Guardian-ship, even during her introduction and training. But now, faced with the monumental architecture, she was starting to think she would have to do her best just to survive the encounter.

This was just a formality, Jacks had assured her. A time for Maddy to meet the Archangels and go through a brief pretraining interview process.

The valet snapped to attention as soon as he saw Jacks's Ferrari.

"Hello, Mr. Godspeed, Ms. Godright," he said. Maddy raised an eyebrow—she'd never been called by her father's last name before. "They're waiting for you upstairs."

Jacks and Maddy entered the elevator. It dinged as the door closed and rapidly ascended toward the main NAS floor. Maddy's stomach lurched. Jacks smiled his warm, angelic smile at her and took her hand in his. She felt briefly comforted.

The elevator dinged again, and the doors slid open noiselessly onto the waiting area. Sleek modernist Italian leather sofas offered Protections and other guests a place to sit while waiting for their meeting with the Immortals. An entire wall of flat-screen TVs played the latest, greatest footage from the Angelcams. Angelcams had quickly become one of the most popular additions to the Angel industry ever, and the technology had already made huge strides in the year since they'd been introduced. All Angelcams now beamed HD-quality footage directly to the NAS TV team, which then provided it to the networks and posted it on SaveTube, where millions of ravenous fans waited to see the next save and who the new famous Protection would be.

The beautiful blond human girl at reception greeted Jackson and Maddy as soon as they stepped off the elevator. She looked like she could be a model in her free time—but her beauty still somehow wasn't on the level of the Immortals.

"Just a moment," she said, smiling, then speaking under her voice into her headpiece. When Jacks looked away for a moment, Maddy saw the girl give her the up-and-down. Maddy gave her a look.

Within seconds the frosted glass doors that led to the offices opened up. Mark's assistant greeted them, speaking faster than Maddy thought humanly possible, barely pausing even to breathe as they walked at a fast clip past the rows of assistants sitting at their desks outside the Archangels' offices.

"Jacks-so-good-to-see-you," he said, shaking Jackson's hand. Then, with a big smile, "Maddy-I'm-Max-good-to-*finally*-meet-you-in-person-they're-all-waiting-for-you-in-the-conference-room-do-you-want-anything-we've-got-waters-and-coffee-in-there-already."

"Um," Maddy said. "Water's fine?"

"*Great!*"

Jackson started peeling off. "Hey, Max, I'll just wait in Mark's office, cool?"

"Already-have-the-game-on-in-there-for-you," Max said. "Need-anything-let-Claire-know." Jacks had described the workings of Mark's office to Maddy to prepare her, and she remembered that Claire was Mark's second assistant, who never seemed to leave the desk directly outside his office. Jacks had joked that he'd never even actually witnessed her leaving for so much as a bathroom break.

Maddy looked desperately at Jacks as he turned away from the conference room.

"*Don't leave me,*" she silently mouthed to him.

"I have to. This is as far as I can go," Jackson said sympathetically. "Remember: you'll do great." He disappeared down the hallway toward Mark's massive corner office, leaving Maddy at the mercy of Max.

"Ready?" Max smiled at her, placing his hand on the steel handle of the opaque glass doors to the conference room.

Maddy took a deep breath and nodded.

The doors opened, and Maddy was met by the gaze of over a dozen Angels, mostly men, all in expensive tailored suits. The view, through a wall of tempered glass, looked out onto Beverly Hills and Angel City beyond. The Archangels were arrayed around a long, gleaming, dark wooden table. All waiting for her. The effect of all these flawless Immortals turning their eyes on her was overwhelming. Maddy felt her legs start to fail, but she just kept moving forward, aided by Max. Maddy recognized Mark among the unfamiliar faces. He secreted her an encouraging grin, and then his face flashed back to serious. An older Archangel near her stood up.

"Our newest star," he said, flashing a million-dollar smile at her. The Archangel reached forward to shake her hand. "We can't tell you how glad we are to see you here today."

Most of the heads in the room nodded in assent, but Maddy also could see a couple more serious faces among the ranks of the Archangels that didn't nod so quickly. Or even at all.

"Please, take a seat," the Archangel said, motioning to the chair at the head of the table.

"Okay, uh, thanks," Maddy said, wishing now more than ever that she had her gray hoodie and iPod earbuds to hide behind. *Okay, uh, thanks??* Could she have sounded any lamer? Why had she ever agreed to any of this? She was starting to bitterly regret her choice. Pure adrenaline filled her veins as she settled in her chair and looked at the prestigious Archangels, the leading lights of the Immortal City, each one famous worldwide, all waiting to hear from *her*.

"Here's-your-water-Maddy-would-you-like-lime?" Max rapidly spit out, filling a glass with ice and pouring Perrier in, finishing it with a lime wedge without waiting for her response.

Another Archangel spoke up.

"Madison, my name is Archangel Uriah Steeple. We've asked you here today just to speak with you during the preliminary phase, before your training. As we all know, your preparation for the life of a Guardian has been less than standard."

"That much is undisputed," an Archangel with a goatee near the end of the table stated. Maddy thought she recognized him from photos as Archangel Charles Churchson, uncle to Steven and Sierra Churchson, who had been Commissioned with Jacks the year before.

The others glared at him.

Archangel Steeple continued undeterred. "But after consulting many of our experts, and conducting some, ahem, tests, there is reason to believe that you may have developed your abilities without even knowing it."

*Tests?* Maddy thought to herself. *How could they have conducted tests?*

"In fact, there has been some speculation in the Angel medical community that you might even be able to develop *unique* features due to your mixed genetic code. Of course, these genes might not express themselves right away. In the same way that you're still waiting for your wings to come out, much of this will have to be a wait-and-see game."

Maddy thought of her recurring nightmare, in which her "wings" turned out to be little more than grotesque, bloody appendages, flopping around uselessly.

"Mark—I mean, Archangel Godspeed," Maddy said, "should have been the first to tell you that I'm uncertain of my own Immortal abilities—"

"But many of us aren't," one of the two female Archangels interrupted. Her hair was a dark lustrous brown, and her voice was rich and warm as she trained her gaze on Maddy. "We are, in fact, certain of what you are. Of what you can become."

Archangel Steeple took over again: "You see, with the growing strength of the preposterous, racist anti-Angel movement around Senator Linden, and the way he and his flacks plan to introduce into Congress this dangerous 'Immortals Bill,' which could threaten to ban Angel activities entirely, we're quite concerned. Plus, we don't even know what the Humanity Defense Faction will do next. Those wing-nut HDF activists are constantly persecuting us, led by that crackpot William Beauborg, who won't rest until he sees us destroyed. So after all the backlash we received following last year's demon attack, who better to help us launch the new, friendlier face of Angels than the half-human, half-Angel herself? It's you, Maddy."

The dark-haired woman Archangel spoke again: "The fact that your actual background to become a Guardian is not the norm, and some might even say *less than ideal*, is beside the point, as we think you can quickly adopt the skills necessary to Guardianship."

A snort of derision erupted down the table. It was the goateed Archangel again, Charles Churchson. "'Less than ideal.' That's an understatement, Susan. What we need is a *strong* response to the racist humans and this proposed 'Immortals Bill,' fringe as it may be. Senator Linden and his allies are proposing they extend the bill not only here in Angel City and the United States, but across the globe. We need to limit access to Guardian services until humans understand what we Angels really are capable of, and how much we're worth. Launching some kind of *half-baked* Guardian won't bring us anything."

"Charles, we agreed you'd keep your minority opinions to yourself during this meeting," Mark stated, anger edging his voice.

"Oh, come off it, Mark," a different Archangel said, his voice booming. "You can't silence everyone."

The room erupted into argument. Max stood very uncomfortably near the glass doors.

Maddy looked at the squabbling Archangels. Blood flushed her face. She found she was getting angry. A newfound strength filled her.

She stood up from her chair.

All eyes turned to her as the Archangels slowly quieted down.

"If you didn't think I had what it took to be a Guardian, why did you ask me to start training in the first place?" Maddy said. "I don't know what Angel abilities I have, or will have. I can't say when my wings will come, or even what they're going to look like. I can't even say if I'm going to like being a Guardian. But I can say that the reason I want to become a Guardian is to protect the ideal of doing one's duty, to help mankind."

Maddy's eyes scanned the room, anger loosening her tongue. She felt like she'd been tricked, swindled into coming somehow. Reaching in her pocket, she pulled out her father's Divine Ring. She felt like she was watching herself in third person.

"I know that even though most of the Archangels during the Troubles have since resigned, some of you could have been against my father and mother, what they stood for, and are probably against me now. But I know that this Immortal Ring should mean the same for everyone in this room—even if they are a jerk. And I believe in what it means, too." Maddy put the ring back in her pocket, her hand shaking. "Now, if you'll excuse me, I have more important things to do with my time than get insulted."

And with that, Maddy turned and walked out the glass doors, leaving the roomful of stunned, silent Archangels behind.

She was stone silent in the passenger seat as Jacks rumbled down Melrose back toward the heart of Angel City. She didn't notice the tourists, the oversized billboards with beautiful Angels splayed across them hawking their wares, the palm trees, the boutique stores, all moving past the car windows outside. She felt Jacks steal a glance at her. He started to say something, but then thought better of it.

She finally broke the silence, her fingers tensely digging into the supple leather of the seat. "Oh my God, Jacks, what have I done?"

Jacks looked over at her in sympathy.

"I'm sure it couldn't have been *that* bad."

"Jacks. I told an Archangel he was a jerk."

"Oh." Jacks's eyebrows shot up his forehead. He took a left and burned up La Cienega toward the Halo Strip.

Maddy let out a long breath. In approximately ninety seconds she had destroyed whatever chance she'd had of becoming a Guardian. She was truly surprised to find that she was sad.

It was now too late to join Northwestern this semester. In fact, she wasn't even sure they would let her have a place there at all, since she had given up her spot at the very last minute. She might even have to re-apply *everywhere*. In the meantime, maybe she could start some classes at Angel City Community College (ACCC), which was in a squat gray cement block building within walking distance of Kevin's house. A far cry from the leafy campus she was envisioning in the plush suburbs outside Chicago. She wondered if Kevin would let her start picking up shifts again, even though the new waitress was doing such a good job.

Maddy's phone buzzed in her bag. She was almost afraid to check it.

"You don't have to get that right now if you don't want to," Jacks said, eyeing Maddy with concern.

"I might as well get it over with," Maddy said. She reached in her bag, pulling out the phone. Her stomach flipping, she looked down at the screen.

It was a text from Mark.

It read: *"You're in."*

# CHAPTER SIX

Darkness reigned along the Angel City street, an unnatural quiet whispering in the fronds of the palms as they rustled in the night above. A block or two away, the occasional car would pass along the sleepy streets, its headlights brightly burning before leaving the night to its darkness and silence. Two streetlamps cast a hard orange glare on the street at the end of the block, and a crisp white security light shone right in front of the building. The rest was shrouded in darkness.

The darkened palms, shifting softly back and forth with the warm night wind, were the only witness to the two dark figures that crept silently toward the offices.

Without exchanging a word, they moved quickly along the sidewalk, passing the thick glass doors of the impressive building and heading to a service door off to the side. One, slightly shorter, carried a boxlike object under his arm. Both wore dark masks that covered most of their faces. Etched perfectly on the glass façade of the structure were the words ANGEL ADMINISTRATION AFFAIRS.

The two paid no attention to the lights still on in the fourth-floor offices. With complete precision, the two dark figures worked in concert. The first placed the metal box on the ground, opening it slightly. His hands reached inside, his fingers working quickly at some unknown task. The other stepped to the service door. Looking back and forth first, he pressed a gun-like object to the steel door. He pulled the trigger. The device obliterated the door's metal lock. The *THWOOMP* of the mechanism echoed into the night. But then all was quiet.

The figure crouched at the box turned to look up at his partner by the door. The latter nodded slightly. Closing the box, the squatting figure carefully lifted it under his shoulder once again and moved to the door. He waited.

The man with the gun device holstered it and then placed the palm of his hand flat against the steel of the door, softly. He pushed with the slightest of pressure, and the door swung easily open, its hinges squeaking slightly.

The two quickly stepped across the threshold into the pitch-black hallway beyond the door. Two crisscrossing flashlight beams disappeared into the dark belly of the building.

The alarm began, a high drone. It carried through the quiet night. A dog began howling in response, followed by another. Slowly, lights began to flicker on in the occasional apartment down the street, someone peering suspiciously out the window, only to think better of it. An elderly man with insomnia opened his door and craned his head to look toward the source of the droning alarm.

Nearly a minute after disappearing into the doorway, the two figures emerged from the dark interior of the building, the alarm still insistently wailing. Neither was carrying the box anymore—it had been left inside.

When later questioned by the Angel City Police Department, the only thing the sole witness—a paralegal who had come downstairs to stretch his legs and get some fresh air—could say for certain about the events was that he had seen two shapes moving across the street. The rest was unclear—he hadn't been wearing his glasses, after all. Those had been sitting on his desk up on the fourth floor, where his entire team and an outside group of temp workers had been working late into the night to meet a deadline for the Angel lawyers. There were at least 135 workers on the floor. The overtime pay was good, the witness explained tearfully.

Quickly scanning the street to check if it was clear, the two dark figures moved at a trot down the sidewalk toward a residential neighborhood. Reaching the corner of the dark residential street, they went separate ways without a word, one turning right toward Beverly, the other going left toward Melrose.

The street was once again abandoned, the alarm wailing over an empty scene.

A security guard who had been drowsing in his old silver Toyota Corolla finally woke to the noise of the alarm. Sputtering and muttering, the overweight guard drew himself up out of the reclined driver's seat and opened the car door.

"*Goddammit*," he cursed under his breath as he collected himself. How long had he been napping? It couldn't have been that long. But now the alarm was going off—this could mean his job. Scanning the street, everything seemed normal except for the alarm. He fumbled for his long flashlight and flipped it on. Stepping down the sidewalk, he walked under the towering glass façade of the building. He reached the glass front doors and checked them. They were still locked snugly tight. The guard's brow cinched in concentration. He shined the light slowly inside the glass of the doors, its beam moving back and forth across the lobby, but he could see no movement.

He felt at his waistband but couldn't find the keycard for the side door into the lobby. Must have left it in the car. So, reaching to his waist, he pulled up a huge steel ring that had at least two dozen keys attached to it. Narrowing his eyes, the guard began going through the keys. He tried one, and then another, but none of them fit. Exasperated, he continued looking through the keys for the right one, then thought better of it.

Dropping the ring back to his side, he started stepping carefully through the short, manicured bushes that edged the front of the building, shining his light through the glass inside. The beam shone weirdly into the dark, empty building, reflecting off the shiny floor of the minimalist lobby, casting fractured, monumental shadows.

Suddenly the searching beam found something out of place, only a few feet inside the glass wall.

"What the hell?" the guard muttered to himself, looking at the black metal box through the glass. Scratching his head, the guard walked back to the front doors. He pulled a huge ring of keys from his pockets and began searching for the right one. He tried one. Not right. He cursed. Tried another. This one didn't fit either.

The legal workers from the fourth floor started emerging from the stairwell into the dark lobby, which was illuminated by flashing alarm lights. Bleary-eyed from too much work and too little sleep, they stumbled into the lobby, grumbling, dozens of them.

"Must be another false alarm," a man with a stained white shirt and a brown tie complained under his breath. "Should have just stayed upstairs with Phil and the others."

Many of the office workers just stood in the lobby, yawning, waiting for the alarm to be reset, looking at the vending machines. There'd been two false alarms in the past month. Some of the workers had begun exiting the building through the side door with their keycards to get a bit of fresh air before heading back up to their late shift. They stood outside, just feet away from the sheer glass walls of the building, the ANGEL ADMINISTRATION AFFAIRS lettering just above their heads.

The alarm continued to drone.

Then, in a panic, the security guard began yelling at the workers, rushing toward them with his flashlight.

"Move! Move! Get away!" the guard shouted. "For God's sake, mo—"

Before he could finish his sentence, he was incinerated in a hellish firestorm of flame and glass.

The front of the lobby exploded outward onto the street in an enormous, ballooning orange cloud as the bomb detonated. The forty or so people just inside the doors never even knew what happened as they were instantly reduced to fiery ashes. The entire glass façade with the ANGEL ADMINISTRATION AFFAIRS lettering burst outward in the fire of the bomb, and the force of the inferno instantly pulverized those unfortunates still standing on the sidewalk. Light from the flames reflected off the millions of shards of glass as they shattered, falling like razor-sharp snowflakes, tinkling, along with whatever remained of the dead office workers, onto a row of burning parked cars. Flames from the cars licked angrily at the sky, roiling black smoke and fire up into the dark.

One woman, her face covered in dark soot and crimson blood, had been saved because she had been standing behind a car. She screamed in agony, her leg a mess of blood and bone. Another man rolled on the lawn, his flaming clothes melted to his body. Most of the others weren't so lucky, the front sidewalk a scene of mayhem and carnage beyond what even the most terrorized imagination could envision.

Somewhere in the distance, a police siren began. Then another. The building alarm itself had been abruptly silenced by the blast.

The trees in front of the building rocked back and forth, their palms flaming and sizzling bloodred in the night.

# CHAPTER SEVEN

The offices of the NAS, where Maddy had been just yesterday, now transformed into a kind of command center. Inside a small auditorium that also served as an enormous conference room, Archangels perched around a massive table, their eyes gaunt from concern and lack of sleep. Many high-profile Guardians sat in seats in the circular auditorium, along with a number of human lawyers, who were seated just behind the main table. A number of chisel-jawed, black-suited Angel Disciplinary Council Agents stood discreetly at the exits of the auditorium, ensuring safety. Frantic assistants flitted in and out of the room. Phones rang constantly. Footage of the smoldering carnage that had been the front façade of the Angels Administration Affairs building a few blocks away played on the massive projection screen at the head of the room. Pillars of smoke swirled up from the glowing ashes of the wreckage on the screen.

A technician readied equipment for a video conference with Angel branch headquarters in Paris, London, Rio, and Beijing.

In the far corner, Mark Godspeed looked contemplatively out the tinted windows that formed a gleaming wall—a wall that looked down onto Beverly Boulevard from many stories up. Golden morning sun filtered through the thick glass. Behind Mark, the newscast scrolled the latest fatality count for the bombing: eighty-three and growing—all humans, but the attack had clearly been on the symbolic seat of Angel business.

Archangel Holyoake brought his fist down on the solid oak table with a thump, causing the half-drunk cups of coffee on the table to shake. Holyoake was a hulking figure, his bulk contained under a steely blue suit, powder blue shirt, and silver tie.

"We have to come out strong. This bombing is a frontal assault, and we need to respond accordingly! We cannot be seen as weak!"

A female Archangel shot Holyoake a glance. "William, how many times do we have to go over this? We have no solid idea where this threat is coming from, or who it could even be. No one is claiming responsibility yet. Jumping to conclusions now would be foolish and would open us up to serious criticism further down the line."

"We need to practice restraint," Archangel Steeple agreed.

A deep voice erupted down the table. It was Archangel Charles Churchson, who stood up to address the assembled Angels. Mark turned his head slightly toward Churchson as he spoke, although he still maintained his gaze out the shimmering window.

"Don't play dumb. It must be Senator Linden and his people. It's the logical next step for their organization, even if he is running a presidential campaign," Churchson said gravely. "He's campaigning on an anti-Angel platform, and some are starting to listen to his lies. The proposed 'Immortals Bill' would be the single most dangerous threat to Angels since the Great Awakening. He's fueling hatred, turning humanity against us. They're making a power play, and they won't stop until we're totally rendered toothless, intimidated, and weak. Some violent act like this was bound to happen. The question is, what will we do about it? Stand by and watch as they attack our prized institutions? Or something else."

More than a few heads at the table were nodding in agreement with Churchson.

Mark Godspeed turned all the way around to the assembled Angels in the room and spoke. "Regardless of what's decided here today, we must ensure safety and security for Angels across Angel City and the world. Whatever it takes."

"Mark's right," Holyoake said. "And part of ensuring safety is ensuring that the investigation is done properly and that we bring the perpetrators to light. That's why we must conduct the inquiry entirely. We can't trust a human police force. With the growing influence of Linden and his agents of hate, we can be sure there will be moles in all the human agencies."

Mark disagreed. "We do have friends within the police department. Perhaps we can use their resources, as well."

"We cannot trust them. Period," Archangel Churchson said. He turned to the bank of nondescript men sitting along the wall. "How has our closing out of the police been going?"

One of the lawyers responded. "The scene was sealed for Angels-only access shortly after ACPD arrived from the 911 call. The police complied."

"Good," Archangel Churchson said. He took a drink from his coffee mug and set it back on the table.

The glass doors to the conference room swung open. Jackson Godspeed stood there in a gray hoodie and dark blazer. A number of Angels turned to the door, surprised to see him.

"Jacks, what are you doing here?" Mark said. "I thought you were with your mother and sister."

The world's most famous Angel scanned the room, seeing Archangel Churchson's nephew, Steven, along with a couple other Guardians from his Commissioning class last year. His cheeks burned hot with anger and embarrassment for a moment as he thought about how he hadn't even been called for this most important of meetings. He addressed his stepfather.

"I'm a Guardian, aren't I? Even if I can't fly right now," Jacks said. "I've sworn to uphold and protect the ideals of the NAS."

A few of the Angels uncomfortably studied the table in front of them rather than match Jacks's direct gaze.

Mark stood up from his chair and walked over to Jackson. He put what was meant to be a conciliatory hand on his shoulder.

"Jacks, you'll be no good to us at all if you don't get better," Mark quietly said. "You need to focus on your recovery. Get your wings back."

Jackson's gaze floated past his stepfather and up to the devastation and disaster of the bombing playing on the screen. Fury and determination combined in his glinting blue eyes.

"No, Mark. I want to help. I *need* to help," Jacks said emphatically. "I want to bring whatever monster did this to justice. I have to be useful somehow. Just doing anything. You've got to put me to work."

Mark seemed about to protest again when a voice spoke. Faces turned. It was Archangel Churchson.

"Let him stay."

# CHAPTER EIGHT

Maddy's alarm woke her from a strangely dreamless sleep. It was her first day of training to become a Guardian Angel. Turning her head, she looked again at the Angel City sign perched above the Hills. It seemed different today.

Maddy stepped into the bathroom, turning the shower on scalding hot. She looked at herself in the mirror as the water heated up. *You are not scared, Maddy. You are not scared.*

She shook her head. She couldn't lie to herself. *You* are *totally scared, though!*

Taking off the T-shirt she slept in, Maddy turned her back to the mirror and looked over her shoulder before she stepped into the shower. Her Immortal Marks, delicate and fair, shone on her bare back. Recently the marks had become even more pronounced, and Maddy could swear she even saw them give off a sparkling light every now and then.

•  •  •

After showering and toweling off, Maddy had to choose what she was going to wear for her first day of training. Against her best efforts to discourage him, Jacks had insisted on taking Maddy shopping on his dime—she would be getting her first Guardian-training stipend check soon, along with an enormous signing bonus, which itself would be more money than she'd ever dreamt of seeing in her life, but the Angel lawyers were still working on the contracts. Maddy was still trying to decide how far to give in to Darcy's insistence on various photo shoots and endorsements. She had heard that Nike was interested in a special "Maddy" shoe, even.

She'd laid some of the new clothes Jacks had insisted on buying her across the back of her old wooden desk chair. She slipped into a skirt and then squeezed into a finely cut shirt by a designer whose name she couldn't pronounce. She closed her bedroom door and looked at herself in the full-length mirror that hung on the back.

She had to admit that the clothes had a certain charm. If she were *really* going to admit it, they looked great—the salesgirl had definitely known what would look good on her. But Maddy looked at *herself* behind the clothes and saw how uncomfortable she appeared, like she was afraid she'd rip something just by sneezing. She seemed stiff and awkward.

Walking to her closet, Maddy rummaged around for a bit before ultimately coming up with what she was looking for, her old favorite pair of jeans. She slipped off the skirt and put the jeans on. Now just to find the other piece. . . . Pawing through a small pile of clean laundry near the door, Maddy found it: her gray hoodie. Finishing her trademark uniform, Maddy looked at herself in the mirror. She was so much more relaxed, it was almost shocking. Jacks may complain, but Maddy wasn't going to start her first day as an Angel wearing clothes she didn't feel like herself in.

She did grab one of Jacks's purchases, a pair of Dior sunglasses she secretly loved. Sticking them on, Maddy flipped off the light switch and headed downstairs. Stealing a quick glance out the front window, she was shocked to see the largest crowd of paparazzi she'd had to contend with yet.

When the Archangels announced last week that Maddy would start training to become a Guardian, the response from the media had been quick and overwhelming. The press had been focused on the shocking bombing of the Angel offices and the grisly casualties, but now a scintillating and unheard of story started replacing the somber coverage of the violence: the future Guardianship of an ordinary girl from Angel City. A! and ANN and almost all the other networks quickly put together hour-long specials about Maddy. Fox ran a new episode of *American Protection* as a lead-in to their "Maddy" special. The networks had gotten their paws on old yearbooks and showed the worst possible pictures Maddy could have imagined, including a disastrous one from seventh grade, or "The Year of the Braces," as she shuddered to think of it. Old classmates she didn't even really remember were interviewed, talking about Maddy like they had been best friends for years. Practically everyone who'd ever met Maddy seemed to be getting in on the action. Worst of all, Maddy thought, was how each of the specials went into gory detail over the dramatic events around Jackson's Commissioning: Jackson saving her, the Dark Angel attack, the deadly freeway chase, Jackson's mangling at the hands of the hired demon, and her own near-death.

The Angel blogs were even worse, running over every piece of gossip they could pick up. Every other hour, it seemed like Johnny Vuitton had some new "blind" item, and with everything horrible that came up, Maddy would get a breathless text from Gwen at college in Arizona.

As for Maddy's publicist . . . Darcy was beside herself every day: her office was being swamped with requests, but Maddy was still turning down interviews, photo shoots, and appearances.

"Maddy, just be *reasonable*," Darcy had pleaded yesterday, practically on the verge of anxious tears. "For the love of whatever you believe in, *please* let me do my job!"

But Maddy, for now, was steadfast—she wanted to focus on her training. With the spotlight trained on her, she was going to need every last bit of concentration as she prepared to become a Guardian.

She ran past the paparazzi to Kevin's old station wagon, slamming the door shut and peeling out of the driveway as quickly as she could. Once away from the clustered pack of photographers, she turned on the radio. DJs on every channel seemed to be talking about her.

*"Angel fanatics across the globe are beside themselves today as Madison Montgomery Godright, the human girl formerly only known as superstar Jackson Godspeed's girlfriend, steps into the spotlight as she begins her Guardian Angel training in glamorous Angel City! Maddy, who is the only part-Angel, part-human ever known to exist, still doesn't have her wings yet—but that isn't stopping the Archangels from getting her into training with other future Angel nominees, like Jacks's bestie, Mitch Steeple, and the sexy Australian Emily Brightchurch! Stay tuned all week as we cover all angles Maddy, the girl who became an Angel!"*

Maddy flipped to another channel, but it was more of the same. The host, Jason Shipley, had a raspy voice, but that didn't disguise his enthusiasm.

*"For years, hopefuls around the country, and even the world, have moved to Angel City in hopes of someday becoming a Protection and joining the sexy and elite circle of Immortals! But now they have an even bigger dream, as this week former waitress Maddy Montgomery starts training to become an Angel! And* Angel Magazine *is offering a cool $1 million for the first photo of Maddy's wings! So if you're in the Immortal City this week, have your camera ready and you could have a great payday!"*

One million dollars? Maddy hadn't known that. A stab of anxiety hit her as she imagined having her wings come out in public. She hoped against hope that she'd have some kind of control when they decided to make their debut.

She pulled up to the guard shack that led to the entrance to the Angel training campus. The security officer leaned down, eyeing the old station wagon suspiciously over the brim of his black hat.

"Hi," Maddy said, smiling tentatively.

"Who are you here to see?"

"Um, no one—I mean, I'm here myself—I mean, I'm here for training."

"ID?" the guard barked. Maddy could see another guard in the shack. It looked like he had some kind of rifle slung across his shoulder, too.

She handed her California driver's license to the guard. As soon as he read the name on the plastic ID, his expression brightened.

"Oh, right this way, miss," he said brightly. "I didn't recognize you. Never can be too careful, especially with those HDF wackos making more threats everyday."

Although the Humanity Defense Faction had yet to claim responsibility, the general consensus was that they must have been involved in the bombing, given that for years they'd been calling for the dismantling of the NAS, by violent means if necessary.

The gleaming gate lifted silently, and Maddy drove onto the campus. Just inside, there was another pair of black-clad armed guards—the Immortals kept their training absolutely secret, and they weren't taking any chances, especially not after the bombing. Leafy trees lined a drive that ran past a series of bungalow offices that had been built in the '30s and kept in pristine condition. A series of gardeners worked on the immaculate lawn, trimming each blade of perfectly green grass. Monumental palm trees stood in the distance.

The front building was a giant corner bungalow that housed the training head's office, where Louis Kreuz, an Angel immigrant from Central Europe, had been ruling the training grounds for as long as anyone could remember. At first Maddy had wondered why he had such an "un-Angelic" last name, but then she figured out it was simply German for "cross." Kreuz was famous, Maddy knew from Jackson, both for his tirades against Angel trainees and instructors alike as well as for his astonishing success at transforming the most unlikely Angels into overnight superstar Guardians. (He was also notorious for having an expensive Cuban cigar dangling from his mouth at all times. An old joke in Angel City was that he smoked them even in his sleep, leading to considerable difficulties for Mrs. Kreuz.)

Maddy followed the drive around the side of the bungalows to the parking area. Her first impulse was to park in the visitor section, but a sign directed her to an area in the small lot reserved for "Nominees in Training."

Past the offices stood two rows of low but imposing white buildings that looked to Maddy like enormous hangars. There must have been at least a dozen of them, gleaming under the sun. If anyone wanted to know how the Angels kept their training so secret, here was part of the answer, at least.

Maddy pulled her uncle's station wagon into a free spot. She checked her bag one last time, making sure she had everything she needed—including a new blank journal from Uncle Kevin, along with her father's training notebook. She got out of the car into the blinding sunshine and looked at her vehicle parked incongruously among those of the other young Angels in training: Porsche, Jaguar, Range Rover, Porsche, BMW M3 . . . and Kevin's old station wagon with 220,000 miles on it. She saw he still hadn't taken the Angel City High School honor student bumper sticker off. Maddy idly wondered if they had "My Kid Is an Honor Student at the Guardian Angel Training Academy" stickers.

A golf cart whizzed up to Maddy, piloted by a young woman just a few years older than Maddy.

"Ms. Godright? I'm Sadie. Mr. Kreuz wishes to see you." Her voice was sharp and clipped. She was so beautiful that Maddy thought at first she must be an Angel, but there was something earthbound about her that made Maddy decide she was human.

"Mr. . . . Kreuz?" Maddy sputtered. "Now?"

"Yes. He specifically requested I come fetch you as soon as you arrived on the grounds. And Mr. Kreuz doesn't like to be kept waiting."

The ride on the cart only took thirty seconds, looping around the back of the other low-slung offices to the front bungalow. Along the way, they passed two Angels Maddy would've bet anything were Guardians in training, a guy and a girl. She also would've bet anything they glared at her as she passed by.

Sadie led Maddy through double doors into the plush offices. They were as well appointed as the NAS headquarters, but much more classic, with a '30s art deco flair. Maddy felt like she was stepping back to a more glamorous time in Angel City's past.

A receptionist sitting at the front desk gave Sadie a hand signal. Sadie nodded and quickly opened the door to the inner office, motioning for Maddy to walk in.

"Mr. Kreuz will see you now," Sadie said. Maddy took a few timid steps in, and Sadie pulled the door shut, leaving Maddy alone in the room.

From behind a tremendous cloud of smoke, a shorter, somewhat portly Angel emerged, cigar first. Maddy realized she hadn't even ever seen an overweight Angel. In fact, he might have been the most un-Angelic Angel she'd ever met. Louis Kreuz wore a sleek herringbone suit and gold tie and had a thin mustache. He stomped toward her.

"You must be the Godright girl," the man said loudly, brashly, putting his hand out to shake. "I read about you. You're famous."

Maddy timidly put her hand forward, and it disappeared in his meaty paw as he shook it up and down.

"I'm Louis. But you probably already know that. If you were dumb, you wouldn't be going through Guardian training. We'd just jump you straight to Archangel." Louis Kreuz laughed heartily at his punch line. The phone on his desk beeped and a light flashed green, indicating a call was coming through. With irritation he turned his head to the thick oak doors. "NO CALLS, YOU NITWITS!" he shouted at the assistants through the doors.

Maddy took a second to look around. She found herself in a plush, oak-lined room. Just outside the two large windows that swung open onto a garden, glorious purple and pink flowers flourished. Their scent wafted into the room, mixing with the cigar. Old, silver-framed photos of Louis Kreuz with practically every famous Guardian ever lined the walls. Memories from Angel City's Golden Age. They were all signed: "With love always, to Louis," "Louis, where would I ever be without you, darling?" "Louis: you still owe me $10, you lug!" Maddy even saw a picture with Jackson's Aunt Clara, the former "Pearl of Angel City." Jackson had told her once there had even been rumors of an affair between the two of them, which the newspapers, radio, and newsreel films at the time had been as eager to exploit as the blogs and ANN would be today.

Kreuz looked at Maddy. "You mute?"

"What?" Maddy started.

"You mute? You haven't said nothin'."

Maddy's face flushed. "Well, I just want to tell you what a great opportunity it is—"

Kreuz's face turned serious. "Save the canned lines for the interviews on ANN. You think you're ready to become a nominee?"

Maddy gulped. "Yes," she said firmly.

"Well that's good. Because I don't. In fact, I told them as much when they sent you along to me. What's a half-Angel, half-human who's never had a day of training and hasn't even gotten her wings yet going to do here? But they insisted. And everybody's got a boss. Including me. Only difference is mine goes by the name Gabriel, he's on the Council of Twelve, and he started a little thing I like to call Protection for Pay. You mighta heard of it."

Maddy was at a loss for words. She tried to stare at the same spot on the carpet, wishing she were literally anywhere but there at that moment. While she had found courage in the conference room at the NAS with the pretentious Archangels, this direct attack from Kreuz left her feeling small and wounded.

"You're coming in so late in the game, I don't even know where to start. These other Guardians, they practically started trainin' in their mothers' wombs. And now they want to fast-track you over a couple years?" Kreuz snorted.

"I . . ." But Maddy trailed off. He was right. She *was* starting training incredibly late, although she knew she wouldn't be Commissioned for at least two years at a minimum.

The short, powerful man looked at her, taking a large puff off his cigar before blowing out an enormous cloud of thick gray smoke.

"That ain't to say you can't do it. Just know I'll be watching you. Closely."

With that, he walked across the office and back around to sit at his enormous walnut desk, where he began checking e-mails on his silver-and-black PowerMac, a small concession to modern days. He still puffed away on his cigar.

Maddy stood there, frozen, unsure what to do. After a moment, Kreuz looked up at Maddy, annoyed.

"What are you still doing here? You got training to do."

Blushing in confusion, Maddy turned around and walked out the door.

Sadie was standing by the receptionist, one hand poised on a box of Kleenex. Maddy's hands were shaking from the encounter, but Sadie almost seemed disappointed that Maddy wasn't more crushed. She moved her hand away from the Kleenex and, leaning down, picked up a brand-new laptop that was sitting on the desk. It had the initials MMG engraved on it.

"This is yours," Sadie said as she handed it to Maddy, who had never had her own brand-new computer before—Kevin had only been able to buy used ones for her. And she certainly had never had her own new $2,000 MacBook Pro.

"Well, thanks," Maddy said, letting out her pent-up breath and examining the object in her hands.

The receptionist spoke into her headset: "Churchfield on two." Then, after patching the call through to Kreuz: "Gary, you're on with Louis."

From inside the office, Maddy could hear Kreuz starting to yell on the call.

Sadie looked at her watch.

"We're running late. Let's get you to your first class."

Maddy nodded, looking for a brief moment over her shoulder to the door that led back into Kreuz's office as his muffled yelling continued.

She was astonished to find that the hallways inside the office and classroom buildings that flanked Louis's enormous office were all marble. They passed door after door of Angel instructor offices and old classrooms, and Maddy wondered how Northwestern would've stacked up. Sadie finally stopped outside a door. Maddy looked through the window into the classroom. A younger Angel in a tan corduroy jacket with elbow patches perched on a desk, looking over some notes. The room looked strangely conventional. And otherwise empty.

"Where's everyone else?"

"Oh, Mr. Kreuz felt that you should have private tutors, especially to begin with. That way you wouldn't feel as behind as you would with the rest of those who are training to be Guardians. It's really for your own good."

Maddy's brow creased as she tried to figure out what kind of game Kreuz was playing.

"Okay. Private tutor. Got it." Maddy thought about how she'd never had a *private* anything, much less a person dedicated to teaching her. "Anything else I should know?"

"That about covers it. If you need anything, you know where to find us," Sadie said. She put her slight hand on Maddy's shoulder and squeezed it in encouragement, the first friendly sign she'd given Maddy. "And good luck."

The door opened with a creak as Maddy pushed it and stepped into the classroom.

The corduroy-clad Angel shuffled his notes together and looked up. "You must be Maddy. I'm Philip. We'll be working together for a while."

Maddy shook his hand and settled into a chair, nervously lowering her book bag to the ground. She found she was actually anxious to discover what her first lesson in being a Guardian was going to be: freezing time like Jacks could do? Some cool trick where she got to dial in to a Protection's frequency and wouldn't have to have the disturbingly random and hard-to-act-upon "static" images that had been with her since childhood, like the one of the boy in the fire? Something even more useful and amazing she couldn't even imagine?

"We may as well get started," Philip said. Maddy leaned forward, her eagerness showing despite herself.

Reaching down to a bag at the foot of the table with both hands,

Philip pulled out an enormous textbook. He threw it on the table between them, where it landed with a thundering *thud*. The book was old, a dark olive green, and had no pictures or graphics on the outside. Maddy thought it must be at least two thousand pages long. Simple black lettering was pressed into the front cover of the book: *ANGEL AERODYNAMICS*.

She reached forward and timidly flipped the book open. The pages were crammed with text, with only the occasional graphical aid. There were also endless formulas and algorithms: calculus and algebraic figures spread across the pages. Maddy had to stifle a groan.

"This should keep you busy for some time," Philip said calmly. "I'll be back in three hours to see how you've done on the exercises in the first three chapters." The Angel rose from his chair to leave the room.

"But—" Maddy started.

Philip turned at the door, his ear cocked, with a wicked look on his face.

"Yes . . . ?"

"Nothing," Maddy said after a moment, remembering what Kreuz had said to her and resolving not to show them any weakness. "I just remembered I *do* have a calculator on my phone. I don't like to use the ones on these computers. Thanks!"

Smiling tightly, Philip left the room.

With a sigh, Maddy opened the book. She looked at the copyright page: 1957. The book was older than Uncle Kevin! This was a far cry from the sexy and flashy Guardian training she thought she was going to encounter on her first day.

Maddy started work, and although the text was dense, she was surprised to see that some of the formulas weren't as difficult as she had first thought. She had always been near the head of the pack in her math classes, and she'd aced the AP calculus exam.

She had barely done the first exercise in the chapter when her iPhone buzzed in her bag. Pulling it out, she saw it was a text from Jacks. It read: *"Angel Aerodynamics?"*

Fingers flying, Maddy wrote back: *"How'd you know?"*

Jackson: *"Haha, everybody gets that first. Don't worry, it gets better!* ☺ *Can I take you to dinner after in celebration of your first day?"*

Maddy thought for a moment, wondering if she wouldn't have too much homework to do after her first day. She remembered Jackson's advice to her the night he had come to her room to take her flying when they had first met: "Just do it to *do* something."

Maddy: *"Okay. As long as you aren't embarrassed by a date who's doing square root calculations during dessert."*

Jackson: *"Pick you up at seven."*

Maddy flipped the phone to silent and went back to work.

Three hours later, when Philip came back, Maddy still had the *Angel Aerodynamics* book open and was writing in her notebook. The jacketed Angel raised an eyebrow and smiled mercilessly as he eyed Maddy. "Still working, I see? Don't worry, this is difficult for even our most . . . *practiced* Angels."

Maddy put her pencil down and closed the massive textbook. She looked up at Philip.

"Oh, I just finished early so I thought I'd do chapters four and five, too—I like to work ahead. I was just starting chapter six when you walked in, but I can do that next time."

She smiled sweetly at Philip.

At that moment Sadie arrived and whisked Maddy away to her next class. She had a stack of other books for Maddy, including *Practical Flying for Guardians, Second Edition*; *Time Manipulation in Guardianship*; as well as *The Book of Angels*, a biblical-era book. Maddy thought it was a strange choice, but apparently it played into an Angel history class—

which, she found ironic, she would be taking for a second time, having been forced to study angel history at ACHS.

As they stepped out into the blinding sunshine, Maddy saw a group of beautiful young Immortals walking together toward a canteen on the grounds. She could've sworn they looked over at her, followed by a snatch of laughter. Sadie glanced at the Angels from the corner of her eye.

"If you're wondering about lunch, you just tell me what you want and I'll have it delivered to the class. Mr. Kreuz feels it would be best if you have working lunches, at least at first, since you have so much ground to cover."

Maddy didn't respond. She thought about the cigar-chomping boss, and anger flushed through her—he was trying to keep her away from the other Guardians in training! She pushed the thought from her mind, trying to focus on the task at hand: surviving her next class. She wondered what boring thing they'd try to throw at her this time: translating ancient Angel texts from Latin into modern English? Memorizing every Archangel since 1910? Reciting the NAS's charter and constitutional amendments, year by year?

Caught in this storm of thoughts, Maddy turned the corner and almost ran directly into a female Angel who was in the middle of a sentence. Her Australian accent was unmistakable: ". . . even *believe* what's going on here now? Next thing you know we'll be taking applications from anybody off the street who thinks—"

The beautiful, lithe Angel, who was walking with another potential Guardian, stopped short. "Oh, hi, Sadie," Emily Brightchurch said.

Sadie cleared her throat. "Emily, this is Maddy Montgomery. You'll be seeing a lot of her around here."

Maddy, flustered, stumbled on her words. "Nice to meet you, Emily." Of course she knew who Emily was—an Australian Angel transplant who had come to Angel City that year to finish her training—though they'd never officially met. Emily was one of the most gossiped-about Angels in this year's nominee class, and her earthy sex appeal was undeniable. She had caused a scandal by appearing in a series of arty, provocative black-and-white Bulgari ads on billboards along the Halo Strip, just across from the Chateau Marmont. She had flaunted the jewelry and her Immortal Marks—and nothing else—in the ads, and the billboards had caused more than their share of near-accidents on that stretch of Sunset Boulevard. She had deep-red hair, the hint of a few sun freckles, and an absolutely perfect complexion.

The sexy Angel looked Maddy fully up and down, and gave her a plastic smile that wasn't meant to fool anyone.

"*Hi*, Maddy. Hope you're getting settled in. We're so happy you're joining us, even though it's at such a late, late stage." Emily flashed the fake smile even brighter. "Everyone is so impressed that you're willing to try despite your . . . difficulties . . . to be a Guardian when the rest of us have been training for so long."

Totally taken aback, Maddy stuttered out a few shocked words. Why was the privileged Angel being so . . . snotty? Maddy had never done a thing to her!

"Be a sweetheart and say hi to Jacks for me, would you?" the Aussie Angel added. "Ta!" Emily turned to her companion Angel, who was eyeing Maddy with thinly veiled disdain. "Let's go, Zoe. The others are waiting."

The two female Guardian trainees whisked away into the sunny afternoon, leaving Maddy speechless in their wake.

"So glad you're getting to know some of the other Angels," Sadie said as they stepped into the golf cart.

"Yes. Me too," Maddy said grimly, looking over her shoulder as the two Angels joined the other group and disappeared into the canteen.

Crossing the grounds in the cart under swaying palm trees, Sadie and Maddy soon turned down a road that led between the enormous white hangars Maddy had seen when she first arrived. Each one looked exactly the same, save for individual painted black numbers. They were low and hidden by a screen of trees behind the thick walls that surrounded the entire training campus, so you would never know they were even there. No frills. But obviously something was going on in them. Sadie parked the golf cart outside the building marked #5.

Going into the building was like stepping into a pool of darkness. The sunlight outside contrasted with the inky blackness inside the building. After a few moments, Maddy's eyes began adjusting to the dark, and she saw she was in a large room, one that was still only maybe one-tenth the size of the entire hangar. It was tiled from floor to ceiling in individual TV screens, like the inside of a dome. A number of computer monitors glowed along a control panel to the side, and in the middle of the room loomed a large metal platform. No one was present except for one Angel. She stood up, smiling genuinely to greet Maddy. Maddy suddenly recognized her as the female Archangel who had spoken up for her at the meeting at the NAS.

"Hello, I'm Professor Archangel Archson," she said. "But you can call me Susan." With her olive complexion and rich, dark hair pulled into a bun, Susan seemed at first glance like another impossibly gorgeous Angel, but there was an accessible side to her that Maddy immediately sensed.

Sadie excused herself, leaving Maddy and the professor alone together. Susan offered Maddy a cup of tea, which she politely declined.

"Well, if you don't mind . . ." The woman poured herself a cup of the steaming brown liquid, mixing in a few drops of honey and fresh-squeezed lemon. She smiled warmly again at Maddy.

"You look confused," Susan said. "Sometimes we Archangels teach classes. It keeps us close to the incoming classes of Guardians."

Maddy tried to smile back, but the fact that her teacher was not just an Angel but an Archangel made her feel even more nervous.

Susan looked at Maddy. "Tell me what you know about frequencing."

Maddy's mind went back to what Jackson had told her, as well as her own experience with the phenomenon—her own strange visions, Angel "abilities" dating from way before she knew she was part Angel, the grisly premonitions that would overrun her at random times.

"Well, every person has a frequency. It's unique. And every Angel has the ability to pick up on these frequencies."

"That's right," the professor said, nodding encouragingly.

"But normally it's like static, if you don't know the frequency. It doesn't make sense, it's all jumbled. That's what used to happen to me . . . before I knew."

"Every Angel has this, except you weren't aware. And every Angel has to learn how to control it. Some have to work very long and hard at it, and some may never even master it. Did you know that?"

Maddy shook her head.

"I've gone over your case file. Apparently you're already well on your way." Professor Archson looked at Maddy. "I bet you didn't know that either, did you?"

"No, I just always thought I was a . . . freak."

"I know what you mean. Visions started interpolating themselves with me at a much younger than normal age. I'd become so disturbed that my parents thought of sending me away to Angel boarding school as young as age seven. I thought I'd never master frequencing, not have those terrifying images own me. And now here I am, teaching them. You're not a freak, Maddy. You're just one of us."

Maddy nodded, her blood chilling for a moment as she recalled the premonition of the boy in the striped shirt, reaching out to her from fire at the homeless shelter.

"Are you okay?" the professor asked.

Maddy regarded the kind Angel in front of her. "Professor Archson, can I still have that tea? It sounds good."

"Sure." The professor poured her a cup. "And remember, it's Susan." She leaned forward in her chair. "Now, should we get started?"

Susan turned to her computer. She typed a few keystrokes, and a deep rumbling started in the room. An eerie blue aura began to fill the space, and Maddy realized it was coming from the mysterious metallic platform in the middle of the room. Susan led Maddy toward it. The blue gleam from the sphere began to grow brighter, and Maddy thought she even felt some heat emanating off the gleaming skin of the metal.

"This is what we call a frequencing modulator. Professor Crosstone, who helped found these grounds, built the first crude prototype, and I have since perfected it." Susan reached her hand close to the sphere. The blue light seemed to slowly gravitate toward her hand as it neared. "If you're on it, it vastly amplifies the frequencies of those within a certain range. It's like throwing darts at a board and all of a sudden having the bull's-eye made ten times bigger—it's a lot easier. You can then practice on isolating and identifying frequencies, sharpening your skills. Which, if all goes well with your training and becoming a nominee, you'll use the day you meet your Protections."

Maddy stepped closer, the blue luminescence from the sphere illuminating her face. She looked at the hundreds of screens surrounding her. They were still all dark.

"What about them?"

"As the modulator brings in frequencies, we project them on each of these screens, graphically. The neural feedback of isolating them both in your mind and through the projections of the screens makes the learning process twice as effective."

Susan stepped away from the platform, leaving Maddy there.

"Want to take it for a spin?"

"Sure," Maddy said uncertainly.

"That's what we're here for," Susan said, laughing. "Don't worry, it won't bite."

She walked over to the small control area and began typing in some keystrokes.

"Stepping it up to full speed," Susan's disembodied voice came over the intercom.

Maddy felt the slightest bit lightheaded, but otherwise nothing seemed to change. The screens surrounding her remained blank.

"I'm going to stop talking for a while," Susan's voice said through the intercom. "What I want you to do is quiet your mind. And then start listening with it. I know this may sound strange, or difficult. But just start to *listen*. We don't expect anything amazing this first time around; it's enough just to understand that there are always frequencies out there to listen to, even if they are jumbled. Take as much time as you need."

"Okay, Profes—I mean, Susan. I'll try to do my best," Maddy said. Closing her eyes, Maddy tried to focus. All kinds of thoughts began rushing through her mind: what Louis Kreuz had said to her, how Uncle Kevin was handling her being gone, what the other Guardians in training thought about her, how she might need to get her own car, whether she'd swapped the laundry from the washer to the dryer. Maddy had never even really realized what her own mind was constantly churning over. It seemed to be amplified by the frequency modulator.

After what seemed to her like an eternity, her thoughts began to calm down, until there was a kind of clearing in her own mind. Taking a breath, she tried to begin to listen with her mind. To her astonishment, Maddy began to hear and feel things outside herself. At first they were far off. Then they became closer. They were a disordered tangle of voices, images, senses. Maddy could almost feel them, taste them herself, if only for the briefest moment. This was the static. She had felt this before, but never on command. Only at strange moments, seemingly by chance. And not this strong, either, except for the few times she'd had an actual vision, like last year when she foresaw her own death outside the high school party just before Jackson had saved her.

"Opening the frequencies," Susan said.

Suddenly, one by one, the screens began flickering to life: this one showing a man in a meeting with a boss, this one a woman buying roses at the florist, this one a teenager sitting in traffic on Angel Boulevard. As each of them hit Maddy, her mind was overtaken for a moment, and she felt like she was *there*. Until the next frequency came upon her. Soon the TVs all around were coming to life, as Susan opened more and more frequencies into the modulator for Maddy to deal with. The voices and noises in the frequencing room became loud, unruly, cacophonous.

Maddy remembered what Susan had told her about isolating and identifying frequencies. With total concentration, Maddy tried to unravel the chaotic images in her mind, one at a time. If she focused extremely hard, she could isolate one, but then it would be gone. Slowly she was able to grab on to one and start to keep it there. The energy she suddenly felt was tremendous.

"That's enough for today. We'll try isolating specific Protections next time."

But a puzzled look flashed across Susan's face as she saw that more and more TVs were coming to life, and the entire room was now filled. Maddy was drawing more frequencies even though Susan had stopped adding them to the modulator.

Maddy's eyes closed. The chaos of voices and images in her brain was incredible. Without even thinking about it, her brain started sorting each frequency strand and filing it away as its own. At long last, Maddy had just one main strand left.

And it was Susan's.

As soon as she locked in on the frequency, it was as if the world switched from black and white to color as she was able to see Susan with perfect clarity. Maddy's own perspective shifted entirely. Suddenly Maddy saw Susan frantically running up the platform to Maddy, who was collapsed, unconscious on the steel deck. It was all as clear as day.

The experience was overwhelming. Maddy felt as if she had suddenly been ripped out of her own body. Adrenaline and almost feverish excitement flooded her body.

"I see you! I see you!" she shouted.

"What? That's impossible!" Susan's voice was loud and insistent, but it seemed a million miles away. "Maddy, be careful. You're not ready!"

"I see you!" Maddy shouted again, swept away by this incredible feeling of the moment. Suddenly she felt extremely lightheaded. The edges on her vision of Susan darkened rapidly to black. Her entire sense of balance and presence had disappeared. Almost as if in slow motion, Maddy felt herself crumpling sideways, her body unable to follow her simple commands.

With a sickening *thud*, her body struck the smooth metal platform. Instantly all the TVs went black.

Susan, in a panic, ran toward the platform—just as Maddy had seen in her brief vision. Her face paled as she saw Maddy crumpled and unconscious. She leaned down over Maddy, who slowly came back to consciousness.

Blinking her eyes, she looked at Susan.

"Maddy, are you all right?" the Angel asked.

Maddy nodded slowly, sitting up. She rubbed her elbow where she'd fallen onto the hard metal.

The instructor shook her head. "It's amazing, Maddy. I thought it would take weeks for us to get to this point. And here you did it in minutes." Susan led Maddy off the frequency modulator. "I think that's enough for today, don't you?"

Maddy touched her side, wincing a bit. "Yeah, maybe that's a good idea." She laughed. "Only I could hurt myself just standing. I thought the dangerous part would be once I get my wings and start flying."

A strange expression passed across Susan's face, and she looked away, examining a computer monitor. "Oh?"

"What is it, Susan?" Maddy asked nervously.

Susan took a deep breath and looked back at Maddy, light lines of concern crossing her still-youthful face. "It's really nothing. But I know the Archangels and other doctors have told you that your wings will be coming in just like an Angel's. From what I've seen in the charts, your Immortal Marks have developed enough that wings should be emerging literally any day. And I know this is what the media expects now, too. But the truth is we don't know when or, really, *how* you will . . . mature. There's no reason to expect anything will be different. But this is a whole new world for us."

Cold, sharp anxiety washed over Maddy like a sneaker wave at the beach.

"Different?" Maddy said, remembering her recurrent nightmare of those almost demonic appendages, deformed, unwanted. Had her dream been some kind of harbinger of what was really going to come, no matter what the Angel specialists or Jacks or anyone told her?

The professor turned away again, distractedly making keystrokes on a small keypad linked to a monitor. The insistent blue light in the room slowly started to flicker and fade.

"I shouldn't have said anything. I'm sorry. We have no reason to believe anything will be different at all, Maddy." The computer screens powered down. Susan turned back to Maddy, a big smile on her face, pulling up enthusiasm. "Now what do you say we go find some lunch, seeing as Sadie seems to have gone among the missing?"

"Sure," Maddy said, gathering her bag. Susan opened the door, and the shocking sunlight poured into the dimly lit room. But Maddy's mind was far away. Still turning over this word, and what it might mean for her: *different*.

# CHAPTER NINE

The man walked down the dark back alley, passing overflowing Dumpsters that reeked in the still-hot night. His shoulders slightly hunched—a bad habit. Above, in the hazy night sky only a few blocks away, the lights of the sleek office skyscrapers shone above downtown. Although heat from the sunny day still radiated off the bricks and asphalt in the back alley at night, the man wore an overcoat, his hands thrust deep in the pockets. He preferred it that way.

The soles of his battered loafers stuck to the asphalt, which was covered with the residue of waste and garbage that never seemed to get scrubbed away.

Downtown in the glorious Immortal City. Once upon a time, the Angels were an integral part of downtown, drinking in swanky bars, dining at old-school steak restaurants, holding Angel events in the ornate auditoriums, driving their beautiful, glamorous cars underneath the towering buildings that were being erected almost every week. But that was years ago. Now every night it became an abandoned camp for the homeless and hopeless, a teeming ground for roving criminals and those who didn't want to be found. It seemed like a lifetime away from the manicured, glorious lives of the beautiful Angels—but their sparkling houses on the hill were only a five-minute drive away.

"*Spaarrre* some change, mister?" a man slurred, pulling a swig of liquor from the brown paper bag between his legs. "Barely survived the Angel City Mission fire and hav—*hiccup*—haven't been able to sleep a wink since. The dreams, I tell ya."

The voice came from beside the olive green Dumpster, startling the man in the overcoat. Looking down, he saw a scraggly man with a bloated face and red nose, his hair and beard matted. The man was dressed in what seemed to be a collection of filthy rags. The bum's image reflected in the standing man's wire-rimmed glasses.

"Maybe next time," the overcoat man said before moving on.

He soon reached an unmarked door in the alley. His fist moved forward and rapped on its metal surface.

After some shuffling behind the door, a slat opened up behind a metal grate, which was at eye level. A pair of dark eyes inspected the man outside suspiciously.

"Closed." The man's voice inside boomed into the alley before he slid the slat shut again. The alley lay silent.

The man in the overcoat reached forward and banged on the door again. This time harder.

"I'm here for Rusalka."

The slate behind the metal grate stayed halfway open.

"Oh, it's *you*," the man inside said. "Wait here."

The slat closed again. He was gone for maybe thirty seconds. All of a sudden, the sounds of multiple deadbolts unlocking came from inside.

The door into the alley opened. The man inside was wearing a white wifebeater, which stretched against his sizeable gut. It was tucked into a cheap pair of gray polyester slacks.

"Why didn't you say it was you? Freddy said you was coming. We've been waiting . . ." The man in the wifebeater trailed off, his eyes growing wide.

The man in the overcoat had pulled out a Smith & Wesson pistol with one hand. Slowly, the other hand reached into his inner coat pocket and pulled out a badge.

Detective Sylvester smiled briefly at the look on the man's face. Sometimes he enjoyed doing his job.

"Rusalka down there?"

The man nodded mournfully.

"Show me," Sylvester said, motioning with his pistol.

The man led the detective down the dismal hallway to a room. About six men sat around the table, a pile of chips in front of them, each studying a hand of poker. The room was hot and smoky from acrid tobacco smoke, and many had unbuttoned their shirts. They sat over their cards, sweat dripping from their brows.

Looking up, they saw Detective Sylvester standing there with a gun.

The men all calmly put their hands in the air. Sylvester motioned for the man in the wifebeater to go stand over by them.

"All I want is to talk to Rusalka."

A balding man with a thick mustache slowly put his hand of cards facedown on the table and stood up.

"Let's go to my office," Rusalka said, leading the detective into an adjoining back room. "You won't need that." He pointed to the gun still in Sylvester's hand.

"If it's all the same to you, I'd like to keep it handy," the detective answered.

"Suit yourself," the balding man said, lifting one eyebrow. He preceded

Sylvester into a shabby small office. The desk was covered with papers and old betting digests from the horse races. Old humming fluorescent tubes lit the room from above. It smelled like stale sweat and halitosis. Rusalka closed the door behind them.

"You want one?" the sweating man asked, pulling a pint of liquor and a pair of small glasses off a shelf behind him.

Sylvester shook his head. The man poured a short drink and gulped it down all at once.

"What can I do for you, detective? I haven't seen you down here in fifteen years. Since you helped take down Ellis and Perez."

The look in Sylvester's eyes changed. Only slightly. But enough. As if he were remembering something far off.

"I need information," Sylvester said, taking the chance to wipe his glasses clean. He put them back on and looked at Rusalka.

"What kind?"

"A couple weeks ago, a guy you had working as a lookout during one of your nighttime 'business transactions.' Travis Fittum. He disappeared, yes? A guy living down at one of the residential hotels on Skid Row. And sometimes the Angel City Mission, if he couldn't raise the hotel money. The same mission that burned two weeks ago and caused the deaths of eight women and children. Fittum was a former associate of yours whom you were giving a second chance." He looked at Rusalka's face. "You surprised? Ten dollars can buy a lot of information around here."

Rusalka looked unblinkingly at Sylvester. "If you think we'd be so dumb as to take out a guy like that and bring cops like you sniffing around, you've lost even more than what they say you have."

Detective Sylvester slightly stiffened.

"The guy disappeared," Rusalka continued. "Like *poof*, gone. We didn't even pay him yet, and he was disappeared." Rusalka shook his head. "Big deal. Just a bum. We were giving him a second chance, and he blew it. He was at a fleabag hotel this week, back on the street the next. Probably got tired of waiting and wanted to find another way to get his fix for the night."

Sylvester shook his head. "We'd normally say the same thing, except his best friend filed a missing person's complaint. He never showed up. This guy's looked everywhere. All the normal haunts from Spring Street past Mateo. And turns out it's the night before the deadly fire just down the block. We have one witness, not entirely credible, who puts him in the Angel City Mission shelter early that morning, say six o'clock."

Rusalka shrugged. "Since when did you start worrying about missing bums?"

"When a dozen go missing in one week, even the ACPD starts to take notice." Sylvester looked at Rusalka. "Do you remember anything out of the ordinary from that night?"

"Nothing. It was a hot night. We wanted to get out of there. We didn't know where he went. We weren't going to form a search party. If he couldn't stand on a corner keeping watch for an hour without getting loaded, he didn't deserve his twenty bucks."

"And you saw nothing else? You don't know anything about the other disappearances?"

"You're chasing ghosts, detective. This is downtown. You know that. It's different from the west side."

Sylvester was deep in thought.

"Now, if we're done, I'm hoping you'll excuse me. I'm one queen away from a full house," Rusalka said, motioning toward the card game outside.

The detective stood up and followed as the man led them out of the dingy room and into the smoky card game.

"Now where were we . . . ?" Rusalka asked the other men as he reached the table.

"I'll show myself out," Sylvester said, walking past the man in the wifebeater who had let him in.

Sylvester stood outside in the dark alley, taking a deep breath. He coughed, his nose burning from the thick pollution from all the trucks running on the freeways that encircled downtown like a noose.

Pulling a handkerchief from his pocket, he cleaned his glasses again and mopped his brow.

Another dead end. Shouldn't have been surprising. The detective's higher-ups in the ACPD had thought he was wasting his time by taking this case. A dozen missing, mostly homeless men and women from Skid Row, half of them John and Jane Does, right around the same time as this fire at the homeless shelter: not exactly front page news after the mysterious bombing of the Angel offices just a week ago, and not exactly a high priority for the police, either. The Angels had pull in their namesake city.

But Sylvester couldn't help feeling something was going on. And if there were twelve *reported* disappearances, how many *actual* disappearances were there? Sure, it could have been coincidence. But things were happening elsewhere. And Sylvester had learned to trust his intuition. Higher-ups in the ACPD had quietly urged the detective to quickly wrap the case up so it could simply be moved to a dead-end file in missing persons and they could label the fire as an accident, since the examiner wasn't sure it was arson. But Sylvester wasn't ready to move on. Not just yet.

The detective's cell phone rang from inside his jacket. Sighing, he reached into the breast pocket and pulled out his phone. He checked the caller ID: it was headquarters.

"Sylvester here," the detective barked into his phone. He listened to the tinny voice on the other line. "Right now? I'm all the way downtown."

He paused to listen again.

"Yes, I understand," he said. "I'll be there in fifteen."

When the elevator doors opened on his floor at the ACPD, Detective Sylvester found himself facing his old partner, Bill Garcia.

"What's going on, Bill?" the detective asked.

"Your guess is as good as mine. Susie and the kids and I were just sitting down to dinner when I got the call. I just got here."

Sylvester simply nodded.

The two police officers began walking together through the open bullpen of cubicles that served as command for the Homicide Division of the ACPD. Sylvester's mind wandered briefly back to the year before, when he had been tracking the demon that had been murdering Angels along the Walk of Angels.

He thought of the night he was taken off the demon case, when he'd had a cubicle in this very room. His dismissal from the case had come by direct order of the Angel authorities. His bosses had planned to boot him back downstairs to deal with petty larceny, but instead of going home that night, he'd tracked the demon to Angel City High School, just in the nick of time—it had cornered Maddy and Jackson. Then, after his plan to help the girl and wrongly charged Angel escape Angel City had failed, the detective found all hell breaking loose on the freeway when the demon attacked the convoy of Angel vehicles. With grim purpose, he had driven to the NAS headquarters and challenged the Archangels to act—before it was too late. Some people in the department had called him a hero. In his eyes, he was just doing his duty and didn't want a fuss.

After Sylvester's vindication during the demon crisis last year, all had been forgiven, and the detective had even been given a little more authority, along with his own office off the main cluster of cubicles.

He'd become golden in the department. His office was small, the coffee-maker didn't work, and the blinds looked like they came from 1982. But it was a good space for working on cases.

Taking a breath, the two police officers stepped into the office. Captain Jim Keele smiled broadly when he saw them. He knew how to lay it on thick when needed.

"David, Bill, come in," the captain said, a steaming cup of coffee on his desk.

"Captain?" Sylvester said expectantly.

"You want to know why you're here. Understandable." Keele put his elbows on the table and grinned tightly. "You may have heard about the bombing of the Angel offices last week."

Garcia raised an eyebrow. "You'd have to be living under a rock not to know about it, sir."

"So you both understand the importance of this case. And right now we have no leads, except for a drowsy office worker on a smoke break who thought he maybe saw something. This is making things . . . difficult for us. For the department. A big black mark on our police work. Our lab hasn't been able to pull anything of value from the site, and we're standing around twiddling our thumbs."

"We're running labs, Captain? What about the Angels?" Sylvester asked. "From what I've heard, they're confident they can find those responsible. They're insisting they can handle it themselves. They're convinced it's the Humanity Defense Faction, or some kind of splinter group."

"He's right, Captain," Sergeant Garcia said. "You sure you want to go against the Angels on this thing?" Garcia added, "We stay out of their way. I thought that was ACPD department policy if they gave the say so."

Captain Keele clasped his hands together in front of him. He leaned forward on the desk. "I can't say from where, but we're getting pressure on this thing. It doesn't matter if the Angels think they can handle this alone. We're doing our own investigation, whether they want it or not. You've seen what's going on with Senator Linden, the support he's gaining across the country. Some winds may be changing in the department. This goes high up. Higher than you would even dream. As you can imagine, politics are involved. Which is why we're keeping this close."

Detective Sylvester narrowed his eyes, looking through his glasses at the captain. "About time at least some of our commanders got out of the back pocket of the Angels." He motioned to Garcia beside him. "So what's our role?"

"David, we're bringing you in special to handle the investigation from now on. Sergeant Garcia, you will be assisting in the investigation. You two were world-beaters last time around with the demon killings on Angel Boulevard. Let's see if you can do it again."

Detective Sylvester pulled off his glasses and cleaned them with a handkerchief. Calmly, he put them back on and looked at Captain Keele: "You know how many homeless have gone missing this week now, Captain, before and after that fire? I just came back from downtown. We could be dealing with some sort of serial kidnapper or murderer or perhaps arsonist. We need to be focusing on this, as well. Maybe I could split—"

The captain cut him off. "*One hundred and one percent* of your time is to be spent on this new case, Detective." He took a sip of his coffee. "We have a mass murder, you investigate the murders. Not ghosts out on Skid Row. Have I made myself clear? Do you not see these stripes?" he said, motioning to the bars sewn into the uniform on his shoulder, indicating high rank. "Now, if I'm not mistaken, you have some police work to do. You are dismissed."

● ● ●

Sylvester went home, but he wasn't looking to relax: he was running two investigations now, whether Keele knew it or not.

The dark spires of the Blessed Sacrament Church rose beyond the window of the detective's apartment, which was in a classic Spanish-style Angel City building from the 1920s. The detective found a glass and placed two ice cubes in the cup.

Opening a bottle of twelve-year Scotch he kept on top of the fridge, Sylvester poured himself a drink. The amber of the liquor spooled with the melting ice. He swirled the ice once, then twice, and took a drink, letting the warmth drop down his chest.

Sitting down at the couch, he turned on the small TV he sometimes pulled out from the closet. He'd had to buy the digital-to-analog converter in order for it to work anymore. Somehow it seemed more sensible than getting one of those flat screens. He took another sip of his drink.

As it warmed up, the TV showed footage of people huddled under blankets, being ushered away from a scene by emergency workers.

"*. . . and officials worry that at least fifty have died in a train-derailing accident at St. Pancras Station in London. This comes just a day after an electrical storm in Northern Germany caused a series of fatal accidents along the Autobahn outside Hamburg.*"

Sylvester was watching the TV with one eye, the other on the case file in front of him. A correspondent was reporting from inside St. Pancras Station, which was a combination of sleek, futuristic European styling and lighter neo-Gothic arches and details. The reporter was standing on the platform in front of a twisted and crumpled Eurostar train. It didn't look strange for a derailment, although the reporter was saying that these modern trains had an impeccable safety record.

But Sylvester suddenly stiffened.

Standing up with the glass in one hand, he took a sip while turning the volume up with the other hand, all the while his eyes fixed on the screen. He got closer to the television and peered as the woman continued speaking.

*"Experts say they have little evidence for technical failure in the high-speed train, and forensic investigators are working to find some cause for the terrible accident in London today."*

Sylvester leaned even closer, almost as close as he could to the screen. Behind the woman standing on the platform, behind the train wreck itself, along the red brick walls, were marks. Deep in the brick. They were so consistent as to almost look like stripes—or claw marks. Sylvester studied the image on the screen until it cut back to the anchors in the studio.

In a daze, the detective walked back to his couch and sat down.

The voice from the TV prattled on:

*"And up next: how Angels and Protections in the Immortal City are taking Senator Linden's latest jump in the polls only five weeks before the election and after the Council threatened to retaliate against the Immortals Bill. Is the senator as dangerous to Angels as many claim?"*

He reached for the remote and turned the TV off.

Sylvester drained his glass and pulled his laptop—a piece of technology he'd begrudgingly allowed the department to give him—out from under a stack of papers. After opening the computer, he searched for "St. Pancras," and dozens of hits came up. He began scanning the images of the accident.

The clear, hideous gashes in the brick walls of the train station appeared again and again in the images. No one on the Internet seemed to comment on them; apparently they assumed the crashing train had made them. But the detective knew better.

He had seen marks like that once before.

Last year on a prison cell wall, dripping with blood.

# CHAPTER TEN

Jackson looked out the tinted car window and took a breath. A dull sound could be dimly heard from outside, almost like being underwater. He looked over at Maddy, who anxiously peered out the window. She took a big breath. Jackson wondered if she'd ever really get used to it. He'd been born into it, while the attention and chaos was being thrust upon her suddenly.

The valet opened the door, and any sense of quiet dissolved into shouts, hollers, and screams. Jacks and Maddy stepped onto the red carpet to the event on Santa Monica Boulevard. A mass of photographers pressed against their barricades, shouting, their cameras flashing, their voices competing with a throng of diehard Angel followers who screamed in delight as they saw Jackson and Maddy pull up.

The red carpet correspondent for A! gleefully announced to her viewers back home: *"Angel City's 'It' couple, Jackson Godspeed and Maddy Godright, have arrived at the event tonight!"*

The whole mess was held back by a cluster of security personnel who kept things in line for the Angels as well as Protections who were arriving.

Maddy and Jacks took their first steps along the carpet, adjusting to the blinding flashes.

Taking a deep breath, Jackson tried to summon the memory of what it had been like. Before the injury. He began walking down the carpet, trying to hide his still slightly noticeable limp. The crowd could sense something was slightly off—this was one of just a handful of official public appearances he'd made since he'd been injured. Nevertheless, Jackson turned, looked out into the adoring crowd, and waved, getting a large cheer from the fans. He smiled widely in appreciation.

Suddenly he heard a cheer just as big, if not bigger, as the one he had received. He saw that Maddy was no longer by his side—she had stopped and was signing some autographs.

"*Maddy! Maddy!*" the photographers screamed. "*How was your first day of training? Jacks! Jacks! Jacks! Are you giving her any tips? Jacks, when do you think you'll be back as a Guardian? Maddy, when are you going to get your wings?!*"

Maddy and Jacks just smiled and lightly waved at everyone, making their way down the red carpet.

"Over the shoulder! Over the shoulder!"

Maddy had enough experience to know by now what this meant. She cocked her body slightly away from the photographers on the edge of the carpet and looked back over her shoulder at them.

"Who are you wearing?"

"It's a new designer named Fluxe from Paris," Maddy said. She smiled as widely as she could as Darcy and her new assistant, Christina, met them and shepherded them through the on-carpet interviews.

After a few interviews, Jackson and Maddy walked into the main event space, which was a lavishly decorated courtyard. Delicate, twinkling lighting was strung across the elegant space, as huge platters of oysters, bottles of champagne, and steaming platters of seared scallops all streamed by, served to the beautiful Angel clientele, who indulged themselves with the best the Immortal City had to offer. The ruckus just outside now seemed to be a thousand miles away.

Every head turned as Jackson and Maddy entered the space.

A waiter with a tray of drinks somehow materialized at their side. Jacks pulled two full glasses off. "Thank you," he said to the waiter before the man disappeared into a cluster of Angels across the room.

Maddy looked suspiciously at the drink in Jackson's hand as he offered it to her.

"You've finished your first week of training. We have to celebrate!"

"I still have a long way to go," Maddy said quietly, thinking of what the professor had told her about the conflicting theories on her wings. And how totally out of place she felt at Guardian training. How much she had to learn. "And I have to wake up early tomorrow. I think I'll stick to sparkling water."

Jackson leaned down and kissed behind her ear. "Maddy, you are going to do great. You already *are* doing great. Did you see how everybody looked when we walked in? They're looking at you. They're seeing what I've seen in you all along. I can see the Angel coming out in you. Embrace it."

"I guess so," Maddy said uncertainly. Looking at Jackson's flawless features, she wondered, as she had so many times, how she could even measure up to this Angel perfection. But Jackson's eyes were so eager. Maddy squeezed his hand. "I mean, I know so. I know what you're saying, Jacks."

Jacks wrapped his arm around her waist and turned away from the partygoers so that they had a private space on the periphery of the crowd.

"How was the treatment today?" Maddy asked. "Dr. Liebesgott has been trying out some new method, right?"

A shadow crossed Jackson's face at the mere word *treatment*. He couldn't help it, Maddy knew. The Angel tried to keep his upbeat attitude, but his tone gave him away. "It's going fine," he growled. "But I don't want to talk about it. Anyway, Mark's helping me find other ways to be useful. If that's even possible." He seemed to realize he was sounding a bit gruff and brightened his tone. "Let's see if we can find Mitch and my sister."

Maddy wished she hadn't said anything, but it worried her so much to see Jacks struggling every day and not getting better. Each day she hoped he would turn the corner to full recovery and rejoin the ranks of what she knew he wanted more than anything: to be a Guardian. What she herself was now training to become, she reflected uncomfortably.

Leading her by the hand, Jacks took Maddy across the courtyard as they looked for Mitch. It was true, everyone *was* staring at them. But Maddy was kind of used to it by now. Jacks glanced over toward the bar and saw his sister.

"I'm going to ask Chloe if she's seen Mitch. Do you want me to bring you a seltzer?"

"Sure," Maddy said, kissing him in thanks. Jacks started walking through the crowd. In his wake, Maddy heard a female voice say clearly, "How is she going to make a save without any wings? Take the bus to try to make it in time?"

There was no mistaking the Australian accent.

Shrill laughter came out of the small group of Angels clustered around Emily Brightchurch, who was standing with her back to Maddy just a few feet away. Emily was wearing a short skirt with a pair of towering Fendi heels that complemented her fierce crimson hair—and made her legs seem to go forever. She turned around, oh-so-casually.

"Oh, *hi*, Maddy. It's funny, we were *just*—"

"Emily," Maddy frostily replied. She didn't want a confrontation. Not tonight. Maddy unconsciously pulled at the right strap of her dress, which was digging into her shoulder.

The Aussie sex symbol looked Maddy up and down. "Is your dress too small? There is a lot of pressure to size down here. And, you know, being an Angel takes a lot of work. I haven't seen you at the gym lately. Just some friendly advice. The camera adds ten pounds."

Maddy breathed through gritted teeth. "The dress fits just fine, thanks. The strap was just twisted. And some of us don't have to work out for our figures."

"Or maybe that's just what they think." Emily smiled bitchily, her voice dripping with malice. "And how are your wings coming? We're all very concerned about your well-being. It must be *so stressful* being in Guardian training and not even knowing if you'll be able to fly. If you need anything, just let us know. We'd be *so happy* to help."

Before Maddy could put together a reply, Jackson materialized at her side with her seltzer.

"Mitch just showed up," he said. "And I had to stop the bartender from serving my little sister a vodka tonic." He rolled his eyes.

"Well, if it isn't Jackson Godspeed," Emily said, undressing him with her eyes. Maddy smoldered angrily next to Jacks, trying to hold her tongue.

"Hey, Emily," Jacks said, looking mildly uncomfortable.

"Come on, Jacks, let's go hang out with Chloe," Maddy interjected.

Jackson nodded, noticing the tension between the two girls. Wisely, he held his tongue.

"Don't be a stranger, Jacks," Emily said, smiling slyly. "And I'll see you at training, Maddy. That is, if they let you back in?" There was a peal of laughter from Emily's hangers-on, but as Jacks opened his mouth in angry protest, Maddy grabbed his arm and turned him away from the group. As Maddy and Jacks threaded their way through the crowd over to the bar on the opposite side of the room, Maddy felt Emily's eyes watching them.

"What's wrong?" Jackson asked quietly.

"Nothing, it's fine," Maddy said.

"Mads, I know you. And I know when things aren't fine. Did she hurt your feelings? You can't let her get to you; she's always been a little . . . aggressive, I guess."

Maddy was silent, looking out into the crowd. A sharp wave of laughter came from the direction of Emily and her cronies. Maddy stiffened.

"Do you want to get out of here?" Jacks asked, squeezing Maddy's hand, knowing when his girlfriend wasn't having a good time. "I know a nice place. It's up in the Hills, where the Angels live. And there's ice cream." A slight smile danced around the corner of his mouth.

"Don't we have to stay?" Maddy scanned the glittering courtyard for Darcy. She wasn't exactly *afraid* of their publicist. But in close quarters, she didn't want to see her mad. There was a reason Darcy always got what she wanted.

"We appeared, didn't we? That's what making an appearance is. And then we leave."

"Okay, but—"

Taking her hand in his, Jackson whisked Maddy out a side door of the courtyard.

Jackson's house was dark as the headlights of the Ferrari sliced across the slumbering home and came to a stop in the garage.

Jacks flipped the lights on room by room as they entered his place. Maddy adored Jackson's beautiful new home up in the Hills off

Empyrean Canyon Drive. She took her heels off and walked barefoot into the house. She was starting to calm down after her run-in with Emily.

The lights in the massive kitchen flipped on, revealing two platters of fresh cookies under plastic wrap on the marble countertop. Jacks laughed. "Apparently Juan thinks I might starve. He's always having Lola bring some cookies over from Mom's house." Jacks pulled back the plastic on the trays. "Chocolate macadamia or"—he tasted the other type of cookie—"peanut butter."

Maddy wondered what the Godspeed fans would think if they could see him now, standing in his sexy slim-cut suit, simply eating a cookie in his kitchen.

He turned to Maddy. "What kind do you want?"

"Both, obviously. We've been dating a year and you don't know me by now?" She came up behind Jacks and scooped her arms around him.

Jacks laughed. "There should be some milk in the fridge."

Maddy opened the Sub-Zero and looked in, the tip of her nose getting cold. Everything was organized, color-coded. It still was amazing to her how the house manager systematized everything from when the gardeners came to what order the cheese went in the refrigerator. She didn't know if she could ever get used to having everything done for her like that. But for Jacks it was the most unremarkable thing in the world: it was just the way he had grown up and how things happened in his new place he had by himself.

Maddy extracted a carton of milk from the fridge and poured them two glasses. She took a long a swallow.

Jacks looked at Maddy, who was still in her "event" dress, and chuckled, his eyes warm.

"What?" Maddy asked, wondering what she'd done.

"You've got a milk mustache."

Blushing, Maddy wiped the liquid quickly away with her forearm. Jacks leaned in and kissed her.

"It was cute," he said. He put some of the cookies on a plate and grabbed his glass of milk with the same hand. Jacks flipped the kitchen light off. "Let's go to the theater. I've been DVRing a bunch of those old movies you like."

Maddy and Jacks snuggled in together on the couch in the dark room, still wearing their clothes from the event. A blanket covered their legs and they nibbled on cookies, the glare of the black-and-white movie on the TV flickering across them in the dark room.

"You feel nice," Maddy said.

"Thank you?" Jacks said, laughing.

"I mean it. It's nice to feel you here. To have you here. It feels like . . . support." Maddy looked up at the Angel she loved. "It doesn't matter what the others think. As long as I have you."

"Don't let them—"

"No, I mean it. I feel like you won't let me go."

"I couldn't even if I wanted to. From the moment I saw you in the diner, I haven't been able to let you go. Not for a moment."

Maddy slowly nodded, then leaned in toward Jacks, kissing him, then pulling back. Jacks moved in and kissed her, longer this time. Their breaths seemed to intermingle.

Maddy's pulse began racing, and her eyes deepened.

"Jacks, I've been thinking . . ."

"Why are you looking at me that way?" Jacks said. "Maddy, you know I've always said there's more than enough time. I want you to be ready. I can wait."

Although Maddy could hear Jackson's words, she could also tell by his breath that he was having a hard time controlling himself.

"What if we don't have to? Wait, I mean," Maddy said. As she said the words, a pang flashed through her as every insecurity she'd ever had seemed to parade in front of her brain.

But instead of pondering the anxieties, she just arched her back, and her lips met Jackson's again as he pressed her against him. Her breaths came hot and shallow, as she felt the definition of the Angel's strong, lean body under his shirt, against hers. Jackson ran his hands lightly under her shirt and along her Immortal Marks. The marks began to tingle under the sensation of his fingertips. She giggled for a moment.

"That tickles," Maddy said, pulling back for a second. "In a good way." Then she drew a sharp breath in as they kissed again. Maddy threaded her hands into Jackson's hair as the kiss deepened. With the other hand, she unbuttoned Jackson's dress shirt, then began to tug at the bottom of his undershirt, and he peeled it off. She could feel the almost searing heat coming off the Angel's chest and torso as it heaved.

Then, trembling, Maddy's body seemed to simply melt into Jacks's. There seemed to be no difference between the two of them. Jackson separated his lips from hers and kissed her ear, and she felt his warm breath against her.

Was this how it was going to happen?

Maddy's pulse raced as every atom in her body started pointing toward one answer: yes.

Pulling back, Maddy met Jackson's gorgeous blue eyes, which were only inches away from hers. She placed her hand on his chest and could feel his heart pounding underneath her fingertips.

"Jacks," Maddy said.

The two slowly lowered down on the couch, until Maddy could feel the full weight of the Angel on her. A buzzing energy coursing through her tingling body, she let Jacks pull her in for another kiss.

After maybe fifteen seconds, Maddy realized what the buzzing was. Her phone was ringing.

She pulled out of the kiss, her breathing heavy. Maddy's eyes darted over to her iPhone, which was ringing and vibrating dully across the floor.

"It can wait," Jackson said, nibbling at her lip.

"You're probably right," Maddy said, managing a smile. The phone stopped ringing and went to voicemail.

"See? They can just leave a message," Jackson said.

Jacks leaned down and lightly kissed her, and soon they were back where they started. Maddy shivered as Jacks ran his hands along her Immortal Marks again. It was almost too much.

Suddenly the phone began ringing again. Its insistent buzz broke Jacks and Maddy away one more time.

"Maybe it's important," Maddy said, anxiously casting her eyes over to the phone again. She propped herself up from the couch with one elbow and pushed her tousled hair behind her ear.

Jackson sighed. "If it's really important, they'll just leave a message and you can call them back. You're Maddy Montgomery. Whoever it is needs to cater to your schedule." The phone stopped ringing again. But then came the alert that told her there was a text message. And another.

The word *schedule* triggered something in Maddy's mind. She looked at the clock hanging above the sink.

"Oh no," Maddy said.

The phone began ringing again, its sound at this point almost deafening in her ears.

"What?" Jacks himself now sat up.

"It's Darcy. I totally forgot I have a phoner with *Angels Weekly*. We've been trying all week to schedule."

"*Now?*" Jacks said, incredulously. "It's night."

"It was the only time we could fit it in. Darcy's been trying so hard to get me this cover. I have to pick up, Jacks. It's important."

Jackson looked down on her, his face a mask of poorly hidden disappointment. He sighed. "Fine, do what you need to do."

"Jacks, please don't be angry. I—this is my job. You of all people should understand." Jacks looked away when she said this, his eyes flashing angrily. "Jacks, Jacks." She cradled her hand under his chin and looked at him directly. "I'm sorry. I'll make it up to you, I promise."

And with that she slid out from underneath him and dashed over to scoop the phone off the counter.

"Darcy?" she said, answering the phone. "I'm so sorry, I had the ringer on silent . . . Steve is on? Oh, so great to hear your voice again, Steve, I've been *so* looking forward . . ."

Jacks sat on the edge of the couch, leaned over, his elbows on his knees. He watched Maddy as she walked to the massive window, beginning the phone interview. He could see her smile in the reflection of the glass, mixing with the neon lights of Angel City below.

Sighing, Jacks picked his crumpled shirt off the floor. *At least there's something else I could be doing,* he thought wearily. He pulled on his shirt and, picking up his phone, hit the button to call Mark.

# CHAPTER ELEVEN

The lights of the Porsche cut a line of illumination across the parking structure as it climbed to the rooftop level. The top level was empty at this hour, except for one other car. Night had fallen on Angel City, but the stretch of Angel Boulevard just a couple blocks away was buzzing with activity. The neon signs for glamorous hotels, along with towering billboards, gleamed in the night above the palm trees and tourists taking in the sights. The famous Divine Records building rose just beyond that, the Angel City sign presiding over it all on the hill.

The Porsche rounded the edge of the rooftop lot and pulled parallel to the other car. Its 350-horsepower engine idled for a moment, echoing across the roof. The engine turned off. The lights stayed on. Archangel Mark Godspeed stepped out of the car.

Detective Sylvester was already out of his vehicle, looking out at Angel Boulevard. The neon from the world-famous street reflected in the lenses of his wire-framed glasses. A helicopter roared over the scene, deafening for a moment before quickly disappearing into the evening, its searchlight cutting down across the innumerable streets and alleys of the Immortal City.

Suddenly the rumble of another engine echoed up the top of the parking structure, and Jackson's Ferrari emerged and parked angled next to Mark's Porsche. The detective raised an eyebrow.

Mark walked up to the detective's side. "This is a little cloak-and-dagger now, isn't it, David?"

"I don't want any complications. Distractions. I don't know whom I can trust," Sylvester said.

"And you think you can trust me?"

Sylvester looked at him and shrugged. "I've got no one else." The detective glanced over as Jacks emerged from his car. "I didn't know your stepson was coming."

Mark shrugged. "He wants to be involved. He's smart. We can use him."

"Hello, Jackson," Sylvester said as Jacks reached them. "It's been a while."

Jacks nodded. "I never got to properly thank you for what you did for Maddy and me last year."

Sylvester shook his head. "Don't mention it."

"You look tired, David," Mark said.

"It's been a long few weeks."

Mark got to the point. "I heard they put you on the bombing case. Sorry to hear that. According to our own NAS investigators, there's practically no forensic evidence. A lot of dead ends. The Council and the Archangels are less than convinced that a human police force will be going after these perpetrators with sufficient force. Which is why we're preferring to handle the investigation ourselves."

"The investigation . . . and the justice?" Sylvester said. "Whose side of the law are you on?"

"We're on whatever side protects us, David," Mark said. "You have to know that."

"I read all the statements, and there seems to be nothing solid to go on. They all sound the same," Jackson said, changing the subject. "There's got to be something there, though. Innocent people *died*. We need to bring the bombers to justice."

Mark and Sylvester exchanged a look. Mark seemed taken aback. He had been underestimating Jackson's motivation.

Sylvester cleared his throat. "Well, you're right. I double-checked the initial ACPD work, reinterviewed all the neighbors, and questioned HDF informants across the region. So far, nothing. Then again, I don't have access to the Angel files on the case," he said pointedly, looking at Mark. "The main body of the HDF is still denying any connection. We may have to go straight to William Beaubourg himself." He was referring to the infamous leader of the Humanity Defense Faction, who had been released from San Quentin prison the year before.

"Even I know Beaubourg's hiding in plain sight in Malibu since he got released from prison," Jackson said. "In the middle of all the Angels. Could be bad for his health. The organization of the HDF moves vertically, so his lieutenants can't be far."

Mark gave Jacks a surprised look.

"I told you I wanted to help," Jacks said to his stepfather. "I've been researching."

Sylvester raised an eyebrow. He was impressed Jackson had unearthed this information. Behind his fancy car and designer clothes, it seemed he might have some real grit.

Mark coughed into his hand. "But, David, if you asked us here in the middle of the night to try to get more information," Mark said, "I'm sure you know more than I do—"

"This isn't about the bombing," Sylvester said. "Well, at least not directly."

Mark's gaze sharpened. "Go on."

"It's about London."

"London?" Jacks asked, puzzled. He studied the detective's face.

"For some reason, I didn't peg you for the traveling type, David," Mark said.

"I didn't take a trip." The detective looked at Jackson and his stepfather. "You may have heard about the Eurostar derailment at St. Pancras Station?"

"It was all over Twitter," Jacks said.

"I may have read something about it," Mark said.

"Something's going on," Sylvester said. "I think there are Dark Angels once again among us."

"Demons?" Jacks asked, a chill rippling down his back as a muscle memory of the demon's searing grip hit him. "But you yourself said the one that attacked me had gone back into hiding."

"That's true. But I think there may be more. Different demons. The marks inside the station were consistent with the marks in the cell last year after the demon came for its soul payment. Eyewitness accounts spoke of an incredible heat and steam shortly before the accident. These aren't coincidental. And there have been other . . . incidents . . . that I've been coming across on the Internet. From Asia to South America. And in the Pacific Ocean, too—that disappearance of the F-18 last spring. And something else . . . downtown. These incidents are growing. I think bringing the Dark Angel forth last year created a kind of crack. There have even been . . . children killed."

Mark's ears perked up at the word *children*. "David, don't let your past start clouding your judgment."

Jacks gave his stepfather a questioning look.

"I resent the implication, Mark," Sylvester said coldly.

"I'm sorry." The Archangel didn't sound sorry, though. He went silent in thought for a moment. "More demons? But why would they start coming now? Last year we faced a Dark Angel. A rogue. The demon did his grisly job and left. But his kind have otherwise remained hidden since the Wars. It doesn't make sense."

"I don't know why. There are just too many variables right now." Sylvester looked at the Archangel.

"What can we do?" Jacks asked. His encounter with the demon last year had been the worst experience of his life. No way was he letting anyone else go through something similar, if there was any way he could help prevent it.

"I'm going to need the aid of the NAS," the detective said.

Mark looked uncertainly out into the night. "David . . . I made an error in not trusting your intuition last time. I misjudged it, and you. I've already apologized, and I'll apologize again. But if you want me to go to the other Archangels—"

Sylvester cut him off. "If what I'm fearing is true, the collective powers of the Angels need to be pulled together immediately to stop it. We have no idea how big it could get. You need to tell the other Archangels and bring this to the Council as soon as possible."

Mark shook his head. "David. I trust you. But what proof do you have?"

"Proof? Dark Angels are just like deadly wisps, nightmares and fires in the night, gone as soon as they've destroyed. The proof is in the body count. Do we need more deaths?"

"He's right, Mark," Jacks said.

"I want to help you," Mark said. "I honestly do. But there's only so much I can do without proof. Dissension has hit the Archangels regarding how we need to deal with this bombing and the anti-Angel movement in general. Things are getting shaken up. You've seen the Council's response to Senator Linden's Immortals Bill. Well, it was a mistake to come out so strongly. Big chunks of support for the Angels in this country are starting to fade and disappear. Yes, the Angel networks are still airing all the same adulatory stuff. But there's something shifting in this country outside of Angel City, in how Americans feel about the Angels. There is a lot of fear among my colleagues. That's why Maddy has become so important to the Angels. We need to focus on positives, not negatives.

"My influence on the Archangels isn't as strong as it once was," Mark continued. "The others aren't going to want to stir up trouble chasing ghosts, tales from the Bible, unless there is incontrovertible proof about what's going on. Until then, they'll feel we need to show a united, strong front."

"But it's not a story from the Bible. There was one here just last year!" Jackson said, his tone sharpening.

"It's true," Mark responded. "But enough questions were raised about Angels during the demon crisis last year. We can ill afford to dig up problems now, unless it's something that's a direct threat. This is something that sounds like a scary story from *The Book of Angels*, David. And we're too old for scary stories. Right now we're focusing on discovering who was behind the bombing and eliminating that threat. Not supposed Dark Angels a half a world away."

"Demons don't leave behind a smoking gun, a fingerprint, a chain of phone calls. They simply destroy." Sylvester smiled sadly, shaking his head. "Don't you understand, Mark? By the time it's a direct threat, it'll be too late. If what I think is happening is actually happening . . ." He put his hand on Mark's shoulder. "Thank you for taking the time to meet me tonight."

The detective walked to his car and opened the door.

"I'll do what I can, David," Mark said, his voice louder. Sylvester paused. "I can promise you that. I'll be in touch. But things are just complicated."

Sylvester smiled the sad smile again before getting all the way into the car. "They always are in this city. Goodnight, Mark, Jackson." He nodded at both of them.

Jackson and Mark watched as the headlights of the cruiser started descending into the parking structure, ultimately disappearing into the levels below.

# CHAPTER TWELVE

In the days and weeks that followed, Maddy plunged deeper into training, even if now she had a vicious, whispering doubt that she was ever going to get her wings, despite what the Angel doctors had been promising her. The Guardian training campus seemed like an island while the Angel media howled outside. Although not a peaceful island.

The more time Maddy spent in training, the more she realized that the other Guardian trainees were resentful of her getting dropped in their mix—with, perhaps, the exception of Mitch, Jackson's longtime best friend. Even though Maddy would train for a few years, that wasn't very long compared with how long most of the other potential nominees had been training. The NAS was giving her a big leg up, and the others knew it.

And Emily Brightchurch was the worst.

Just into her second week of training, Maddy was studying in an open classroom on the training grounds when Emily showed up. The redhead walked in and closed the door. Maddy looked up.

"Hi, Maddy," Emily said.

"Hello, Emily," Maddy said coolly, remembering how the Aussie Angel had treated her at the party the week before. Emily had also been tweeting a lot lately, and one of her tweets was from the night of the event: "*When a girl has someone who's TOTALLY out of her league #Makes-MeCrazy.*"

"I'm glad I found you. Alone," Emily said. "It's about time we had a chat."

"Is it?" Maddy said, her adrenaline starting to flare.

"Yes." Emily flashed her a thousand-watt fake smile. "I'm not sure if you noticed or not, but we just wanted to make sure that you knew nobody wants you around here." She batted her eyelashes. "In case you were confused."

Maddy's face flushed. She stared the girl Angel down. "Thanks so much for the message, Emily. I really *was* confused. I hope you haven't gone to too much trouble to deliver it. I know it must have been hard for you to stop taking your clothes off for money and come over here."

Emily narrowed her eyes at Maddy and sucked her breath in through her teeth. Her voice, when she responded, was low and sharp: "If you think I'm just going to stand by while you pollute the Angels and ruin Jacks both at the same time, you're more than just a half-Angel freak. You're a fool. And I've got people who will help me."

Maddy looked at the Angel in front of her, taking a moment before responding. "Jacks is *mine*," she said firmly. She looked the Angel up and down. "You're not me. You're not even Vivian," she said, referring to Jacks's ex. "Frankly, she's a much better bitch than you."

"Watch me." Emily flipped her hair and huffed out of the room.

Maddy's eyes followed the Angel as she left, knowing that Emily wasn't going to just disappear forever (however appealing that might be). Maddy was going to have to keep an eye out. Sighing, she tried to return her focus to her homework but found it almost impossible. Although everyone might not be as vocal as Emily, Maddy knew the Aussie temptress spoke for a lot of the nominees when she said Maddy wasn't wanted at Guardian Training.

And as if the prospect of not getting her wings, Emily's threats, and the resentment of her fellow potential nominees weren't enough, Maddy had another thing to worry about. Through hints her professors dropped, Maddy knew Louis Kreuz was keeping a very close eye on her progress. She had to show him she could hack it as a Guardian nominee. She seemed to work twice as hard as everyone else—she had so much to catch up on!—and her car, a brand-new Audi S5 she had bought as soon as she got her first check from the NAS, was always the last one still at the lot at night, the other Guardians in training having already left to go enjoy life as an Angel in the Immortal City.

After one of these late evenings at training, when even the guard was surprised at how long she had stayed, Maddy stopped in at a chic furniture showroom to finish picking the pieces she wanted for her apartment, which was going to be just a few blocks from the Halo Strip, down the canyon from Jackson's house. She had a few more weeks, and then she'd be able to move in. Although she knew Kevin would miss her dearly, she'd only be a ten-minute drive, and she bet that deep down her uncle might enjoy being able to walk out to get the paper in his robe in the morning without being greeted by a dozen photographers.

The furniture dealer had arranged for a private showing for Maddy. A woman in all black with some kind of Nordic accent showed Maddy a flurry of pieces. Maddy yawned, trying to pay attention. Everything looked the same to her, and was probably too expensive. But Jacks's mom had said this was the best place to go. Her mind was elsewhere, back on training, since she was having a difficult time even getting a start in her Elementary Time Pockets class.

"Thees one would be seemply stunning, an elegant but moderna addition, do you not agree, Miss Montgomery?" the Danish woman coolly stated, pointing at a sleek sofa that looked like it had come straight out of its own photo shoot.

"What?" Maddy said, snapping back to the present. Her eyes focused on the sofa. She realized she didn't really *know* what she liked and didn't like. She'd never even thought about this stuff before. Were there always so many decisions in the world of the beautiful Immortals? "Oh, yes, definitely. I'll take that one."

By the time Maddy left, she was too late to meet up with Jacks for a bite—he'd promised to accompany his mother, Kris, to an Angel charity event that Mark couldn't make. As Maddy's Audi zipped down Sunset back toward Kevin's, she was kind of glad to have an empty social calendar, actually; she was exhausted, and she was looking forward to an evening in. Plus, ever since the dinner after her first day of training, Jacks had seemed somehow different. Not in a bad way, but just *different*—a little more serious. She and Gwen had talked for hours about it on the phone but hadn't really come to any conclusions. Gwen had made the shockingly un-Gwen statement, "Well, he may be an Angel, but he also is just a boy. And boys are strange sometimes." They'd left it at that.

Maddy had found when she talked to Gwen that it was a strange contrast, like channeling the ordinary life she could have had at college, worries about finals, fights with dorm roommates, dining halls, college parties. It was so close to having been Maddy's life. But it contrasted sharply with Maddy's extraordinary life now. The life of a Guardian Angel in training. Something she could never have imagined just a year ago.

Inside Kevin's house, Maddy threw her bag down on the front table and poured herself a glass of OJ from the fridge. It was quiet. She let out a sigh, her body slowly relaxing. She flipped on the TV, moved a laundry basket, and plopped down on the couch, wondering if her new one would be as comfortable as this old monstrosity. Probably not.

Maddy flipped through the channels: Angels, Angels, more Angels. She went to the "normal" news channel. There was a talking-heads debate on. The topic: Angels and human relations. Maddy sighed, but paused for a moment. The graphic at the bottom of the screen read: "*Senator introduces Immortals Bill.*"

A square-jawed male anchor in the news studio spoke:

"*Senator Ted Linden, whose presidential campaign as a third-party candidate has been growing its support dramatically, formally introduced a landmark piece of legislation to the Senate today. It is being called the Immortals Bill. The legislation would ban nearly all Angel activities, including supernatural acts of flying, strength, and speed, under penalty of prison until the entire Angel system can be reassessed, which some say could sideline Guardian Angels for years. Experts say Linden will have a tough time getting enough votes to pass the bill, but he remains confident. He has even gone so far as to propose limits on Angelic powers across the globe. Some prominent international leaders have stated that they support Linden's reforms being carried throughout the world, including many in Western Europe, who have historically been much more critical of the Angels' politics and lavish lifestyles than politicians in the United States and Angel City.*"

Senator Linden, a handsome man in his fifties with a shock of gray-black hair, appeared on the screen at a fundraising event in front of a crowd of supporters waving American flags. "*I will not rest until I see this piece of legislation passed, and America made safe from the pernicious influence of Angels again. My first act as president will be to sign this bill into law and simultaneously establish a Global Angel Commission with our allies across the world.*"

The image cut back to the anchor in the studio.

"*Reaction in the Angel community has ranged from shock to dismay to anger. We are awaiting an official statement from the NAS.*"

The anchor turned to a different camera.

*"Next up: you won't believe this year's Power List of the Immortal City's Angels. Did your favorite make the cut? But first, the weather."*

Maddy turned the TV off, feeling perturbed. Like Linden, she supposed, she felt that the Angel system of Protection for Pay was somehow corrupt. You shouldn't only get to be saved if you're rich enough to afford it. And if she ever made it through Angel training, she was going to figure out how to fix that system, to give more humans an equal chance at being protected. But at the same time, Angels *did* save people. The work they did, at the end of the day, was good. She didn't understand why Linden felt as aggressively as he did, unless it was just to make some noise and win some votes.

Maddy realized she had gotten a strange headache from watching TV, and her back was starting to hurt, probably from slouching on the couch. She got up and found herself a little dizzy. Maybe she'd draw herself a bath.

Upstairs, Maddy closed the stopper on the tub and turned the knob all the way to hot, the steaming water beginning to fill up the basin. Below, Maddy heard the back door close—Kevin must be home.

The mirror began to slightly fog. The tub was nearly a quarter of the way full, light, white wisps of steam rolling up toward the ceiling from the scalding water. Maddy began to take off her clothes, but she felt lightheaded again. Leaning forward, she gripped the edge of the sink to steady herself. A pain shot through her back, and she felt even more lightheaded.

What was happening?

At that moment, Maddy felt the most excruciating pain since the knife had driven into her gut months ago on the roof of the library tower. Two separate pains, equal distance from each other. On her back.

Maddy let out a terrible cry and fell to her knees.

She could only think of one word: *wings*.

*Please let them be normal, please let them be normal.* Maddy's mind raced as she doubled over in pain again. The entire bathroom, swirling in steam, began to quaver and ripple before Maddy's eyes as her consciousness flickered in and out.

Maddy yelled again, the pain almost unbearable. It felt as if her back was suddenly on fire where her Immortal Marks were.

As if from another world, Maddy heard Kevin's footsteps echoing on the stairs.

Tears streamed down her face. Helplessly she tried to lift herself off her knees. She swore she could feel tiny droplets of warm blood running down her back. She just wanted it to end.

All of a sudden, Maddy heard a quick *rip* as the back of her sweatshirt violently tore. An enormous *whoosh* shook the room as two wings emerged from her back, scattering shampoo bottles from the side of the tub, blowing back the shower curtain, ripping a towel off a shelf, before settling, tucked against her back.

Maddy kneeled, gritting her teeth. Her wings hovered, extended behind her. She took a deep breath. And then another. The terrible pain had subsided as soon as the wings emerged.

And now she could *feel* them.

She gasped as a knock rapped on the bathroom door.

"Maddy!" Uncle Kevin shouted through the door. "Are you okay?"

Maddy still leaned over, her newly formed wings curled up tightly against her. She panted, gritting her teeth. "I'm fine, it's nothing, Kevin. I'll let you know if I need any help."

"Are you sure?"

"*Yes!*"

Of all nights, Kevin had decided to let Samuel actually handle things at the diner!

"You're *sure* sure?" Kevin asked, concerned. He had heard her cries.

"*KEVIN!!!*"

"Okay, okay," she could hear Kevin muttering through the door. His steps slowly descended down the stairs.

The tub was almost overflowing now, and Maddy scooted over and turned the faucet off.

Carefully, slowly, Maddy stood up, trying not to knock anything over and trying to understand this new feeling: there were two new appendages attached to her body.

*Did she dare look?*

She turned to the partially fogged mirror. Just by her thinking it, her wings slowly expanded, stretching out so she could see them.

They weren't monstrous; they were beautiful.

Maddy's wings were smaller than those of most Angels she'd seen and, uniquely, were shaped more oblong than normal Angel wings. They were delicate and sleek, almost like hummingbird wings. To Maddy they seemed almost lighter than air.

Maddy gasped: silver threads seemed to come alive and move throughout the wings. They also had a slight purplish glow. She turned around and craned her head to look at her back and see the entire span of wings. Beneath the shredded holes in her sweatshirt, she could see the faint glow from the base of her wings, where her Immortal Marks normally were. She turned back to face the mirror.

She reached and touched her own wing. The feathers were sharp, insistent. They were hot to the touch, alive, electric.

She had wings.

Maddy looked down at the floor—there were only the slightest few drops of blood, nothing near the terrible mess she had dreamt of. Her wings had already apparently cleaned themselves off, just as she had seen Jacks's do in the rainstorm following her save. They gleamed.

Cautiously poking her head out into the hall, Maddy made sure that Uncle Kevin had, in fact, disappeared downstairs. She crept down the hall to her bedroom and quickly closed the door. She had some thinking to do—it wasn't every day you grew wings, after all.

Maddy picked up her phone and saw that she had a missed call from Jacks. She paused, looking at the name JACKS on her call log. What was she going to say: "Hey, I just got some wings. Want to go get pizza?"

She set the phone to silent and placed it back on her desk.

A light, warm wind gusted through Maddy's open window, sending a few papers tumbling end over end in her room. She noticed that she could slightly feel the breeze on the feathers of her wings. She walked to the window to close it, but paused as she looked out at the hills beyond. They had sunk into twilight, the Angel City sign blazing like a beacon. The soft wind blew again. She closed her eyes, feeling its warmth against her cheek.

Maddy opened her eyes and stepped closer to the window. Then, as if automatically, her right foot stepped onto the windowsill. Then her left foot. She looked down, feeling as if she were in a dream.

Everything in her body told her: *do it*.

Maddy leapt from the window.

The sick feeling of gravity smashing her stomach up into her throat, like the sheer drop of a rollercoaster, hit her. White-hot adrenaline tore through her body as the ground below rushed toward her. A scream began to grow from within her. Then, suddenly, almost as if under their own power, she felt the wings behind her flap once, then set. Just as she was about to hit the ground, she leveled off, careening past the oak in the backyard, sending early leaves scattering. Then, with a taut strength powering through her wings, she flapped awkwardly above the diner and was flying off through the Angel City night.

The warm night air whipped her hair and clothes as Maddy tried to use her wings to move toward the Angel City sign just up the hill. She gained more and more elevation as she tested her wings, which seemed to respond to her, even though they felt like something that wasn't really part of her. Her flying was stilted, awkward, not like the graceful flight she'd experienced with Jackson.

Higher and higher she climbed, passing the Angel City sign, until she at last turned to look back on the Immortal City. It was a vast grid below her, millions of lights, each one representing a person, a dream. She could clearly see Angel Boulevard down below her, a glittering neon slash burning in the night.

A shout of sheer delight escaped Maddy's lips. She couldn't help it, even if it was awkward.

She was flying.

Thrusting her wings, Maddy rose even higher, and then dove, banking down the hill. She buzzed over the tops of the tall palms, experimenting with letting her hands tuck beside her, flowing with the airstream. The exhilaration of it completely overwhelmed her. This wasn't like when she had gone flying with Jacks. This was totally different. She felt *powerful*. She felt a surge of energy that she had never felt before. Something in her *turning on*. An *awakening*. A feeling that this was who she was. This is where she had always belonged. This really was the *new* Maddy.

She closed her eyes, and slowly twisting in the dark air, she let the freedom course through her entire body, her entire being. It was unlike anything she had ever experienced—she was untethered from the earth. She opened her eyes and looked out again at the twinkling lights of the Immortal City. Everything seemed so insignificant from up here. Everything in perspective.

Pumping her wings hard, she shot further up. She attempted to spin right, hard, and her wing froze for a moment. Maddy panicked as she began plummeting toward the ground a thousand feet below. Her wings flapped back and forth, almost uselessly. It only took a few moments for them to correct themselves, however, and she was flying along again, trying to maintain a straight course. She definitely had some learning to do.

Trying to gain some speed, Maddy turned right again to follow the Angel City freeway as it threaded its way up the hilly Cahuenga Pass. The cars seemed miniature from this high up, mere toys. As she neared the top of the hills toward the canyons, she clumsily banked left, toward Jackson's house. Mansions sped by underneath her, islands of light in the narrow dark canyons below. She thought she recognized the Godspeed residence as she weaved her way forward, toward Jackson's own house in the canyon.

Soon Maddy was breathing hard, the muscles in her back beginning to ache with exertion. They grew tenser and tenser. Maddy didn't want to turn back—the entirety of the city stretched out below her, and she could even see the dark sea beyond Venice Beach and Santa Monica, almost beckoning her. But she knew that she wouldn't be able to last much longer flying, and she needed to get back to her house. She'd have to show Jacks another time; she wouldn't be able to surprise him the way she'd hoped.

Sighing, Maddy looped widely left and turned back toward her house. She couldn't think of anything she wanted to do more than continue flying in the welcoming, balmy night—except maybe fly side-by-side with Jacks—but she knew she'd need to get her wings in shape for longer flights, and also learn some technique. Peering into the distance, she could see the neon sign for Kevin's Diner and set her course for it—obviously no street signs could guide her way, so she had to position herself by landmarks.

Reaching closer to home, Maddy dropped further down, toward the tops of the trees and houses. If she could help it, she didn't want to be spotted as she came in and landed at her uncle's. She hadn't seen any camera flashes or heard any shouts when she left, so she was hopeful she hadn't been seen leaving, either.

It was about then that she realized she didn't know how to land.

Almost faster than you could keep up with, Maddy whipped over the diner and dropped down into the backyard. She dropped more quickly than she wanted, and she fell through the oak. Leaves ripped and a few branches snapped as she popped out the bottom of the tree and landed with a thud on the grassy yard, her butt smacking the grass. It slightly knocked the wind out of her: she'd have to practice that one.

Still out of breath, but smiling in the afterglow of her first flight, Maddy stood up and dusted the leaves and grass off her behind. She began to walk into the back door of the house, but, looking up, she saw her window was still open.

*Why not?*

Maddy smiled to herself, and with a jump up and two inelegant pumps of her wings, she clattered in through the window. She landed just inside the sill with a *whoosh* as papers scattered, magazines flapping open with the gust of air. She landed slightly on her toes, and she leaned over with one hand to steady herself as she came to a rest before falling over and knocking her desk down with her.

Maddy's chest heaved. Still doubled over, she couldn't help stealing a quick peek at herself in the full-length mirror on the back of her door. The back of her hoodie was shredded—she was going to have to invest in a lot of new clothes. But that's not what Maddy noticed.

She was glowing. She looked sexy. She liked it.

# CHAPTER THIRTEEN

Maddy was pretty sure she'd remember the next day for the rest of her life.

That's when it really all changed.

She woke up early, earlier than usual—more like when she used to get up for shifts at the diner. Bleary-eyed, yawning, she heard a consistent low buzz of voices. Puzzled, Maddy padded her way to the front of the house on the second floor and snuck a peak out the window.

"Maddy!!!" Uncle Kevin yelled from downstairs.

"Uh-oh." She suddenly remembered she now had wings.

Somebody must have gotten a picture.

If she had thought the paparazzi were bad before. . . . It was as though Uncle Kevin's house had come under siege overnight. She was pretty sure even the helicopters she heard were shooting overhead footage for the breathless, nonstop coverage of *Maddy, the girl who had become an Angel*. A chopper roared past, rattling the plates downstairs.

Maddy's hands automatically moved to her back, but the wings were withdrawn. She knew if she looked in the mirror, she'd just see her Immortal Marks, shimmering, waiting.

"Uncle Kevin . . . something happened last night," she loudly started explaining as she went downstairs.

The day was a whirlwind. Footage had cropped up on SaveTube that claimed to show Maddy flying across Angel City around the same time she'd had her picture taken the night before: handheld, fuzzy video of an Angel with oblong wings and a gray hoodie, flying across the glowing letters of the Angel City sign. The clip already had more than eleven million hits.

The video of Maddy's wings had raced across the Internet within seconds, and every Angel fan was cooing over their unique shape and delicate, darker coloring. On Angel Boulevard, a Maddy impersonator had already created fake wings that looked like hers and was taking pictures with tourists on the Walk of Angels.

Maddy didn't even want to look at her iPhone, which she had kept on silent—it was a minefield of missed calls and texts.

She hadn't told Jacks before bed last night, and now she regretted it. There was just something that felt almost like gloating now that she had her wings, and Jacks couldn't even fly. But she saw that Jackson had already sent her a message:

*"Mads! You were flying! You looked great. Call me when you're up!"*

Maddy's brow creased in thought—he wasn't mad that she hadn't told him before it broke on the blogs and on TV? Did he not feel like she had kept something from him? Thinking about it made Maddy's head hurt. She told herself she'd deal with it later, when she had some time to think.

Gwen had also texted from college: *"Girl, you are like SO BIG right now!"*

By far the biggest number of calls and texts had come from Darcy, who was ecstatic that her client had finally gotten her wings. *"We're going to get DOUBLE for every appearance now, do you know that???"* one of Darcy's jubilant texts had stated. No matter that Maddy hadn't even done any "appearances" at all yet.

Darcy's most recent text surprisingly didn't even make Maddy too anxious: *"Everything's lined up for magazine. It starts at ten, don't be too late. TEXT ME TO CONFIRM!"*

After what had seemed like days and days of negotiations between her and Darcy last month, Maddy had agreed to do a bit of publicity. She knew she was going to have to start making concessions to the Angel way of life soon if she was going to become a Guardian. So she agreed to do a photo shoot with *Seventeen* right after she got her wings. And apparently Darcy had taken that literally to mean *right after*. Maddy had to smile—Darcy was on top of her stuff.

On her way out to the shoot, Maddy remembered to text Jacks: *"It was so great. Can't wait to tell you about it in person. Now I'm a slave to Darcy. Hopefully she won't make it too painful! ☺"*

After somehow making it through the roiling mass of photographers and fans outside Kevin's house, Maddy drove to the address in West Angel City where Darcy told her the studio was. Her route took her past Angel Boulevard, and with a shock, she realized the gigantic four-story screen was playing the shaky SaveTube footage of her flying the night before, with the crawl underneath: "OVERNIGHT ANGEL SENSATION MADDY MONTGOMERY GETS WINGS!" She slunk slightly down in her car, hoping she could just get all the way to La Brea without being recognized and mobbed.

The photo shoot didn't seem so bad. In fact, Maddy was more than a little surprised to realize she was enjoying herself. Suddenly she couldn't quite remember what she had been so opposed to in the first place. She even helped pick out one of the outfits. The energy of the cameras, of the people primping and fussing—it had the same feel as flying had the night before: exhilaration. And extending her wings didn't hurt as much this time.

She was allowed to keep her photo shoot clothes, and on her way out she couldn't help noticing the paparazzi. Impulsively, she paused just long enough for them to get their shots of the amazing skirt and top.

All the attention today, the focus on her at the photo shoot, her future as a potential Guardian: after years of being the wallflower at ACHS, Maddy had to admit it was kind of nice to be treated like the belle of the ball for once.

If she was choosing this path, why not enjoy it a little?

Early light clouds had cleared and it had turned into a classic Angel City day by the time she left the shoot and drove east along Melrose—crystal blue skies, a warm wind rustling the fronds of the swaying palms lining the street as the sun bore down on the beautiful Angels, Protections, and those who wanted to *be* them. The guard at the entrance to the Guardian training campus just grinned when Maddy pulled up.

"Congratulations," he said, lifting the gate to let her in.

"Thanks," Maddy said, smiling back. Was there anyone in Angel City who didn't know about her wings by this point?

Sadie was waiting for her in the parking lot with her trademark golf cart.

"Mr. Kreuz would like to see you," she said in a sugary voice.

Inside Kreuz's office, his second assistant leaned over her desk, listening to a phone call on her headset as she took notes. She lifted her finger up, signifying it would be just a moment. Maddy could hear Kreuz's voice rise and yell every once in a while from the other room. He kept Maddy waiting for only a few minutes, during which time no less than ten "Maddy Montgomery" blog alerts went off on her phone, and Darcy e-mailed her to let her know how fantastically she'd done at the *Seventeen* shoot.

Maddy could tell from the relative silence in the other office that Louis had finished his phone call, and a minute later Sadie showed her into the training boss's office. He sat in his chair over his desk, splitting concentration between his laptop and a stack of papers. He wore a pinstriped suit and shiny brown Italian leather loafers. His cigar chugged out massive plumes of smoke, like an old-time smokestack.

He didn't look up as Maddy came in.

Maddy started to speak, but her tongue caught in the back of her throat. She just stood there, planted a couple of feet inside the now-closed door, wondering how awkward Kreuz was going to let things get. She studied the photos on the walls, the details of the oak paneling, the plushness of the thick carpet. After a minute or so, Kreuz finished signing a document and finally spoke, still without looking up. His voice came like a clap of thunder: "*Wings*, huh?"

Maddy, who had thought she'd be ready, found herself tongue-tied.

"Yes, I, uh—"

"Think you're special?" He looked up narrowly at Maddy, his meaty hand using his lit cigar to point at her. "Every Angel has wings, you know that."

He looked back down, shuffling through another paper and puffing on his cigar. After a moment, he peered up at Maddy again, who stood stock-still.

"You know the worst thing an Angel can do?" He arched an eyebrow.

"I don't know," Maddy admitted.

"Believe her own press," Kreuz stated.

He leaned back in his chair and spun slightly so that he could see out the window and look at the manicured grounds of the Angel training facilities.

"My job is to make sure that my nominees go out there, get Commissioned, and are the best Guardians they possibly can be. I come from the golden age of Guardians. Things were different. There was no question what an Angel stood for in this town. Nowadays the scandals and the public appearances and events and the rehabs and the reality shows, and Angels make millions and millions outside of Guardianship in endorsements, products, and anything else we can dip our wings into. But for me, it's about the saves. No matter what."

He turned away from the window to face Maddy.

"Do you think you're any different, kid?" he asked.

"No, Mr. Kreuz."

His dark eyes scrutinized her. She felt like a bug on a pin.

"You've got friends in high places. They're trying to push you through. I've seen some of your scores. You're doing fine in Aerodynamics, Frequencing, doing okay in Theoretical Protections. But you're *weak* in other areas." He pointed his menacing cigar at her again. "You gonna try to tell me you ain't weak in some spots?"

Maddy gulped, feeling the slightest bead of sweat on her forehead, her face flushing. "No."

"Good," he said. "I also wanted you to be aware that I've received some . . . information . . . that *distresses* me, to say the least."

"Information?" Maddy asked. One name flashed through her mind: *Emily*. But what could Emily possibly have told Kreuz? Her mind raced a mile a minute.

"Yes. I'll be looking into the situation personally. If I need you, you'll hear from me." Kreuz kept his gaze on her for a moment, then looked back down at the papers on his desk. "Now go learn how to fly. I saw you in that video; you got a lot of work to do."

Twenty minutes later, Maddy found herself staring into an enormous space the size of at least a few football fields inside building #7, one of the hangar-like structures built past the offices. The vast expanse in front of her looked like an obstacle course, except instead of just running along the ground, the obstacles were built on the walls and ceiling, too. Bright lights arced across the course, and an enormous air conditioner hummed, pumping chilly air into the building as the sun baked outside. She saw hoops arranged in jagged lines, vertical gaps between two blunt walls, a dramatic Angel-made valley full of jags and crannies, and even a strange plastic corkscrew-type length of Angel-sized tubing.

The whole thing would have been overwhelming even *without* Maddy being totally distracted by what Kreuz had told her about the mysterious "information."

"Welcome to Proving Ground 1. My name is Professor Trueway. We're beginning with basic agility work," the instructor, who Maddy had heard was a former Angel Disciplinary Council Agent, said. Although he wasn't wearing his futuristic batwing armor, the black jumpsuit the flight instructor wore reminded her of the ADC garb somehow. She shuddered to recall the ADC's pursuit of her and Jacks through the skyscrapers downtown. The agents had been incredible fliers—almost as good as Jacks.

Maddy herself was wearing a flight-training uniform that was black with gray trim, and although it wasn't really Spandex, it was close enough to make Maddy feel a little body conscious. The back had slits for wings to expand without damaging any of the fabric.

The instructor continued: "This goes against some theories, which say you should teach an Angel straight speed first. But after losing a couple Protections in the '70s, we rethought a lot of the curriculum, and agility now begins flight training."

A door off to the side opened up, and Emily walked into the room, wearing her flight uniform. You could see every curve on her body as she stood next to Instructor Trueway. She was stone-faced.

"I trust you know each other?"

"Oh, Maddy and I go way back," Emily said.

"Wonderful," Trueway said, totally oblivious to the thick-as-tar hostility that hung in the air between the two girls.

The instructor held a small control in his hand. He typed in a code, and a strange whirring occurred on the course. "We'll start you on the easiest level."

Out of the corner of her eye, Maddy saw the slightest of sardonic smirks creep onto Emily's mouth.

To Maddy's astonishment, portions of the obstacle course began to flip like segments on a cube, rotating around so that an entirely new face was exposed in each section. There were far fewer hoops and obstacles on this level, and the jagged valley had been replaced by a calm, undulating hillock.

"Emily has been so kind as to demonstrate the proper technique for these courses." He motioned to the Aussie Angel. "Emily?"

"No problem," she said. Maddy's hair blew back as Emily's wings suddenly ripped out, spreading open. She looked at Maddy. "Should be quite easy."

Emily leaned slightly forward, on the balls of her feet. Her wings were not fully spread, maybe 60 percent. Maddy noticed immediately how much bigger than her own wings they were.

"As you'll see, for correct takeoff technique, Emily is looking directly forward with relaxed shoulders. Her wings are only—"

Before the instructor could finish his sentence, Emily had beat her strong and sharp wings, once, twice, and then was off like a slingshot. Maddy's jaw literally dropped as she saw how fast Emily could fly. The young Angel twisted, dipped, and turned with ease, her flowing red hair whipping behind her, as she screamed to one edge of the course, then back, dipping over a series of hills, flying through a line of suspended hoops, and then rotating sideways to fit through a large gap between two walls. She was almost a blur.

Before Maddy even really knew it, Emily was landing next to her and the instructor, having finished the course in less than fifteen seconds. She wasn't even out of breath.

"That's how you do it," Emily said, narrowing her eyes at Maddy, her incredible wings spreading out behind her. "This is kids' level. Should be pretty easy. Well, at least for a full Angel."

It was going to be a long afternoon.

"Now your turn," Instructor Trueway said.

Butterflies in her stomach, Maddy stepped forward on the balls of her feet like she'd seen Emily do. Emily's gaze felt like it was burning a hole into her. Maddy took a deep breath, then flapped her wings, once, twice . . .

And flew five feet and careened over on her right side as she crashed into a heap.

Emily burst into laughter, but then cut it short as the instructor gave her a sharp glance.

Maddy blundered and fumbled her way through her first agility flying class; she soon found out the floor, ceiling, walls, and obstacles were made of very soft foam as she crashed, miscalculated, and generally looked like a fool out there. Her wings, which had felt kind of okay the night before, now seemed not to want to listen to orders as she tried to make turns and quick changes in elevation to fly between a gap or through the hanging hoops.

Luckily, Emily had to leave for a class pretty soon after Maddy started training, so she didn't have the glare of the Australian Angel beating down on her every mistake the *whole* time—just the stern face of the instructor, who may have looked pitiless, but who actually had some encouraging things to say to Maddy. But also, to her embarrassment, she'd seen that Professor Archangel Archson had walked into the room and was watching how things were going from the back of the space; Susan had seen how clumsy Maddy had been.

As Maddy stood, out of breath from the exertion, looking at the course before trying one more time, she thought of Kreuz's snide comment about her flying ability. *I will* master this, she vowed.

Leaning forward on the balls of her feet, looking left then right to check the width of her wings, Maddy was about to start the course again when the instructor put a hand on her shoulder.

"Maybe that's enough for today," he said, giving her his first smile of the day. "You've made a lot of progress, yes?"

"I can go one more time . . . but if you insist," Maddy said, secretly grateful she could take a break.

As she walked toward the exit, she was met by Professor Archson. Maddy's face turned red for the thousandth time that day.

"I was terrible," Maddy blurted out miserably.

A look of compassion passed across Susan's beautiful face. "You were great, Maddy. For your first day, you were wonderful," Susan said, smiling warmly. "But—"

"But?" Maddy's stomach plummeted further.

"But that doesn't mean you couldn't use a little help. Angels, we're born with wings. But you need to learn to fly, just like humans do in planes. It's not totally natural for you, and I think it will take you a lot of practice." Maddy's professor looked at her. "And maybe some training." Professor Archson took her smartphone out and pulled up a contact. "I'm going to e-mail you the contact info for a pilot I know," she said, fingers flying. "His name is Thomas Cooper. He's very talented. He might be able to help your technique."

"Okay," Maddy said, feeling defeated and wondering how a human pilot could do anything to help her fly as an Angel. But she guessed if her teacher was suggesting it, she might as well try it.

"Good. I'll tell him to expect your call," Professor Archson said, smiling. She put a friendly hand on Maddy's shoulder. "Don't worry, it will get better."

Once outside the training facility, the warmth of the afternoon sun penetrating her skin, Maddy started rubbing all her sore spots—she'd taken a beating in there. But she'd kept it up. She craned her face toward the sun, closing her eyes behind her sunglasses, letting the rays of California sun soak in.

She checked her e-mail on her phone and saw that Gwen had sent her a link on SaveTube through her college e-mail account.

"*Can you believe this*???" Gwen had written.

Maddy watched the clip on her phone: it was breakneck HD Angelcam footage of a female Angel Maddy had never met bursting through the cab of a Porsche Cayenne and pulling a girl to safety just as the SUV tumbled over a freeway median into the path of a semi truck. Maddy watched the footage again—it already had a million hits—thinking about her lame showing in agility flying training and wondering how she would ever be able to do something like that.

"Maddy?"

The voice startled her. She opened her eyes and turned.

It was Mitch, Jackson's best friend, stockier and more square-faced than Jacks. If he'd been a bit cool toward Maddy when they first met, that had been forever wiped away when she saw him help attack the demon on the library tower. Among this year's class of nominees, only Mitch was friendly toward her.

"I heard about your wings. That's pretty cool. How'd it go in there?" he said, motioning toward the massive white hangar behind her.

"Oh, you know . . . pretty good," Maddy said, trying not to let the truth color her voice, but it quavered a bit.

Mitch clapped a big hand on her shoulder.

"I'm sure you did great. Everybody has to start out somewhere. Plus, don't worry, you have Jacks to give you some tips. Has he ever shown you his awards?"

"Awards?"

Mitch laughed. "He always is trying to be all modest. But he's got a closetful of awards and citations somewhere, best flying this, best flying that. He has, like, five records in the agility course, and almost all of them in the speed course. A lot of instructors said he might be the best flyer they've ever seen."

"Oh," Maddy said, nodding slowly. "I don't think I really knew that." She thought of the doctors, specialists, everyone working to repair his wings. And the lack of progress.

"You and Jacks coming to the *Angels Weekly* party next Thursday? It's the biggest event before Commissioning. Everyone's going to be there. Maybe even Vivian—I know how much you miss her!" Mitch said, grinning. "But, seriously, you guys should come."

"I don't know," Maddy said, feeling tired. "I'll have to talk to Jacks."

Mitch laughed. "Jacks doesn't have to come. You know how he sometimes gets about events. You're your own Angel."

Maddy had never thought of it that way. "We'll see. I'm only part Angel, remember? They still might not let me in." She hugged Mitch goodbye and they split ways, the athletic Angel waving at her as he walked off toward the parking lot.

As she watched him disappear under the towering palms that lined the drive, she thought about what he had said, about what Jacks had accomplished before he even became a Guardian. What Jacks must be going through every day now.

And she also thought about the last comment Mitch had made. It struck her as strange, but also true in some ways.

*Your own Angel.*

•  •  •

These thoughts swirled in her mind as she drove toward Jackson's parents' house, her aching and bruised body protesting after the day of awkward crashes while training. Jackson had told her to meet him at the Godspeed residence, since he had to pick something up for his mom. Maddy had changed back into her skirt and top from the photo shoot—would Jacks notice?—and was listening to a playlist she'd made a few nights earlier on her brand new MacBook Pro, drowning out the sounds of traffic and congestion around her in rush hour traffic before she crossed Sunset and started heading up into the Hills. Slightly annoyed, Maddy realized that Jacks had both called and then texted her a couple times during the drive asking where she was. It wasn't like him to be so needy.

"*Coming*," she had texted back twenty minutes ago, and then put her phone to silent, enjoying the music and the drive as she wound her way up the Hills after leaving behind the traffic on the Halo Strip.

By the time she reached the Godspeed house, dusk had settled over the Angel City basin. The last of the sun was a thin orange thread hanging along the horizon; it signified the end of her first full day with wings. Maddy took a big breath as she parked her Audi behind Jacks's Ferrari. It was strange—where were everybody else's cars? She checked her phone: no text back from Jacks.

The house was oddly dark. *That's weird*, she thought to herself as she walked toward the impressive structure. Through one of the windows she could see there was a solitary light on across the other side of the house. Maddy thought back to the first time she'd come to the home, when the ADC agents were taking Jackson away. That was also the first time she had met Kris and Chloe. Not exactly ideal circumstances to get acquainted with your boyfriend's family.

Reaching the front door of the home, Maddy reached for the

doorknob and realized the door was cracked open. The hair on the back of her neck instantly stood up. The door was *never* open. Looking left and right for anything unusual, Maddy gently pressed her fingertips against the door. With a torturous creak it slowly swung open onto the foyer and entryway. It was dark and silent inside.

Adrenaline pumping through her veins, Maddy took one step forward. Then another.

"Hello?" Her voice carried into the darkness. She wished she had been paying more attention instead of just skimming the aerial combat part of the textbook last week in training—but she hadn't even had wings at that point, after all. As Maddy stepped forward, she could *feel* her Immortal Marks growing warm, starting to ache. Every part of her was alert.

Maddy took another step into the dark foyer.

"Hello? Jacks?" she said.

All of a sudden she heard the sound of someone *behind her*. And they were moving quickly. Turning in a panic to meet the attacker, she found—

"*SURPRISE!!!!*" a chorus of voices burst out.

The lights in the home instantly blitzed on, turning the scene blinding white for a moment before Maddy's eyes could adjust. She was face-to-face with Jackson, who was stepping toward her with a bouquet of flowers! He took her in his arms and spun her around.

"Congratulations, Maddy!" he said. Her heart pounding in her chest, it took Maddy a moment to realize what was happening. It was a surprise party! She looked around and saw that everyone was there: Mark, Kris, Uncle Kevin, Chloe, and even Mitch—he had done such a good job of not saying anything! As Jacks spun her around, she saw all their smiling faces. They were there for her.

"I don't know what to say . . ." Maddy said, her face burning in embarrassment at the sudden unexpected attention. At the *Seventeen* shoot earlier in the day, she had felt confident and alive, but now, with her friends and family, she once again felt awkward and the unwanted center of attention.

"Don't say anything, then," Mark said, stepping up to shake Maddy's hand, smiling wide, before embracing her. "Welcome to the Angels."

Uncle Kevin stood off to the side, looking mildly uncomfortable but also proud. Mark looked over his shoulder at him. "You have your uncle and Jacks to thank for this. I just showed up for the cake," Mark joked. The Archangel stepped aside and motioned to a large gourmet frosted cake shaped like wings—like *Maddy's* specific wings, oblong and with a slight purple cast. They had had it custom-made that day.

Jackson was grinning at Maddy. "We're really happy for you, Mads." He reached his hand down and touched her face lightly with his thumb. "You're going to do us proud." Jackson leaned in close to her ear and whispered: "You look beautiful, by the way!"

Uncle Kevin gave his niece an awkward hug. "I know you hate surprises, but, well, this young Angel thought maybe you wouldn't mind this one so much," Kevin said, motioning to Jacks. "It's a big day for you, after all." Maddy's uncle looked deeply into her eyes. She knew he was thinking about her mother and father. Once again Kevin was there to witness something in place of her parents.

Mark's phone rang, and he pulled it out to see who was calling. His face turned grave. "If you'll excuse me, I need to take this," he said as he walked out of the room. Kris's eyes followed him with concern.

"Probably the Immortals Bill," Jacks said under his breath to Maddy. "He's been fielding calls all day."

Jackson's sister, Chloe, walked over, munching on a carrot stick.

"Your outfit is super cute! We should totally go shopping sometime."

"That'd be great," Maddy said warmly. Although she knew they'd probably be followed by a camera crew filming the second season of *Sixteen and Immortal*, which was now *Seventeen and Immortal*, of course. It had taken Jacks's sister a little while to warm up to Maddy, because Chloe had idolized Jacks's ex, Vivian.

Jackson leaned in. "See, I told you she'd start to come around."

After about half an hour, when everyone was eating cake, Jacks and Maddy took the opportunity to sneak off to the deck, which held the stunning view of all of Angel City. Jacks grabbed a sweatshirt from his old room for Maddy so she wouldn't be cold—it had started to get a little chilly. Maddy slipped the sweatshirt on over her head, breathing in deeply; Jackson's scent was always so overwhelming, but also so comfortable. Sitting on the cedar bench, she drew her knees up to her chest and leaned against him as they looked out at the panoramic view of the Immortal City.

For a moment, she looked up at his face. It never seemed to change, no matter if he hadn't gotten enough sleep or anything: it was always perfect. His steady features always filled her with some kind of confidence. In him.

Jacks pulled her closer, slightly squeezing her shoulder.

"Ow," Maddy said, rubbing it. "Agility training was a little harder than I expected."

Jacks laughed. "Just wait until you have to deal with the advanced course. The first time I tried it I felt like I couldn't fly for a week I was so sore."

Maddy rolled her eyes. "I'm sure you were great at it. Mitch told me about all your awards."

"What awards?" Jacks said innocently, smiling, his blue eyes twinkling.

"Stop always being so modest!" Maddy said, playfully pushing at him.

Jackson laughed for a moment, but then grew quiet, looking out at the sprawling view of the Angel City basin ahead of them. Maddy stole a glance up at his face—it had turned serious.

She knew he was thinking about his wings again.

"Maybe you can help . . . teach me. How to fly?"

Jacks peered into the distant Angel City night. "Even if I could fly now, I'm not sure what there is to teach. You kind of just do it. I mean, it's built in. As part of being an Angel."

Maddy thought about how that was somewhat true with her—she'd been able to fly intuitively at first—but also how some things seemed not to be natural at all. Jacks had never had to think about it, so how could he teach it? He had always had his wings, as long as he could remember.

All of a sudden Maddy's heart felt impossibly tender as she thought about this Angel, who had sacrificed almost everything he had spent his whole life being groomed for in a mere moment under a knife on top of the library tower last year. What that must feel like for him.

"Jacks?"

He looked at her with a questioning face.

"Thanks. For tonight. And everything." She squeezed his hand and then nestled in closer against him as the breeze slightly picked up.

All of a sudden the sliding glass door to the house opened up. It was Jacks's sister.

"What is it?" Jacks asked, a little annoyed at his younger sister interrupting.

"You guys should come in here," Chloe said. Her face was serious as she spoke.

Maddy and Jacks got up and walked into the living room. All the party guests were standing, watching the large TV, holding their drinks or plates with a slice of cake, but not eating.

On the screen was Archangel Charles Churchson, with his trademark goatee, wearing a crisp dark suit with a powder blue tie.

The Archangel looked squarely at the camera and began speaking: "Good evening. My name is Archangel Charles Churchson, and I am spokesman for the National Angel Services and its Council. Gabriel and the Council have given me the following statement to read regarding recent political developments."

The Archangel looked down at a paper in his hands. It had the raised seal of Gabriel and the Council upon it. He began reading the statement. "'If the so-called Immortals Bill is passed into law by the United States Congress and, by extension, the Global Angel Commission, we cannot guarantee the safety of any human authority who attempts to apprehend an Angel. And we will take measures to neutralize any threats by whatever means necessary. We hope lawmakers will consider long and hard what the Angels have added to society before taking such an action and potentially putting their own kind in harm's way.'" Archangel Churchson looked up from the paper and looked gravely at the camera again. "Thank you."

Churchson turned and walked off camera, leaving only an empty space where he had just stood.

The camera cut back to the newsroom, where the stunned anchors were waiting. Voices and murmurs floated through the room among the guests as Kris leaned over and used the remote to turn off the TV. Mark was silent.

"Jacks, what's happening?" Maddy asked.

"We need to protect ourselves, Maddy," Jacks said. "Linden is a nut. You don't know how dangerous he really is. I mean, look at the bombing."

"The bombing was terrible, but that doesn't mean that all humans should have to pay for it, at least until they figure out who did it!" Maddy protested.

"There are many facts you don't know, Maddy," Jackson's stepfather said. "Some of Linden's more radical ideas are spreading across the world. Angels all over the globe could be unsafe. And that could mean you, too. The public is being led down a dangerous path by this extremist. It's a hard decision, but we have to be allied together."

"But Archangel Churchson just made a threat against humans. That's insane," Maddy said, appalled. "Angels are supposed to *protect* people."

"We need to protect ourselves first," Mark said. "Only then can we continue protecting the humans. Right now what the Archangels have chosen is to protect the humans from themselves. This should be seen as a wakeup call to stop moving toward extremism and hate."

"I think he's right, Maddy," Jackson said. His unwavering gaze met hers.

Maddy glanced over at Uncle Kevin across the room. He wore a troubled expression.

Jacks walked over to his stepfather, and they began speaking together under their breath.

Maddy's brow creased in thought. The Archangels were threatening humans? What next? Jackson seemed so sure that what Churchson and the Archangels were doing was right. But did Jacks really know what was best?

For the first time, the slightest shadow of doubt began to darken Maddy's mind as she watched Jacks and Mark talk across the room.

# CHAPTER FOURTEEN

Even in the midst of the political uproar that followed Archangel Churchson's statement, Angel City had Angel-gossip business to pursue. The next day, Jacks watched from the side of the set as Maddy blinked under the glaring lights. TV crew members shuffled past Jacks, coiling cables, assistants with clipboards and headsets dashing by. Darcy wandered back and forth wearing her trademark black pantsuit. She was juggling two BlackBerries and an iPhone as her assistant struggled to take notes. It was a new experience for Jacks being off to the side of the cameras. Sitting on a stool on stage, Maddy shifted nervously, adjusting her Balenciaga skirt. Taking a sip of her water, she looked over at Jacks uncertainly. He silently mouthed: *"You're doing great."*

And she *was* doing great. Despite obviously being very nervous before the taping started, she'd had only a couple of awkward moments, and she'd quickly moved past them. Jacks was sometimes shocked at how quickly she was transforming before his very eyes. The reserved, thoughtful girl he'd known for the past year was still there, but she had both literally and metaphorically grown wings.

A voice boomed directly beside Jacks. "And we're back in FIVE, FOUR, THREE," the burly floor manager said before turning silent and motioning "two" and "one" with his hands to indicate that the show was back on from commercial break. The lights on the cameras turned on, and the smiling host of the show turned to Maddy and began speaking once again, flashing his perfect white teeth.

"We're back with who some would argue is the biggest overnight sensation Angel City has ever seen: Maddy Montgomery Godright. In her first television appearance! She has catapulted from graduating Angel City High School to already ranking in the Power List among the Immortal City's elite and landing her first magazine covers in less than three months. And she just got her wings. Plenty of girls and boys across the country dream of becoming a Protection. But to become an Angel? Almost unbelievable. She's a shooting star, folks, and who knows where she'll land?" He turned to Maddy. "So, Maddy, tell me, when did it all change?"

Maddy cleared her throat, looking unfortunately like some kind of deer in headlights. Jacks held his breath. "Um . . . can you repeat the question?"

"When did it all change?" the host said, unblinking, his gigantic, bright white smile fixed on his face.

Jacks watched Maddy just off stage. She sent a quick glance his way. "*You can do this*," he mouthed to her. Maddy took a deep breath and looked into the bright lights, which he knew were blinding her but which made it seem like she was looking into the audience.

"Well, Taylor, I'd have to say it all changed the moment I realized that I had the chance to make a difference in people's lives. That I wasn't just going to be a waitress anymore, that I could help people. That I could save people. Like someone saved me once. That's why I joined the

Angels, because I believe in their core traditional values." She glanced over at Jackson again.

The host nodded thoughtfully.

"Now I know you can't talk about training. Very hush-hush. But do you ever feel, I don't know, *unique* being the first non-full Angel on the way to becoming a nominee for Guardianship? With your fellow nominees like Mitch Steeple, Hailey Wentcross, and Aussie hottie Emily Brightchurch?" The host put on a big smile. Jacks's ears perked up—this hadn't necessarily been on the list of questions.

Maddy thought of the chilly reception she'd gotten from Emily Brightchurch. How she often found herself separated from the rest of the Angels for "special" training because she needed to catch up. And how Louis Kreuz himself seemed to have it in for her.

"Well, if you mean, um, do they treat me differently as a part-Angel, part-human, no, I haven't felt anything like that at all. They're all extremely supportive," she lied. She smiled big right back at the host.

"Well, that's just great to hear," the host said. "And how is it learning to fly now as the first half-Angel, half-human? We're all dying to know."

Darcy, who had been distracted by something on her iPhone for a moment, perked up immediately, her eyes going wide. She looked over at the host, murder in her eyes, making a cutting motion across her neck: *WE AGREED NO ABILITIES QUESTIONS.* The host ignored her and smiled out at the audience.

Swallowing for a moment, Maddy looked out into the blinding lights toward the expectant crowd.

Then she smiled coyly.

"That's a trade secret, Taylor," Maddy said. "A lot's been going on in training. All I can say is that I plan on living up to the full potential of my Angel abilities. And there might even be a surprise or two." She winked out toward the studio audience.

The audience cheered loudly.

"*That's wonderful,*" the host said. "A lot of people across the country and the world are waiting for that day when you'll be Commissioned a Guardian. And speaking of surprises, I hear you're here with a *special guest* today?" The host looked over at the edge of the soundstage.

Jackson's eyes grew wide. "*No, no,*" he silently mouthed, trying to stop them.

The host turned to the audience: "Folks, why don't we give a hand and get *Jackson Godspeed* out here?"

The APPLAUSE light lit up, and the crowd started clapping and cheering. Maddy motioned with her hand for Jacks to come out, and Darcy gave a little shove. If he had felt slightly awkward for two seconds, it didn't show as soon as Jacks got on camera. His instinct, natural charm, and training kicked in. He strode onto the set confidently, looking like the perfect Angel he was in his tailored suit. He raised a hand and waved at the audience as they cheered his arrival.

He shook hands with Taylor and then sat down on a stool next to Maddy that an assistant brought out on stage for him.

"Thanks, Taylor, good to see you."

"Great to have you back on, Jackson. It's been too long!"

Jackson looked into the white, glaring studio lights. It *had* been a while. He blinked, letting his eyes get used to them.

"So . . . you two have been dating for almost a year now?"

"That's right, Taylor."

"And are things getting a little more . . . serious now that Maddy has her wings, Jackson?" Taylor asked, raising an eyebrow. All kinds of unfounded rumors had been swirling that Jacks had proposed marriage now that Maddy had gotten her wings.

"You know, we're both really young," Jacks said, "and Maddy is focusing on her training right now. But we really enjoy spending time together." Jacks smiled his perfectly practiced smile and took Maddy's hand in his.

Although Maddy's face was turning red despite her best attempts to hide her embarrassment, she still was able to smile and nod in agreement. She looked into Jackson's eyes.

"He's a good Angel to have around," Maddy said.

"*AWWWW*," the audience collectively said.

"And speaking of Guardian careers, Jackson, we're all waiting to hear when Jackson Godspeed will be back out in the spotlight, saving people."

Jacks actually felt a bead of sweat form on his forehead. His pulse quickened, although he tamped down any nervousness.

"Well, you know, we're just stepping back and seeing how things go. As you know, I had a, uh . . ."

Jacks trailed off. The lights had started to become even more and more blinding in his eyes. Why were they so bright? "I had a, uh . . ." Jacks was stumbling over his words. Although Taylor kept his grin ever fixed on his face, the audience was starting to murmur in discomfort.

Maddy leaned over to Jackson and whispered, "Jacks, are you all right?"

It was like two things had happened simultaneously: it was as if the white light had taken over Jackson's entire vision, and as if he were underwater in the "therapy" tank, the same "therapy" that never seemed to help his wings get better. He flashed back to trying to fly just the day before after therapy. In excruciating pain, he'd managed maybe ten feet before he'd dropped back to the earth, grinding his teeth in agony and shame. Now in the studio, the world pitched and reeled before him. Jacks grabbed the edges of the stool he was sitting on. Maddy's voice was distant and sounded like it was underwater. But the voice slowly drew him back to reality.

Everything snapped back to focus instantly. Sharply.

Jackson coughed into his fist and looked at the host. "Sorry, Taylor, I had something in my throat. What I was saying was that, as we all know, I had a setback, but I'll be back soon as the Guardian Angel the world knows and loves."

The audience began clapping, and Jackson flashed a ten-thousand-watt smile at them and waved thanks.

"That's just so *wonderful*," Taylor said. "You heard it here first, folks, Jackson Godspeed on the mend and on his way back to saving lives and being in that glamorous spotlight of the Immortal City. We *can't wait*."

Taylor turned back to Maddy. "Thank you so much for coming on, Maddy. We expect great things! Just promise you won't get too big to come back when you become a Guardian!"

"Oh, don't worry about that, Taylor," Maddy said, turning toward the audience and smiling. "I may become a Guardian but I'll always just be me. I still will just want a burger and milkshake at my uncle's diner."

The audience went wild at this, clapping and cheering.

"That's just *terrific*—America's sweetheart is still going to be the girl next door." The host quickly turned to the other camera: "Up next, an exclusive peek inside the home of *American Protection* winner Lindsey Gonzalez to see how she's handling her first year in the glamorous world of the Angels and Protections! Don't go anywhere!"

The lights above the cameras went off, signaling commercial break. Jacks stood up from the stool, just wanting to get off the stage. That kind of lapse had never happened to him before. He was *Jackson Godspeed*, after all—he had been practically raised in front of cameras.

Taylor turned to Maddy, grasping her hand. "Thank you *so* much, honey."

"Did I do okay?" Maddy asked.

"You were *just great*," the host said. His eyes were shining bright, and he was smiling. He was obviously charmed by Maddy. "This might be our highest rated show all year!"

"Wow, thank you," Maddy said, laughing.

Jacks remained slightly to the side, his hands in his pockets.

"Oh, and, Jacks, thanks for coming on. Really great to see you," Taylor said, almost as an afterthought, shaking Jackson's hand quickly.

Darcy was upon them in two seconds, hustling them off the stage toward the green room.

"Absolutely amazing. And you looked *gorgeous*, Maddy."

"Do you really think so?" Maddy said.

"*Absolutely*," Darcy said, putting her hand on Maddy's shoulder.

Maddy looked at Jacks expectantly—he knew how she liked his opinion on things.

Jacks put on his best smile. "Darcy's right, Mads. You nailed it there—you're a natural-born Angel. And you looked great."

Maddy blushed.

Darcy's assistant ran up to Maddy and started taking off her microphone. Darcy took the opportunity to pull Jacks quickly to the side.

"What happened out there, Jacks?" she whispered under her breath.

"I . . . I don't know." He thought about that sense of total blindness under the lights, combined with a strange pitching back and forth. Just thinking about it made him feel like he was going to be seasick. "I just . . . maybe didn't sleep so great last night."

"You've got to let me know if you're not . . . not feeling well or something." His publicist tried to put a smile on. "I mean, just so we're all on the same page, okay?"

"Sure, Darcy," Jacks said, slightly irritated but trying not to show it. He wasn't on drugs, for heaven's sake.

A call came in on Darcy's iPhone.

"And it begins," she said, a smile flickering across her face as she answered. "Hi Terry . . . are you crazy? We won't take less than double for that. This is *Maddy* we're talking about." Darcy lifted her finger to Jacks as if to say, "Just one second."

Jacks wandered off to the side, the set still buzzing. He leaned against the wall, watching the bustling activity around him.

After the taping, Maddy and Jacks decided to get a late lunch at Angel City hotspot Urth Caffé. Jackson and Maddy had gone more than a few times to Urth; even though it was always a madhouse, Maddy liked the outdoor seating area.

The paparazzi outside Urth had somehow been tipped off—probably by Darcy—about the arrival of Jackson and Angel City's hottest new nominee, and they began shouting. Urth's security personnel helped corral the photographers on the sidewalk as Jacks and Maddy started walking up toward the entrance of the café.

MADDY! JACKS! MADDY!

MADDY! JACKS! MADDY!

MADDY! MADDY!

MADDY!

A reporter for a popular blog was doing a video segment outside Urth when he saw Jacks and Maddy arrive. "And just showing up at Urth Caffé is Angel City "It" couple Maddy Montgomery and Jackson Godspeed."

Jacks winced before he could help himself. Normally it was "'it' couple Jackson Godspeed and Maddy Montgomery"—not the other way around.

A girl, maybe sixteen, called out in a shriek: "Maddy! Can I just get your autograph??"

Maddy paused with one foot on the steps. Jacks watched her, curious to see what she'd do. She turned and walked up to the girl.

"Sure," she said, smiling, taking the pen and paper that the girl held outstretched in her hand.

Another teenage girl ran up on the other side of Jacks. "Excuse me, Jackson?"

Jacks turned. The girl held a digital camera in her shaking hands, her eyes wide and Angelstruck. Security raised an eyebrow at Jacks, but he shook his head at him, letting him know it was okay.

Jacks smiled warmly at the teenager. "Would you like to take a picture with me?"

The girl's eyes darted quickly to Maddy, then back.

"Actually, well, do you mind taking a picture of me with Maddy?"

The edges of Jacks's smile faded almost imperceptibly, the mask of his face tightening as he tried to hide his surprise and the dawning feeling of . . . what was it?

"S-sure," he said, his lips translating more than he would have liked the colliding emotions inside him. The girl flashed a bright smile and skipped over to Maddy, who was signing an autograph for another girl.

"Um, she wants a picture with you," Jacks said flatly.

"Oh, okay," Maddy said, distracted by the pen and paper still in her hand. "Just give me a second." She finished signing another autograph, then stood with her arm around the girl, and Jacks took the picture.

"*Thankyousomuch!*" the teenager sputtered. She and her friend started walking away down the sidewalk, then shrieked in glee together as they realized what had just happened. Their voices were clearly audible to both Jacks and Maddy.

"*Oh-my-God-I-just-got-Maddy-Montgomery's-autograph!*"

Jacks turned to Maddy abruptly. "Are you ready?"

"Oh yeah, sure, let's go in."

The café was filled with Angels, Protections, and all their hangers-on. All eyes turned to Maddy and Jacks as they entered the outdoor seating area. A low buzz started as people began talking excitedly. The whole energy in the space changed as soon as they came in.

Jacks and Maddy sat down at a table near the corner. All of a sudden there was the screech of chairs being pushed back, as two people got up across the outdoor seating area. In an instant, Jackson recognized Vivian Holycross, along with Emily Brightchurch. He stiffened, hoping they'd just leave without making a scene.

"What are *they* doing together?" Maddy said, preparing for the worst.

But the gorgeous Angel girls made their way out without approaching Maddy and Jacks, though they did whisper together and laugh while looking in Maddy's direction.

"Well, I guess that wasn't too bad. Emily at least didn't stab me or anything," Maddy said, laughing a little bit. "Although I bet she and Viv have a lot to talk about." Maddy was in good spirits after the TV taping. She looked at Jacks, who was silent, seemingly staring off into space. "Jacks? Are you okay? I mean, I know my joke wasn't that funny, but . . ."

Jacks looked around the café at the other Angels sipping their lattes, eating their salads, chatting, flirting, laughing. He'd been at that café more times than he could count. He knew so many of the people sitting just a few feet away, Angels he'd come of age with, and he was here with Maddy. But right then he just felt . . . empty. Alone. He couldn't explain it. It was like how he had felt when he had gone on stage at the taping. It just happened on him. And he felt afraid.

Jackson Godspeed wasn't used to feeling afraid. He began to really, truly, think about the possibility his wings might never be fixed. A cold hole opened in his stomach.

"Jacks?" Maddy leaned forward across the table and took his hand in hers.

"I'm fine," Jacks said, snapping out of his reverie.

Maddy looked at him with concern, squeezing his hand. "Are you sure? You seemed a little off this morning, too. Is there anything I can do?"

"It's nothing!" Jacks said, his voice rising. A few customers at the other tables turned their heads toward their table, noticing, and began whispering under their breaths.

Maddy looked at him in shock—Jacks never raised his voice at her. Ever.

He glanced back and forth, realizing he was drawing attention.

"It's nothing," he said, more quietly this time. He pulled his hand back from Maddy's.

A look of pain and confusion crossed Maddy's face. Suddenly Jacks's phone buzzed with a text. A strange look crossed his face as he read the text and then put the phone down.

"What was it?"

"Nothing."

"Jacks," Maddy said. "No secrets. Remember?"

He sighed. "It was from Emily."

Anger flooded through Maddy's veins. "Why is she texting you? How'd she even get your number?"

"I don't know. It's stupid. You know how girls like Vivian and Emily can get. Vivian probably gave it to her. I deleted it. I'm not writing back. They're just trying to get at you. They knew you'd be sitting right here when I got it."

Maddy seemed to realize her raised voice had drawn the attention of the tables of Angels and Protections around them. "She never stops."

Jacks scanned around the courtyard of the café. He suddenly had the impulse to get away from all those eyes, the Angels watching. Even Maddy herself.

"Are you okay, Jacks?" Maddy asked.

"Sure, I'm fine," he lied, trying to keep his voice light. She seemed to believe him.

Maddy glanced over at her phone on the table and suddenly realized what time it was. "I'm going to be late! I almost forgot—I have my first flight lesson with that pilot. Professor Archson thinks it's going to help."

Maddy stood up and kissed Jacks on the cheek. "I'll talk to you after, 'kay?"

"Sure," Jacks said, his mind swirling with the day's events. He managed a weak smile at her. "Have fun."

Maddy slipped between the tables of beautiful Angels, toward the street. Jackson watched her go.

He let out a long sigh and looked at the menu in front of him. Although he'd been hungry just a little bit ago, now he had no appetite. A waitress showed up, eying the solo Jackson Godspeed.

"Just coffee for me," he said, handing the menu to the waitress.

# CHAPTER FIFTEEN

The small airstrip was on the far edge of Burbank, on the other side of the freeway from the glitzy Angel facilities. Maddy pulled in next to a guard shack, and the guard waved her through, barely looking up from his phone as he opened the gate.

Dust swirled on the old runway as she parked her Audi between an '87 Dodge pickup and a Toyota Corolla with peeling white paint. A small hangar lay off the side of the airfield. Stepping out of her car, she realized how much hotter it was over here than in Angel City. A blazing wind rolled over the mountains that loomed behind her.

Walking toward the hangar, Maddy noticed a young man in a khaki naval-service dress uniform step out from the hangar, wearing aviator sunglasses and a stony expression. He had a striking jawline and chiseled cheekbones. He was tall and his shoulders were broad, his glossy hair dark though not as close-cropped as she thought it would be for some-one in the military. The pilot was also younger than she thought he'd be—maybe just twenty-one. Maddy smiled in a friendly manner as she approached him, her heels clacking on the asphalt. His face remained unchanged. She guessed he must be her instructor.

Maddy was here on this dusty airstrip because of Susan Archson's suggestion that she might need to learn to think like a human pilot. Maddy wasn't entirely sure, though, how airplane training was going to help. She wasn't going to be flying a plane; she was flying *herself*. But Susan had prevailed and said the young pilot was the best around and would be happy to work with Maddy.

Now, on the tarmac, she was meeting him for the first time. Reaching the boy in uniform, she put out her hand.

"Hi, you must be Tom, er, Lieutenant Cooper. I'm Maddy Mo—"

"You're late," the pilot said, looking down at his watch. His voice was deep and direct. Almost cold. He examined her outfit incredulously: heels and a skirt and a flirty top she'd had her stylist pick out for her since she had an appearance later.

"I, uh," Maddy floundered. She checked her phone; she hadn't realized she'd been running so late. There had been so much to take care of before this appearance later tonight that she'd let the time get away from her . . .

"I'm sorry, I had to meet with Darcy before, and she was stuck at an event with another client, and—"

"Darcy?" The pilot raised an eyebrow above his aviator shades. "Who the hell is Darcy, and what does she have to do with your flight training?"

Maddy looked at him, speechless.

Tom examined the expression on Maddy's face. "Yes?"

"Nothing. I just expected someone a little more . . . courteous," Maddy said, standing taller, looking directly into the glinting mirrored glass of the pilot's shades.

A tight smile spread across his face. "You're the one who's late and you're talking to me about courtesy?" Tom said, shaking his head. "*Angels*," he said, as if to himself, in disbelief. He turned to the hangar. "Now come on, we can stand out here in the sun all day or get to work. You've wasted enough of our time."

"Bu—" The pilot had already turned and was walking back into the hangar. Flustered, Maddy called to him: "You'll get paid the same no matter how late I am."

He spun on his heels, an insulted look crossing his face. "Paid? Ms. Montgomery, this isn't for money."

The pilot led her to a chipped metal table off to the side of the hangar. An old chalkboard was set up next to it on a rolling stand. The old desk chair squeaked when Maddy sat in it. The young man sat down opposite her at the desk and took his sunglasses off. Maddy was immediately struck by his eyes—they were a deep green. He didn't blink.

Maddy glanced over at the single-engine Cessna next to them just inside the hangar.

"Is this your plane?" she asked.

"I'm allowed to use it, yes. My normal aircraft is a little . . . faster."

"So when do I fly?" Maddy smiled, trying to start their relationship over on the right foot.

"*You* don't."

Maddy froze for a moment.

"Not yet," the pilot continued. "Not until I say so. *If* I say so."

Maddy's eyes blazed rebelliously. Something about this pilot made her flare up inside. "And this is supposed to help me? I'm not sure I need help, anyway. I've just got a slow start flying is all."

"Not from what I've heard."

"Professor Archson said you were good, but I still don't see how this is going to help me," Maddy responded after collecting herself.

The pilot rapped his fingers lightly on the metal top of the desk.

"I was one of the youngest ever to graduate the Naval Academy, got top marks across the board in all aviation categories, and finished head of my group at the elite U.S. Navy Strike Fighters Instruction Program. I've flown over thirty-two F-18 missions from my aircraft carrier, which is now positioned in Angel City Bay." His voice was calm and his gaze unwavering as he spoke. Maddy thought she remembered from a Military Channel show her uncle was watching that an F-18 was one of the military fighter jets. The most expensive and prestigious airplanes in the fleet.

Tom continued. "Susan apparently thinks you need to learn how a pilot sees, feels, and thinks, and she believes I can help. Although, to be honest, that might be pretty hard for somebody like you."

"You don't know anything about me, *lieutenant*," she said quietly.

The pilot was silent.

"What did I ever do to you?" Maddy said after a moment.

"*Do?*" Tom asked, his green eyes flecking with gray. "Do you think I want to spend my time teaching some prima donna *Angel* how to fly when I could be helping someone who actually appreciated it, needed some help? Are you sure you wouldn't rather have a tutor on how to spend money and pose for photographers?"

Maddy eyed him. "Well then, why are you doing it?" she asked.

"Because I have to. Susan asked me. And it looks like you have to as well."

"You *have* to? Why?"

"That's strictly none of your business," the pilot said.

Maddy crossed her arms. Silence hung heavy in the air between them. A fly buzzed, lazily circling up toward the ceiling.

Tom stood up and walked over to the chalkboard. He flipped it over with a squeak, revealing a side already marked up with chalk. It was covered with diagrams and equations covering aerodynamics, velocity, yaw, trim.

Maddy's eyes narrowed at the board, her arms still crossed. "I've already learned this stuff."

"Not my way, you haven't," Tom said, turning back to the chalkboard. "If you learn this, I can help you wrap your head around how to maneuver your body in the air. But if you're going to be stubborn, you'll always stay where you started. Which, from what I understand, isn't the most graceful place."

Maddy opened her mouth to come back with a snappy reply. But she stopped short as she looked into Lieutenant Cooper's serious eyes and thought about her struggles on the training course. Maybe he was right. Maybe he could help her maneuver her body in the air.

"All right," Maddy got out, fighting her rebellious streak.

"Good," the pilot said, turning back to the chalkboard with the slightest smirk on his face. "Let's start."

# CHAPTER SIXTEEN

The buzzer panel for the building was faded and covered in filth, the names and unit numbers barely readable. Sylvester's eyes ran up and down the list, trying to discern one name from the other. Some of the names were written in Russian letters, and the detective tried to piece together what they might mean. Others were written sloppily in black marker.

Sylvester's investigation into the grisly Angel bombing had taken him through all the official ACPD reports that had been filed, all the traditional HDF informants and their statements. He'd uncovered nothing new. But Sylvester had other resources. He pressured an HDF operative who was close to the group's leader, William Beaubourg himself. Sylvester had used her as an informant for years, off the books and out of the ACPD database. And the detective had gotten one word out of her: Minx. That's all she'd say about the bombing. But maybe it was enough.

Garcia had radioed in the name "Minx." There were maybe two dozen Minxes in the Angel City database, but only one that seemed right to Detective Sylvester. It was on a dingy industrial block on the outskirts of abandoned downtown.

Minx Watch and Clock Repair.

Now Sylvester stood outside the address. Could be another dead end. Afternoon sun beat down on the cracked sidewalk. The rumble of steady traffic on the freeway just a couple blocks away created a dull white noise. A homeless man pushed a shopping cart toward the detective, one of the wheels squeaking terribly. The man saw Sylvester, instantly—and correctly—took him for police, and crossed the street. Sylvester looked toward the north and figured most of the homeless disappearances he'd been following had happened only twelve blocks north of here.

Since he'd been pulled off that non-Angel case, at least ten more destitute men and women had disappeared mysteriously off the streets or out of fleabag residential hotels. Yet the ACPD hadn't even detailed anyone else on the case since Sylvester had been reassigned. The detective got an ache in his kidneys just thinking about it. He wasn't going to let that case just die now that he was on the Angel bombing, so he'd dropped Sergeant Garcia near Skid Row and asked him to question anybody who might have seen anything involving the disappearances. It was risky having Bill work on that off-limits case, but Sylvester wouldn't be able to live with himself if he didn't.

But today he had to investigate the bombing. Leaning further in, Sylvester peered through his glasses at the numbers and found the one he was looking for: 1C. There was no name next to the buzzer number, just a description: WATCH AND CLOCK REPAIR.

Sylvester pressed the button. Only a few seconds later, the door buzzed, unlocking.

The detective entered a large, dingy hallway. Sylvester easily found the door inside: 1C. The words WATCH AND CLOCK REPAIR were etched on the dirty frosted glass of the door. The detective entered.

He was met with a terrible mess. Stacks of old clocks sat atop each other on the scratched glass countertops, more stacks of old plastic clocks were propped against the wall, and various clock parts were scattered around. The storefront was lit dimly, and old-fashioned jazz was playing on a radio in a backroom somewhere. He noticed a brass bell in front of him. He pressed down, and the ring carried loudly through the store.

After a few moments, a man emerged from what was probably the back office. He pushed aside a tattered old green curtain with gold trim and began lumbering up to the desk, breathing heavily through his nose. He was short and wore a stained brown apron over a white button-up shirt. The apron bulged over his belly. His thinning, wispy hair was matted to his scalp with sweat. The most remarkable feature about the man was his elaborate pair of eyeglasses, which were more like a visor attached to his head with a black rubber strap; a number of moveable magnifying lenses and loupes were attached to the front of the glasses, able to swing back and forth to provide the right enlargement of detail for the eye.

The man wiped his fingers on the apron and looked at Detective Sylvester as he approached the counter. His brown eyes were exaggerated and bulbous through his thick glasses. As he smiled, his yellowed teeth shone out at Sylvester.

"Can I help you?" the man asked.

"Mr. Minx?" Sylvester said.

"Yes?" he said.

Sylvester reached into his pocket. "I'd like to have a watch fixed," he said, pulling out a wristwatch. Its glass face was beautiful, trimmed with gold, and the numbers inside almost were art deco in a 1930s kind of way, harking back to the heyday of Angel City.

The man took the watch in his hands and inspected it through his glasses, holding it up to the light. The light danced and refracted in his glasses.

"This is a beautiful piece, yes, yes. The inner workings are quite complex, but durable. A different era, a different era. I haven't seen one like this for quite some time, Mr. . . . ?" He dropped his gaze back to the detective.

"Sylvester. Detective Sylvester, ACPD." He reached into his other pocket and produced his badge.

"Oh?" Minx attempted to hide his surprise, continuing innocently to look at the watch. He glanced into the backroom, just for a moment, then his attention was back on the watch. Sylvester studied the man in front of him. "And is there something else, Mr. Sylvester? I have the feeling your visit might not just be about this timekeeping piece."

Sylvester looked at the man squarely.

"A bomb."

Minx didn't miss a beat. "A bomb, Mr. Sylvester? Nasty devices. Liable to do much damage. But why would I know anything about a bomb? I'm a simple watch repairman, running my simple shop." He smiled innocently again at the detective, his eyes distorted through the lenses.

Sylvester leaned in quickly toward the fat man, spitting fire, his words sharp and fast. "Yes, a bomb. The one that turned the front wall of the Angel Administration Affairs office into thin air and fire. And killed ninety-two people. Ninety-two counts of murder. I'm not going to waste time going back and forth pretending you aren't what we all know you are. A bombmaker." Minx flinched just a little. "And I know your anti-Angel sympathies."

Minx opened his mouth in a big yellow-teethed smile. "You have your facts wrong there, Mr. Sylvester. It is true, I would weep no tear if the Angels were to disappear from the earth tomorrow. But I also cannot bear the tyranny of *human* politicians, businessmen, lawyers, and the police state. They should all be cleared away."

Sylvester studied the man in front of him. "An anarchist."

"To use one term." Minx coughed and placed the watch down on the glass display case. He looked at the detective. "I did not make your bomb, Mr. Sylvester. You could investigate for some time and find no trace, I promise you that. There is a man, though. He might be interested in talking with you."

"Who?" Sylvester asked.

"I can't give you a name. All I can say is that, when the time is right, he may appear."

"Do you always talk in riddles?"

"Not always. Just with policemen." He grinned again.

Sylvester placed a card flat on the glass counter. "I'll give you a couple of days. Then I'm coming back for you. With friends."

Minx looked at the card, thumbing it in his hand. "It is funny to meet you this way, Mr. Sylvester. At one point you were quite notorious down here, you know."

"That was a long time ago."

"True. Does time mean less for you than for the rest of us? Or have you . . . adapted since you lost your wings?"

Sylvester gritted his teeth, looking at the man standing amid the strewn stacks of clocks and gears. "I'd say it's about the same. More or less."

"Some of us may pity you. Others, not so much. Myself, I still haven't decided." Minx looked at Sylvester. "I hope you aren't neglecting your other investigation."

Sylvester raised an eyebrow. "What?"

Minx raised an eyebrow. "The homeless disappearances are concerning us. It's not like the Angels to 'slum,' as they say."

"The Angels?" Sylvester said. And who was *us*? A strange feeling began to spread in Sylvester's stomach.

Minx brushed off the question.

"Dig far enough and you can find some who may have witnessed *something*. If they can even be made to talk," Minx said. "A man named Gerald Maze might be a good place to start."

"Why are you helping me? I thought you hated police?"

"There are some things that can be hated more than even the police, Mr. Sylvester. As hard as that may be to believe," Minx said, grinning again. "The police are just the symptom of the larger sickness, Mr. Sylvester, the institutions. But cracks are appearing. Demon sightings. The rise of the Godright girl, half-human, half-Angel."

"Maddy." Sylvester blinked at the name. "But how do you know all this, if you're just a bo—"

Just before he said the word *bomb*, a sudden bolt of realization struck Sylvester. His thoughts raced back and forth over details in his head. Were the bomb and homeless disappearances somehow related? But how?

"The disappearances, the growing unrest throughout the country, the strange occurrences across the world. The bomb. You yourself have been interested in London, St. Pancras, I believe." The nutty bomb-maker smiled through his glasses.

"You think . . . these are all connected?" the detective said. The startling potential of a link between the events sent his detective mind into overtime. He struggled to comprehend it all, but the meaning still lay flickering just outside his understanding.

"The time of the Angels may be coming to a close, Mr. Sylvester," Minx said. "But then again, so may the time of the humans. It is foolish to take sides. Let the powerful destroy themselves, and then we can pick up the pieces after clearing away the garbage of this society."

"The homeless aren't just trash to be taken away," Sylvester growled.

"*You're* the one implying that, detective." Minx grinned from behind his weird glasses.

Detective Sylvester noticed for the first time *The Book of Angels* sitting off to the side of a pile of old clocks. The apocryphal book with its famous prophecies didn't seem likely reading for an anarchist who hated Angels. It was the kind of stuff the crackpots read from the corners while people quickly walked by, trying not to pay attention.

"Violence never solved anything."

"I think you're quite wrong there, Mr. Sylvester. Quite wrong." Minx coughed hard into his hand and wiped it on his apron, grinning again, his wild eyes peering through the lenses and loupes. Sylvester felt like taking a shower.

"Remember. I'm giving you seventy-two hours," Sylvester said.

Putting his jacket on, Sylvester began walking toward door.

"*Detective*," Minx said.

Sylvester stopped and turned around to face the bombmaker. Minx was holding the watch in his hand.

"This may take me some time to adjust. I want to make sure I do a fine job on such a beautiful piece."

"That's fine, take as long as you want," Sylvester replied. "I just want the job done right."

The frosted glass rattled on the door as Sylvester walked out, Minx still peering at the watch through his strange glasses as the detective's footsteps faded down the hall.

That evening, Detective Sylvester walked down the hall of his old building, floorboards creaking under his loafers as he made his way to his apartment. He had a plastic bag with a container of green chicken curry from his favorite spot in Thai Town, which was just down Angel Boulevard from all the tourist shops and the Walk of Angels. He was looking forward to eating it. And getting some rest.

It was eerily quiet, the hallway empty except for a neighbor, an older

Mexican woman, walking her Pomeranian. The small dog yipped at Sylvester as they passed.

"You have a visitor," she said, nodding down the hallway.

Sylvester looked up and saw Jackson Godspeed leaning against the door to his apartment. *Interesting*, Sylvester thought.

"I hope you haven't been waiting long," he said.

"Not too long, detective," Jacks said. "I would have gotten your number from my stepfather, but . . . well, I didn't want him to know I was visiting."

The detective opened the door to his apartment and fumbled around in the dark for the light.

"Please, come in and take a seat."

Jacks entered the modest apartment and looked around at the walls that had given him and Maddy refuge almost a year before, after Sylvester had saved them from the demon in the high school. He sank down into the couch. He was holding a small envelope in his hands.

Sylvester put his keys and the Thai food down on the side table. He pulled a chair over from the kitchen and sat down.

"What can I do for you, Jackson?" the detective asked.

Jacks offered him a small manila envelope, placing it on the coffee table.

"Inside is a zip drive and a DVD. On the drive are all the statements the Angels' investigating committee has received, and that DVD has video surveillance from outside the Angel Administrations Affair on the evening of the bombing."

Sylvester sat up. "I thought the Angels said there was no surveillance video that survived?"

Jacks just gave him a look.

"Thank you, Jackson," Sylvester said. He opened up the envelope and examined the black thumb drive. "But why are you doing this?"

"Because, after what you did for Maddy and me last year, I trust you. And I think it doesn't matter *who* solves this case. As long as it gets solved. I'm not sure if there's anything you can use. But you might see something we haven't." He took a deep breath. "My stepfather doesn't know I'm here, like I said. I got a lot of this info from his laptop. He thinks it's nice for me to have a . . . hobby, I guess." Jacks's voice was bitter for a moment. "Since I can't protect anyone right now. But he sees it as just that, a hobby. He doesn't understand that I'm looking for a *purpose*. Or something like that."

Sylvester nodded silently, his respect for the young Angel increasing.

"I'm not even sure myself what it is. But not being able to save, not being able to fly, I feel so helpless—useless, I guess. Like someone who's not supposed to be there anymore. Now just a burden." Jackson's eyes grew dark and contemplative.

"I'm sure that's not true, Jackson," Sylvester offered.

Jackson didn't respond. He looked around the apartment. At the printed-out articles. A map. The stacks of books around the living room. Sylvester's obsessions.

"Detective . . ." Jacks began slowly. He motioned around. "Why do you do it?"

The detective's face was serious. Almost gaunt.

"Mark mentioned something about your past when we saw each other last time. Was it from when you were an Angel? I know from what you told me last year that you made an unsanctioned save, and lost your wings. And I know"—a look of pain came across Jackson's face—"what it feels like not to be able to fly. But what happened? Behind the rumors and the discrediting and losing your wings. What really happened?"

Sylvester let out a long breath. Pulling his glasses off, he polished them with the white dress shirt he wore under his rumpled sports coat.

"It seems so far away now," Sylvester said. "Even though I think about it every day. It's difficult for me to talk about."

Jacks looked up at the detective. "Maybe it could do some good."

"Maybe." The detective walked to the kitchen and came back with a glass of Scotch, neat. "I was a Guardian. Around the same time your real father and your stepfather were both also coming up as Guardians. It was a great time for the Angels. Each year more and more Protection policies were coming in, and the NAS wasn't nearly as controlling of things as it is now. Not as corporate. It was a golden age for Angels in America, in my opinion.

"I lived in a house up off Laurel Canyon. Not as much a house as a mansion."

Jacks involuntarily raised an eyebrow as he glanced around the detective's current humble apartment.

"Yes, I too once lived like the Angels, Jacks," Sylvester said. "My bonuses each year kept getting larger and larger. I was young, only twenty-two, twenty-three. I loved the Angel life and it loved me. I had a girlfriend I was in love with. Sylvia. She was about to be Commissioned.

"I didn't have much to do with humans. I generally stuck to Angels and the Angel events. The way my father did, and the way his father had taught him. But then a child changed my life. She was eleven, maybe twelve. This was when I was still a new Guardian. She was the daughter of my housekeeper. Her father had left them, moved to Texas when she was just a baby. She and her mother lived in the side guesthouse on my estate.

"Penelope—that was the girl's name—she and I would sometimes play chess. She'd win half the time, and I wasn't letting her. She was smart. And she would make me laugh. I'd never had any siblings and it was . . . fun . . . to have a laughing kid around. I wasn't much more than a kid myself, frankly. I often helped her with her schoolwork. After a short while, I started to think of her as a member of my own family. And something about that girl made me start to think, just a bit, mind you, about the selfish Angel life I was living."

Sylvester paused to take a drink of his whiskey. He stared at his distorted, amber reflection at the bottom of the glass before beginning the next part.

"It was a beautiful day. The most beautiful day you could ask for in Angel City. Especially in those days, when the pollution was much worse.

"Penelope and her mother, Maria, were on their way to visit relatives in East Los Angeles. They insisted on taking the bus, even though I offered to drive them. I think Maria would have been embarrassed if I saw where their family lived." Sylvester shook his head. "That's what being an Angel causes in other people."

"What happened?" Jacks asked.

"The driver of the bus was on the freeway when she had a diabetic seizure. At sixty miles per hour, the bus began plowing toward the edge of the overpass they were crossing.

"I had the vision. Of Penelope and her mother's death. It was brutal, searing my mind. I saw her frequency instantly. It was of her dying under the crushing weight of the bus as it toppled off the overpass and onto the road below. She was, of course, not a Protection. Maria could have worked and saved for thirty years and never have afforded a Protection policy. I know now this is why my father didn't want me consorting with humans. Not because he was a snob.

"Before I knew what I was doing, my wings were out. I blasted through the plate glass window of my home to fly to the speeding bus on the freeway. I was there, Jackson. I had made it in time. In a blur, I was beside the bus, ready to make the save, as the bus smashed through the concrete like it was papier-mâché and plunged straight off toward the streets below.

"But I—" Sylvester's voice broke for a moment with years of emotion. "I hesitated. Just for a moment."

Jackson shivered.

"I thought about the consequences. Of making the unsanctioned save. Of losing my wings. I hesitated. Instead—instead of just saving her. I was thinking of my miserable *self*. Instead of that beautiful girl. It was just a moment. But it was enough.

"The bus began collapsing onto itself with force against the pavement, like an accordion. I shot down and used my time-bending to freeze the accident. It took everything I had in me. Chunks of concrete hung in midair, enormous sparks were flying up from the crumpling front of the bus on the street, frozen in space. The terrified expressions of those on the street below were fixed on their faces. I still remember everything as clear as yesterday. I smashed in through the bus window and found Penelope and her mother there. They were frozen. Her hair was floating up toward the back of the bus. Shrapnel and purses and eyeglasses and blood were floating back up there, too. All frozen like a snapshot. And I was too late. Penelope's bottom half was already crushed. But she had a strangely peaceful look on her face. I just looked down at her legs and lower torso mangled in the metal, and I started to weep. The bus began to slightly shift as my grip on the time-bending began to slip. I ripped open the metal, reached down, and pulled Penelope and her mother from the wreckage just as the bus smashed fully down and toppled over.

"I kneeled on the sidewalk and had Penelope over my knees. Her eyes opened for a second. She was conscious and saw me. And you know what that little girl said to me? 'It doesn't hurt.' She died in my arms."

Jacks looked at the detective, his blue eyes wet. He didn't speak.

"Maria survived her injuries but was never the same. She was heartbroken. She got a settlement from the city and the bus administration and moved back to El Salvador. Every Christmas I get a postcard.

"The NAS was able to conceal from the public the fact that an unsanctioned save had been made. But I was punished immediately. The ADC took me that night. Not that I cared. Pulled me out of a bar downtown, where I was hoping to obliterate myself. After how I'd failed to save Penelope . . . I didn't even want to live anymore. My girlfriend, Sylvia, begged me to fight, but I knew it was useless. She ended up getting Commissioned as a Guardian in Rio de Janeiro. I've never seen her since. They've made sure of that. And they took my wings.

"I joined the ACPD. Changed my last name to what was then my middle name: Sylvester. I tried to start a new life to cover my guilt and shame. Thought I could bury myself in the department. A rumor circulated at ACPD that I'd missed the save of a Protection and that that's why I was disgraced, all washed up. If they'd only known how much worse it was than that."

"I'm . . . sorry," Jacks said. "I shouldn't have brought it up. I—"

"There's no way to have known, Jacks," Sylvester said. "That is why I do what I do. Not because any of it could ever bring an innocent child back, or erase what I did when I didn't save Penelope in time because I was thinking of myself. But somehow, some way, I can at least make the account slightly more even." He knocked back the rest of his drink before putting the glass down with a clink. "Jackson, you've saved someone you loved and almost paid the ultimate price. But you saved her. Never forget that."

Jackson's thoughts streamed back to Maddy. His voice was studied. "I won't."

"And now, if you'll excuse me, I have to eat my dinner before it gets too cold."

Sylvester and Jacks stood up.

"Thank you for this," the detective said, motioning to the manila envelope sitting on his coffee table.

"I just want to help. Even though it feels like no one else believes I have anything to offer anymore. I at least need to try, I guess." He dropped his eyes again. "Anyway. Thank you, and have a good night," Jacks said, walking out the door. Sylvester closed it behind him.

Sylvester sat down on the couch and opened the container of Thai food, which was still satisfactorily warm. He started digging in with a plastic spoon, his mind swirling with the history he just told Jackson. Drawing in a deep breath between bites of curry, the detective tried to shake it off. Reaching into his bag with his free hand, Sylvester opened up his laptop to start watching an episode from one of his favorite TV shows—he had a weakness for a couple of BBC series. Even though he was mostly a traditionalist, he had to admit that being able to stream was pretty nice.

The computer was open to his email, and he saw he had a number of new messages. Mostly mass e-mails from the department, with some spam. But the latest was only a few minutes old. And it was from someone simply called "A Friend." The e-mail address was just a series of nonsensical letters in front of a gmail.com domain name. The subject line read: "Please Read Me, Detective."

Puzzled, Sylvester opened the e-mail.

Inside was simply a link to an online newspaper—no other sign or note of who could have left it for him. Sylvester clicked the link.

It opened an article about the fire and collapse of a brand-new high-rise apartment complex in Beijing, which had been designed by a prestigious Swedish architect. The Chinese tragedy had happened a week before, but officials had only been coming out publicly with details over the past day, after everything was cleaned up. Over five hundred had died in the horrific accident.

In the article was an eyewitness photo taken as the building burned. Sylvester cleaned his glasses, leaning closer to the screen to investigate the photo. The building was on fire, smoke roiling from the glass windows, residents streaming out in a panic. It was horrible. But what was Sylvester supposed to see? He continued looking, and looking, but could find nothing.

Frustrated, he zoomed in further on the photo on the screen, which only began to slightly pixelate.

And then he saw it—far off on the side of the building in the background, unnoticed, there were flames. But these were a slightly different color, the smoke darker, the fire more intense. If you didn't know what to look for, you'd never have noticed anything in the chaos.

Sylvester looked even closer. A jolt ran through his body.

If he examined as closely as possible, he thought he could see eyes burning darkly in the fire. The eyes of a Dark Angel.

# CHAPTER SEVENTEEN

Jackson's Ferrari rumbled under the Immortal City sun as he slowed along Ventura Boulevard in Angel Oaks, looking for his destination. He rarely came out to the Valley, and he didn't know his way around this part of town as well. Last night's visit with Detective Sylvester was still resonating in Jackson's brain as drove down the street, looking for the unfamiliar address. The detective's tale had haunted Jackson's dreams that night.

He wanted to somehow help further with the investigation. He may not be able to serve as one of the Angels, but he could still help his kind. That's what he *should* be doing. Instead of doing things like *this*, out in the Valley. Caught in his thoughts, Jacks missed a turn. He grumbled as he pulled a U-turn.

At last he saw it. *Wow. You really couldn't miss it*, he thought. He pulled around the side of the building and parked near the back. The thrumming engine of the car went silent as he turned off the ignition key. Jacks sighed as he looked out the window at his job for the day.

Out in front of the modern, curved-glass-and-steel showroom of the giant car dealership was strung a number of multicolored balloons, along with a large banner that read GRAND OPENING in big lurid letters, hanging over sparkling Range Rovers and Porsches.

Was this what it had come to? Jacks tried to remain positive. He thought about how he had a long road ahead of him and tried to chase away thoughts of just a year before, when his image had been splayed across buildings across Angel City. Darcy had convinced him that this car-dealership opening was a great appearance, that they really wanted Jackson to make it a glitzy event. And his publicist said he needed to do whatever came his way, to "get back out there." But Jackson was still reluctant.

Stepping out of the sports car, he scanned the parking lot for Darcy—where was she? She was always early.

All of a sudden, Christina, Darcy's assistant, materialized at Jackson's side.

"You're here, Jackson, that's just wonderful," Christina said, keeping one eye on her phone. "Now let's get you in to talk to the owner, Mr. Rahimi, who's so excited to meet you before the event begins."

"Where's Darcy?" Jacks asked, looking around.

"She's with Maddy, of course," Christina replied, tapping at her BlackBerry. "But I'm here for anything you need."

"Oh," Jacks said. Now Darcy wasn't even dealing with him directly?

"JACKSON!" A voice boomed loudly. A tan man in a sleek suit approached Jackson, all smiles. "Willy Rahimi, so terrific to see you. Welcome, welcome. Would you like a snack? A glass of wine? A Perrier?"

"No, I'm fine, thank you," Jacks said uncomfortably as the big man shook his hand up and down a few times too many. Jackson could see that on the other side of the lot, underneath the balloons, was a little table set up for him to sign autographs. There was a small line of people waiting patiently. Above was a sign: MEET JACKSON GODSPEED.

Mr. Rahimi looked over to Jackson's car. "No Maddy?" he said with a nervous chuckle. "We were hoping maybe she might just happen to come along. Heh."

For a second Jacks looked back at his Ferrari—his potential escape. Darcy's assistant picked up on it.

"Jackson is *so* excited to be here today, Mr. Rahimi," Christina said. "Come on, Jacks, just this way."

Swallowing his doubts and pride, Jackson walked over toward the cheerful balloons and table, where some people were waiting.

A teenaged girl accompanied by her dad was at the front of the line. She had a pink cast on her broken wrist. She introduced herself as Aimee. Smiling, she had her dad take a picture with Jacks and had him sign her cast.

"Thank you," the girl said, starting to turn away. "Before I go, one last thing, though," she said bashfully.

"Yes, Aimee?" Jacks asked expectantly.

"Can you tell Maddy hi for me?" she asked hopefully, looking up at Jacks with batting eyelashes and her broken arm.

"Oh. Uh, of course," Jacks said, forcing a smile. "She *is* pretty great, isn't she?"

The next person in line was even more blunt as Jacks signed a Nike Wings poster from his campaign a couple of years ago. The young man asked point blank: "What's it like being with Maddy?"

"Maddy's going to be a great Guardian someday," Jackson answered through set teeth. This was getting a little too personal. "Next?"

The rest of the event continued pretty much the same way, Mr. Rahimi standing behind Jacks and shaking hands with potential customers. And Jacks getting asked by everyone about Maddy.

"You were great out there," Christina said as she walked Jacks back to his car after he finished his contractual hour appearance.

His shoulders and neck taut, his entire body feeling just wrong, Jacks came to a firm decision. "I'm not doing one of those again."

"But—" Christina started.

"I don't care what Darcy says. *No*," he said. "This isn't what I've been working for my entire life—to be a . . ." He couldn't even finish the sentence as he waved his hand toward Rahimi's car dealership. "No," he repeated, slamming his car door shut, wheels squealing as he peeled out of the lot.

"So you'll watch me this time," Tom said to Maddy. The array of gauges, dials, lights, and meters in the cockpit was dizzying. She had studied the instrument panel from the book the pilot had given her, but facing it right now was a daunting prospect. Still, she thought this time she'd get a chance behind the controls.

"But this is our second lesson already. How am I supposed to—" she blurted.

"Maddy. This is my show. I know you're used to getting your way everywhere else out there." His hand gestured over to the hills that stood between them and Angel City. "But here, what I say goes. If you don't like it, you can get out right now."

Maddy bit her tongue, although it took everything she had. Something about this pilot just got under her skin. She wanted to impress him, but he was making that impossible.

"Okay," Tom said. "So I have one commandment: Do. Not. Touch. The. Controls. Period." Tom looked at her.

"But what if we're, like—"

"Even if I have a heart attack and I'm keeled over the controls and we're plunging to our deaths, don't even try it."

"I can fly on my own, you know. I have wings," Maddy said defensively.

"I've read the report. I think that depends on your definition of 'flying.'"

A slight smile broke through the pilot's normally serious expression, and Maddy felt suddenly better. His words might sound mocking, but underneath, it was as though he understood what she was going through.

"Let's go." The propellers suddenly roared to life, a raucous whirlwind outside Maddy's window. After a brief taxi, Tom lined the plane up along the small runway. In fact, now that Maddy thought about it, the runway seemed *really* small. She realized she'd never flown in a plane this small before.

"Are you sure this is long enough to—" Before she could finish her sentence, she was pressed back in her seat as the aircraft began speeding forward. Her nails dug into the side of the seat as the end of the runway approached.

With a quick lurch, the Cessna lifted off the ground, and then, after a quick ascent, it leveled off. The weightlessness lifted Maddy's stomach up into her chest for a moment. She peered down as the earth receded below them.

She looked over at the young pilot. His eyes flipped from instruments to the sky in front of him and then back again. His hands moved quickly, smoothly. It was simple, automatic for him, manipulating the controls. He looked like he was just tying his shoes. It just seemed so effortless. Maddy couldn't explain it, but as they banked to the left, it seemed almost like he and the plane were fused somehow. She began to see why he had come so highly recommended from Professor Archson. After their first lesson, Maddy had done a Google search on "Tom Cooper fighter pilot," and dozens of results had come up: he had graduated summa cum laude from the Naval Academy in Annapolis with a degree in history, had been selected for the prestigious Navy Strike

Fighter Tactics Instruction Program, and had gotten many accolades for his flight prowess. She even found some of the navy message boards, and they were calling him the greatest pilot of his generation.

"When reaching sufficient altitude, you have to decrease the—"

"Angle of attack," Maddy said, finishing Tom's sentence. "That's the way to ensure stability."

Along the horizon, the peaks of the mountains extended into the distance, poking out of a low line of wispy clouds.

Tom looked over at Maddy, raising an eyebrow. "That's right," he said. "But what if you want to also assume zero bank angle?"

"Since this is fixed wing, I use the gyroscope to observe yaw and use the controls accordingly."

"Good," Tom said, looking over at Maddy from behind his aviator shades. "You've been doing what I asked."

Maddy suppressed a smile. *Ha.*

"Now watch me. The key is to integrate all the information at once: the tension of the controls, what you're seeing, what the instruments are telling you, what your intuition is telling you."

The plane gracefully climbed and rolled to the right, through a bank of clouds that had rolled in from the ocean. Above the clouds was crystal blue sky as far as they could see. They both seemed taken with the sight for a moment.

"How did you learn?" Maddy said at last, breaking the spell.

"To fly?"

Maddy nodded.

"I may not have wings like an . . . Angel," Tom said. "But ever since I was a boy flying the crop duster with my uncle back in Pennsylvania, we knew something special happened when I got up in the air. I was a natural-born flyer. They couldn't keep me out of the air."

Maddy studied him. "What do you have against Angels?"

"I don't have anything against Angels," Tom said. "Susan referred me to you, didn't she?" He looked down across the horizon. "Now please pay attention as I make this maneuver."

"You're changing the subject. Every time something about Angels comes up, you get this look on your face."

The young pilot glanced over. "I'd prefer not to talk about it. My politics are my business. Let's just say I don't agree with everything the Angels stand for."

Maddy's thoughts cast to her long discussions with Jacks about this, and the process she went through to choose joining the Angels over college.

"I don't agree with everything either," she said.

Tom looked at her incredulously. "You're becoming a Guardian."

"So I can get a chance to maybe change things," she said, color rising in her cheeks. "I resent your tone. You don't know anything about me."

Tom looked over at her. "I'm sorry. You're right. I hope you can change some things. I really do, Maddy."

A brief patch of turbulence shook the plane, then smoothed out. She tried to bring the topic around to less controversial subjects.

"So you flew so much with your uncle you became a professional pilot?"

"Nothing seemed more natural."

"And now you fly . . . jets?" Maddy asked.

He nodded. "F-18s. And I'm here in Angel City testing a new proto-type off my aircraft carrier in the Angel City Bay. Next-generation fighter."

She remembered the awards and accolades she'd come across when she did a search on the pilot. She looked over at Tom. Even though he was serious and put on airs, he was just a boy a couple years older than she was. A boy with a lot of responsibility. And he was helping her—even if he did feel obliged.

"Lieutenant Cooper," Maddy said. "I know we may have gotten off to a rocky start. But thank you. I mean it."

Tom looked over at her uncomfortably for a moment. She had caught him off guard. "Of course," he said hurriedly. "Now what about when a precipitous drop in altitude occurs and you need to . . ."

The polished steel elevator doors in Maddy's apartment building slid open with barely a whisper. She stepped out into the hallway, her cheeks glowing from the sun of the flight lesson, her hair windswept. She was met by Jacks, who was standing in the hall outside her apartment.

"You're late," Jacks said.

She checked the time on her phone. He was right. "Oh. Only ten minutes, Jacks," she said. "I had my flight lesson and it went longer than I thought."

She opened the door and threw her bag down.

"How's that going?" Jacks asked, following her inside.

"Good. I think. Although the pilot still won't let me fly. And other training stuff is okay, too." She poured herself a glass of orange juice from the fridge. "Except I can't really bend time yet."

Maddy cast her glance to her father's old notebook, which was on the side table with her other books. At night she had been studying it. It was filled with useful tips and tactics for mastering the training subjects. But she'd only managed to bend time briefly, just for the slightest moment, not enough to successfully pull off a hard save under pressure. Or do anything as complicated as when Jacks froze the policeman's bullet in Kevin's Diner the year before.

"You won't have that class for another couple of years, anyway. It's very advanced," Jacks said.

"Well, I still want to try, Jacks," she responded, taking a gulp of her OJ.

Jackson didn't answer. He walked over and turned the TV on.

". . . *numbers for Senator Linden's presidential bid continue to rise day-by-day. The increasing verbal threats from Angels have drawn more and more supporters to his camp. Self-described 'former Angel addicts' are flocking to the charismatic politician, who claims he will clean up the, quote, 'Angel—'*"

The TV went black. Jacks had turned it off, shaking his head.

"I don't know why you watch that station sometimes," Jacks said.

"What, PBS? I like the shows with the lords and ladies and stuff," Maddy said defensively.

The phone in Maddy's bag buzzed. With one hand still sipping her orange juice, she pulled it out and checked it: a text from Darcy.

"Oh no," she said.

"What?" Jacks asked.

"I totally forgot I have the *Teen Vogue* gala at the museum tonight," Maddy said.

Jacks looked at her evenly. "I told you I wanted to do something."

"I know, I'm sorry. It's just that this came up and it seemed like a good thing to agree to. Why don't you come with me?"

Walking to the window and looking out, Jackson let out a long breath. "I . . . I don't know. I don't know if I feel like it."

"Why not?"

Jacks spun around. "I guess I didn't realize that events had become so important to you."

Maddy's face burned. "It's not the event that's important, it's just part of the process. It's part of what I have to do to get the respect of all these people whose world I'm supposed to be joining. You told me this yourself, Jacks!" Maddy was frustrated, embarrassed, and angry all at once. "You wanted this for me, Jackson. Becoming a Guardian. And now it's almost here. Isn't this what happens?"

Jacks bit his lip and turned back toward the window. Silence lingered between them. On the horizon, an ACPD helicopter crisscrossed the sky.

At last, Jacks spoke. Bitterness and hurt edged his sardonic voice. "I didn't get invited."

"What? Of course you're invited," Maddy said, walking closer to him. "I mean, are there even invitations?"

"Yes. Everything you go to. Darcy has them. They . . . didn't invite me."

Maddy stepped back and leaned against the counter.

"So go as my date."

Jacks's face darkened. "Do you understand, Maddy? They don't *want* me there. And that's not all. Even though Mark would never come out and say it, I can just tell that he is having to fight more and more for me, the way my wings aren't recovering. It's being held up as proof that Angels aren't so amazing after all. Everything's fueling that crackpot Ted Linden's presidential campaign and the Immortals Bill. I bet most of the Archangels would be happy if I just disappeared."

"Jacks, don't talk like that," Maddy said, feeling miserable. "I won't go. I'll just stay here. We'll do something else." She approached Jacks and held his two hands in hers.

But he slowly shook his head. "No. You should go. Darcy will be pissed if you don't."

"I don't care what Darcy thinks. And I don't care what the Archangels think. Or what Senator Linden thinks. Or what *anybody* thinks, except you, Jacks."

Jacks shook his head. "I'm sorry, Maddy. I'm sorry I brought up the other stuff. You should go; you need to go. I'm going to be mad now if you *don't* go. This is all my own stuff I'm trying to deal with."

"But—"

"No *buts*," Jacks said emphatically. "I want to look on ANN tonight and see footage of"—he put on a Tara Reeves voice—"'gorgeous *Maddy Montgomery coming out to shine with the stars.*'" Jacks smiled and laughed a little.

Maddy looked at him. She felt upset and confused and didn't know what the right answer was, or even if there *was* a right answer. Was Jacks being selfish? Was she being selfish? She felt exhausted all of a sudden. "Are you . . . are you sure?"

Jacks nodded, running his thumb along her cheek. "I've been meaning to spend some time with my mom, anyway, and I know she's home tonight. Not a big deal." Jacks smiled more, swallowing his disappointment ever deeper.

That night at the event—an Angel-studded gala on the rooftop of the Angel City Art Museum—Maddy was the center of attention, wearing a spectacular Alexander McQueen dress she and her stylist had been planning on. She smiled and took pictures along the red carpet and did brief interviews with ANN and A!, which had correspondents waiting to pounce on the hottest Angels.

The autumn air was starting to crackle with energy as the biggest event of the year was just a month or so away: Commissioning Week. Emily and Mitch were both going to be Commissioned, and Maddy was hoping that for at least a week or so, the spotlight wouldn't glare so brightly on her. She couldn't even imagine how nervous she was going to be in a couple of years when her own Guardian assessment was going to take place. So much attention was already on her.

She glanced around the event: anyone who was anyone in the Angel world was there, but Maddy had the strange feeling they were all looking at *her*. She kept up appearances, trying not to stumble in her Louboutin heels, which she was slowly but surely mastering, but she had a bad feeling. She walked over to the edge of the roof, where there weren't so many people, and pulled out her iPhone. She saw she had a text from Gwen: "*Look at this* . . . ☹," with a link to a blog posting with pictures already up from the *Teen Vogue* red carpet just thirty minutes ago.

"*Maddy One Step Behind!*" the headline read.

It showed pictures of Maddy arriving at the red carpet that night in her McQueen dress. And then it showed pictures of Emily *the night before* wearing the same exact designer dress.

Emily had already tweeted—from the other side of the party: "*Don't you hate girls who are just copiers? Get your own style!*"

The Aussie Angel had somehow found out that Maddy was planning on wearing the McQueen dress to the *Teen Vogue* event and wore it just to make her look bad!

Looking back over her shoulder into the main bustle of the party on the rooftop, she saw Emily's friend Zoe with another group of young Angels, all rolling their eyes and laughing at Maddy. Maddy's cheeks burned. She felt like a bug on a pin. She had been walking around the party, not knowing that everybody thought she was just copying Emily.

Sighing, she looked out onto the dark hills and the Angel City sign, which was barely visible in the distance. The gala glittered behind her. She thought about Jacks, whose pride wouldn't let him come with her tonight. Because no matter how badly she felt for Jacks, she realized that's what it was: his pride.

As Jacks was on her mind, a disconcerting thought suddenly arose in her head, very clearly.

*How long can this go on?*

# CHAPTER EIGHTEEN

The next morning, Maddy looked out the window of the helicopter at the auburn desert flats below her and couldn't help but smile to herself at the irony: they were using the chopper to fly her out to the desert, so that then she could practice flying. Angel efficiency at its best. The roar of the blades overhead was dulled by the headset she wore.

"Almost there," the voice crackled over the radio in her ear. Below her, the seemingly never-ending development of Angel City had butted up against mountains and then finally given way to vast tan, parched desert that stretched now as far as she could see. It was incredible to her. She'd driven through with Uncle Kevin once when they'd visited some relatives in Nevada, but being above it gave her a sense of the scale of the whole thing.

The Angels had a top-secret proving grounds out here near the military bombing ranges, but not even the military were allowed to trespass on the Angel training grounds here in the desert. Maddy soon saw a gleaming silver structure in the distance, just inside what looked like tall cyclone fencing.

"Dropping the bird down," the pilot said, landing them on the helipad next to the building. Sand and dirt swirled around angrily as the helicopter touched down. Maddy pulled her hood close around her and jumped out of the chopper into the churning grit, following her flight instructor, former ADC Agent Trueway. It was time for Maddy's more advanced speed training.

She might be able to get by without knowing time manipulation—there were some Angels who weren't too great at it—but there was no way she'd make it to Guardian without getting the hang of flying. It was crunch time, and Maddy knew it.

Maddy and her instructor, Trueway, were met by a tall, muscular Angel in ADC uniform—when not prepping Guardians, the agents performed their advanced tactical and flying training out here in the desert. Junior ADC agents stood guard at the building. Maddy felt a slight shudder run down her spine as she saw the black uniform but tried to chase it from her mind. She noticed the entire grounds were surrounded by twenty-foot-tall electrified cyclone fence.

They were led into a black truck, which drove a short distance down a gravel road until it reached a paved clearing. In the center of the paved clearing was a metal pylon, which reached about twenty feet into the sky. More pylons continued as far as Maddy could see, each about a football field's distance apart. Far off, it seemed as if they started zigzagging a bit.

"Ready?" Trueway said to Maddy as they reached the paved clearing. Maddy looked at him and nodded. She slipped off her hoodie so that she was wearing only her flying training gear—a nylon-and-cotton formfitting uniform that had openings for wings. It wasn't too weird, but it made Maddy, who had never been particularly athletic, feel self-conscious. She stepped out of the truck and looked into the distance at the pylons.

"Maddy, now normally when we bring Guardian nominees here, it's just to hone their already God-given instinct as an Angel to fly. We train for more speed, smooth over some rough patches. Essentially help them become the best flyers they possibly can be." He scrutinized Maddy through his sunglasses. "Now, with you it's a little . . . different."

Maddy's cheeks flushed as she recalled her repeated embarrassments during agility training, her inability to master the basic techniques necessary to fly gracefully and smoothly. All the while, other Guardian nominees had basically come out of the womb knowing how to fly properly. It was like learning how to walk while all the other students were world-class runners.

"My goal with you is to get you to a basic aptitude and hope that nature takes its course from there, assisted by continued supplemental training. Okay?"

She nodded, although that was not what she wanted to hear. Maddy wanted to hear that she was going to learn to fly like a Guardian. Today. Not tomorrow. Now. She was tired of feeling different from the rest. Even her lessons from Tom hadn't seemed to be making too much of a difference, although they hadn't reached the stage where she flew the plane yet.

It wasn't even her fault that she couldn't fly as well as other Angels, and it wasn't fair to get shown up by someone like Emily, who'd had every advantage that being an Angel could bring throughout her life. Maddy was just a nobody; she knew nothing.

Trueway pointed at the line of metal poles that extended into the distance. "Each pylon represents a station along the way for the time trial. You have to fly within ten feet of each one for it to register. Breaking each leg down, we're able analyze an Angel's performance and see what sections can be improved upon." Her instructor handed her a small earpiece to put in. "I can communicate with you through this. Normally we'd start working for speed, but since you're, uh, new to this, we'd better just begin with having you run the course. Any questions?"

She shook her head.

Maddy's instructor held up a device a little bigger than a phone. "We monitor your progress and times here."

"Okay."

"Whenever you're ready, start on the mark." Trueway pointed to a perfect red circle painted on the smooth concrete. "The clock will automatically begin as soon as you lift off." Maddy stepped onto the mark.

A wind blew across the desert flats, shaking the dry scrub. The sun glared over the whole scene as Maddy prepared herself. She could do this. She could. She tried so hard to concentrate, thinking about everything she would do. What had Jacks told her? *Just fly?* That was easy for him to say—he was born with the ability.

"Remember, poised on the balls of your feet," Trueway said.

Maddy leaned slightly forward, lightly.

*WHOOSH.*

Her wings suddenly extended from behind her back, sliding noiselessly through the specially designed slits in the back of her training gear. Maddy groaned in pain, dropping to a knee. It was getting better, but it still was incredibly painful each time she spread her wings. Another difference between her and full Angels.

The other Angel with their group moved forward to help her, but Trueway put his hand in front of him as if to say it was okay.

Maddy pulled herself up, dusting off her knee, and leaned forward, poised on the balls of her feet again.

"Good, good," Trueway said. "Now launch."

Leaning forward, one, two enormous flaps and she jumped up. The wings suddenly propelled her forward and Maddy was flying off the mark, her sneakers lifting from the asphalt. The muscles in her back burned with effort. She raised herself up twenty feet with four powerful thrusts and then set her wings, trying to gain speed. The desert ground sped beneath her. Her breath came sharp and ragged. She was wobbly as she attempted to jet straight toward the first pylon in the distance. Maddy tried to remember flying with Jacks.

"Come on," she said under her breath. Still struggling to maintain a straight course, Maddy flew by the first pylon, which had two lights on it. It turned green, signifying she'd passed within ten feet of it.

A little confidence growing, Maddy set her sights on the next one, getting slightly faster. She was still struggling to maintain a straight course, however. She concentrated as hard as she could, but it still felt somewhat unnatural. Passing the second pylon, it turned green, and Maddy found the pylons beginning to zig and zag slightly, like slalom gates, across the desert landscape.

Setting her teeth, Maddy neared the third pylon, her wings flapping desperately as she tried to make the hard right turn toward the next marker. She overshot the mark and awkwardly had to circle around to get to the fourth pylon. The light turned green, but Maddy was pretty sure she was breaking some kind of record for slowest flight ever. With determination, she exerted as much energy as she could to gain speed toward the fifth marker.

The pylon grew closer and Maddy suddenly wobbled, midair, and flew wide of the mark, off to the left. She looked back at the pylon: the red light came on. She had failed.

"Bring it on back. We'll try it again," Trueway's voice said over the earpiece.

Maddy circled around back to home base, trying to figure out in her mind where she had gone wrong. Trueway watched her approach through a large pair of field glasses. Landing, she drank some water and collected herself, making sure her ponytail was tied tightly.

"Ready again?" her instructor asked, his eyes hidden behind his sunglasses.

She nodded, stepping onto the mark again.

"This time try to . . . flow with it a bit more. Drop your starboard wing and lean in to bring you around that pylon."

Maddy nodded that she understood—and she did understand, physics-wise, how that would work—but she wasn't sure she *felt* it. Maybe this time she could. She set her jaw and leaned forward on the balls of her feet.

"Anytime you're—"

Before Trueway had finished his sentence, Maddy was off. She looked down at the desert scrub as it zoomed underneath her; she was actually gaining some speed this time. She smiled as she got to the first pylon, passing it quickly, and then on to the second. Both lights turned green. Maddy got to the third pylon, but this time she didn't overshoot it, and was able to turn quickly and start gaining speed for the fourth. Passing it as well, she made a sharp turn toward the fifth, which she'd missed last time.

She smiled. She was starting to get the hang of it. Bearing down, she started gaining as much speed as she could. Beads of sweat broke on her forehead, her ponytail whipping behind her as she neared the fifth marker. Almost there. . . . The metal of the pylon glinted in the direct sun as she zoomed toward it.

She thought of what he had said: *Now drop starboard wing, lean in.*

Suddenly Maddy began rolling in midair, her wing dropping too much as she flew directly toward the metal globe atop the pylon. Red-hot pain shot through her body as her right wing caught the side of the pylon, which jerked her violently into a spin.

Tumbling in thin air in a dizzying freefall, Maddy screamed as the desert floor rushed to meet her.

She landed hard with a crunch on the dry bushes of the desert ground. The wind was knocked out of her, leaving her stomach hollow and her chest in pain.

"Maddy! Are you all right?" Trueway spoke on the earpiece.

Maddy sat up, miserably dusting herself off next to a cactus. She looked at the pylon above her. It didn't even seem to recognize her presence, even though it had brought her low.

"I'm okay," she croaked, barely able to speak, still trying to get her breath back.

"Maybe we should try some easier exercises," the voice crackled in her ear. "We'll send the truck to get you."

"Sure," Maddy said, defeated.

Maddy was silent on the helicopter ride back to Angel City that afternoon, dirty and dusty from the humiliating day at the proving grounds. She didn't even know where to begin. Instructor Trueway insisted she was making progress, but she still felt like some toddler learning how to walk.

The only thing she knew was that she had to figure it out, and sooner rather than later, if she was going to be a Guardian.

She checked her phone when she got back to Angel City and saw that Jacks hadn't texted her back from the morning. That was unusual for him, although she knew he had a long day of doctor's appointments. Kevin had called and left a voicemail—very Kevin, no texts for him—probably asking when she was going to come over for dinner.

After showering off the desert grit, Maddy tenderly sat down on her couch, sore all over from the fiasco of the day's flying training. She grabbed her laptop off the couch and flipped it open, massaging her aching neck with her free hand. Her browser was still open from last night, when she'd been perusing Johnny Vuitton's Angel blog and reading the public's comments on the dress debacle.

Maddy's mouth literally dropped open. And stayed there.

An outside observer would have thought Maddy had somehow been frozen in place, a peaceful statue. Far from being calm, adrenaline coursed through her veins and her blood screamed in her ears. She was so shocked she simply couldn't move.

The blog headline read:

"MADDY DOING SO WELL IN TRAINING SHE'S GETTING COMMISSIONED THIS YEAR! BOMBSHELL ANNOUNCEMENT FOR AMERICA'S SWEETHEART!"

Breaking out of her spell, Maddy rushed to open another blog. And then three more. And then the ANN homepage. They all had the same story.

Maddy's phone began ringing.

And ringing.

And ringing.

Within twenty minutes, Maddy was at the Godspeed house. She was glad to see Mark's Porsche in the driveway. She let herself in the door.

Coverage of her early Commissioning was blaring on the TV. Mark, his tie slightly undone and his jacket thrown over the back couch, stood there watching the events play out on ANN. A strange look hovered on his face as he turned to Maddy.

"Jacks isn't here, Madison. Were you supposed to meet here? Did you try his house?" He motioned to the TV. "I'm assuming you've heard about your historic Commissioning?"

"I'm here to talk to you, Mark. *What* is going on?"

The TV played a series of photos someone had managed to get a hold of that showed Maddy through her school years. She tried to ignore it.

Mark looked at her. "The NAS feels that, given your progress, there's no better time than now to get you out there as a Guardian."

Maddy's hand unconsciously moved to the bruises on her arm from her hard fall earlier in the day during flight training.

"Progress, Mark? Do you know how I did at the desert proving grounds? I couldn't get past the fourth pylon. I can barely fly."

Mark's eyes darted to the bruise and back up to Maddy's face. She could read conflict in his steely eyes.

"What's really going on, Mark?"

The Archangel sighed and lowered his voice, leaning in close to Maddy.

"There is a strong contingent—very strong—among the Archangels that thinks waiting to Commission you is just a waste of time and momentum. Given your special . . . position."

"You mean my popularity?" Maddy said, getting to the point. This was no time to be humble. Something bigger than her was happening.

Mark narrowed his eyes. "Being an Angel is about a lot of things, Maddy," he said. "Yes, making saves is a large part of that. But pleasing the public is also one of those things. Without public support, we Angels are going to have a hard time keeping Linden and his racist cronies at bay."

"So basically I'm a great PR opportunity."

Mark put his hand on Maddy's shoulder. "We need to remind people of the reason they fell in love with Angels in the first place. And why they need us still. Rekindle that romance. Capture the thrill. The opportunity. You embody all that, Maddy. Whether you like it or not. It's bigger than you, now. You're going to be a Guardian in two weeks."

Maddy let out a long sigh. "But what if I can't? What if I'm not good enough?" Her voice became quieter. She looked up at the Archangel. "What if I'm not ready?"

"Well, you're going to have to be."

# CHAPTER NINETEEN

If Maddy had thought things were hectic before, her unforeseen Commissioning this year threw everything instantly, irrevocably into overdrive. It suddenly seemed that the amount of media coverage had doubled overnight, and Maddy was the name on everybody's breathless lips.

The NAS had made the right bet: Maddy was becoming the biggest thing for Angels in decades. She was doing wonders for Angel publicity: her picture was everywhere; she was in demand from everyone; she even suddenly had her own action figure that came with the kid's meal at a popular nationwide hamburger chain. For the first time in weeks, the story about Senator Linden and the Immortals Bill faded a bit into the background as everyone re-remembered the excitement of Angels, now that someone who had been born a human was officially joining their highest ranks.

As the Archangel spokesmen kept saying on TV, "*Maddy stands for the best and brightest, our new generation of Angels. She's made so much progress, we're all just eager to get her out there saving Protections and thrilling her fans!"*

And so Maddy Montgomery Godright, recently graduated from Angel City High School and formerly a morning shift waitress at Kevin's Diner, was their "It" girl. It was dizzying.

"Maddy, honey," Darcy had said, looking seriously into her eyes, "you have hit the jackpot."

Maddy wasn't so sure about the jackpot, however, especially as the crush of photographer and interview requests grew to smothering proportions. And if she already wasn't a favorite among the other Angels, now all of them except Jacks officially hated her. Especially those in training. They all but hissed at her when she walked by, and Emily's friend Zoe had stopped her in a hallway and told her to her face she didn't deserve it and everyone knew it. Emily herself had been keeping up a stream of thinly veiled insults on her Twitter feed. Even Mitch had been a bit chilly to Maddy.

*It's not my fault!* she wanted to shout out to them. But she knew it wouldn't do any good. It didn't matter who was behind her early advancement to Guardianship—the other nominees were going to resent her bitterly no matter what.

And Jacks? His reaction to her early Commissioning had been strangely quiet.

So then one afternoon less than a week from Commissioning, sitting in the nice air-conditioned comfort of her luxury apartment, Maddy suddenly felt like she couldn't breathe. At all. Like there was a vise on her chest and the vise was getting tighter and there was no way to get out. She gasped for air.

She realized she was probably having a panic attack. Looking at the blogs, watching A!, checking Twitter—the tsunami of being nominated to Guardian after such little training had suddenly overwhelmed her.

Catastrophe, embarrassment, shame, and failure all crashed into her head at once. And capping it all was an image in her mind's eye of her tumbling down forever, out of the clouds, her wings flapping helplessly.

In a cold sweat, Maddy dug through her purse, searching. After fumbling through a number of canisters of lipstick and makeup—how different her life had become in just a year—Maddy found it. The card read: "U.S. Navy Aviator 1st Lieutenant Thomas Cooper." And a phone number.

A bored voice answered the phone. "Navy."

"Is Tom, I mean, Lieutenant Cooper there? This is Mad—his tutee."

"Hold, please."

The phone clicked over, and patriotic hold music played in Maddy's ear. Her pulse was still racing from the panic. She tried to catch her breath.

The phone clicked over. Tom's voice was on the line.

"Hello, Maddy?" the pilot said, the line crackling slightly. "Is everything all right? Our next session isn't scheduled until Thursday, and it's Sunday."

"I need your help," Maddy blurted into the phone before he'd even finished his sentence.

Avoiding the paparazzi, Maddy crept in the back door of her uncle's diner—she still had the key—and walked through the back hall toward the dining room. She took a glance through the open door at the cluttered office as she walked by. Kevin had been meaning to clean it for about a year. She shook her head. Some things never changed.

She was surprised to find the kitchen empty. Where was her uncle?

Stepping out into the main dining room, she found Tom was already there, sitting in a booth in the corner. Kevin was standing by the table, his apron still on, chatting with her tutor.

"Speak of the devil," Kevin said as Maddy walked up.

"Hey," Maddy replied, giving him a hug. "You've met Lieutenant Cooper?"

Tom looked up at Maddy with his green eyes. He was wearing a leather motorcycle jacket over a dark T-shirt, old jeans, and boots. This was the first time she'd seen him out of uniform.

"Thomas was telling me about the jets he flies—really interesting stuff," Kevin said. "You remember how much I liked the Air and Space Museum when we went that year, Maddy?"

"Just another day at the office, sir," Tom said. "And please, call me Tom. Only my mom calls me Thomas. And that's when she's mad at me."

"Well, then, please, call me Kevin," Maddy's uncle said. "And don't forget—not everybody's office is a supersonic jet."

Kevin looked over at the waitress, Jana, who was giving him the eye. "Looks like duty calls. Let Jana know if you need anything else. Nice meeting you, Tom."

"Nice meeting you, too, sir."

Standing there, relaxed, Maddy realized that she felt instantly more at ease around those who weren't Angels, like Kevin. And even Tom. It was like taking a vacation from her new life. Sometimes there were things that only humans understood.

"So this meeting is unorthodox," Tom said, looking at her expectantly. "But I told Susan I would help you. And it sounded like you need it. So here I am."

"I'm sorry, I know you're probably busy with your own work. I just didn't know what else to do," Maddy said. The pilot's face remained inscrutable.

"Of course I saw the news. Everyone has. They've moved your Commissioning to this year? Is this—your call—about that?"

Maddy nodded.

"One second I think I have a couple of years to get used to flying," Maddy said. "Get used to the idea of being a Guardian. How I'm going to start making my mark. Helping to work to reform some Angel practices from the inside out. And now, all of a sudden, they say I'm going to be a nominee. A year ago they were calling me an abomination. Half-human, half-Angel. Now I'm their best hope?"

"You're different than them, Maddy," Tom said, sounding suddenly impassioned. "You know that. Not everything's been given to you." He seemed to recollect himself. "I guess I have some strong opinions about Angels. Now's probably not the time for me to share them, though."

Maddy remembered their first meeting, when he was so cold to her. "I know, I'm different," she said. "But I can't even fly properly yet. I'm still not getting it. Even with your lessons. It's like I'm unteachable. Even Jacks"—she noticed Tom's expression slightly changed when he heard the name—"can't help me. He doesn't know what to say." She looked down at the old Formica on the table. "I can flap around. It's kind of like flying. But just not like an Angel."

"The Angels, it's in them already. They don't have to work at it," Tom said. "It's like a bird trying to teach a fish how to fly. The bird really can't even explain it, it just knows. So you need to have more faith in me. And yourself."

"I guess so," Maddy said hesitantly, trying to imagine the conversation between the bird and the fish, and instead getting a mental picture of the bird eating the poor fish.

"You're ready, Maddy."

"What are you suggesting?"

Tom's green eyes deepened. "You may want to get a coat."

The headlights of Tom's truck climbed over the ridge as the sun set along Angel City. Maddy sat in the passenger seat as the pickup made its way to the private airfield out past the Valley. The owner of the field, wearing a big belt buckle and a cowboy hat, greeted Tom like a son as they pulled into the small gravel lot next to the field. It was closed for the day, but he had come down especially to open it up for Tom.

"She's all fueled up, ready to go," the man said, pointing to the small plane on the small runway.

Soon the Cessna climbed into the sky, Maddy's stomach dropping as she sat next to Tom in the cockpit and they quickly gained elevation. For a brief moment, the image of Angel City disappearing below them caused Maddy's mind to flicker back to that first night Jacks took her flying.

The orb of the sun burned with color as the plane crossed it. The Cessna was silhouetted black against the sinking blood orange disk.

Yet again, Tom seemed so confident, calm, and at home behind the controls of the plane—he was a natural. He turned, glancing at Maddy for a moment from behind his aviator glasses before looking forward again. Flying was a joy for him.

After a couple of minutes, they leveled off, heading northwest along the coast toward Ventura County and Santa Barbara. Tom turned to her again.

"Okay, I'm going to let you take the controls."

"*What?*" Maddy said incredulously. "I thought—"

"You're flying the plane now," Tom said, letting go of the controls in front of him.

"Are you crazy?" Maddy said, slightly panicking. The yokes floated in front of them, untouched. The plane continued flying straight ahead.

"You better fly, or we're going to have some problems."

"I can't—"

The plane began tilting slightly, and Maddy instinctively reached forward, grabbing the controls to right the plane.

And it was incredible.

Maddy could feel the plane respond. Tom was right.

When flying with her own wings, Maddy had tried to figure everything out, because it didn't feel natural to her. But now, holding the controls of the plane in her hands, she was able to understand the natural way wings kept aloft—whether on a plane or an Angel.

"This is amazing!" she yelled. She felt an invigorating sensation of freedom.

"You're doing great. Hold it steady," he answered, a grin in his voice.

Maddy pulled the yoke back, and they began climbing even higher. She tilted it right, and the agile plane banked right.

"Okay, easy, easy. Now feel the lift. You know it from the books and what I've told you. But just let the lift keep us up. Get familiar with it, at ease."

"It feels so strange . . . but so right!"

"Maybe you were born to fly after all," Tom said, the slightest smile spreading across his face.

Patiently, Tom walked her through the applications of the basic flying principles as they continued northward. After a while he looked out west to the seemingly unending Pacific Ocean as the last of the light began vanishing in the distance

"Naval twilight," Tom told her. The glimmering edges of purple and red were fleeting on the horizon. "Time to go home. Can you get us headed there?"

Gripping the yoke harder, Maddy pressed on it, banking them back around toward Angel City.

The dark churning waves of the Pacific crashed on the beach below them as the plane gracefully soared in a circle back to the invisible lights of the Immortal City. How different it was from her flying with her wings earlier in the day! The grace and ease she experienced was incredible. She felt as if she had control. Maybe even a little bit of skill. She couldn't believe it—it was like something had shifted in her brain and body when she took control of the plane. She somehow intuited what was needed for her to fly with her own wings. It was going to feel natural. *Like this*, she told herself.

Tom took back the controls as they neared the city and potential air traffic. It was entirely dark as he finally touched the plane down on the runway with a screech of tire on the tarmac.

In the truck on the way back, Maddy let the bouncing of the pickup soothe her as they drove along. Traffic was bad on some of the freeways, and Tom turned the radio on, tuned to the news station.

*"Expect delays with protests across the city this evening, starting at ACX airport as presidential candidate Senator Ted Linden arrives for a two-day fundraising tour through Southern California. And his first stop? Angel City, the worldwide center of Angel culture and home to those Senator Linden has targeted with his anti-Angel Immortals Bill."*

"Linden's coming here?" Maddy asked, thinking of the party at the Godspeed house and Archangel Churchson's cold statement. "Pretty bold."

Tom merely raised an eyebrow. He looked for an exit off the trafficked freeway.

*"The Immortal City, home of the gorgeous Angels and legions of fans who love them, may seem an unlikely place for the senator to raise funds for his presidential run. But spokesmen for Linden say anti-Angel sentiment in the region is only growing by the day as the Council makes threats against humans. An official Angel statement denounced the visit by the senator as yet 'another stop on Teddy Linden's hate-filled agenda.'"*

As he whipped the truck off the freeway, Tom turned the radio off and the two rode in silence. To avoid traffic, he took them through a beautiful back route around Griffith Park, the trees lit by the spearing headlights of the old truck. The traffic seemed a world away. Tom was quiet, and they just enjoyed the drive after the flight.

After the winding drive, Tom pulled the truck into the side street near the diner where Maddy's Audi was surreptitiously parked.

"Tom, er, Lieutenant Cooper, thank you so much," Maddy said as he put the pickup in park, the engine idling. Steam rose from the exhaust pipe in the early autumn evening. The inside of the cab was dark, but they were lit by the glare from the streetlight. "I can't even begin to tell you how much you've helped me."

"Of course," Tom said, "anytime." His voice was a little more serious than usual. Maddy looked over and saw that his eyes were getting more serious, too. "Your uncle told me about your parents, Maddy. I'm sorry."

Maddy nodded her head silently in the passenger seat. Where was he going with this?

"My parents were alive," Tom continued. "But they weren't exactly there. My dad left before I was even born. My mom raised me by herself. She was always in and out of the hospital. She never talked about my dad. Every year I received a check for $400 in an envelope with no return address." Tom looked up at Maddy. "I'm sorry, I don't know why I'm telling you this."

"It's okay," Maddy said. This was a side of Tom she hadn't seen. That he hadn't wanted her to see, with his uniform and rules and giving her a hard time.

"And I always had to work, too. Like you. Mom couldn't earn. She was usually too sick. Luckily, as I got older my uncle let me have some of the crop-dusting jobs myself, just as long as I didn't tell anybody. I worked day and night, and studied too. I got into the Naval Academy at seventeen. Nobody had as many flight hours when they arrived as I did.

Others had the pedigree of military families. But I had the experience.

"The Angels wouldn't understand. They may work hard, but it's different for them. They have a big something to catch them if they fall. Money. Prestige. Power. We haven't had that, Maddy. You may be half-Angel. But to me you're all human. For the right reasons." He looked at her. "I'm not anti-Angel. I'm just pro-honesty. Pro-human."

Maddy nodded, thinking about how much time she'd spent studying in high school while everyone else seemed to just goof off and have fun. And now, being the first half-human, half-Angel to be nominated for Guardianship. How many seemed to be against her.

"So I just wanted to say that I can relate," Tom said. "To being the underdog."

"Thank you . . . for saying that," Maddy replied. "Sometimes I think I forget where I am. Where I've come from."

"I admire you, Maddy."

No one had ever told Maddy they admired her. Now that her fame was growing, everyone seemed to want to get closer to her, to be near her, to learn about her, to somehow *be* her.

But no one had said they admired her.

"Thank . . . you," she said.

"Friends?" he said, putting his hand out.

"Friends."

The two shook hands, smiling.

Maddy was halfway out the truck door when Tom's voice stopped her.

"And Maddy?" he said.

She turned and looked at him.

"Don't let anyone tell you that you don't know how to fly. You're a natural."

Maddy flushed, her red cheeks half-illuminated by the truck's dome light.

"Thanks," she said.

Maddy watched the truck's taillights disappear into the quiet Angel City evening. She figured she would just head home—it was near the dinner rush at the diner, and after all that had been happening, she was too tired to deal with being recognized tonight.

It was then that she felt her phone buzzing in her bag. She pulled it out and saw she had numerous missed calls. All from Kevin.

"Hello?" she said, worried.

His voice was pretty serious: "Are you back from flying?"

"Yes. What's—"

"You better get to the diner."

And he hung up. Maddy's imagination blazed. She began quickly walking the block to the diner, wondering what in the world could strike Kevin so serious as to make a phone call during the dinner rush.

The first thing Maddy noticed was a number of men wearing suits standing underneath the glowing Kevin's Diner sign outside. They wore dark sunglasses and had small transmitters in their ears. This wasn't a strange sight in Angel City—they could've been security for any Angel event, and Maddy had dealt with them a lot over the past year. But this was outside her uncle's decidedly non-Angel restaurant. And these men were different. They seemed a bit more on edge, their suits a bit boxier. Like there might be guns under them.

They stared straight ahead as Maddy walked into the diner.

Kevin, wiping his hands on his apron, met her at the entrance. The restaurant seemed empty.

"Kevin, what's going on?"

Her uncle led her toward the back booths, talking under his breath.

"I don't know how he found us, but . . . well, he's waiting," Kevin said.

"*Who's* waiting? What's happening?" Maddy asked.

"Just, well, you'll see," Kevin said. He led Maddy to the furthest table in the back and motioned for her to sit.

Maddy slipped into the booth and found herself facing a man in a navy Brooks Brothers suit, red tie, and a big smile. His hair looked perfect. With a shock, she realized who it was.

"Hello, Maddy. Let me introduce myself—"

"You're Senator Linden," Maddy interrupted cautiously, her eyes darting to the men in the dark suits standing behind them. She examined the senator. He had a strong jaw, but his eyes had a certain lightness to them. He was still a handsome man. She thought of all the things Jacks had said about Linden's campaign. How stakes were growing by the day. How it was one of the biggest crises to face Angels since they came out of hiding over 150 years earlier.

"Yes, I am. You might not be aware of this, but I was friends with your father, Maddy."

Maddy remembered the rainy night a year before, when Jacks had saved her and the ADC agents were closing in. Uncle Kevin pulling out an old, secret album. She'd seen a photo of her father with a young Ted Linden.

"You worked together," Maddy said, remembering that conversation. "What do you want from me? Are you trying to get my endorsement? Even you should know that's a long shot."

The senator didn't seem ruffled by his cool reception.

"I didn't come here for your support, Maddy. This is an unscheduled stop. I came here today because I did know your father, Jacob Godright. And respected him very much. He was a great Angel." Linden's voice trailed off, as if he were remembering something very painful. "And so I thought I owed it to you. I simply thought we should talk. I want you to know why I'm doing what I'm doing."

"Why?" Maddy said. She had to admit that she was curious about how he could go from working with Angels to banning them outright.

"The Angels' PR machine is good, I have to give them that. I'm painted as a bigot. A hatemonger. But I don't hate the Immortals. I've loved some of them. I loved your father dearly, like a brother. I hate the system. The system is so unfair and corrupt, it must be dismantled."

"But reform can happen," Maddy said, although her voice was somewhat uncertain.

Senator Linden was firm. But his voice was filled with regret. "We don't have time for that. I've tried it before. Time and time again. But the Angels won't do their part. I don't see any other choice. I don't want it this way. I'm an idealist at heart, Maddy. But I have to be a pragmatist in my actions. It's the only way to save us both: humans and Angels. I have an obligation to shut it down. I wish it weren't this way."

Maddy absorbed Linden's words. She wasn't sure how she felt about them. But she was starting to see how he had marshaled so much support, so quickly. It wasn't just some kind of anti-Angel spirit sweeping the country. When he was there, you could *feel* his conviction. Even if you didn't agree with him, it was almost intoxicating.

A young man in an ill-fitting suit appeared at the counter. He spoke under his breath: "Senator, we need to be moving along. We have the dinner at Palisades Riviera in two hours, and we need to stop at the community center in West Angel City along the way."

Senator Linden nodded. "Just give me one more moment with Ms. Montgomery here. Or Godright."

The young man nodded and disappeared around the corner.

"Maddy, you come from both worlds, Angel and human. I know this must be difficult," the senator said. "I just wanted you to know I understand that. Whatever happens, it's not personal. And I wanted to meet you. I'm glad I have—your father would have been proud." A far-off look came across the senator's eyes as he remembered another time, another place.

Words came rushing out Maddy's mouth. "I still think reform can happen. That *I* can help make it happen."

The senator considered what she had said for a few moments.

"Maddy, I know your heart is in the right place." His eyes searched hers. "But honestly, no matter what you think, you'll never be able to reform the Angels from the inside. They'd never let you. If you're honest with yourself, you'll know that what I'm saying is true."

A pang stabbed Maddy's body as she heard these words.

On some level, did she agree with what Senator Linden had said? Was it in fact going to be impossible to effect change from within the Angel organization? She had thought that from within was the only way *to* bring about change. But was she entirely sure?

"Now I should go before my staff has a meltdown," Linden said, standing up and smoothing his blazer. "Who knew being a politician was mostly being babysat by a pack of high-strung people?"

"Kind of like being an Angel," Maddy said aloud before she could stop herself.

The senator put his hand out toward her. Maddy hesitated a moment. His smooth hand hung outstretched in the space between them.

Maddy shook his hand. He gripped hers firmly.

"You have your father's eyes," the senator said. "Goodbye, Madison. Let's hope we meet again under more favorable circumstances."

# CHAPTER TWENTY

Jackson and Mark sat next to each other at a gleaming oak table in the conference room of the medical center. Across from them was assembled a panel of four doctors, wearing crisp white lab coats over their shirts and ties. The room also doubled as a library, and the walls were lined with volume after volume of handsomely leather-bound books and journals.

Jacks wasn't looking at the doctors or anything else in the room, though: his gaze was through the window at the sunny day outside. Birds flitted about, squirrels scurried back and forth with prize nuts, and sprinklers chattered along the green lawns as they watered the grass.

The tall doctor with a neatly trimmed beard whom Jackson's step-father often played golf with cleared his throat.

"Jackson?"

Jacks kept looking out the window. After a long moment, he answered without turning his head. "Yes?"

"So you understand . . . what we've told you?"

Jacks spun in his chair and put his hand down gently on the table. "Yes, doctors, seems pretty clear."

A pained look crossed Mark's face.

Jacks stood up and put his hand out. "Thanks for your time." He nodded to a shorter Angel doctor with auburn hair. "Dr. Liebesgott, safe travels."

The doctors all shook Jackson's hand, grave looks on their faces. Jacks's smile, on the other hand, was bigger than life. It confused them as they filed slowly out the side door to their offices.

The smile remained on Jacks's face until he and Mark had reached the hallway, which is when it turned to disgust. Jacks took five quick steps and then spun on his heels to the right, punching the thick wall. His fist instantly flared in pain.

"Jacks," Mark said, reaching forward. Jacks started walking further away down the hall.

"Over," Jacks said in anger and sadness. "It's over."

"Jackson, wait." Mark caught up to him, grabbing his shoulder. "We don't know that yet. We can get a third opinion, a fourth opinion, a fifth opinion. They themselves said it's not a hundred percent."

"How long can we fool ourselves?" Jacks began walking again, his footsteps quick and angry.

"It's not fooling ourselves. There is a new treatment from England. We can find more doctors, another clinic, a—"

Jacks stopped and turned to Mark, his eyes and voice were brimming with emotion.

"Mark, they said I'll probably never fly again. What was the term he used?" A mocking tone edged his voice. "Oh yes, I think he used the term *miracle*."

Mark looked Jacks squarely in the eye. "There have been those before, Jackson. There have been miracles."

Jacks looked at him almost mockingly. "Not in my lifetime, Mark."

Jacks turned and walked the rest of the way down the hall, pushing open the heavy oak door that led outside. Mark watched as sunshine poured into the dim corridor and then vanished as the door creaked shut again, Jacks disappearing into the sunny afternoon.

Outside in the blinding sun, Jackson put on his sunglasses and squinted off into the distance, past the well-manicured garden and fountains outside the medical building, into something more abstract. Something more terrifying. His stomach felt cold and vacant.

Ahead of him, his life seemed to stretch out to infinity. Empty. A series of meaningless daily rituals, adding up to nothing, meaning nothing. If he couldn't be a Guardian, what good was he? He knew now that the parties, the clubs, the attention in Angel City—all of that would never fill a life in which he couldn't do what he was sure he had been born to do. He couldn't live on those empty events. Not after Maddy had shown him the deeper side of life, which was helping people. Not after saving Maddy, and being saved by her. He thought about Sylvester's story of how he had lost his wings, and the young girl the detective hadn't been able to rescue. Penelope. Maddy had saved more than Jackson's life that night on the library tower.

Yet now he was doomed to lose any chance at all.

Jackson's fists were unconsciously clenched at his side, trembling, his fingernails digging bitterly into his palms.

Suddenly he spun around on his heels, sensing someone behind him.

It was Archangel Churchson. He smiled at Jackson from behind his trademark salt-and-pepper goatee, wearing a perfectly tailored Hugo Boss suit. Off to the side, Jacks could see a couple of very built Angels in dark suits and shades. Out-of-uniform agents? Archangels didn't usually have bodyguards.

"Hello, Guardian Jackson Godspeed," Churchson said. He smiled.

Jacks looked at him speechlessly, having been startled out of his dark thoughts.

"Is everything all right?" Churchson asked, his eyes scanning Jacks's pale face.

"Just some bad news, I guess you could say," Jackson said.

"Well, I'm sorry to hear that," Churchson said. He put his hand on Jackson's shoulder and squeezed it warmly. "We don't like our Guardians having to deal with hardship."

Jacks gave a short, bitter laugh. "I don't think it's correct to call me a Guardian anymore."

Churchson's brow knitted in concern.

"This doesn't have anything to do with your wings, now, does it, Jackson?" he said.

Jacks didn't answer. He couldn't bring himself to.

"Well, so wonderful we just happened to run into each other this afternoon. There's something I've been meaning to bring up with you," Churchson said, looking over at his security detail for a moment before focusing his attention back on Jacks again. "What would you say if I told you that we have a way for you to fly again . . ."

# CHAPTER TWENTY-ONE

The day after Senator Linden's visit to the diner proved to be the last day that Maddy had an ounce of free time, as she and the rest of that year's nominees inexorably hurtled toward the final assessment for Guardianship—and getting their own all-important Divine Ring. That ring brought the highest level of fame and fortune and the chance to save lives as one of the fabled and beautiful Guardians of Angel City. Maddy could see that even the more confident Angels at the training grounds were getting a little nervous as the date approached.

As much as she didn't want to admit it, Senator Linden's visit had shaken Maddy up. He seemed like such a strange connection to have to her father, but besides her Uncle Kevin, he was now the closest. The stop at Kevin's Diner hadn't been on his official agenda for the Angel City visit, and no paparazzi had followed Maddy to her uncle's diner, so it hadn't hit the media at all, which was a blessing. She couldn't even imagine trying to explain *that* to Darcy. And the senator could've easily somehow used it for some publicity. But she suspected he wanted it to be in the papers and on the blogs as little as she did.

The Angel news channels were cranking up coverage, and the blogs were alive with gossip about upcoming Commissioning Week. Most of the buzz was about Maddy's historic Commissioning. The irony to Maddy was that everyone just assumed she'd be recommended for Guardianship, no problem. The news and blog people were more worried about the designer of her skirts and which event she was going to. But she knew she was by no means a shoo-in, even though the NAS had bumped her up to this year. Mark Godspeed had told her she obviously had enough votes within the Archangels to be made Guardian. But to even be *eligible*, she had to be nominated for Guardianship by the training board. No matter how much support the Archangels put behind her, she had to be able to perform.

Added to all this, Jacks was, for some reason, more distant than usual. This would have normally bothered her, but Maddy didn't even have time to think about it too much as she prepared to face Kreuz and the board of instructors and somehow balance the even bigger crush of blog, TV, and social media attention.

As the days before the assessment grew near, Maddy had her final session with Susan Archson in the now-familiar frequencing room. Susan was wearing her normal white lab coat over a classy black dress. Maddy stepped onto the circular platform of the frequency modulator. The tiled room full of screens surrounded her, and they began to flicker on, one by one, as they drew frequencies from Protections across the board. The voices of all the people grew until they were an almost unbearable din.

Maddy let her mind open, quiet. The frequencies and visions poured in instantly this time. And unlike her first time, it didn't create any pain. The cacophony in her mind was incredible, but she let it all wash over her, taking deep, long breaths.

"Candace Waldman," Susan said.

Maddy's mind quickly and neatly unconsciously threaded through the hundreds of Protections getting frequenced, all of the screens quickly darkening until she had isolated one: Candace. Maddy was transported as she saw the humdrum activity of Candace walking her dog down the street, waving at a neighbor.

Susan called more names off, and each time Maddy isolated the frequency quickly again—it had become second nature.

"Incredible!" Susan exclaimed, making a final mark on the digital tablet in her hand. She began shutting down the system. "Your speed is some of the best I've ever seen, Maddy. Your frequencing ability outstrips ninety-nine percent of Guardians."

Maddy blushed. "Really?"

"Really," Susan said, smiling warmly. "You've made such progress. You're special, Maddy, just like I said."

Maddy flashed back to her first day of training, when she'd felt totally . . . how had she felt? *Exposed.* That was the word. She didn't know that at the time. But meeting Kreuz, and sensing the superior attitude of her fellow Guardians, how they sniffed at her as she passed . . . she had felt exposed, somehow. She had been afraid—afraid of what her abilities *wouldn't* be, and, if she were honest, what her abilities *would* be. She had felt like the slow kid put in a class full of geniuses. Except instead of being nerdy, these geniuses were beautiful, perfect Angels.

Yet Susan had been there for her.

"I'm proud of you," Susan said, putting her hand on Maddy's shoulder. Her eyes grew serious. "We, I mean, *I* have high hopes for you. More than you can imagine."

"Thank you," Maddy said, starting to feel a little emotional. She felt a bond with Susan. Out of all the Angels—besides Jacks, of course—Susan understood her the most.

"I'll be sad to see you go," Susan said, her eyes glimmering. "But you have some lives to save."

Maddy's last flying session was the next day. Following her Cessna flight with Tom, Maddy had been practicing flying the obstacle course on off-hours, taking advantage of an extra set of keys Susan had snuck to her. She used the principles Tom had taught her, and she found herself getting better each time. He had been right: she'd needed to learn flying the way a pilot does. She might be part-Angel, she might have wings, but it didn't come naturally to her. She needed to learn to put one wing in front of the other.

Instructor Trueway was waiting for her in indoor hanger #7 for their last flying session. The blinding overhead lights arced over the indoor course, which extended far into the distance. Emily and Mitch were just leaving as Maddy arrived. Maddy looked out and saw that the agility course had been set to "Difficult."

"Hey, Maddy!" Mitch said, seeming more friendly than he had the previous week. "Ready for assessment? Almost as brutal as that first interview with Tara Reeves post-Commissioning."

Maddy laughed to hide her nervousness. She had to hand it to Mitch: although you could tell it made him uneasy that Maddy was being advanced toward Guardianship so quickly, at least he was trying to be a good sport about it. Better than some other Angels she could mention, like the one right next to him.

"We were just getting a workout in. You know, kind of polishing our skills, since we've been training for *years*," Emily said snootily, looking back at the course. "Don't worry, he'll set it back to beginner's level for you."

She walked up close to Maddy and spat at her under her breath: "What you're doing is a disgrace. You're a fraud. I just wanted to tell you. And we're not going to take it lying down."

Emily stepped away and turned to Mitch, raising her voice again. "Come on, Mitch, I've got a four o'clock with Valerie."

"Thanks for letting me know, Emily!" Maddy said, beaming a big fake smile at her.

Mitch, who was clueless about what had just happened between the two girls, simply smiled and waved goodbye.

Maddy turned to Trueway. He was going over notes on a clipboard. He gave her a serious look.

"Maddy, as you know, we've had some . . . difficulties in honing your flying skills. There are challenges we've never had to face before in training one of our nominees. And now there's this . . . unprecedented . . . potential promotion. Now I'm not saying that I absolutely can't recommend you for Guardianship, but it certainly is in question right now."

A shot of adrenaline ran through Maddy. It was time to apply everything she'd learned. Now or never.

"I understand. I'm ready."

The instructor reached to adjust the course in front of them.

"And can we do it on intermediate?"

Trueway raised an eyebrow. "Are you sure?"

Maddy nodded. "Yes."

The huge platforms along the floor and ceiling began rotating, using the complex hydraulic system the Angels had designed.

Steep walls, a long tube tunnel that took a number of turns, a narrow gully that quickly climbed up toward the ceiling, as well as a number of hoops gleaming in the bright light—these all appeared as the course set itself to intermediate.

A blast of air rippled her ponytail sideways as Maddy's wings extended quickly. She only grimaced slightly this time—the pain lessened with every unfolding.

*You've got this*, Maddy told herself.

Instructor Trueway looked at her. "Ready when you are."

Leaning forward—her wings beating once, twice—then Maddy was flying along the agility course. The ground blurred underneath her as she approached the first obstacles. It was the fastest she'd ever gone on the course, but she had to make an impression. The first few segments were easy hoops that Maddy flew through, making turns to pass through each one. Kind of like a warm-up. Ahead was a series of walls extending from both the floor and ceiling, which she had to fly in between. Concentrating, Maddy lowered her speed and used the hard, sharp beats of her wings to maneuver through the walls. Once on the other side, she was able to pick up some speed, moving toward the far end of the course.

She had to fly down into a gully, which was so narrow that she had to pull her wings in as close to her sides as she could; for once her smaller wings were an asset instead of a hindrance. The gully climbed up to the ceiling and started circling over. Doing an inversion, Maddy flipped over near the ceiling and rocketed down toward the next section, in which she had to zigzag back and forth between a series of massive poles, the most technical part of the course. She gulped for air, starting to tire with the effort as she neared the final stretch. Her ponytail snapped from side to side as she whipped back and forth between the poles and onto an open stretch.

The mouth of the tunnel appeared. Maddy dove straight into it, setting her wings. It was narrow, but not too bad. The lighting inside was a spiral of LEDs, guiding the Angels through the twists and turns. Maddy grunted, using her concentration to avoid crashing into the sides as she zipped through.

She was actually *doing it*. She trusted her wings; she knew that when she did one thing with them, it would result in a consistent outcome.

Tom had shown her that, through the constants of physics and aerodynamics. She had of course known it, but now she *felt* it.

The end of the tunnel appeared, and Maddy tore into the bright light of the open air. Only one section left: the final series of hoops, which were arranged in a difficult spiraling pattern. The hardest part of the course.

Maddy decided to increase her speed.

The hoops hurtled at her quickly, and Maddy let her pilot instinct take over, setting her wings like a plane's. With her speed, she began spinning laterally as she flew through the hoops. She couldn't believe it, how fast she was going through them! Her mouth opened in a delighted smile, and she gave a shout of glee.

She shot past the final hoop, spun slightly to level herself off, and then dropped down dramatically right in front of Instructor Trueway. She was panting, catching her breath. Maddy couldn't believe how well she'd done. It blew away anything she'd ever done on the course.

"Good," Trueway said, making a note on his iPad.

*Good?* That was it? Maddy wanted to hear that she was in, that she'd done it, that she was recommended. A big *"Congratulations!"* But if she thought she was going to get that from Trueway, she was mistaken. The instructor's face was blank as he put his iPad away.

"I'll see you Friday," he said, walking out of the hangar.

The day of the assessment finally came. Maddy had tried to sleep, but she'd mostly just tossed and turned the whole evening. She had set her alarm early, almost as early as when she woke up for a shift at the diner. Yawning as she padded around her apartment, she was surprised to find she kind of missed the way early morning felt. The way her body felt, the way the world felt. The sun rose over the Angel City Hills. A warm breeze passed through the palms. Another perfect day in the Immortal City.

Although the paparazzi and media were getting even more frantic, and there were tons of events and appearances Darcy was trying orchestrate, Maddy had tried to take it easy that week, going to only one event, a launch party for one of her fellow nominee's fashion lines. She and Jacks had only hung out once during the week, but then, she had been really busy.

She took a shower and put on a black pencil skirt and gray top she'd bought at Fred Segal just the day before. The outfit was fashionable and sleek, but also a little conservative; she'd gotten it specifically for the assessment today.

Putting on a pair of heels, Maddy stood in front of the mirror. She smiled at her image. At the very least, she looked the part to become a Guardian. Some days it shocked her that it was actually *her*, Maddy, looking back in the mirror.

Just then she got a text. She was surprised to see it was from Tom. He had remembered what day it was.

*"Remember: You're a natural. Break a wing!"*

The guard at the gate to the training grounds cheerfully greeted Maddy as she pulled up. "The big day, eh, Ms. Godright?"

"Sure is," Maddy said, trying to be cheerful herself, although it felt like a thousand butterflies were flying loop-de-loops in her stomach at the moment.

As Maddy stepped out of her Audi in the parking lot, she peered up into the cloudless sky.

Across the perfectly blue atmosphere, far, far up, two fighter jets screamed across the sky, leaving two crisp white trails behind them. Maddy idly wondered if one of them was Tom.

Sadie rolled up almost noiselessly in her golf cart.

"They're ready for you," Sadie said, her perfect white teeth sparkling in the morning sun.

"Great," Maddy replied, smiling forcefully. Looking around, though, she was confused. "Wait, where's Jacks? He said he was going to meet me here."

"Yes, yes," Sadie said, pulling a bouquet of flowers from the seat of the golf cart. "These are for you. Jackson isn't feeling well and couldn't make it." Sadie looked at her watch. "We should get going. They are waiting."

"Oh." Maddy took the bouquet of assorted flowers in her hand as she climbed into the golf cart, trying to hide her confusion and hurt. She looked at the card.

GOOD LUCK TODAY, MADS. LOVE, JACKS

Disappointment washed over Maddy—was he really sick? Why hadn't he told her directly? He was supposed to be there!

Maddy didn't have time to think about it. Before she knew it, they'd arrived and Sadie was leading her into the small auditorium built into the end of the bungalow offices. The room also served as an event space whenever the training facility was holding some occasion or party or there was a presentation from an Angel expert.

Sitting at a long wooden table that had been placed at the front of the room were Louis Kreuz, Susan, Trueway, and Philip, the tweedy teacher she'd met the first day of Guardian training, whom she'd been quietly battling with ever since. Looking to her left as she entered, Maddy was surprised to see Jackson's stepfather, Mark, sitting in the auditorium seats further up. He gave her a subtle thumbs-up.

Sadie seated Maddy behind a smaller table in front of the board of instructors. There was a bottle of water and an empty glass on the table. Maddy didn't think she'd need it: she knew that there was to be no more discussion. The decision would simply be made.

"We're here today to either recommend or deny Madison Montgomery Godright's nomination to Guardianship," Louis Kreuz said. "As you know, Maddy came to us much, much later than normal for training. And her unique situation creates other considerations."

Maddy anxiously glanced back toward Mark, but he wore a look of pure confidence.

"We have had our discussions. Now that the potential nominee is here, it is time for us to recommend or deny. The decision must be unanimous. Is the board ready?"

All three other instructors nodded.

"We'll begin with Archangel Archson," Kreuz said.

"Recommend," Susan said brightly, smiling at Maddy.

"Phil?"

"Recommend," Philip said, coughing into his hand.

"Trueway?" Kreuz said, narrowing his eyes.

Maddy looked at her flight instructor, former Agent Trueway. He eyed her without emotion. Maddy's heart was pounding up through her throat as she waited for him to speak.

"Recommend," he said.

Silence hung in the room as Maddy looked at Louis Kreuz, who for once didn't have a cigar in his hand. It needed to be unanimous in order for her to move to Commissioning.

Kreuz looked at Maddy and began addressing her. He was strangely much more formal in this situation, as if he felt the gravity of the situation.

He cleared his throat.

"This is a special situation in our history in the training of Angels. A half-Angel, half-human, brought to our facilities for training and Guardianship. And now promoted to nominee after only a short period of training. Unknown territory. We have no idea how she will react in a save. If her inner Angel will truly win out during the save . . . or if her weaker human side will prevail."

He cleared his throat again, loudly. He continued: "It looks like the minds of the other members of this board are to recommend," he said. "And I have no choice but to go along with their view.

"Madison Montgomery Godright, you are recommended for Guardianship."

# CHAPTER TWENTY-TWO

Sylvester awoke from a strange dream, sitting up in bed. In the dream he had been following someone down a fetid, dark alley, the buildings reaching to the top of the blue-black sky. The alley never ended. It just kept extending and extending, Sylvester never getting any closer. The figure in front of him always remained the same distance away. Every once in a while, the figure would stop and turn around. Sylvester couldn't see his face.

"Hey! Hey!" Sylvester would yell. He would reach for his gun, but it wouldn't be there. And the figure would continue running. And Sylvester would keep going down the never-ending alley.

The only thing that changed in the alley was that it got hotter. A lot hotter.

The ring of his landline woke him. The old-school telephone rang again. And again. In his white undershirt and boxers, the detective fumbled for the light, and then the telephone.

He looked at the clock: 4:34 a.m.

"This is Sylvester," he grumbled into the phone, rubbing his eyes.

"You were looking for me, detective?" a strange voice said on the line in a hushed tone.

Sylvester sat up straight.

"Could be. Who's this?" Sylvester scrambled to put his glasses on, along with getting a pad of paper and a pen.

"It's about the bombing. Minx . . . he told me about you. That you might be able to help me."

"Yes, yes, of course," Sylvester said. "I can help. Now where are you?"

There was silence on the line. Sylvester could hear the man breathing. "No. It's too dangerous. We need to meet somewhere public."

"The train station," Sylvester offered.

"No, they're watching. The Angel Wax Museum. In the lobby. Noon. Come alone."

"How will I recognize you?"

"I'll know you, detective. Noon. Come alone, or you'll never hear from me again."

"Who are—"

Before the detective could finish his sentence, the phone clicked dead—he'd hung up.

Sylvester slowly placed the receiver down. He sat on the edge of the bed in the room that was dark except for one bedside light, his mind running over the strange turn of events.

For a moment he laid back down on his bed, but his eyes remained wide open. After only a minute or so, he let out a large sigh and got up, walking to the kitchen to make the first pot of coffee of the day.

At eleven thirty Detective Sylvester was on Angel Boulevard amid throngs of tourists, in the heart of Angel City. He was wearing a shirt just picked up from the cleaners and a pair of shoes he'd had resoled down at Raoul's on Santa Monica. He felt all right. He was ready for this case to break open.

The reports and DVD surveillance that the Godspeed kid had slipped him from the Angel investigation didn't give him too much info, aside from confirming for Sylvester that there were two bombers, working in tandem. He hadn't been able to glean anything further than that, though. The case had remained slow up until the call early this morning.

Sylvester walked his way around fans snapping pictures of the stars on the Walk of Angels; the empty spot where it was rumored Maddy Montgomery's star might go drew an especially huge crowd. Looking down as he walked along the glittering sidewalk, Sylvester noticed names of Angels past and present that he had known over the years. As he got closer to the Angel Wax Museum, he came across Jackson Godspeed's star. No one was taking pictures of it. Sylvester shook his head.

He reached the wax museum. In the very front of the building, surrounded by glass so everyone could see it from the street, was a new wax statue of Maddy with her shorter, oblong wings with the fine silver threading that ran along them. Groups of people were excitedly lining up to enter.

Sylvester walked down Angel Boulevard a little further, then back, slowly letting his old police instincts take over as he read the crowds. It was fairly busy for a weekday, with double-decker buses blowing by, throngs of tourists, vendors selling maps to the Angel houses in the Hills, those hawking T-shirts reading "SAVE ME," the Angel impersonators whom you could pay to get a picture with. Above the whole scene hung massive billboards with half-naked perfect Angels selling perfumes and clothes, along with garish neon signs. Every once in a while, some remnant of old Angel City would peek through the chaos, giving Sylvester a sense of the city he once knew. One he had been proud to be an Angel in.

Looking up, Sylvester saw three-story footage of Maddy's arrival at a red-carpet event across town. She smiled perfectly as the flashes surrounded her.

At eleven fifty Sylvester walked to the ticket desk and purchased one adult ticket for entry to the wax museum. He walked into the lobby, scanning the crowd slowly. No one seemed out of place, or otherwise nervous, just your general crowd of Angel City tourists.

Some of the more popular wax statues were in the lobby, including Vivian Holycross in the outfit she wore to last year's Commissioning, one of classic hunk Owen Holymead, and one of Gabriel, one of the founding members of the Council of Twelve. Gabriel appeared wise and almost glowing in his white robes. Behind him was a wax statue of an ancient Angel in Grecian battle dress, holding a copy of *The Book of Angels* in his hand.

The detective walked down one of the hallways. It was uncanny, how many of these wax Angels he had once known in real life. Seeing their statues was like seeing ghosts from his former life.

After a few minutes, the detective made his way back to the lobby. He checked his watch: eleven fifty-eight. Two minutes. He pulled off his glasses and wiped them with his shirt. A nervous habit.

The detective eyed the visitors moving between the wax Angel statues, trying to discern who would be meeting him. He looked at a bench off to the side, where a man in his thirties was reading a copy of the *Angel City Times*. Was that him? Then the man stood up and walked out the door of the wax museum, hugging his wife and small child, who had been using the restroom.

Sylvester continued watching the crowd, his pulse quickening as he glanced down at his watch and saw it had reached noon. A tour bus must have just let out on Angel Boulevard, because a huge group of people began streaming in. The faces in the crowd mixed with the perfect wax Angel faces.

Suddenly, in his peripheral vision, Detective Sylvester saw a man in a dark suit on his left, and then another on his right. They were moving fast. Directly toward him. Adrenaline pounded in Sylvester's veins as he started at a dead run toward the exit.

Instinct took over, but before Sylvester could escape the men, an iron grip clasped down on him from behind and pulled his hands together, binding them together in plastic zip-ties.

Five square-jawed men in suits were on him in seconds as he struggled in his restraints.

Struggling and panting, Sylvester's eyes grew wide as, through the glass, he spotted a black Suburban idling at the curb on Angel Boulevard. They led him toward it.

# CHAPTER TWENTY-THREE

The thick, hard plastic restraints dug into Sylvester's wrists, rubbing them raw as he attempted to break away from his captors. Blood pounded in his ears, survival instincts taking over.

Tourists stared slack-jawed as these men in suits hoisted the struggling detective toward the front exits of the wax museum.

It'd been a set up.

"What are you doing? I'm Detect—"

"Be quiet!" the square-jawed man holding him barked, pushing Sylvester forward.

"Step away from Detective Sylvester!" a voice resounded through the open glass door to the museum. It was Sergeant Garcia, in plainclothes. He pointed his service revolver at the man next to Sylvester. His aim was steady.

In horror, Sylvester watched as the men in suits suddenly drew pistols from inside their jackets, beginning to turn them on Garcia.

"ACPD! Drop your weapons! ACPD! We will shoot!" The voices

seemed to come from everywhere at once.

Within a moment, the entire lobby turned blue, as uniformed ACPD officers rushed from all corners upon the men holding Sylvester. "Drop your weapons or we will fire upon you!"

Sylvester smiled: Sergeant Garcia had his back.

Scrambling to lay their guns on the ground, the outnumbered men in suits screamed "FBI! FBI, for God's sake, FBI!"

The suited men stepped away from Sylvester, who still had his arms bound behind him, as they pulled their federal badges from under their suit jackets while keeping one hand in the air.

"FBI? *Jesus Christ.* Who are you!?" Sylvester yelled at them.

"Us? Who the hell are *you*?" the tallest of the suited FBI agents yelled back to Sylvester as he slowly laid his government-issued nine-millimeter handgun on the cool marble floor of the wax museum.

"Detective Sylvester, ACPD," Sylvester panted. A uniformed cop was behind Sylvester, cutting his hands free from the plastic restraints. Dozens of ACPD officers were now frisking the outnumbered FBI agents, checking their badges, chaos all around.

A senior FBI agent suddenly arrived on the scene, his beard stubble grizzled and long wrinkles running across his forehead.

"Senior Agent Wilkins, Special Crimes," he identified himself. "What the hell's going on here with my investigation?"

His hands free, Sylvester walked up to this lead FBI agent, red coloring his face.

"*Your* investigation? Goddammit!" Sylvester yelled, spinning around on his heels.

"Come on, David, calm down, calm down. It's okay," Garcia was trying to pull him back.

"We're all on the same team here, detective," the senior FBI man said.

"Are we?" Sylvester demanded.

"My men detained you as a matter of safety and precaution."

"Precaution for what? *Senior agent*, you just pissed all over my meet-up with a confidential informant in a high-profile case! I'm going to have your ass for breakfast!"

The FBI man looked at Sylvester. "Informant? You mean Jesse DeWinter?"

"I don't have his name. We were supposed to meet here at noon. He's gone now, though, spooked forever!"

Wilkins shook his head. "Jesse DeWinter died instantly at eight forty-four this morning when his car struck the median at high speed heading eastbound on I-10 near the Washington Boulevard exit. He was pronounced dead at the scene."

Sylvester reeled. "Dead?"

"We searched his apartment shortly after. We've been keeping an eye on him here in Angel City as a potential political radical. We found a photo of you, along with this note."

Wilkins reached into his coat and pulled out a photo of Sylvester that had been printed from the Internet, along with a small scrap of paper: "Wax Museum—noon."

"It was a meet-up," Sylvester said quietly, sitting down on the bench. "He was coming in . . . someone found out."

"HDF literature and bombmaking materials were found in his car—or what remained of the car after it burned," Special Agent Wilkins said. "We had our suspicions. Now it's a pretty open-and-shut case that the HDF was behind the bombing. The next step is to move into the HDF organization itself."

Sylvester shook his head, hands plunged into the pockets of his overcoat. Was that it? After Minx obviously sent DeWinter on to Sylvester himself. Why would he be turning against the HDF now? Whom did he fear?

"Forensics is running tests on the residual bomb material, but early results say it's a one hundred percent match to the bomb used earlier this month."

Sylvester absently looked out the glass walls at the waves of pedestrians walking down Angel Boulevard. Tourists were stopping outside the front glass wall and taking pictures of Maddy's wax statue through the glass.

"Of course it's a one hundred percent match," Sylvester said softly. "I bet it wasn't even damaged in the fiery accident."

"It's just a shame we couldn't talk to DeWinter before his accident. It would've been helpful," the FBI lead said.

Sylvester, breaking from his mental fugue, looked at Wilkins through his wire-framed glasses.

"Accident?" he said. "Obviously, it was no accident."

# CHAPTER TWENTY-FOUR

The day of Maddy's Commissioning arrived, and the media was calling it the "event of the century," or even the "event of the millennium." Maddy Montgomery Godright would be the first part-human, part-Angel ever commissioned as Guardian Angel.

Commissioning Day was preceded by nonstop breathless coverage of Maddy's stratospheric rise. "Maddicts," as they called themselves—a lot of them former "Jacksaddicts"—had camped out just like they had for Jackson's Commissioning the year before, dreaming that they too secretly had an Angel parent and would one day have wings and rise to fortune and fame.

Starting at dawn, news helicopters hovered restlessly above the scene. Angel Boulevard had been closed overnight in preparation; workers had turned the sidewalk and street in front of the Temple of Angels into a backdrop worthy of an Angel Commissioning. Enormous plastic Divine Rings were placed near the entrance, and massive bleachers were erected for the lucky few who would get a firsthand view of the glamorous

Angels and their annual event. The scene was teeming with media, as usual, with correspondents from A!, ANN, all the news networks jockeying for best position as the workers unfurled the red carpet.

Meanwhile, security was more pronounced than last year. Big, bulky men in suits with earpieces seemed to be all over the scene, supplementing the already strong ACPD contingent. After the still unsolved bombing of the Angel building, the Angels were taking no chances whatsoever. Even Tara Reeves was searched as she walked into the media area, an indignity she put up with without complaining too much since she saw what a great position she had again for her exclusive Angel Television stage, which was erected at the beginning of the red carpet.

Tara smiled dazzlingly into the camera, wearing a fiery red dress.

"The day you've been waiting for all year is finally here! The red carpet is perfectly rolled out, the bright lights are turned on, and the Divine Rings are ready as the fans swarm the Temple of Angels. And they're all waiting for the Commissioning of Maddy Montgomery Godright, America's new Angel sweetheart! Along with Angel favorites Mitch Steeple, Emily Brightchurch, and the other twenty nominees, this is being called the Commissioning of the Century. And feeling the energy around here, I'm not going to disagree! The world's most beautiful Angels and Protections will be here tonight, and you're going to see it all live, with me, your host, Tara Reeves. You don't want to go anywhere as we bring you the Commissioning, right now, from the heart of Angel City!"

Dusk began settling, and enormous searchlights were fired up, humming. They shone into the air, visible from miles and miles away. And now the Angels began arriving, one by one, on the red carpet. They waved and smiled dazzlingly, looking flawless and glamorous in their expensive designer gowns and tuxedos. Fans yelled for autographs and pictures as the famous Angels did on-carpet interviews with the TV hosts.

An *ooh* rippled through the audience as Vivian Holycross arrived with her date Julien Santé. Vivian had taken a year off from training and would be eligible for Commissioning next year. She was wearing a dress Julien had had handmade by a friend in Paris who designed for YSL haute couture. Julien himself was wearing a crisp tuxedo behind a pair of YSL sunglasses.

"I'm just so happy to see Emily get Commissioned!" Vivian said, leaving no doubt she was *not* there for Maddy's benefit. "And I'm just so happy to be here with my man, Julien. He's a great Guardian with *so* many saves already this year."

No one doubted who she was comparing Julien to, either—there had actually been betting pools in Las Vegas on whether Jackson Godspeed would even show up at this Commissioning.

Unexpectedly, two of the U.S. House representatives for Angel City, Juanita Perez and Paul Wheeler, arrived on the red carpet. Juanita was bedecked in a sparkling silver gown. She was there to show support for the Angels after Senator Linden and some other high-profile politicians had decided to create an alterna-Commissioning where they'd be playing a game of softball and then barbecuing at the senator's estate on Eastern Long Island instead of watching or attending the Commissioning.

"I want the American people to know that in spite of some bad apples, we in the government support the Angels one hundred percent, knowing that they are a strong part of our country, provide so much for our nation's economy, and are out there every day saving lives. And they are now facing racist attacks in the form of horribly violent bombings," Representative Perez said. "I'm proud to represent Angel City in Congress and help spread the word to Washington about all the good the Angels do! God bless the Angels, and God bless America!"

Representatives Perez and Wheeler smiled widely, waving at the crowds.

The Godspeed family showed up—Mark, Kris, and Chloe. Mark would of course be sitting front and center with the rest of the Archangels, and would be placing the Divine Ring on Maddy's finger himself. Chloe had outdone herself. Being another year older, she had felt justified in getting an even lower-cut dress that showed off her Immortal Marks—she'd flown to New York City with Kris just to get it—and the cameras flashed as the teenage Angel showed herself off.

"In some ways we feel like Maddy's part of our family, and we're just so pleased for her," Kris said, smiling sweetly. She was, as usual, classy and sophisticated, drawing the admiration of middle-aged women across the world with her mix of know-how and sexy grace.

Then the nominees began arriving, with Mitch Steeple leading the pack. Mitch was wearing the customary tuxedo as he walked the carpet, his shoulders broad and chest boxy. He had been waiting for this day all his life—even though Jacks had beat him to it by a year.

Tara caught up with him and got a sound bite.

"I'm just proud to be joining the Guardian ranks this year. It's been my dream to get that ring, no matter what. And now that day has come. Can't wait to start making saves and thrilling the fans. Thanks, Tara."

The fans cheered loudly and a thousand flashes went off as every new nominee arrived on the carpet.

Emily Brightchurch's blazing fiery orange hair contrasted wildly with her sleek black dress that showed every curve, and photographers' jaws dropped as she walked her way down the red carpet. But in the midst of her interview with A!, a roar came from down the carpet. The host almost lost track of what he was doing as he turned his head to see if *she*, Maddy, had arrived.

She had.

Emily's face darkened in fury as the host quickly threw coverage from her interview to Maddy's arrival.

"Just getting word that *Maddy* has arrived." He turned to Emily. "Thank you so much, Emily. Now back to Tara to cover America's sweetheart as she walks the carpet."

The whole scene turned blinding white with flashbulbs as Maddy stepped onto the carpet, Jackson Godspeed by her side. Just behind her was Uncle Kevin, looking very uncomfortable in his tuxedo and in front of so many cameras. The fans exploded in screams as they saw Maddy, pounding their feet along the metal bleachers.

Maddy stepped cautiously up the carpet—would she ever *really* find this normal?—and waved at the fans and photographers in front of the Temple of Angels. She was wearing a red de la Renta dress that Kris and Chloe had helped her pick out.

Tara's gushing was nearly hysterical.

"Maddy, tell me where you got this dress?!"

"Well, actually Jackson's mother, Kris, and his sister, Chloe, brought me to the designer. It's unique, one of a kind."

At the sound of Jackson's name, Tara turned to him for a brief second.

"Wonderful to see Maddy's boyfriend here, showing his support! But back to you, Maddy. Do you have any idea who your first Protections will be? And what about these rumors you might be involved in next season's *American Protection*?"

Maddy looked over and saw Darcy mouthing, "*Be vague.*"

"Tara," Maddy said, laughing as best she could. "You know I can't comment on any of that. But everyone should know that I promise my first save will be memorable."

"Everyone's on the edge of their seat!" Tara practically squealed. "Maddy, your rise has been unprecedented, and fans all over the world look to you for guidance. What would you say to them?"

Maddy paused slightly and considered her words seriously. "I'm just so grateful to be here. And so grateful for any good I can do. That's what's truly important. Not all the glitz and glamour. But the chance to change people's lives. That's what I'm becoming a Guardian Angel for."

Tara turned back to the camera. "And Maddy, showing the humility and down-to-earthness that has made her a household name in mere months! I almost can't stand it, I'm so excited—America's Angel sweetheart, everyone! Don't go away, as we have the Commissioning ceremony from inside the Temple of Angels soon!"

Maddy wasn't oblivious to the fact that Jackson's body was tense, nor that he had been all but ignored by Tara, who would have murdered small children to get two minutes of exclusive interview with him just twelve months before. Maddy reached for his hand.

"Come on, Jacks, let's go in," she whispered.

With a final wave to the screaming fans, Maddy and Jacks disappeared inside the Temple, walking under the arch that Jacks had passed the year before. It read: DO YOUR DUTY.

They were ushered through the depths of the Temple of Angels to Maddy's dressing room, next to those of all the other nominees. Her stylist was waiting inside, prepared to put the ceremonial robe of the Guardian on Maddy; the formal robe was one thing that hadn't changed for the Guardians in hundreds of years.

As the stylist fitted the robe properly around Maddy, Jackson couldn't help but smile.

"What?" Maddy said, worrying she looked silly.

"Nothing," Jackson said. "It's just that you look so much like an Angel right now."

And it was true. As the stylist stepped back, Maddy was able to see herself in the mirror: she looked more Angelic than she'd ever even dreamed of in her life. As if her inner Angel half was truly coming to life under these robes, her very skin almost seeming to glow.

"You're beautiful, Maddy," Jackson said. He came over and squeezed her hands tightly.

"No kissing!" the stylist admonished, worried that Jacks would smear her makeup.

Maddy looked up at Jacks, nervous, starting to breathe more quickly.

"You're ready," he said calmly. "Don't let anybody tell you you're not."

Maddy leaned her head on Jacks's chest. "I wouldn't be here without you, Jacks. . . . Thank you for everything. Thank you for being you."

Jackson looked at her, his eyes mysterious. "I should get going," he said.

"Oh, do you have to?"

"It's about to start. I'll see you up there. You're going to do great. Don't worry." He gave her hands one last squeeze and then disappeared into the hallway.

Maddy looked at herself in the mirror again, waiting for the personnel to come get her. *You can do this, you can do this*, she told herself. This was just a ceremony. She could handle this. She *could*.

Maddy checked her phone and saw she had two texts. One was from Gwen: "*I'm so proud of you girl! Don't forget us little people!*" Maddy smiled and wrote back: "*Never! I love and miss you. Wish me luck.*"

The other text was from Tom. It read: "*Break a wing up there tonight— remember to credit me and the U.S. Navy for all your success in flying.*"

Maddy texted back. "*Haha, I will. Thank you, Tom. Nervous but ready!*"

His response came almost instantly. "*Nothing but faith in you.*"

Maddy smiled and put the phone away.

She looked at herself in the mirror one more time and thought back to those numerous days in the ACHS halls, when she was just another anonymous girl in a hoodie and earbuds. Although she didn't totally want to get caught up in all the hype, well, it was nice to be the center of attention, to look so beautiful. To feel so . . . wanted, if she were honest with herself. She may as well enjoy this moment. Right?

A light knock came on the door. Maddy looked toward it, taking a deep breath. Was it time? "Come in," she said nervously.

The door squeaked open, and there stood Louis Kreuz, the head of Angel training. A dark cloud crossed Maddy's face. She was done with training. What was *he* doing here? Did she still have to put up with him?

"Can I come in for a second, nominee?" He was wearing a crisp tuxedo with a jaunty collar. He held a Cuban cigar in his heavy mitt, but it remained unlit. A rare compromise to fire codes.

"Mr. Kreuz, I'm really just trying to—"

Kreuz let himself in and closed the door behind him. "It'll only be a second, kid." He smiled at her.

Maddy sighed. Kreuz was holding a small case in one arm. He opened it and held it out for Maddy.

"Here, take it. Please."

Puzzled and a bit wary, Maddy looked into the case. It was lined with velvet, and inside was a golden and purple silken sash. It was of the Godright class. She gasped.

"It's for you," Kreuz said. "You know, to wear."

"I didn't know any had survived," Maddy stammered, pulling it out of the case.

"Here," Kreuz said, helping arrange the sash so that it draped over her neck.

Maddy felt a tingling as the sash fell over her. As if it were sending energy to her.

"There aren't too many, but, well, I managed to have one set aside." Kreuz coughed. "It was your father's."

"But how . . . ?" Maddy said, tears starting to well in her eyes. "Or why, even?"

Kreuz put a hand on Maddy's shoulder. He looked Maddy in the eyes. "Your father was the best nominee I've ever seen. Until Jackson Godspeed, actually. Your dad was hardworking. Talented. Smart. Fast. A natural-born Guardian. And also stubborn. In some ways he felt like a son to me." Louis's eyes cast off to the past. "You remind me a lot of him."

"But you were so hard on me," Maddy said, remembering the meetings in his office, when he had basically told her she would fail.

"I'm sorry," Kreuz said. "But any less than perfect would've been enough for your enemies to stop your Guardianship. And I could tell when I first met you, you had more of your father in you than even you might imagine. I knew I had to challenge you harder than anyone else could challenge you. And all I could do was hope you'd be up to it." He smiled at her. "And you were."

Maddy looked at the Angel in front of her, her entire perspective of him changing rapidly.

"I wanted to apologize, too, for ever even mentioning some false . . . allegations that were brought against you," Kreuz said. "You know I have to investigate every charge of misconduct, regardless of who it is or how much hooey it may seem."

A bolt went through Maddy. "Emily," she said. "What did she say?"

Kreuz didn't respond directly. He just looked at her thoughtfully.

"Keep your eyes open, Maddy. That's my best advice about that one."

Maddy nodded. "Thank you, sir."

"Now, having delivered my special package, it's time for this old Angel to find his seat upstairs." Kreuz adjusted his bowtie. "You know they have a special seat with my nameplate on it. Moved it from the old Temple and everything. Perks from old Angel City." He smiled.

"But I want to know—"

"No more time for *buts*," Kreuz said, waving his hand as he left the dressing room. "Now get up there and become a Guardian."

Someone with a headset arrived directly after Kreuz departed and guided Maddy to her position in line, at the end. Just like Jacks had said he'd been the year before. It wasn't until Maddy was lined up with the rest of the nominees backstage that she really began to feel nervous. Her palms were sweating and her heart was beating hard. She realized at that moment she'd never even watched a Commissioning on TV before, much less been in one.

The main room of the Temple waited just beyond the doors. The music struck up as the commercial break ended, and a woman's voice echoed into the back hall, where the nominees were waiting.

"*Ladies, gentlemen, and Angels, welcome to the 143rd annual National Angel Services Guardian Commissioning. And now, please let's all welcome the nominees for Guardianship!*"

Maddy's heart began pounding in her chest. *This was really happening*. She reached up and felt the Godright sash that hung from her neck. It comforted her.

The doors swung open and the audience cheered. The twenty nominees filed down the main aisle of the Temple, each being announced as they crossed the threshold.

Finally: "*Madison Montgomery Godright*," the voice announced as Maddy stepped into the Temple itself. Maddy felt instantly overwhelmed by the grandeur of the space—a row of columns ran along each side of the aisle, leading to the front stage, on which sat enormous screens. Screens that were presently showing Maddy's face as she slowly walked toward her seat on stage.

For a second, seeing her face that big on the screens paralyzed Maddy. But then she realized she actually felt good. She was happy.

She smiled wide, and the boisterous crowd responded with large cheers on both sides as she made her way down the aisle. She walked on stage with the other nominated Guardians, passing the altar where all twenty Divine Rings sat, along with a neat stack of twenty envelopes.

She took her assigned seat, still trying to take all the pomp and circumstance in. The last fading light from outside filtered in the enormous stained glass windows that hung over the whole scene.

Looking out into the audience, Maddy saw Jackson sitting in the third row, next to his mother and sister. Jacks looked at her with a beaming smile. Even from this distance, his looks and presence were nearly magnetic to Maddy. She felt so *lucky*. And next to the Godspeeds sat Uncle Kevin, still messing with his tuxedo.

The female voice announced the arrival of the Archangels. They ceremoniously filed into the Temple in their deep crimson robes, taking seats in the first row. Once the Archangels had been seated, the lights grew low and the giant screens on stage began playing a kind of highlight reel or tribute to all the nominees, with their names and a shot of them looking into the camera and smiling before showing footage of them in action. As usual, the clips weren't long, and Maddy kept waiting for her sequence to show up. She saw Mitch's, in which he showboated for the cameras and showed his all-American side, and then some clips of Emily Brightchurch's fancy flying and sexy appearances at Angel events. The reel had gone through all the nominees before it finally reached Maddy.

They showed clips of Maddy smiling at events—though she noticed worriedly they always used angles from which you couldn't see Jacks by her side—debuting her wings at that first photo shoot, and even embarrassing photos of Maddy in her waitress uniform and in school.

Although these latter images had clearly been photoshopped a bit, they got across the point that though Maddy might be the world's hottest new Angel, she was still just the "girl next door."

The video cut to footage of Maddy's smiling face that they'd shot last week. The camera held the shot, and the crowd started cheering louder and louder. Maddy couldn't believe they kept holding on her smiling face even longer, as the crowd applauded more and more.

Finally text appeared on screen: OUR MADDY.

Having been whipped to fever pitch, the crowd erupted in their loudest cheering yet. The Angels knew Maddy was a true phenomenon—that since she was half-Angel, half-human, the fans really felt like she was part of them, that they had access to Angels themselves. And the NAS knew how to market its stars.

Maddy felt a small hole burning in the back of her head. She turned back, and although it was pretty dark, she could see Emily staring directly at her, giving her the stinkeye. Maddy turned her head forward, not bothering with the Australian's envy.

"THIS YEAR'S GUARDIANS," the screen flashed, before fading to full black.

Although Maddy hadn't ever watched a Commissioning, she knew what was coming next: the Council of Twelve in what had become their one public appearance per year.

On the screens, light slowly faded in, and you could start to make out twelve robed figures sitting in a semicircle. A bit of murmuring rippled through the crowd: the Council wasn't sitting in its normal small chapel. This seemed to be a more open space, with dark Grecian columns on each side.

There sat the twelve True Immortals, the original Angels who had gone public, developed Protection for Pay, and made Angel City what it was today. They remained obscured in the shadows of the carefully stage-managed lighting of the live footage of them from a remote, undisclosed location. After a moment, one stood up, his gorgeous golden robe shimmering under the light: Maddy knew this would be Gabriel.

Lifting his head, Gabriel faced the cameras. Maddy gasped, having never seen an image of him. Even only on screen, his presence was something that took her breath away. His face filled the screens on both sides.

Gabriel's stature hadn't changed with age, and he seemed larger than life. His trademark white hair was perfectly poised on his head as his Angelic eyes looked at the audience. Maddy could swear he was looking right at her, just for her.

Gabriel began speaking.

"May you young Guardians flourish with our blessing, on this historic Commissioning," he said. His voice was thunderous in the now-hushed auditorium. *Historic?* Did he mean her, Maddy? Many of the other nominees on stage glanced at her.

On screen, the rest of the Council nodded in approval as Gabriel spoke. Without ceremony, Gabriel turned around and took his seat with the rest of the True Immortals, the applause of the audience rising to fever pitch as the lights came back up in the Temple.

The time was coming. This was what they had been waiting for.

Archangel Mark Godspeed walked on stage and stepped to the microphone by the altar. Jacks's stepfather cleared his throat and began speaking.

Maddy stole a glance out into the audience and saw Jacks. His eyes seem to be saying *almost there.*

"Each year we meet here to celebrate the best and brightest that we Angels have to offer, those Angels who would be Guardians, those who would take an oath to offer their lives in service to the Protections we serve at the NAS. And each year they remind us why Angels remain honorably willing to render their Immortal services to mankind, sworn to protect the ideals of the NAS, the Council, and Angelkind."

Applause peppered the auditorium. Representatives Perez and Wheeler nodded in approval.

One at a time, each nominee was called to the altar by Archangel Godspeed. Each nominee stepped up, took their solemn oath, and received their Divine Ring from Mark. Emily was one of the first, and as Mark placed the Divine Ring on her delicately gorgeous hand, she turned to the audience, her blazing hair flaring. The crowd *oohed*. When Mitch received his ring, he gave a thumbs-up to the crowd, kissed the ring, and pointed to the sky.

Soon everyone but Maddy had been called up.

"Now, at last, we have the historic Commissioning of Madison Montgomery Godright." Maddy flinched when she heard her full name—it was always so strange. "Maddy, please come up here," Mark said.

The Archangel could barely be heard over the din as the crowd erupted in cheers. Maddy stood up and walked to the red-and-gold altar under the spotlight. Mark had to motion to the audience to calm down. They finally quieted. Maddy felt every single eye in the Temple trained upon her as Mark began speaking.

"Madison Montgomery Godright, do you offer yourself in the service of mankind?" Mark looked at Maddy.

"I do," she said.

"Do you swear," Mark continued, "to keep safe, at all times, those under your protection?"

"I do."

"Do you take this burden of your own free will, to do this good work on this earth?"

"I do," Maddy said.

Maddy looked down at the dark velvet that held her Divine Ring. Mark lifted it from its holder and carefully slid it on Maddy's finger. She held her breath.

"I hereby commission you Guardian Madison, of the Godright class."

Maddy looked down at the Divine Ring on her finger, which dazzled under the bright lights. Turning, she faced the audience. Their cheers grew, pounding in the Temple. Their adulation was deafening and overwhelming. She saw Uncle Kevin clapping as hard as he could, tears in his eyes. She spotted Jackson in the tumult, using his fingers to whistle loudly.

With poise and grace, Maddy lightly waved at her audience, her smiling face and sparkling ring magnified on the giant screens behind her. The cheers somehow grew ever louder and louder. The crowd was now out of their seats and on their feet.

She had really done it.

She was Guardian Madison Montgomery Godright.

# CHAPTER TWENTY-FIVE

Early the next morning, Maddy stood in the glass conference room of the Archangels at the NAS headquarters in Beverly Hills, facing the wall of windows that ran from floor to ceiling on two of the four walls. Just below, on the street, was the mad hustle and bustle of the Angels, Protections, and those who would be them. Maseratis, Bentleys, and Porsches crawled in stop-and-go traffic, as slack-jawed tourists stumbled their way to Rodeo Drive and the boutiques where all the beautiful Angels shopped. Maddy noticed that not the slightest bit of noise made its way up into the conference room from the street below. It was like she was in a perfectly sealed bubble, her own world away from that noisier, messier world below.

The door to the glass conference room opened and Max, Mark Godspeed's manic assistant—although he seemed slightly calmer; maybe he'd adjusted his medication—poked his head in.

"Hi, Maddy. Archangel Godspeed wants to know if you're ready. Your first Protection is here."

Maddy nodded, sitting down in one of the chairs facing the door.

She poured herself some of the sparkling water in front of her, took a sip, and drew in a deep breath.

Mark soon entered, holding the door for a sixteen-year-old girl in a designer pink mini. Diamond earrings sparkled in her ears.

"Oh my God, it really *is* you," the girl said, running up and throwing her arms around Maddy. "This is . . . amazing."

Maddy stiffened, totally unprepared for this girl to just invade her space. But, then again, if her parents could afford a Guardian, she was probably used to getting what she wanted. Always.

"Please, take a seat, Ms. Westfield," Mark said, offering a chair. He sat just off to the side as the girl sat down.

*Westfield?* Maddy thought she knew about the Westfields—they'd first made their money in oil near Santa Barbara in the early twentieth century and had owned half of Angel City, practically. She and Gwen had even taken a field trip to the Westfield Mansion, which was now a historical landmark, when they were in middle school.

"I'm Vanessa," the girl said, looking Maddy up and down. "Am I really going to be your first Protection?" Eagerness danced in her eyes, complemented by the light flashing in her diamond earrings.

"One of the first, yes," Maddy said, looking at the heiress. She probably could have hired twenty Guardians, and her family still would've had plenty of money left over.

"This is *so incredible*. Wait until my friends hear about this, they are going to be *so jealous*."

Maddy bit her tongue, knowing that this was part of the process. "We're glad you're so pleased, Vanessa."

"Maddy? You're like the biggest ever," Vanessa said. "I can't wait for us to go shopping together!" The girl's eyes flickered with delight as she thought about the prospect of her every move with Maddy being caught by the paparazzi.

Maddy wanted to point out that shopping together wasn't in the contract, but instead she said, "That'd be great."

*It's all about pleasing the Protections when you first meet them*, Mark had said. *Keep them happy.*

Mark said, "Now please just relax for a moment, and—"

"I've done this before, with Lance, remember?" Vanessa interrupted Mark. "Even though no one knows what you guys do." Vanessa settled in her chair. "Ready."

Maddy looked over at the heiress, then closed her eyes. Using the technique Susan taught her, she opened her mind and let Vanessa's energy come in fully. She then began the process of disentangling the frequency from all the others nearby. The energy was buoyant, mostly happy, and just a bit mean. Soon Maddy had a clear lock on Vanessa's frequency.

"We're good," Maddy said, opening her eyes and smiling again. She was surprised at how easy it had been.

Squealing, Vanessa pulled out her iPhone. "Okay, can I just get a picture?"

Maddy looked at Mark. He nodded, telling her to play along.

Vanessa came around the table and then leaned next to Maddy, taking the picture with her phone. She checked it. "I'm totally tweeting this right now!" she exclaimed. "Maddy, thank you so much!" She threw her arms around Maddy again, and then bounded out of the room, led by Max, who was standing by. The door closed and the room was silent again.

Maddy had her first Protection.

Jackson's stepfather looked at Maddy: "Are you all right?"

"I am," Maddy said. "Now who's next?"

Over the next couple hours, Maddy met five more Protections. They ranged from another wealthy teenager to an older woman who had been married to a man who had started a donut empire. All were absolutely thrilled to have Maddy as their Guardian; Maddy was clearly the hottest Angel on the planet right now. There was only one Protection who had any problem with her. His name was Jeffrey Rosenberg. *The* Jeffrey Rosenberg. The billionaire.

Rosenberg was considerably overweight. His belly rounded underneath his tailored jacket, straining the buttons as he walked into the room, sweat on his brow. He was accompanied by his assistant, a young woman with a short pixie haircut, A-line skirt, and white blouse.

"Mr. Rosenberg, meet Guardian Madison Godright," Mark said. "Maddy, this is Jeffrey Rosenberg."

Mark was being overly nice as he sat Rosenberg down, Maddy thought. Entitlement just oozed from the billionaire's pores. Maddy found it mildly repulsive, and given enough exposure to it, she might find it *very* repulsive.

Still, she let herself go and let Rosenberg's energy wash over her. After having met only a handful of Protections, Maddy could memorize their frequency within seconds now. It was getting easier each time. Even though Rosenberg left her feeling gross. This was her *job* now.

Settling his girth in the seat, Rosenberg's eyes drifted incredulously over Maddy, all the way down to her Louboutins, and then back up. She smiled tightly.

"I didn't want the one that was half," Rosenberg finally said.

Mark shot a quick glance at Maddy that seemed to say, *Be calm.*

"I can assure you, Maddy is as capable as any other Guardian, and she possesses skills I haven't seen in years," Mark said. "You are in good hands."

"I want half off my protection plan." Rosenberg's voice was flat. Maybe borderline ruthless.

"Jeff, you know that's not an option," Mark said, trying to maintain his composure.

The billionaire flared his nostrils as he looked at this part-human, part-Angel across from him, the slightest wisp of an arrogant smile on his face.

Maddy'd had enough.

"If you don't want to work with me, that's fine," Maddy said. "Because the truth is that there are a lot of people out there who need help. And you, sir, don't look like one of them."

Silence reigned in the room. Mark sat, frozen. Jeffrey's assistant was totally silent, her eyes the size of golf balls—she'd probably never seen someone tell off her boss like that. As for Rosenberg, he just sat there, not moving a muscle, looking directly at Maddy, as still as a statue. Ten seconds passed. And another ten. The tension in the room was thick and oppressive.

Then Rosenberg did something Maddy never could have seen coming. He laughed. He came to life, his laughs small and gurgling at first, and then transforming into long, wheezing peals of laughter.

"I like this one. She's got nerve," he said, nodding at Maddy.

Rosenberg got up and, without saying another word, waddled back out into the hall, his assistant by his side. His laugher trailed behind him like an eerie echo until it was lost in the general murmur of the office.

"You okay?" Mark asked.

Maddy nodded, but Rosenberg's presence still lingered in the room, and in her mind.

The final two Protections were a couple in their thirties; the husband had started a popular website, and the wife did a lot of human charity work. They'd just bought their third house.

They were polite enough, and happy to have Maddy as their Guardian, but just like the others, they were rich and entitled.

Maddy felt their frequencies quickly, and after exchanging a bit of chitchat, they left quietly, thanking her for her time.

Max came in with a printout of the list of all her Protections, along with their contact information, background, et cetera. Maddy felt kind of strange looking at it. Like there was something she was forgetting, and couldn't remember.

"Max?" Maddy asked as he picked Mark's empty water glass off the conference table.

Mark's assistant looked at her expectantly.

"Have you gotten any word on the status of the Protection charity programs I wanted to start for the disadvantaged? Jacks was going to have Mark present it to the Archangels?"

"Oh, we're definitely working on that, don't worry, Maddy," Max said, smiling. "Can I fill you up there?" He poured her some more sparkling water. "It's definitely one of Mark's big priorities right now. But, as you know, anything involving Guardians and Protections also involves lawyers. We just need to make sure that we're not infringing on anyone's contracts and that every *i* is dotted. You know how these things go. They just take time." He smiled even wider.

"I actually *don't* know," Maddy said. "But if you say it's happening . . ."

"Oh, don't worry about that. It's definitely one of Mark's big priorities right now," Max repeated. "Should I call down so your car's waiting?"

Maddy was absentmindedly looking out the window again, watching the people on the street.

"No, it's okay," she said. "I think I want to go for a walk."

Downstairs she wandered toward the front door of the building, passing the sandwich chain café that was inside the lobby. She thought she recognized someone and paused. Inside the cafe, Jeffrey Rosenberg's young assistant was at the head of the line, digging in her wallet for enough money to pay. After a minute she shook her head, blushing, and pushed the sandwich back at the cashier before walking toward the exit, head down.

Maddy felt a cold sensation settle over her body at the sign of the girl's tightened straits. Suddenly, in total clarity, Senator Linden's conversation with her at the diner came into her mind. How he believed she would never be able to reform the Angels from the inside. And how she had felt this morning as she'd looked her wealthy Protections in the eye.

She swiveled. The clack of her heels resounded across the lobby as she walked to take the elevators downstairs to her car.

She drove fast, maybe even recklessly, to Jacks's house, who she knew would be home by now after his scheduled session at the Angel doctors. Chloe was in the living room watching TV when Maddy entered the house with the keys Jacks had given her. Jacks was in the kitchen, making a turkey sandwich.

Chloe's eyes took in Maddy's suit. "You look amazing in that, Maddy. Nice choice!"

Maddy tried to smile at her but found she couldn't. She walked toward Jacks.

"Hey, I wasn't expecting you 'til later. You done at the NAS already?" Jacks seemed caught off-guard in some way.

"Jacks, you told me things were going to change," Maddy said.

"What?" Jacks looked over and saw Chloe surreptitiously trying to eavesdrop from the living room. He opened a sliding glass door to the deck, and they walked outside. Jacks slid the door closed so that they had privacy. It was a blustery day, and wind whipped their clothes in gusts as they stood outside on the deck overlooking the canyon.

"Maddy, what's wrong?"

"My Protections. It's all the same as it has always been. I know it takes time to bring progress," she said. "But I was supposed to change it. And nothing has changed."

"Maddy, calm down," Jacks said, putting a hand on her shoulder. "Now what happened?"

"Nothing . . ." Maddy said. "I mean, nothing, but everything. You should've seen him Jacks. He was so . . . smug."

"Who?"

Maddy just shook her head, thinking of Rosenberg. She wanted to cry, but she wasn't going to let those tears happen. Jacks pulled her into an embrace.

"Mads, the charity program you've been talking about putting together is going to help get Guardians to disadvantaged people across the country," Jacks said. "But that takes a long time; you can't change things overnight. Especially with the Angels. When the change comes, it's going to be huge, opening up Protection to so many more. Just like you wanted. But to pay for that, we also have to keep getting Protections that *can* afford to pay. You know this."

Maddy leaned against Jackson's chest. "But meanwhile, the threats the Council has made against Senator Linden and, well, against humans have been pretty serious, Jacks. It's changed a lot of people's minds, and a lot of people are starting to join his cause." She paused. "What if he has a point? That the Angels *do* have too much power and influence? That Protection for Pay is ultimately corrupt?"

Jackson stiffened against her.

"That's what Linden *claims* for the Immortals Bill. That it will be temporary while they investigate Protection for Pay. But the ban on all Angel activities would be open-ended. It could take years before anything was decided, and the case would probably have to go before the Supreme Court. And what until then? It's illegal to be an Angel? For me to be me?" He narrowed his eyes at Maddy. "And, do I need to remind you, illegal for you to be you?"

Jackson gently put his hand up to her cheek. "This isn't about the money, or any of that," Jacks said. "It's about basic Angel rights, Maddy."

"I'm just . . . I don't know," Maddy said, a tumult of emotions fighting inside her. "There's just so much going on."

"You've been under a lot of stress. Think about that. There's a lot of change happening. And you're taking on a lot of responsibility. You just met the people whose lives you may one day have to save. Don't add more pressure than is necessary. Just enjoy your first year as a Guardian and worry about the other stuff later, once you're settled in."

Maddy had to admit she had been feeling a bit more on edge than usual. Maybe Jacks was right. She couldn't tell anymore. For the moment, she just let Jacks hold her to him, the wind lashing against them, sending her hair streaming in all different directions as she pressed in closer. But her mind flitted back to the conference room, to the entitlement of her Protections. And how she was feeling like she was failing at her goal before she'd even begun. She was becoming a Guardian like all the rest.

Jackson gazed down at her. He seemed to be weighing his words. He took a deep breath.

"Maddy, there's something I've been meaning to tell you . . ." Jacks said, his voice trailing off quietly.

The Angel looked down expectantly at Maddy. But her eyes were far off. She was distracted, her mind turning over and over what happened back at the NAS headquarters earlier in the day.

"I just can't believe how *arrogant* they were," Maddy said, slowly coming back to the present. She looked up at Jacks. "I'm sorry—did you say something?"

"No, nothing," Jacks said stiffly. "It was nothing. I was just telling you it'll be okay." He pulled her closer again. "It'll be okay."

She wanted so much to believe him.

# CHAPTER TWENTY-SIX

Detective Sylvester put on the second pot of coffee of the night, stretching his back and yawning as the hot water percolated slowly through the machine. Outside his apartment, the voices of a couple arguing echoed up from the otherwise empty street. It was late already. But he still had hours of work ahead of him.

*Some vacation,* he thought to himself, shaking his head and smiling slightly.

Pouring himself a cup of coffee, Sylvester walked back to his living room. Stacks of files that Sergeant Garcia had delivered sat on his coffee table and on the side tables. A number of books were scattered next to his couch, with bookmarks and notes poking out. There were two tall stacks of newspapers behind the sofa. In the background, the TV played nonstop on the news channel at a low volume. As a new report came on, he turned the volume up.

*"Just days before the election, there have been more calls for investigations into the ties between the violent Humanity Defense Faction and anti-Angel*

*Senator Ted Linden's presidential campaign. This comes after officials identi-fied the culprit in the bombing of an Angel office as a high-level HDF opera-tive with ties to Senator Linden's political party. Election officials say this could derail Linden's bid, along with his Immortals Bill and newly formed Global Angel Commission, for good."*

Sylvester turned the volume on the TV back down. He took a strong pull of the coffee and looked at all the paperwork. The leads. The dead ends. He'd taken some paid vacation time off. Everyone understood, after his work on the bombing case, which was now "solved."

He'd basically moved his office to his apartment. This way he could work his cases—all his cases—away from the prying eyes of Captain Keele. When was the last time he had slept? He forgot. It didn't matter, anyway. This was too important.

No rest for the wicked.

The detective's eyes drew to his wall. A large global map, the kind you might see in an old high school classroom, hung there. All across the map were markings in different colors, in different countries and cities. The markings each had a date and a note. There was also a large map of downtown Los Angeles taped to the wall, with a series of notes and red X's.

On the world map, there was a marking in the blue of the Pacific Ocean off California. It had the earliest date of any of the markings: "F-16 Downed."

There were marks all over the map, even Antarctica, where an electrical accident with a generator at an observation station had killed ten workers. The map also included one neat marking on London—the St. Pancras derailment—and another on Beijing—"Apartment Fire/Collapse."

There was one other marking, this one with a question mark, directly in the middle of Angel City: "Bombing of Angel Administration Affairs Offices."

After Sylvester had learned of DeWitt's death and that the FBI found incriminating evidence of the bombing and Humanity Defense Faction materials, law enforcement had considered the case solved. The investigation now moved to a higher-level investigation into the HDF on conspiracy charges. It was time to infiltrate the leadership with undercover officers and confidential informants. The Angels were special counsel for the operation. William Beaubourg would likely be drawn in. It could get ugly. But it was out of Sylvester's hands now.

Captain Keele was happy just to get one more case solved. It was good for stats. And what was good for stats was good for the captain's promotion to police commander.

The only problem was Sylvester didn't consider the case solved. Not at all.

He didn't voice these doubts to Keele before going on "vacation"—the captain would have a meltdown if he knew Sylvester was still investigating a closed case. Only Garcia knew. Every day he brought the detective new photocopies of documents and files from headquarters to chew through.

Something wasn't adding up—a constant knot in Sylvester's stomach was telling him that. Almost every day Sylvester was putting another red mark on the wall map. Dark Angel sightings that the media attributed to religious hysteria. Terrible accidents with no precedent. And then the continuing trickle of homeless disappearances downtown. Captain Keele had decided there was no pattern, no evidence of murder. The cases had been kicked over to Missing Persons. The files would probably sit there for months before anyone got to them.

And now the pinning of the bombing on the HDF. It had to be a setup. But for what? And for whom? How did it all tie together?

Still sipping his coffee, Sylvester looked at an article he had printed off the *New York Times* website and then walked to the map with the marker. He made a new mark on the map, just off the coast of Brazil: "Ferry Accident."

Yawning, Sylvester walked over to the couch and extracted a Red Vines container from underneath some files. The tub was empty. Shaking his head, Sylvester walked to the coat rack by the door and put on his overcoat. He left the light on; he'd only be gone a few minutes.

It was a cool Angel City evening, the streets quiet and nearly empty this late, except for the occasional homeless person or drunk clubgoer stumbling her way back home. A black Maserati suddenly roared past on the quiet street and was gone as quickly as it came. A light mist hung in the air, seemingly swirling around the streetlights. Sylvester reached the corner newsstand. He nodded to the familiar, overweight man working behind the counter as he walked in. The detective grabbed a bag of Red Vines, along with the early edition of the *Angel City Times*—sometimes he still liked to have the physical paper. All kinds of Angel tourist merchandise and tchotchkes were crammed around the store: little teddy bears with "I ♥ Angel City" sweaters, maps to Angel houses, little mugs with the Angel City sign printed on them.

"Late night, detective?" the man behind the counter asked in a thick accent. He wore a brown polyester shirt, unbuttoned, with a white wife-beater under it.

"Something like that, Chas," Sylvester said. "How's business?"

"Oh, you know, can't complain."

Sylvester nodded, tucking the Red Vines and paper under his arm as he walked out of the store. The arguing couple had disappeared, and the street was almost totally silent as Sylvester reached his apartment building and walked up the stairs to the second floor. His hands automatically found his keys in his pocket and unlocked the deadbolt.

It wasn't until he opened the door and stepped into the pitch-black apartment that he realized the light had been turned off.

Sylvester's hand instinctively went for his gun.

"Looking for this, detective?" a voice from the dark said. Straining his eyes, Sylvester could see the metal of his gun glinting in the reflection from the streetlight shining in the window. He cursed himself—he'd taken his holster off earlier in the night. "Turn on the light," the voice said.

Sylvester flipped the switch, and the apartment was flooded with light. A man in a navy blue windbreaker was sitting in the chair facing the door, training Sylvester's own gun on the detective. Dark circles rimmed his eyes, and he needed a shave.

"Take a seat," the man said, motioning with the gun to the couch.

Sylvester walked to the sofa and sat down, his mind racing.

"Don't worry, this is just a precaution. I'm not here to hurt you." The man's eyes scanned the apartment nervously.

"What are you here to do, then?"

"Talk."

"I'm listening."

The man walked to the curtains and drew them, but left a crack open so he could see out. He moved his chair closer to the window. "It's about Jesse DeWinter."

Sylvester's pulse raced, but he kept his demeanor calm. "What about him?"

"I was his partner in the bombings." The man looked the detective directly in the eyes as he said it.

"HDF?" Sylvester said.

The man laughed. "If you believe that—"

"I never said I did," Sylvester cut him off.

The intruder nodded in respect. "What I have here is . . . a game changer." He pulled a thick manila envelope from his coat and placed it on the one free spot on the coffee table. "Phone logs, a CD with recorded calls, photos. Everything I could get." The man looked at Sylvester with serious, sad eyes. "I put it together after they killed Jesse."

"They?" Sylvester's heart was pounding in his throat.

"Yes, 'they,' detective. 'Them.' Whatever you want to call the murderers," the man said, looking out the window. "*The Angels.*"

"What do you mean? As revenge for the bombing?"

The man looked at Sylvester like he was the stupidest person in the world.

"No. They hired us, detective."

The detective's world became fuzzy for a moment as he realized what the man in front of him was saying.

"What do you mean? How . . ." Sylvester struggled to make sense of what he was being told.

"Archangel Charles Churchson came to us with the job. It was to have stayed just between us, forever. Bomb the offices. Head to Costa Rica on Angel money. That way, Jesse and I could still fund the cause. The cause will take any job. Angels or humans. Our operating expenses are . . . high. But we didn't know all those workers were going to be there. I don't know if Churchson did or not. But the whole deal was supposed to be clean. That was until Churchson decided he couldn't trust us anymore. That's when Jesse tried to find an out. Through you, detective. But he was too late."

"But why would Churchson set up a bomb on his own organization?" Sylvester asked.

"Power. And politics."

"Of course . . ." It all made sense. "He could claim the humans were turning against them and they needed to prepare to defend against the ingrates. Charge them more. And keep Angel City for Angels."

"And also discredit the mainstream anti-Angel movement," the man said.

"The presidential election's on Tuesday. Senator Linden. You know what this could mean."

"It could mean a lot of things," the man said. "Like I said, game changer. I sent a copy of what's in this packet to the ten biggest news agencies in the country. All across the country, news editors will be getting to work and discovering this. People will know the truth. I'm sorry I ever became involved now. But it was supposed to be clean. The building was supposed to be empty. Nobody was supposed to get hurt."

Sylvester let all of what he had just learned sink in. "Who does this touch in the Angels? How far does the corruption go?"

"We only dealt with Archangel Churchson, and as far as I know, that's as far as it goes. I know he has some allies. But he also has many enemies."

Sylvester thought of Jackson's stepfather, struggling to maintain control in the Archangels' orgainzation.

After a moment, Sylvester looked at the tired, weary man across from him. He'd obviously been on the run for some time. "Why come to me? I could arrest you."

The man smiled. "You forget: I have the gun," he said. "Plus, Detective Sylvester, I've heard that even though you're police, you're honorable police. The cause keeps its eye on you. It knows the work you're doing," the man said. There it was, Sylvester thought, the *cause* again. "And I'm leaving, forever. If anything happens to me . . . I just don't want it to fade away. Get swept under the rug." He looked at Sylvester. "Can you promise me that?"

Sylvester nodded.

"Thank you," the man said. He looked out the window again. "I need to go, detective. It's time." He placed Sylvester's gun on a side table. "I trust you won't be needing to pick this up until I've been gone at least five minutes, let's say." He smiled.

As the man stood up, zipping his windbreaker, he nodded nonchalantly at the global map on the wall. "I see you have the seven now, detective."

"Seven?" Sylvester said.

The man began reciting from memory: "'And then when the seven burn across the earth, evil will rise upon you from the West.'"

"*The Book of Angels*," Sylvester said. "I know the passage. The controversial final revelations. They're famous. But their source is also in doubt. Still, many have spoken of a battle between good and evil. What do you mean I have the seven now?"

"The seven continents, detective," the main said. He pointed to Brazil in South America. Sylvester had just marked the first incident in the continent twenty minutes before. "We've been tracking them as well. It's only a matter of time now."

The man began walking out the door.

"You, or your people, sent me the anonymous e-mails about the attacks. Why?" Sylvester said, his mind running quickly. "Who are your people? What do you want?"

"You'll know us when the time is right," the man said, walking to the door. "Goodbye. I have to leave if I want to live to see tomorrow night."

"Wait—"

But the man was already out the door. His footsteps echoed down the hallway.

Sylvester's head swirled with the revelations, implications, and even more questions the mysterious man's unexpected visit had brought.

He couldn't even begin to imagine what was going to happen when the public found out that an Archangel had set up the bombing to stir antihuman sentiment in the Angel community. And Sylvester had thought the bombing had had something to do with the demon attacks. How wrong he had been.

It turned out that the Dark Angels might be coming for something much, much worse.

Sylvester went to his bookshelf. Next to the King James Bible, he had the Apocrypha, which included the Gospels of Judas and Tom. Next to the Apocrypha, he had *The Book of Angels*. It had surfaced in the Middle East in the 1930s and gotten an incredible amount of attention by a public hungry for everything Angel.

Most of it just told biblical stories from the viewpoint of the Angels. Except for the ending sections, which were all new. They were also the bloodiest and the most famous sections, with plenty of demons and carnage. The Angels had put a lot of effort into proving that the later apocalyptic sections in *The Book of Angels* were not ancient, just the work of some crackpot in the nineteenth century. "Scary bedtime stories," as Mark had called them. But there were still many people who believed they were prophecy.

The detective flipped through the yellowed pages and found the passage the man had begun quoting.

*"And then when the seven burn across the earth, evil will rise upon you from the West. The Darkness will come from a pit in the Great Ocean, out of which no light has ever been seen, straight from the depths of the other world. Death will surely find a home with you, and mercy shall be driven out by the hordes of doom. And you will beg for the end."*

Sylvester felt a coldness creep along his spine. He slowly closed the book, and then sat down at his kitchen table.

He reached over for his landline telephone, but then paused. Fumbling in his pocket, he pulled out his old cell phone, a Nokia. Scrolling through the numbers he found it: MARK GODSPEED.

Mark answered on the fourth ring.

"Yes, I know what time it is, Mark," Detective Sylvester said. "I have some news about Archangel Churchson. But you're going to need to help me."

# CHAPTER TWENTY-SEVEN

The day after receiving her Protections, Maddy had to go to the NAS media offices, which were only a few blocks away from the regular NAS headquarters in Beverly Hills, to get fitted with her Angelcam. Although the Angelcam had only been around for a little over two years—and a lot of those two years had been spent in trial and error with prototypes—it was now one of the most popular additions to Guardians ever. Now that they were HD, being able to watch a save firsthand through footage from the tiny camera was almost too good to be true for Angel fanatics. Saves were becoming more and more watched around the world, and every new save on SaveTube was getting millions more hits than the one before. Angel analysts expected Maddy's first save to be the most-watched save of all time. The question on everybody's lips was, when would it happen?

At the media office, Maddy showed up with a piece of jewelry, as they requested: her mother's necklace. "Sorry, it's a little crazy down here," the technician said, pounding a flurry of keystrokes as he finished calibrating her 'cam. He turned to her. "But let's get to work."

The Angelcam was the world's most advanced camera, a trade secret owned by the Angels. It would make a fortune if the technology was released to the public, but the Angels were content to keep it to themselves right now and reap the profits from the footage of their hottest Guardians making saves around Angel City and the world.

After her necklace was fitted with it, Maddy looked at herself in the mirror. You'd never know she had a camera on her. It was almost microscopic. She looked at the monitor next to the technician, and it was showing amazingly clear, crisp, and steady live footage, even though she was shaking back and forth. The technology was amazing. Looking at herself in the mirror, she then looked into the LCD monitor, training the camera into it. On the TV it looked as if there were a thousand Maddys extending forever. She smiled, her white teeth extending into infinity on the screen.

"Guardian, you are ready for your close-up," the Angel technician said, smiling.

The technician's intern, a pimply college student majoring in Angel Studies, suddenly burst into the room, his face in a panic.

"What is it?" the Angel technician asked, looking annoyed at the intern.

"It's, uh, uh—"

The technician pushed past the intern to where a group of Angels and interns were standing in a group, watching something.

Maddy followed her Angelcam technician out the door and found everyone glued to the large TV mounted on the wall of the waiting room. Most seemed to be standing, mouths open, in shock.

On the screen was file footage of Archangel Charles Churchson, in a black tuxedo and bowtie, attending an Angel charity event earlier that year. Maddy recognized Churchson as the goateed Archangel she'd called a jerk during her meeting at the NAS. The one who had been against her becoming Guardian.

Bold script on the screen read: **ARCHANGEL IMPLICATED IN BOMBING THAT KILLED NINETY-TWO INNOCENTS.**

The voice of the anchor back in the studio was announcing: *"NAS officials have denied they had any clue of Churchson's plot, and promise to do everything to help authorities bring him to justice. But Angel observers wonder if the damage done is already too late to fix."*

"What's going on?" Maddy asked the intern.

"Archangel Churchson was the one behind the bombing; he was trying to frame the HDF and make Linden look bad," the intern reported breathlessly.

"*What?*" Maddy gasped.

*"Protests in major cities around the globe have already erupted, demanding justice and a full inquiry into the Angels and their hierarchy. Presidential candidate Teddy Linden has announced a press conference one hour from now. Still no official word from Gabriel and the True Immortals at this time. Stay with us as we follow this shocking scandal and the outrage around the world!*

*"In other news, a group of doomsday activists shut down Metro lines this morning as they claimed . . ."*

"Oh. My. God," Maddy's technician whispered to no one in particular.

Phones across the offices began ringing incessantly. For a moment, no one seemed able to move to go answer them. They all stood stock-still, remaining in disbelief.

The shockwaves from the utterly astonishing revelation that Archangel Charles Churchson had been behind the mysterious deadly bombing of the Angel offices quickly spread out from Angel City and across the world. The idea that an Angel himself—especially an Archangel—could be behind something so odious was deeply troubling to even those who had been consistent defenders of Angelkind and their rights. And the anti-Angel groups found their claims about the corruption of the supposedly perfect Immortals vindicated.

Bizarrely, A! and ANN and some of the other Angel fan networks kept running normal Angel coverage, including specials on Maddy, while most of the regular news stations were running nonstop coverage of the Churchson scandal, interviewing family members of the victims, running profiles on Churchson, and cutting together exposés on other high-ranking Angel figures. The Angel networks were pretending like nothing was happening, even though the presidential election was mere days away. Poll numbers showed the public flocking to support Senator Linden, the Immortals Bill, and the Senator's proposed Global Angel Commission, known as GAC. Maddy didn't know how it was all going to end up. The Council of True Immortals had promised swift retaliation if humans trespassed on the rights of Angels. Everyone was on edge. But, in the wake of this devastating scandal, Mark had told her the "show must go on."

And so it did: Maddy soon got her second wave of Protections, bringing her up to her final number. Like the first batch, they all were very well-to-do and had a sense of entitlement clinging to them. But this time she tried to not let it bother her as much. Because, as Jackson had said, sometimes change took time. Soon, she assured herself, she'd be able to start advocating for some changes, but after she got really settled.

Maddy also didn't want to kid herself: with the shocking revelation of Archangel Churchson's corruption and violence, she was secretly hopeful there would *have* to be some kind of reform on the way. People were demanding it.

Jacks had been very busy recently, and he wouldn't say much about what he'd been doing. But she thought it had to do with his treatments, which seemed to have increased in frequency.

• • •

Then Election Day came. Maddy went over to the Godspeeds' house that evening to watch the results. Jackson, his mom, and his sister were there. Mark was at the NAS offices, preparing to start maneuvering around whatever might happen politically.

A strange pall had hung over Angel City that day, a morning mist that lingered far into midday, lending the afternoon a gray cast. People seemed to walk or drive around with their heads down. The beautiful Immortals were what Angel City knew. What it thrived on. What it felt pride in. And now a large part of the rest of the country might vote against them?

The public revelation of Archangel Churchson's crimes had been catastrophic for the pro-Angel political cause in the final days before the election. Everyone who had been infuriated by the threats of violence from the Council, everyone who had been calling the Angels "fallen," all those who had pointed to the existence of someone like Maddy as a sign that Angels had been hiding things—they all felt a victory that day.

"We cannot let one bad apple ruin an entire system that thrives on goodness and the principle of service to mankind," Mark had said in a press conference. But for many humans across the country, that was not good enough.

At 7:43 p.m., hours before anyone would have predicted, the news networks were already able to call the winner of the election. They cut quickly to footage of the acceptance speech: the man on the screen had a shock of lustrous politician hair, with only a bit of gray starting to show through. His smile was meant to inspire confidence. Confidence in yourself that you'd made the right decision by voting for him.

It was Senator Linden, now president-elect Linden.

*"My fellow Americans, I wanted to speak directly to you, the men and women of this great country of ours, the United States of America, the greatest*

*country this world has ever seen. As one of our earliest citizens said, we are indeed a light upon the hill."*

The president-elect cleared his throat and continued:

*"I want to thank you for the confidence you've put in me. I will do my best to serve you and this country as your next president. Now, I don't think it will surprise you to hear me say that I'm proud to be an American. But it might surprise you when I look westward to Angel City and see something as un-American as the institution of the National Angel Services on our own shores. Well, I want to do something about it. The Angels don't want you to hear about this. They've got their fancy cars and fancy homes and fancy lives to think about. I know many of you have followed these so-called Immortals your whole lives. They've thrilled you, moved you. You might even remember important events in your life around Commissionings, or a particularly memorable save. There is nothing wrong with that. We are all human Americans, allowed to spend our time and liberty however we see fit. The Constitution guarantees this. However, when the Constitution was framed, the Angel question was not on the table. As you know, I've been spearheading the special committee on Capitol Hill over the past nine months that has been investigating Angel affairs. And what I've discovered would shock—yes, shock—you. Much of it I can't disclose right now, but, when the time comes, it shall be made public.*

*"But even without this information, just ask yourself: What is American about conducting all your training in secret? What is American about keeping our own government and military away from the secrets that you hold? What is American about creating yourself as a separate class from the rest of us hardworking humans?*

*"Recent events, such as threats by Gabriel and the NAS Council, Archangel Churchson's disgusting mass murder and deceit, and even Jackson Godspeed's apparent injuries and inability to recover, have raised grave questions about the claims of Angels to having a divine right to be on earth. Scientists*

*and philosophers have been debating such things for decades, but recent research suggests that Angels may not be what we think. What you think. We truly stand at a crisis moment.*

*"Before I go any further, let me say that I stand here today to promise that I do not condone, nor would ever condone, violence against any Angel."* His eyes twinkled. *"Yet I cannot stand by as our sacred institutions of liberty and fairness are trampled on by the Immortals, True and Born alike. My Immortals Bill, which I plan on enacting as soon as possible with the help of the sitting president, will promise imprisonment for any being performing supernatural acts, and dewinging for flagrant offenses. This will stay in effect for as long as it takes to review the current position of Angels in human society. Our allies across the world are ready to honor this bill in their own countries as part of the Global Angel Commission, which will spearhead all human efforts to reform the Angels."*

The TV suddenly went blank. Kris had turned it off. She had tears in her eyes.

"He's lying! He doesn't want reform! He's just the polished front for the HDF," Jacks spit out.

"I don't understand," Maddy said. "They won't really ban Angels. Will they? And taking wings? Isn't it just some kind of strategic ploy to transform Protection for Pay?"

"He's serious. Don't you see? He just wants us dead. They have allies across the world now, there's no place for us to go. They want our power and our money. That's all they see. They don't see the good we do."

Maddy looked worriedly at Jacks.

"You're part of this too, Maddy. Whether you want to be or not," Jacks said. "You're a Guardian now."

"But, Jacks, you know there are things I don't like about how the system works," Maddy said. "And what Churchson did with his bombing, how many were killed . . ."

"I don't like those things either, Maddy. You know I don't." Jacks looked at her with his steely blue eyes. "But there are right ways to deal with reform, and there are wrong ways. The right way is with Angels, by Angels, from Angels. Not from outsiders. Not this way. Not Linden's way."

Maddy was silent. Kris and Chloe started walking out of the living room, Jackson's mother still in tears.

"I just didn't think it would actually happen," Jacks said, almost to himself. "Angels are the greatest force of good the world has ever seen."

"But you don't think anything drastic will happen?" Maddy asked quietly. "I mean, it's the Angels . . . what could they do? The Immortals Bill isn't really going to happen, is it? Even once Linden takes office, there are politicians who won't vote for it . . . right?"

"I've talked to Mark. We don't know what to think," Jacks said. "But soon you might have a choice, Maddy. And I hope you choose the right side."

# CHAPTER TWENTY-EIGHT

Golden afternoon light passed through the blazing orange and red leaves of the oaks that covered the open picnic area on the hillside. Fall leaves lazily spiraled their way down to the grass. The oaks had turned the earth into a carpet of yellow and scarlet. Up above, Griffith Park extended up and over the hills for hundreds, if not thousands of acres: an oasis of wilderness right next to Angel City. A small, woodsy little shack off to the side of the tables served as a café.

It was the day after the election, and Maddy had wanted to ask a certain non-Angel's advice.

Tom had already been waiting at a picnic table for ten minutes when Maddy arrived in a rush. He was wearing old jeans, a T-shirt, and his leather jacket, which Maddy reflected was like his uniform when he wasn't wearing his *actual* uniform.

"I'm *so* sorry I'm late. I got caught in traffic." She remembered how annoyed Tom had been the first time she'd kept him waiting.

Tom sipped his coffee. "I haven't been waiting long. I've been making friends with the squirrels here," he said, motioning to a squirrel that was running to and fro across the leaves with an acorn from an oak tree. "Just don't get him started, or he'll never shut up." As if in response, the squirrel started chirping and then dashed away and disappeared up the rough trunk of a tree.

Maddy laughed. It was so nice to remember there were creatures in the world who couldn't care less about the Angels.

"This park is great," Tom said, looking around appreciatively at the wilderness. "I never would have known it was here."

"I used to come here a lot with my uncle when I was a girl. We would walk up the hill and then go to the Griffith Observatory, and I would look at all the planets. And then we would go get pie at this all-pie restaurant. The Angel City sign is just over there." Maddy pointed west. Her mind cast back for a moment to that simpler time.

"It's quiet," Tom said appreciatively. "And an all-pie restaurant? Sounds good."

Maddy looked around with her own appreciation—no paparazzi in sight. They tended to stick closer to Runyon Canyon Park, which was one of the hottest Angel-sighting spots in town.

"I got you something," Tom said. "For your Commissioning."

"You did?" Maddy said, surprised and slightly uncomfortable.

Tom nodded, reaching into his leather jacket. He had something in his hand. He extended his palm. A set of golden naval aviator wings, maybe three inches across, sat there. They glittered in the fading afternoon sun.

Tom grinned at her. "Well, go ahead, take them. They're for you."

"They're beautiful," Maddy said. She reached forward slowly and took them in her hand. The gold was warm to the touch. The detailing was incredible.

"Turn them over," Tom said.

Flipping the wings over, Maddy discovered he had engraved *NATURAL* on them.

"Your call sign," he said. "If you're ever on the flight deck, just show them these."

"I don't know what to say. How did you get these? Are you going to get into trouble?"

"Don't worry about that. I wanted to get you something to celebrate. I hadn't . . . acquired them by your Commissioning. But now you can have them. I'd be proud to have you on my wing any day."

"Thank you, Tom," Maddy said slowly. Was it okay for her to accept them? Yes, she decided. Tom was just her flying instructor. "It's so thoughtful of you."

"I remember when I first got my wings. How I felt. It seemed like everyone thought I couldn't do it, given my pedigree. But I proved them wrong."

Maddy nodded, holding the small golden wings between her fingers. Autumn leaves continued to fall behind them. A light breeze sent them spinning as they descended to the ground.

"I'm getting a little cold. Should we go for a walk?" Maddy said. She buttoned up her jacket.

They made their way up one of the wide trails, up the hill. Not many people were on the packed-dirt path, so they had some peace. Birds chirped enthusiastically in the trees, and the thicket of oaks gave way to stands of tall palm trees. The palms were so tall and spindly they seemed to extend to the sky itself. Soon the gleaming observatory appeared further up the mountain, a white pearl on the hillside.

Maddy was wondering how to bring up what she'd set up this meeting to discuss, but Tom beat her to it.

"So I guess you know my new boss doesn't like Angels too much?" Tom said.

Maddy gave him a questioning look.

"President-elect Linden. Technically he'll be the commander in chief of the military."

"Oh," Maddy said. "Angels"—she'd almost said *Jacks*—"are pretty upset about it."

"Upset? They have no right. After what Churchson did . . . How many innocents were murdered, just for the Archangel to try to consolidate Angel power?" Tom shook his head in disgust. "Well, it's blown up in their faces. Did you know that just a few hours ago in DC, Congress passed an emergency measure to form the Global Angel Commission with Western Europe, China, Russia, India, Brazil, everyone? Leaders and emissaries are all flying to Washington, from around the world. Linden will be sworn in as the president of the GAC tonight. He'll be leading everyone. All of this is happening at top speed to deal with the Angel corruption crisis. The current president is taking a backseat role. Big change is happening, Maddy. We may be here to witness it." There was a certain excitement in Tom's voice. "Now it's only a matter of time before the Immortals Bill passes. They're calling the Angels 'fallen.' Churchson's crime was like pouring gasoline onto a flame. All Angel activities will be suspended, punishable by jail, while they determine what reforms have to be made. There will have to be huge changes to Protection for Pay. We don't know what's going to happen."

Maddy was completely silent. She remembered what Jacks had told her. About decisions.

Tom looked at Maddy's face. "What? I mean, you're excited for this, right?"

Maddy looked off into the distance.

"We've talked about this before, that you wanted to help bring change to the Immortals. That's why you started, you told me. Well, now you have a chance."

"That's not entirely why I started," Maddy said. "There were many—"

"That's not what you told me. You told me once that a hero will fight for an idea. Now you can use your position to work with President Linden and bring real change. Now, Maddy. Not five or ten years from now. But tomorrow. Think about that."

"But what will happen to the people who need to be protected in the meantime if the Immortals Bill passes while he reforms?" Maddy asked. "There are some Angels who think that the change needs to happen from within. Is Linden's way the right way? I met him, you know, Senator—I mean, President—Linden. He came to the diner. He knew my father."

"You met him?" Tom asked incredulously. "What was he like?"

"Honestly, Tom, he seemed somehow . . . good. Or at least his intentions were. But I don't know in my gut that what he's doing is right. Maybe he's wrong about all this and we're headed toward a disaster we can't even imagine."

"Neither you nor I can answer that. But it may be the only way." Tom's eyes were becoming deep and rich with a kind of fire and conviction as he turned to Maddy. "The Angels could say they're going to change. But how can you ever trust them? They denied that you even existed. They needed to keep their image clean. That's enough for me right there. You said yourself that they called you an abomination."

Maddy felt unsure. She felt an old pain at the word *abomination*. She turned away, looking off to a small grass-covered ravine that had a trickle of a creek running down it.

"Maybe you're right." Maddy was shocked to hear herself saying those words. "I . . . I don't know yet, Tom."

The pilot had come up behind Maddy. He put his hand on her shoulder. "I'm sorry. I didn't mean to upset you. It's just important. This isn't something you have to decide right now. But you may have to make the decision someday soon."

There was comfort in his hand on her shoulder. Maddy felt it represented something real, something concrete, something different. For some reason it also scared her.

Tom looked at her, an unreadable expression in his eyes. "I also just wanted to let you know, if you ever want to take the plane up again, just tell me. Maybe we'll fly all the way to Santa Barbara."

"Thanks, Tom. I appreciate it." She held the wings in her hands. "Thank you for everything. You've been a great friend."

The pilot's gaze remained on her.

"I should go, though. It's getting late."

Maddy turned to start walking down the path, back toward the cars.

Suddenly what seemed like a thousand flashes fell upon Maddy and Tom at once, absolutely stunning them. A herd of photographers charged up the hill, calling Maddy's name.

The paparazzi had found them.

Maddy shielded her face and, stunned, hurried as fast as she could toward the parking lot. Tom, cursing, tried to follow her through the crush of photographers to his pickup. Maddy's mind raced a thousand miserable directions as she imagined the field day the media was going to have with this situation.

But the biggest question in her mind was, how had they found them?

And then she saw, just down the hill where the cars were parked: a redhead getting into a white Porsche and zipping into the sun-spangled afternoon back down into Angel City.

Emily.

# CHAPTER TWENTY-NINE

The media-circus response was swift and ruthless.

Pictures of Tom and Maddy, along with a video of her covering her face as they ran down the hill and Tom threatening some of the photographers, sped across the internet and TV stations within minutes.

*"Maddy Flies High with Pilot Hunk! Devastated Jack Sits at Home, Wings Clipped!"* read the title of the post on TMZ, the first of eight that night. The media had already started doing background on Tom, pulling up everything they could find. Maddy was frantically looking at blogs on her phone while driving toward her house. Damage control was necessary. Very necessary.

She'd texted Jacks and called eight times. He hadn't picked up, not once. All she could ask herself was, what had she done?

Maddy's Audi squealed into her parking garage, and she quickly went to the elevator. Darcy was calling. Again. She didn't know what to say, so she didn't answer.

Once inside her apartment, she turned on the TV to check the damage. And it was bad.

A! was running a graphic of her face, with cutouts of Tom's and Jacks's faces on each side of it. *"AMERICA'S SWEETHEART CAUGHT IN LOVE TRIANGLE!"*

Ew.

She switched over to ANN and was met with commentary from one of the newer Angel "experts," Colleen Theo, who was notorious for being extra sensationalistic. "Maddy clearly hasn't been getting what she needs from fading star Jackson Godspeed, so apparently she's looking elsewhere. And, frankly, who can blame her when she has a sexy decorated fighter pilot like Tom Cooper? He could take me to Mach 2 any day of the week." Colleen creepily looked directly into the camera when she said this. Maddy had to turn the TV off.

She tried to call Jacks again. She paced around her apartment as the phone rang, walking back and forth over the white shearling rug.

Voicemail again.

*I have to go find him. Explain things.*

Maddy picked her keys up from the counter. Opening the door, she almost ran into Jackson.

He was standing there in a blazer with a V-neck T-shirt underneath, his blue eyes piercing her with seriousness. Maddy held her breath.

"Going somewhere?" Jacks asked flatly. He was silhouetted by the hall light behind him.

"No—I mean—yes," Maddy stuttered. "To find you," she finally got out, defeated.

"Are you going to invite me inside or just stand there looking all guilty?"

"I'm not guilt—" she started firing back, but held her tongue for the time being. She moved out of the way, keeping a watchful eye on Jacks as he came in.

"I had to hear from Chloe," Jacks said coldly, shaking his head. "Maddy, what's going on?"

"Nothing!" Maddy protested. "Jacks, I swear!"

"Why were you on a date with that pilot then?"

"It wasn't a date. . . ."

"It looked like a date. The media seems to think it's a date. You know what they're saying about me!" Jackson was furious, his hands curling at his side in anger. "It's . . . it's humiliating!"

"Tom and I are just friends! You know that!" Maddy said.

"*Tom*," Jacks said, scorn in his voice. "Friends? All you ever told me was that you've been training with a pilot to help with your flight skills. You didn't say you were friends. And not that you were going on romantic hikes together." The anger and hurt in Jackson's voice filled it in equal measure.

Maddy moved to Jacks, pressed against him. "Jacks, don't be like this."

He wouldn't look at her. She took his face in both her hands and turned his face to hers. "Jacks, look at me. Look at me. He's been my tutor, and now he's a friend. Tom's just a friend. I *promise*."

Jacks held her gaze a bit longer, and then turned away.

Although she tried to stop them, a few tears began running down her cheeks. She swiped them away with the back of her hand and was able to stop them from coming uncontrollably. "It was Emily, Jacks."

"What?"

"How the paparazzi got tipped off."

"Maddy, you're being paranoid," Jacks said. "Emily's a nice girl. Sometimes she can get a little carried away."

"*Nice girl?*" Maddy said. "Why are you defending her? What's going on, Jacks?"

"Nothing is going on, Maddy. Quit trying to change the subject."

"You just want to think she's a nice girl, Jacks," Maddy said. "But she somehow followed me or something. She sent the paparazzi. Don't you see that this right here is what she wants? To poison us?"

Jackson looked at Maddy. "I'm sorry," he said at last, his voice lowering. "Maybe I overreacted. If you say he's just a friend . . . I have to trust you. Out of anyone, I should know not to always believe what the media says."

Maddy moved closer to Jackson again. He let her embrace him this time. "I'm sorry, Jacks." She pressed her face against his shoulder.

"How did we get here?" Jacks asked, shaking his head.

"I don't know," she said. "I don't know."

"I think you should probably call Darcy now."

"I . . . okay. That sounds like a good idea."

Stepping away from Jacks, Maddy picked up her phone and made the dreaded call to her publicist.

Darcy wanted Maddy out, in public and looking happy, so the next day saw Maddy jaunting all over the Immortal City. The blogs were still on fire over the potential love triangle, and the Angel networks had locked onto it with a death grip.

The day started with very public morning coffee with Jacks, of which the paparazzi caught every moment. Plentiful Angel City sunshine shone down on smiling Maddy and Jacks. When asked about Tom, Maddy said, "He's been a great help in my flight instruction," and left it at that. Although she knew that might sting the pilot's pride, she couldn't worry about that now. She had to salvage things. Maddy and Jacks walked away hand in hand, the photographers' cameras snapping and whirring.

She then went home and changed. Darcy was insisting she make an appearance at the launch of a new Angel organization that funded the arts for young Angels with the help of corporate sponsor BMW. She didn't really want to go, but given the problems she'd just landed on the lap of her publicist, she also didn't want to be too difficult.

"MADDY! MADDY! HOW WOULD YOU CHARACTER-IZE YOUR RELATIONSHIP WITH TOM? WHAT DOES JACKS HAVE TO SAY? MADDY, RIGHT HERE!"

Maddy didn't answer; she just smiled and waved, walking in among the other Angels as the photogs did their thing.

Suddenly, to the side, Maddy saw a group of protesters penned off by metal fencing. They waved signs and were shouting at her and the other Angels as they arrived. The signs bore graphic pictures from the bombing.

They pressed angrily against the barricades, which normally held back rabid Angel fans, not Angel detractors. The ACPD and private security attempted to keep them back from the red carpet, which baked under the hot sun.

They screamed:

"ANGELS ARE MURDERERS!"

"LIARS!"

"WHY ARE YOU HIDING CHURCHSON WHEN YOU'RE ALL GUILTY?!"

"YOU HAVE BLOOD ON YOUR WINGS!"

Maddy's brow knit in concern as she looked at the people so furiously screaming at them. Suddenly a few of the protesters reached into their backpacks and began hurling rotten vegetables toward the Angels. The girl Angel just in front of Maddy received a disgusting *splat* of a tomato that exploded across her expensive, almost sheer dress. She shrieked. Other Angels began dodging the rotten veggies, and Maddy ducked un-der what looked like a putrid yam as the police extended their batons to try to handle the crowd, which was becoming more and more unruly.

In a daze, Maddy rushed into the reception area for the event, where she was ushered toward the back gardens. Calming classical music was playing on the speakers as she passed a priceless fountain that had been designed by one of the twentieth century's greatest Swiss architects. The shouts of the protesters had already faded into the background. All the museum staff had big plastic smiles on their faces, as if they had no idea there was practically a mob scene just outside.

Maddy thought of the fury in the protesters' eyes. And how strange she felt being the target of it. It was unsettling. Didn't they know that she, too, disapproved of the terrible thing Churchson had done? That most Guardians probably also felt awful and hoped they would find the Archangel and bring him to justice?

It was a sunny, warm day, even though winter was just a page or two away on the calendar. The organizers had decided to hold the luncheon in the back sculpture garden of the museum. Maddy looked at the modern art masterpieces sprinkled throughout the garden. The museum itself loomed large in the background like a behemoth, a work of art itself. She knew the pieces were supposed to be very "important," but some of them just looked like a block of black marble, not sculpted at all. One was brass and looked just like a giant balloon animal, the kind you get from a clown when you're a child.

Darcy helped introduce Maddy to all the important people at the event. She posed for more pictures with the BMW backdrop and gave some sound bites about how important it was to fund the arts.

Throughout the event, Maddy's mind kept wandering back to what had happened yesterday, with both Tom and Jacks. She had texted the pilot an apology. Maddy was sure the media had been hounding him all day—she'd seen footage of him getting into his pickup and driving away from base last night with a bunch of photographers taking photos of him. He didn't look too happy to see them.

But Tom was more concerned about her: "*Are you okay? Is there any-thing I can do?*"

"*I'm fine, Tom,*" she had written. And left it at that.

She was also concerned about Jacks. Even though he seemed to believe her that Tom was just a friend, he still had an edge, an edge that, she realized, had been growing in him over recent months. Whenever it was almost too much, Jacks seemed to pull back just in time. Become old Jackson again. The one she felt so calm around, the one who could still turn her into a silly, Angelstruck girl.

A voice came from Maddy's side. "You must be Maddy. I'm Rachel," a young woman said. She was wearing a matching lavender skirt and top. She was blushing. "I'm the event producer, and I just want to thank you so much for coming. Have you been to the sculpture garden before? What's your favorite piece?"

A photographer came up to take some photos, and a few other people at the event stepped closer, curious to hear Maddy's response. Out of the corner of her eye, Maddy saw Darcy eyeing her.

"I . . ." Her mind was going blank.

Maddy stood there, her mouth agape for a moment.

"What I mean is . . ." she said, her words growing faint. But it wasn't because of the question.

"Maddy?" Rachel said. "Are you okay?"

But Rachel's voice was already somehow distant, in some other world. It was like Maddy was going through a tunnel.

Maddy's mind suddenly was overtaken by the clearest of images snapping into focus: the instrument panel in the cockpit of a small jet. The digital screens were crisp. And flashing red. The numbers on the screens were fluctuating wildly. And then out the window. The emerald-blue water. Rushing toward the glass, impossibly fast. It took her breath away.

Maddy saw the water strike the cabin. She saw the nose crumple toward the pilot. There was no time to see more.

The Gulfstream jet disintegrated against the water surface just as surely as if it had been striking concrete.

A spray of water and plane. And body parts.

Maddy was there as it happened, with pity and fear as instant death took the man.

She instantly knew the frequency. That energy, that aloof entitlement. It was now revealed for what it really was: cowardice. She saw the man's eyes, long tunnels with ghosts in them. Then the image widened out, and she saw the bloated, flushed face.

Maddy's eyes shot open, a shriek having just left her lips. Rachel and Darcy and others were standing near her. *Are you all right? Are you all right?* Their voices still seemed far off. Blood roared in Maddy's ears.

She'd seen the face of Jeffrey Rosenberg.

# CHAPTER THIRTY

In the sudden rush of adrenaline, extending her wings didn't hurt nearly as much as it had prior times. The oblong wings reached out, then crouched in toward her body, coiled, ready. Their purplish luminescence pulsed with the rush. Even now they felt like before, like something attached to her body, instead of entirely part of it. Like wearing a very large backpack that, impossibly, seemed to weigh almost nothing.

People in the sculpture garden were speechless, their mouths open in shock.

Maddy crouched, leaning slightly forward as she had been trained. She made a move as if to jump straight up into the air. As she did, she felt the wings flex, with a tremendous *whoosh* of air that blew back her ponytail and whipped her loose hair around her face. She felt her shoes leave the ground. When she looked down, she saw the museum receding until it was no more than a toy box, the cars winking sunlight up at her. Her necklace snapped wildly around her neck. Her heart hammered relentlessly in her chest, and she fought to breathe against the rush of the air as her wings pushed her into the unblemished sky.

Less than graceful, she leveled off and beat her wings furiously against the sky. Below, the world looked suddenly calm and silent. The only sound was the rush of air in her ears. She thought of her training with Tom. It was all for this.

Within a minute, the beach came into view, with the Angel mansions crowded against it. The impressive homes seemed small now, like mere toys. The sunbathers and volleyball players were now as small and insignificant as ants.

The black cruciform of her Angelic shadow flew along the sand of the beach, and in seconds, Maddy was soaring over the Pacific Ocean. She swept her wings back, picking up as much speed as she could with her wings, and squinted into the distance. She could see nothing but brilliant, untarnished blue. It was even hard to tell where the sky ended and the ocean began. Her eyes darted wildly along the horizon, burning in the brilliant glare of the sun, scouring the distance for something, anything.

Then she saw it.

The Gulfstream G4, inbound to the Santa Monica Airport. A plane, Maddy knew, that would soon be at the bottom of the ocean.

Suddenly the private jet banked wildly and climbed, all at once, for a brief moment before stalling into a nosedive. The plane was spinning as it descended, and Maddy had to dive directly down to catch up with it. Her hair tie was long gone. He hair lashed at her face now, but she didn't have time to bother with it. It was all happening so fast.

Her shoes touched the metal of the wing, but the plane was spinning, and the wing turned over and over before she realized what was happening. Maddy clutched the wingtip, her wings flailing to regain control of herself. She felt strength she'd never imagined coursing through her veins, every fiber of her being turning to Angel instinct.

Black smoke began pouring from one of the engines. She'd have to move fast.

Inside, oil billionaire Jeffery Rosenberg was already passed out in the cockpit, his body hunched over the wheel, causing the plane to spin wildly out of control. Maddy grabbed the handle on the cabin door and tore at it with all her strength. The exertion sent pain searing through her arms, but the door ripped free of its hinges with a groan and in an instant was gone into the clear blue sky.

*Wow.* Maddy had of course been taught about the increase in strength and ability during a save, but since an Angel only experiences it during a real save situation, there had been no way to train for it except through simulation. She was surprised that it was both easier and much more difficult than the computer simulations.

Hooking her feet and hands around the doorframe, Maddy thrust herself inside the cabin of the jet with a single, powerful burst of strength. Another hot dagger of pain raced down her back as her wings banged against the top of the doorframe.

*I left my wings out.* She retracted the throbbing wings and looked around, holding on to anything she could in the depressurized cabin. Wind violently smacked at her face. Debris of every kind was tearing loose from the cabin's interior and rocketing past Maddy's head. She made her way up the aisle and reached the flight deck in one swift move.

Maddy discovered Rosenberg in the cockpit, slumped out of his chair and hanging by his seatbelt like a morbid marionette, his face a mask of pain. He appeared to have put on at least fifteen pounds since Maddy had met with him just after her Commissioning, which almost seemed impossible.

His lifestyle was going to kill him sooner than he'd thought.

*I didn't want one that's half.*

She remembered the man's words, spoken arrogantly and with a wave of his hand, as he answered e-mails on his smartphone.

Now the words rang in Maddy's ear as she snapped the seatbelt with her bare hands and pulled Rosenberg's prodigious mass out of the chair. She glanced out the window and saw the white caps of Santa Monica Bay rushing up at them. She had six seconds at most. Maybe less. Threading her hands under the man's arms, Maddy dragged him down the aisle and toward the cabin door as the airframe spun and shook uncontrollably around them. She glanced out another window and saw only churning ocean.

*Three seconds.*

Then Maddy saw her, crouched against the seat, her eyes a blaze of terror: it was Rosenberg's assistant. The one Maddy had met as well.

The girl was going to die.

Before she knew what was happening, Maddy had freed one hand and extended it forward inside the cabin.

She cried out in terrible pain, using every fiber of her Angel being. She didn't know if she'd be able to do it. Time manipulation had never been her strong suit, after all.

Suddenly the water outside the jet, merely fifty feet away, stopped. The jet didn't get any closer. The whitecaps froze in place, droplets of seawater splashed up and froze just above the ocean surface. Maddy grunted in concentration, her body shaking and convulsing as she attempted to maintain the local time bend using the technique Susan had taught her. She was doing it!

In a moment Maddy was by the girl's side, scooping the terrorized assistant up from the floor and over her shoulder. Then, as if in a flash, she was at the door with both Rosenberg and his assistant. The local time bend was starting to shimmer and shudder, Maddy losing concentration.

*Come on, just two more seconds, come on, come on.*

With an audible growl, Maddy shoved Rosenberg through the gaping cabin door and onto the wing. She jerked the assistant out the door and gathered the girl under her arm.

Maddy paused only a moment to look at the fast-approaching water as her local time bend began to dissipate. The waves suddenly began rolling across the ocean, the screaming of the diving jet taking over all sound as they careened to doom. A feeling bloomed in Maddy's stomach that she hadn't yet felt during the save. It crept up through her chest and sat tingling in the back of her throat.

*Fear.* Maddy crouched, exploded off the wing, and rocketed directly skyward as the Gulfstream slammed into the Pacific Ocean. The impact ignited the fuel tank, incinerating the plane as it twisted and shattered with a terrible metal shriek. Maddy glided back toward the coast, Rosenberg still over her shoulder, the girl under her arm. A single thought echoed in Maddy Montgomery Godright's mind as she touched down on the Santa Monica Pier.

*That was close.*


Rosenberg regained consciousness lying comfortably on a stretcher, paramedics tending to him, tourists and onlookers crowding around. He squinted up at Maddy, the pier's Ferris wheel spinning in the background behind him.

"You gave us a scare," Maddy said.

The man looked all around, struggling to put the fragmented pieces of his memory together. "What happ—who are you?" Then he gazed into Maddy's face again, and recognition flashed across his eyes.

"My God. It's you."

Maddy smiled. "Were you expecting someone else?"

"No, I just . . . I just never thought it would happen to me."

"No one does. It was a heart attack. Minor. You're going to be fine.

My Archangel will be contacting you tomorrow to debrief you. Until then, rest easy. They've contacted your family to let them know you're okay."

Rosenberg's face turned ashen. "Lauren," he said gravely. "I . . . I killed her. She was on the plane."

Maddy nodded to their right. Rosenberg looked over and saw his assistant, sitting, covered in a blanket and talking to a Santa Monica paramedic.

"Lauren?" he said, confused. "You're alive?"

He looked at Maddy.

"How . . . ?"

An ambiguous look crossed Maddy's face. "I just had to," she said. "What's . . . done is done. It can't be changed now."

Maddy's mind spun dizzily as she realized she'd just made an illegal save.

The onlookers had grown to an excited crowd. Dozens of cell phone cameras clicked, capturing Maddy *postsave*. Fans screamed as the cameras snapped. A team of Santa Monica police arrived and did their best to hold the crowd back.

"Maddy's first save! Maddy's first save!" some of the onlookers shouted, taking more pictures, unable to believe their good luck in witnessing the historic occasion.

The photos were doubtlessly already being picked up by blogs and news outlets around the world. A strange, inevitable panic entered Maddy. They were taking pictures of Maddy with her Protection, Jeffrey Rosenberg. And his assistant, Lauren. Not her Protection. An illegal save.

"You know what my last thought was?" Rosenberg stammered, his mind reeling with the memory. "I remember thinking, *This is it. This is how I die.*"

The man had tears in his eyes.

"You saved my life . . . and Lauren's."

"Yes, I did," Maddy said, surprised at the emotion coming out of Rosenberg. She'd read his frequency the moment he came into the conference room at the NAS, and she hadn't felt this.

The hot liquid spilled from his eyes, running down his ample cheeks.

Maddy walked over to Rosenberg's assistant.

"How are you?" Maddy asked awkwardly. Lauren looked at her with wide eyes. She was still shaking. The girl knew she should be dead.

"I—I didn't have protection," Lauren stammered. "How did you save me?"

Maddy felt her face screw into an inscrutable mask. Hot tears rushed up toward her eyes. She turned away, looking off the end of the pier to the shimmering blue ocean, which would have been Lauren's unmarked watery grave, her body trapped in the twisted and incinerated jet. Maddy remained silent.

"God bless you," Lauren said, weeping.

Maddy looked over at Lauren, and then to Rosenberg. "God already did."

The crowd was getting more boisterous as word spread that Maddy was on the pier with her first saves. More pictures, more tweets, more Facebook updates—and inevitably more questions about how she saved someone who wasn't a Protection. "But I need to go now."

Applause rose from the crowd. A woman in the front row dabbed at her eyes with a tissue, and a man next to her gave Maddy a hearty thumbs-up. Maddy deployed her wings and, to the thrill of her audience, rocketed elegantly and effortlessly into the cloudless sky.

Soon the pier floated away underneath her, becoming smaller and smaller, set against the vast blue of the ocean.

• • •

Wings spread and taut, Maddy soared back toward Angel City. A cool breeze had picked up, and she floated along the slipstream. Maddy tried to take a deep breath of the cool air. The true enormity of what she had done started to hit her. An *unsanctioned save*. A numb terror crept into her bones as she thought about the Angel Disciplinary Council Agents in their black uniforms, ruthless in their pursuit. They'd be after her, and they would cut off her wings. There seemed to be no way she'd be able to escape them. Maddy figured that if the Angel Disciplinary Council were going to come for her, she may as well make it easy for them by flying. They could have her within seconds if they wanted to. She wouldn't stand a chance. Soon she was over Beverly Hills and could see the enormous black shiny box that was the NAS headquarters.

As she flew ever closer to Angel City proper, Maddy's body began shaking. An unsanctioned save. Punishable by wing removal. And mortalization. Though Maddy figured she probably wasn't Immortal anyway, being only half-Angel. *Funny*, she thought semihysterically, *that was one question that hadn't been addressed in training.*

*Her wings.*

Maddy realized how much she'd actually come to love them, how they really had become part of her. Part of her full identity. For the first time in her life she'd really felt complete, she realized. Her mind cast back to the terrible nightmare of them being monstrous and deformed, and instead how beautiful and perfect they really were when they finally emerged.

And now her wings were going to be taken away in a merciless disciplinary action.

With a shudder, she wondered how badly it would hurt.

But after a few more minutes of flying, Maddy realized curiously that no one was coming. No ADC agents. She had the skies to herself.

Looking off into the distance, Maddy set her course for the Angel City sign and thrust her wings to gain speed.

Maddy landed a couple of blocks away from Kevin's Diner so she wouldn't be spotted by any photographers. She dropped into someone's backyard. The little dog tied up in the back began yipping ecstatically as soon as he saw Maddy land, tugging against his lead.

"Shhh," Maddy said to the dog, putting her finger to her lips before quietly slipping out onto the street.

# CHAPTER THIRTY-ONE

She was soon outside Kevin's. Partially hiding from across the street, she watched the block for a few minutes, monitoring to see whether anyone who looked like one of the disciplinary agents was lingering around. She also anxiously kept casting her eyes to the sky, adrenaline pumping in her veins, convinced that the ADC was going to come any moment to shear away her wings as punishment for her unsanctioned save. But everything still looked safe outside the house.

*Where were they? Were they just toying with her?* Part of her just wanted to cry. But she stopped herself.

Maddy slipped in the side door of the diner and then through the backyard to the house. Finally, she was able to take a breath, although her hands were still shaking in fear of what was going to happen. She had broken the rules. Consequences must be paid. She leaned against the kitchen counter in the familiar setting for a moment, just breathing.

After searching for a bit, Maddy found the cordless phone handset smashed between the couch cushions—Uncle Kevin still had a landline.

She dialed Jackson's cell phone number. No answer. She left a voicemail, telling him to pick up when she called from the landline number. After a minute, she dialed again. No answer. What was he doing? She needed him now, more than ever.

She dialed again.

Still no answer.

Maddy put on an old shirt from her upstairs closet to replace the blouse that was now shredded in the back from her wings, and then went in the back of the diner. She crept up to the kitchen and looked in.

"Maddy!" her uncle said, relief spreading across his face. She could hear the TV in the dining room breathlessly reporting details of her save.

"Just a second." Kevin undid his apron and hung it on a hook just outside the kitchen. He walked into the living room. Maddy peered out and saw him flip the OPEN sign to CLOSED. There was only one table with customers, and they were just paying the bill. They quickly stood up and left.

Maddy looked cautiously out into the parking lot to see if any suspicious characters were outside, but the coast still seemed clear. She walked into the dining room and sat down in her favorite booth, near the back where no one could see her inside. Jana looked at her with big eyes.

"Go ahead and take the rest of the night off, Jana," Kevin said.

The wide-eyed waitress mutely nodded and disappeared to the back, her pumps squeaking on the linoleum.

The Magnavox was playing footage of Maddy's save.

The bottom of the right-hand corner of the screen read: "Courtesy of SaveTube." Maddy was shocked to find it was raw footage from her Angelcam.

*"The controversy continues to grow, threatening now to explode. Angels: saving us, or letting us die? Operatives from an unspecified activist group hacked the Angelcam system this afternoon and immediately released unedited footage of Guardian Maddy Godright saving both a Protection and a non-Protection in a thrilling, spectacular save off the coast of Santa Monica today. So far, no comment from the NAS, but the furor grows across the country."*

It felt uncanny to Maddy as she watched the firsthand footage of herself making the save. It all seemed so quick: the ocean hurtling toward them through the window on the flight deck, Rosenberg's unconscious face, Lauren crouched between the seats, the orange fireball as the Gulfstream morphed into incinerated gas, metal, and nothingness.

Kevin brought two mugs of coffee over and settled into the booth with Maddy. He glanced out to where paparazzi waited on the other side of the street.

"I just couldn't," she said, looking into Kevin's eyes. "I just couldn't leave her behind."

The door chimed, and both Kevin and Maddy turned their heads to the door. To her astonishment, it was Tom.

"Tom," Maddy breathed the name. She was surprised to find relief heavy in her voice.

"I came as soon as I heard what happened," he said, walking in tentatively and nodding to Kevin in that formal yet friendly way he seemed to do everything. "Are you okay?"

"I think so," Maddy said, emotion starting to well within her with the realization of what she'd done. She looked up at Tom with terrified eyes. "They haven't . . . come for me yet. For my wings."

"We won't let them do that," Tom said, exchanging a look with Uncle Kevin. "There's no way they'd be able to anyway: you're just too big, Maddy."

"What?" Maddy said.

"Your save is everywhere. Everyone knows what you did. There's no way the NAS could politically risk coming after you," Tom said.

"He's right," Kevin said. "You know they would have been here already. Remember last time? They were everywhere."

"I don't know . . ." Maddy said, her mind still submerged in fear of the agents in their futuristic black armor. She still remembered the ruthless grip on her throat in Kevin's living room. The unblinking, pitiless eyes behind the mask.

Tom sat down in the booth next to Maddy, opposite her uncle.

Kevin stood up. "I'll get another cup of coffee."

Tom turned to her.

"Maddy, I saw your flying. You were amazing," Tom said quietly.

The report on the television continued.

*"A statement from the White House said there will be a quick investigation into the day's events and that, quote, 'action will be swift.' President Linden won the election as a third-party candidate on an anti-Angel platform, and experts expect the new president to take this opportunity to push forward his mandate."*

"I would've let her die," Maddy said, shaking her head. "That's what they would have wanted me to do." A sick feeling was in her stomach. "What's happened to me?"

Tom had been silent, just letting her talk. He put a calming hand on her shoulder. Then it felt so natural for Maddy to lean her head against his shoulder. She could feel the pilot's body just next to her rise and fall with each breath.

"But you didn't let her die. That's what separates us from them, Maddy."

"Us?"

The door jingled again. Her head still against Tom's shoulder, Maddy's eyes drifted to the door.

It was Jacks.

He looked directly at Maddy with her head on Tom's shoulder, a strange expression crossing his face.

"Jacks!" Maddy said, sitting up. She could feel Tom stiffening next to her, his body coiling up in a defensive posture.

The Angel walked further into the diner, his eyes moving coolly back and forth between Tom and Maddy.

"*What. Are. You. Doing?*" Jacks asked, his neck muscles tensing and releasing.

"She's upset. I was comforting her," Tom said.

"Nobody was asking you," Jacks said.

"He just got here, Jacks," Maddy said. "It's not—"

"What is it then?" he said.

Maddy just shook her head, silently. This was the worst thing that could have happened.

Tom turned and looked at Maddy. "Are you okay? Being here with him?" Maddy put her head in her hands but nodded. "I'm going to leave then. You need to resolve some . . . things. If you need anything, you know where to find me."

"You don't have to go, it's fine—" Maddy was clutching for straws.

Tom smiled grimly. "No, I can tell when I'm not welcome."

"Don't, Tom—you're always welcome," Maddy said. "I'm sorry, it's all just complicated right now."

"Nothing to be sorry for. We can't all be Angels," he said.

"That's not what—"

Tom passed closely by Jacks as he walked to the exit. The Angel and the pilot stiffened as they neared each other.

"You might want to appreciate what you have, rather than take it for granted like everything else in your life," Tom said, mere inches from Jackson's face. The door jingled, and he was gone. The muted, deep rumble of his pickup entered the diner and then slowly faded.

Maddy looked at the Angel in front of her. "Jacks, don't start."

The report on the TV continued. They were replaying Maddy's unsanctioned save on loop.

Jacks glanced up at the TV, then down at Maddy. "Do you know what you've done?"

"I was able to save her. How could I let her die?" Maddy said. "Jacks, I did the same thing you did with me last year."

"It's different."

"How? How is it different?"

"I don't know. It just is," he said.

"I had to save her," Maddy said, shaking her head. Lauren's terrified eyes still haunted her memory. Maddy glanced out the window to the parking lot. "Why aren't they here yet?"

"I don't know. The agents should have been here by now," Jacks said. "With me, they were able to spin the story. Turn me into a villain. Nobody saw what actually happened. There's no spinning now for you. The Angelcam footage was out instantly, everybody knows what happened, and that she wasn't a Protection. If anything happened to you, the uproar would be unforgettable. 'Punished for saving a life.' And the Archangels and the Council, their backs are against the wall. President Linden was looking for anything, any excuse to show that Protection for Pay isn't necessary. That Guardians could be saving anyone out there, that we Angels are supposedly in it only for profit and power, and that we don't care who lives or dies as long as we're paid. Any reason he could get to make a move against us. And you handed it to him on a silver platter."

"But I couldn't leave her. How could we let them die? We could save all of them!"

Jacks snapped with anger. "You may be right. But don't act naive, Maddy! Where do you think it all comes from? Your apartment? Your car? The clothes you wear for the photographers? From nowhere? That you get it for just being you? It comes from Protection for Pay. Pure and simple."

His words cut Maddy deep, like a jagged knife, but she knew they were true. She knew they'd been true for a while. Maddy felt the ground underneath her start to crumble, her sense of self shaken to the very core.

She'd let herself be transformed into the very rich and famous Angel she had once hated.

"I may not even like it. But that's just the way things are," Jacks said bitterly.

Anger and shame loosed Maddy's tongue as she turned on Jacks.

"You talked me into it, Jacks, you brought me along—"

"I'm tired of hearing that, Maddy. You knew what you were doing when you became a Guardian!"

"I did not. You told me it could change!"

"Well, maybe I was wrong," Jacks said.

Silence hung in the large dining room. Orange evening sun was filtering through trees across the street, starting to steam into the front windows of the diner.

Maddy reached for Jacks's hand. The warmth and smoothness of his fingers gave her some comfort. But only momentarily, before he pulled his hand away.

He turned and looked at her, his perfect Immortal features rimmed by the fading sunlight glinting through the window.

"Originally, I was coming to find you here for another reason, Maddy," he said. "It seems almost stupid now."

"What reason?" Maddy asked.

Jacks looked away. He didn't speak for a few moments. And when he did, it sounded like his words were carefully chosen.

"It's my wings," he said deliberately. "The Archangels have found a way for me to fly again."

"What? How?" Maddy asked in disbelief. "That's amazing!"

"There's a new technology. My wings will be part natural, and part . . . metal or something. They've developed the technology for strategic uses. I'm going to become a Battle Angel."

"What technology? I don't understand, Jacks."

"Apparently they've been developing it for years. I was trying to tell you the other day, but you weren't listening to me."

"Jacks, I—" Maddy said.

"Just like you haven't been there for me the past few months," Jacks continued.

Maddy's face burned. She knew he was somewhat right.

"The procedure is happening next week," Jacks said. He looked out the window as brazen red streaks from the sunset cut across the Angel City sky and then turned to Maddy, his eyes glinting in the light. "Maddy, I'll be able to fly again."

# CHAPTER THIRTY-TWO

As Sylvester sat down, he examined the marble frieze that ran around the four walls of the domed hall. Light knifed down from a narrow skylight at the top of the dome, dust motes dancing in the stark sunbeams. The beams glared on the polished marble floor. The frieze, a wide horizontal band running the length of the walls, was stunning in its detail and artistry. In marble relief, it showed the ancient stages of the Angels' history and scenes from the Bible. It also depicted other moments in Angel history that humans would never have known about. There was Greek text under each of the scenes.

One section of the frieze, which was carved in deep red marble and had been restored from an ancient Angel ziggurat, had a language Sylvester had never even seen. He recognized the scene, though: the epic final battle of the Angels over the Dark Angels, who had just become demons. What had started as a civil war had quickly turned into an all-out struggle for Angel survival. Those rebelling, the fallen Immortals, had become grotesque, distorted, and demonic, and obsessed with destroying Angelkind. Untold amounts of Angel blood had been spilled in the Demon Struggles.

The panel showed an Angel in full battle dress plunging the tip of a blessed battle sword into the heart of a demon. Whoever the artist was, he had been extremely meticulous in creating the detailed flame that actually *was* the demon. Sylvester was impressed with his level of skill. And dedication. It must have taken years, just that small section.

His eyes took in the whole scene. He was alone in the expansive hall, waiting.

He had never been here before, but then again, not many had. Not many Angels even knew this place existed, although of course they had heard rumors. This temple had been carved deep out of the earth over a century before. The light high above came from a latticed and intricate skylight at ground level.

The detective coughed. It echoed loudly throughout the marble hall. Reaching in the pocket of his old overcoat, he extracted a throat lozenge and popped it in his mouth.

Soon he heard footsteps. An almost ethereal young Angel woman appeared, walking across the hall. Her skin was milky, almost translucent, her hair so blond it was nearly white, and her eyes a ghostly blue. She wore a strangely modern robe, its golden threaded detail along the seams gleaming as she passed through a beam of light from above.

"The Council will now see you . . . Detective Sylvester."

"Thank you."

Detective Sylvester stood up, picking up his thick folder full of documents, photos, and testimonies. Smoothing his overcoat, he followed the Angel woman across the hall toward two large double oak doors. Each door had a long, black iron handle. She pulled them at the same time. The doors creaked as they swung open, revealing to Detective Sylvester a chapel—he had seen footage of it this year during Maddy's

Commissioning. Thick Grecian columns ran the length of the room, and in the center was a table, shimmering under the candlelight. The Council of Twelve sat around it. Sylvester's breath caught in his throat as he saw the resplendent Twelve, those original Archangels who had brought Angels out of hiding, established Angel City, and founded the entire system on which the Angels ran today.

"David Sylvester," the Angel woman announced before retreating. She closed the doors behind her.

"Welcome, David. Please, approach." The voice was distinctive and authoritative. Gabriel's. He sat at the center of the table, wearing a golden robe that seemed to glow all on its own. He had surprisingly youthful features for the sleek mass of trademark white hair atop his head. Archangel Mark Godspeed sat to the side of Gabriel. He was wearing his normal uniform of designer suit and sharp tie. He had gotten Sylvester the meeting after the detective's heads-up on the Churchson bombing scandal. Godspeed owed him one.

Walking forward, Sylvester had more of an opportunity to see the room. On the opposite wall were two enormous flat-screen TVs built into the marble walls of the private chapel of the Council. Closed-captioned news footage of President Linden's inauguration, as well as Maddy's unsanctioned save, was playing on the TVs. All the corners of the room hid in shadows. The Council watched him as he approached.

Gabriel studied Sylvester with his piercingly sharp eyes before speaking.

"Mark says you know something of importance that may affect the very existence of Angels." He looked at Mark beside him. "It is to him you owe this extraordinary audience with us."

"Thank you," Sylvester said. He polished his glasses on his shirt. "I will get straight to the point. It is my belief that Dark Angels are emerging at a greater and greater rate across the planet. That incidents of death and destruction around the globe have been caused by these demons. I've uncovered dozens of cases that could be linked to these demons." He held the manila folder aloft. "The crack created last year has led to this—they were waiting some time for an opening between their world and ours. For an opportunity. In fact, according to my reading of *The Book of Angels*, I believe demons have spotted their chance first to conquer humanity, and then to overtake Angels and replace them on earth as the dominant supernatural power. It is only a matter of time before the war begins. The war between good and evil."

The detective's words hung in the chapel air. The members of the Council remained silent in their beautiful finery and golden robes. They eyed the detective. Gabriel's gaze remained unwavering on Sylvester.

"Detective," Gabriel's voice was full and slow, magnificent, "you are aware of what's happening right now?" Gabriel nodded to the large screens playing footage of President Linden and the scandal surrounding Maddy's save of Lauren.

"Yes," Sylvester said. "Of course."

"Good. Then you will understand how precarious of a position we are in at this moment," Gabriel said. "The humans are turning against us, their very benefactors. We stand, in short, at a crisis. It is imperative we maintain our rightful place, here, in Angel City, on earth. This threat from the humans is real. It is before us right now. This instant."

Gabriel continued. "Even if we were to believe your hypothesis about the demons emerging, have these Dark ones been harming Angels? It seems in all these cases, humans have been perishing. Not our kind."

Sylvester attempted to control his frustration. He motioned to the thick folder in his hand. "I've seen some of it firsthand myself. The death and destruction. And if you look at these documents, you'll see it's much more than just a hypothesis."

Gabriel nodded, understandingly. "You may be surprised to

know that we are already quite aware of some of your so-called demon incidents."

"And you've done nothing?" Sylvester said, in shock. Mark's face showed he was also surprised by the revelation that the Council might have known demons were operating at will on earth already.

"Although they may betoken the presence of demons," Gabriel said, "we see no evidence they mean to turn on us."

"But you can't believe they won't—"

"We can believe a lot of things. What would you have us do? Ferret out the Dark Angels one by one? There is no surer way to goad them into turning their focus on us. You forget that we Twelve have dipped our swords in demon blood. It is not something we would relish again unless absolutely necessary."

Sylvester stared at the Council in their glowing robes. "The humans won't stand a chance."

A sardonic grin appeared on the edges of Gabriel's mouth. "Humans? As we speak, David, the humans are turning against us in an enormous case of ingratitude and arrogance. The very existence of our way of life is at stake. Once again we have been disappointed by mankind."

Mark looked at Sylvester with regret in his eyes, as if to say he'd done his best.

"That is all, thank you," Gabriel said.

Sylvester stood there, bitterly gritting his teeth. Gabriel turned and began quietly speaking to Uriah, the Council Archangel to his left. Sylvester stood rooted to his spot. Gabriel looked up at the detective, as if at an annoying child.

"*That is all*, detective."

# CHAPTER THIRTY-THREE

Linden had set a press conference for the evening of the day after Maddy's save. The Angels were remaining quiet. No one knew what was going to happen, and a strange stillness hung across the city. Most of the day, Maddy stayed in her old room at Uncle Kevin's, the last bastion of calmness in a world rocked by her unsanctioned save of someone who wasn't a Protection.

Eventually Maddy decided to go out. She could at least go to her apartment and get some of her things to bring back to her uncle's. She felt like staying at Kevin's for a while for some reason. It just seemed more comfortable for her.

A small armada of paparazzi and supporters parted as Maddy drove into the parking garage of her apartment building off the Halo Strip. Some of the fans had signs that read "SAVE ME MADDY!" spurred by the dream that they too could be saved, now without even being a Protection.

Maddy put on her biggest pair of sunglasses and just stared straight ahead as she pressed her way through the churning madness of photographers and fans.

Once she finally made it into her apartment, Maddy breathed a sigh of relief and put the keys down on the side table. She sat on the couch, its fine leather squishing underneath her as she sunk into it.

Maddy's eyes slowly scanned the luxury apartment, the designer furniture, the glossy black granite countertops. Her gaze moved out the window to the bird's-eye view of thrumming Immortal City beyond the floor-to-ceiling glass. A gray marine layer still hung in the sky, sending a dim cast over the city. Her eyes passed to the open bedroom door, to the closet door that wouldn't close because of all her Angel clothes inside it. On the wall was a framed copy of her first magazine cover, for *Angels Weekly*. On the cover, Maddy looked confidently into the camera. *I'm here*, she seemed to say. *I have arrived.*

And for what? Her mind flashed back to the terrified eyes of Rosenberg's assistant, Lauren. Her eyes as she thought she was about to die. And her automatic acceptance of how Maddy was just going to let her. The face of death. How could Maddy have been so blind? She had forgotten her own commitment. What had drawn her to Guardianship in the first place. It wasn't Jackson's fault. It was her own.

She suddenly felt very miserable indeed.

Maddy picked up her cell phone and scrolled through the contacts. He picked up on the second ring.

"Hello?"

"I didn't know who else to call," Maddy said, embarrassed, into the phone.

"I'll be right over," Tom said.

And he was. Twenty minutes later there was a knock at the door, and Tom was standing there.

"Hi," Maddy said quietly.

"Hi," Tom said. He lifted up a bag. "I came up through the back entrance. And I brought you some food. I hope you don't mind Chinese. It was the only thing I saw on the way."

Maddy realized with a shock that she hadn't really eaten anything all day. Tom really was thoughtful. "Thanks," she said. "I guess I should try to eat."

"You're not going to do anyone any good if you starve to death," Tom said. He pulled a plate from the cupboard and scooped some vegetable noodles out of the takeout containers. "The navy trained us to always make sure you've eaten. No matter what's going on."

Maddy took the plate of steaming food. She managed to take a bite or two before putting it to the side.

"I'm sorry about yesterday," Maddy said miserably.

"No apologies," Tom said. "Can we agree on that?"

"Okay," Maddy said. "No apologies."

"He—I mean, Jacks—didn't seem too happy," Tom said. The pilot looked over at Maddy.

"No, he wasn't," she said. "It's just so . . . complicated." Maddy kept her eyes down. "The whole reason I became a Guardian was for an idea—the idea that those who *can* protect those who *can't* protect themselves. Somehow along the way I forgot that." She looked out on the darkening Angel City through the window. "And now everything is changing. I don't know what's going to happen."

"Nobody can predict the future," Tom said.

"He says it's my fault." Maddy glanced up, looking into Tom's eyes.

"It's not," Tom said, suddenly upset. "Because Jacks can never see things the way you and I do. He doesn't understand what it's like. He doesn't understand looking into your eyes and seeing the hurt, and the confusion, lurking behind . . . this beautiful, confident woman. He has no idea, he's just an Angel." Suddenly, like magnets drawn together, they were just inches away from each other. "I can see it, though." She could almost feel his body heat radiating from his skin.

With a shock, Maddy suddenly realized her eyes were closing, and the heat of Tom's breath was tickling her lips. And then his mouth was on hers. Without thinking, she pulled him in, closer, tighter, her lips pressing hard against his as she welcomed the kiss.

After a moment, they both drew back. Her breath was coming hard and shallow. She tried to look into his eyes, but in lifting her chin, her mouth brushed his, and then his lips were against hers again, and as much as she tried to stop it, she wanted it. Wrapped her arms around him and threw herself into the kiss. His fingers laced through the hair at the nape of her neck. It was all she could do to draw back. He must have felt the force of the kiss fading, and her lips withdrawing, because he suddenly withdrew too. Maddy knew she couldn't be close to him any longer.

"We have to stop, please," she breathed.

With the last of her self-control, she backed away until her back hit the far wall, then she slid down the wall to her knees. Stunned.

"I'm sorry," he stammered, confused, "I didn't know that was going to happen." He looked around for his coat. "I should go."

"No, don't—" Maddy stuttered. "I don't know." She sighed. "You don't have to go."

Maddy slowly gathered herself and returned to the couch. As if sleepwalking, Tom sat down on the couch as well.

"I—it's not like I planned it or anything," Tom said, his face slightly burning. "I respect you too much to do that."

Maddy's mind was whirl of confusion. It was as if everything had suddenly flipped upside down in an instant. Everything she felt and believed. That she could have been so attracted to Tom that they suddenly fell into each other's arms.

It was like waking up in her home and suddenly discovering there was a whole other wing of it she'd never even known existed. And it'd been there the whole time. Maddy's world swam before her eyes. Everything she thought true and real was now turned and distorted. But what was the truth?

There was something about Tom that felt real. Solid, tangible, in the glimmering, transient tempest of the Immortal City, where if you were famous, someone always seemed to want something from you, all the time, always. Where you couldn't believe what you saw in front of you—it could simply be tricks of the camera. But the pilot next to her, she felt that he was *real*. She felt a connection to him, a kind that she hadn't felt before—no, not even with Jacks. Like he truly understood what she had gone through. And she realized she'd been feeling this for a while. She just hadn't realized it. And apparently he hadn't either.

"Tom, when we first started training together, why did you say you had to help me?" Maddy asked. "That you owed something to Professor Archson?"

Tom took a breath in. "To Susan? I can't . . . tell you, Maddy. Not now. It's more than I can get into. I will tell you sometime, I promise."

Maddy and Tom sat silently on the couch in the dark room, lit by the flickering blue of the TV in front of them. On screen, President Linden was about to give his press conference. As he neared the podium, he ran his right hand across the front of his suit jacket, smoothing it.

"Should we turn the volume up?" Tom asked.

The podium bore the new seal of the Global Angel Commission. Linden stood behind it, his lips moving but still muted. His hair was, as usual, perfect. The current sitting president of the United States stood behind him, off to the side, along with other global officials and their emissaries.

Maddy hit the button on the remote.

*"It is under the gravest of situations that I speak to you tonight. Many of you may not have agreed with my viewpoints in the past, and many of you may not have even voted for me. But I hope that we can all put our differences aside and agree, as Americans, and global citizens, that something has to be done about the Angel question. The shocking footage of yesterday's save by Guardian Madison Montgomery Godright confirms that abundantly. This save proves that the Angels' insistence on high fees and Protection for Pay is just a ruse, that they in fact can save more than one person at a time, and around the globe thousands are dying unnecessarily due to greed and manipulation by the NAS. Although we know very little about the Angels' methods or training, we have thought since President Grant's time that the Angels could only save a certain number of people. Protection for Pay was supposed to allocate who got saved— not cruelly, without conscience, let others die.*

*"While once we thought that we were the recipients of a great good, we now know that we have been the targets of a much greater deception. It is now, with my powers as president of the Global Angel Commission and president-elect of the United States, that I lead us in this difficult time. In a joint session, what has been known as the Immortals Bill has passed both houses of Congress just moments ago. Simultaneously, across the globe, leaders of the GAC countries have put into effect their own versions of the bill. The Immortals Bill makes the supernatural acts of flying, strength, and speed illegal, effective immediately.*

*"As of this moment, any Angel caught performing a supernatural act, regardless of purpose, will be subject to arrest and prosecution to the fullest extent of the law by federal marshals, duly appointed local police officers, or members of the military. Flagrant offenses may result in the loss of wings.*

*"Thank you, and God bless America."*

Without a further word, President Linden turned and walked away from the podium, flanked by his aides. The pressroom had erupted into a din of shouting and pandemonium on the part of the reporters.

The anchor back in the studio was in total shock, stuttering: "*I think, George, yes, I believe President Linden is done there. And I, uh, believe he just, well, he just* banned *Angel activities under his powers as world leader of the GAC. The Immortals Bill has been passed and signed. Is that what you heard? That's what we got back in the studio.*"

The black remote in Maddy's hand turned the TV back to mute. She and Tom looked at each other, silently. The light from the TV still danced across their faces in the dark.

"You did a great thing when you saved that girl, Maddy. A hard thing, but a great thing." Tom squeezed her hand tightly. But Maddy's hands still felt cold. In fact, her whole body felt a chill as she watched the chaos on the Angel City news station unfold silently on the TV. She slowly pulled her hand away. Tom's face flashed with disappointment.

"I'm sorry, I'm just confused," Maddy said.

"I didn't know, Maddy . . . what I felt for you," Tom said. "But how could I have been so blind?"

Maddy leaned forward on the couch and hugged her knees with her arms, her mind roaring with thoughts of Tom, and Jacks, and of the passing of the Immortals Bill.

Angel City would never be the same again. Forces had been put into play that she could not have imagined a year ago. She had wanted to change things with the Angels, but she had never dreamed it would go this way. This would harm Jacks, Kris, Chloe. *Jacks.* Jacks, who now had his wings back. And now was banned from using them.

Jacks. A spasm of terrible guilt passed through her as she realized what had just happened between her and Tom. Her own swirling, shifting feelings cascaded inside of her.

Maddy got up and went to the window, looking out at glittering Angel City far below. A steady rain had begun pounding the streets outside, and the bright lights of the glorious playground of the Angels smeared through the wet window.

She knew the Archangels and the Council wouldn't just sit back. They had too much to lose.

Maddy knew the Immortals would not just give in.

# CHAPTER THIRTY-FOUR

The next morning was bright and unbelievably clear, only the lightest white wisp of a cloud in the sky. The rain overnight had washed the Angel City streets clean and new and had drawn pollution out of the air, leaving the city feeling fresh. Maddy woke in her old bed at Uncle Kevin's, looking out the window. She had fallen asleep before drawing the blinds and was greeted by the Angel City sign, which used to meet her every morning.

Getting up out of bed, Maddy checked her phone: still nothing from Jacks. They hadn't had contact in two days, since he left the diner after her illegal save. She realized with a pain that this was the longest they'd gone without talking since they'd met.

Maddy stayed downstairs all morning, curled up on the couch in an old sweatshirt, drinking tea and watching the developments on Kevin's new TV. It kept her mind off Jacks. And Tom. There had been no official response from the NAS about the signing of the Immortals Bill, which seemed strange. The world was on the edge of its seat, waiting for a response from the Angels. The networks were still covering Maddy's save, and there were many interviews with Lauren, the girl whose life she had saved.

"*She's a real hero,*" Lauren said, tears in her eyes. "*She could've let me die like any other Angel would have, but she didn't.*"

The footage cut to a reporter standing across the street from Uncle Kevin's house. If Maddy would have opened the curtains, she would have seen herself appear in the image.

The reporter spoke: "*And 'hero' Maddy Godright still keeping quiet, today, two days after her electrifying save of both her Protection, billionaire Jeffrey Rosenberg, and her unsanctioned save of Lauren Donnell.*"

Footage showed Maddy, in sunglasses, driving her Audi into the parking garage at her apartment building. A thousand bulbs flashed as she drove slowly forward.

The reporter standing outside Uncle Kevin's house continued. "*Sources say she's keeping close to relatives and friends in this trying time, as we all wonder what will happen next.*"

All of a sudden, the footage awkwardly cut from the reporter back to the studio.

On ANN, a snowy-bearded anchor in the studio seemed unprepared for this development. He shuffled papers in front of him and looked into the camera.

"*We are, ahem, getting word that the Angels will be making a statement on President Linden's ban of all Angel activities. In an unprecedented move, the Council themselves are said to be delivering a statement. It's been forty years since the Council of Twelve has done anything public except for their annual endorsement of the nominees for Guardianship, or the very occasional odd appearance. And in the past twenty years, they've disappeared from the public eye almost entirely. And, yes, I'm getting word that we are getting a live feed right now via the NAS.*"

The picture on screen cut to a close shot within the larger chapel that the Angels had been in during the footage from the Commissioning. Dark marble Ionic columns ran along each side, a shaft of light falling somewhere from the ceiling upon a stark podium that had been placed in the center of the white marble floor. Instead of being seated, as the public was normally used to seeing them during Commissioning ceremonies, the Twelve were actually standing, as if to represent a united front. Their golden robes almost seemed connected in one glowing whole.

The graphic on the screen read: *LIVE—Council of Twelve Chapel.*

The anchor back in the studio whispered: *"It seems the Council is in the newer chapel. And it looks like Gabriel is walking to the podium. Let's listen in during what could be a historic moment for human- and Angelkind alike."*

One True Immortal stepped forward. It was, of course, Gabriel. He seemed even taller, more impressive than usual as he walked to the podium with the microphone. The Immortals behind him closed ranks, shoulder to shoulder, to fill the hole he left. Gabriel's piercing eyes and sharp features, framed by his famous white hair, looked straight into the camera.

He began speaking.

*"It is with true sadness that I have to stand here today. Unwarranted aggression, envy, and spite have brought us to this point. For almost 150 years we Angels have existed with humans in harmony, doing our divine duty: saving lives. Throughout, we have found a willing and reasonable partner in the United States government, which has always appreciated the invaluable services we provide.*

*"Recent developments have strained that bond to the breaking point. It is true that mistakes have been made. The deplorable behavior of Archangel Churchson shocked us on the Council as much as it surely did you.*

*And there is certainly room for . . . adjustments within the National Angel Services.*

*"But I am not lying when I say that this is not the way to help us reform. And we will not stand by as our divine rights are trampled upon by a newcomer president and his lackey Congress. We have been here far too long for that, I assure you.*

*"Thus it is with great reluctance, but also strong resolve, that I now say we will not allow any action to be taken against Angels. Retribution will be swift, effective, and immediate. We are a united front of supernatural stature. Humans have yet to see an Angel at war, but if President Linden and his Global Angel Commission have their way, they shall see one soon enough.*

*"Thank you. And good afternoon."*

The almost empty bowl of granola and yogurt Maddy was holding on her lap fell out of her hands. Her eyes were wide in total shock. The bowl rattled on the floor but didn't break.

On screen, Gabriel stepped back into the shadows toward his fellow Council members as they nodded in assent, his skin nearly luminescent. The footage from the chapel began to fade to black.

The bearded anchor back in the studio was in disbelief as they cut back to him, his mouth hanging wide open. *We're back on. Okay, we're back on. And, yes, an official statement from Gabriel and the Council of Twelve. And it seems . . . it seems, folks, that Gabriel just threatened some kind of Angel . . . military action against the government if the international ban is enforced. Marcy, can we confirm that with the NAS? Okay, yes, and you saw it here, Gabriel promising, quote, 'swift, effective, and immediate' retribution."*

Maddy's hand managed to find the remote and mute the TV. *An Angel war? What would that even look like?* Maddy asked herself.

Her iPhone buzzed on the table in front of her. Jacks was calling.

Maddy looked at the black vibrating phone like it was a snake about to bite her. Her mind raced immediately to what had happened with Tom the night before. After the second ring, she picked up.

Jackson's voice was serious, urgent. "I need to see you."

"Okay." She breathed the word out before she even knew it.

"Is there any way you can get out without being followed?"

Maddy peered through a crack in the brown curtains and saw the three-ring media circus still set up outside. "I don't know, maybe. They'll see my car."

"Slip out on foot. Meet me just up the hill on Ivar Avenue in twenty minutes."

Putting on an old pair of sweats and an even older hoodie, Maddy was able to walk straight out the front of the diner and sneak out the back of the parking lot between the bushes before anyone across the street noticed. Her pulse was beating harder and harder as she slipped onto a street parallel to Ivar and began walking a few blocks north, her sneakers crunching the fallen leaves underfoot.

Jacks's voice had been urgent, distraught: *I need to see you.*

What could he say?

Maddy didn't even know where her feet were taking her, they just kept moving. But as her feet moved, one after the other, she felt somehow as if they were leading her to some kind of destiny. The residential street was quiet in the early afternoon, and she didn't have too much trouble keeping herself unrecognized.

She reached the meeting point, slightly up the hill on the tree-lined street. She anxiously looked around, not seeing Jackson. Just a minute later, Jackson's cherry red Ferrari squealed to a stop next to her.

"Get in," Jacks said. Sunglasses hid his blue eyes as he opened the passenger door from the inside for her. Maddy got in the car and felt the six hundred horses roar under the engine as they peeled their way further up the street. After a little searching, Jacks found a dead end further up the hill and pulled to a stop. The engine died, and he stepped out of the car. Maddy soon followed.

Jacks stood there in a T-shirt and jeans, pacing back and forth at the end of the shabby road. It dead-ended to a guardrail, beyond which was grass and a gentle slope down to some houses below. No one was near. Jacks ripped the sunglasses off his face and looked at Maddy. Maddy had never seen his beautiful eyes set in such gaunt pain and anxiousness.

"You know the Council—" Jacks started.

"I saw," Maddy said sadly. "I saw Gabriel."

"So then you know . . . war is inevitable."

She looked at him uncertainly. "Does it have to be, Jacks?"

"Maddy, under the GAC ban, if you or I even *flew* right now, we could be taken by the police or military. Technically if we even had our *wings* out. Do you understand what that means? We can't be Angels. This is about Angel rights."

Jacks paced again, then stopped by Maddy's side.

"I came here for one reason and one reason only. To get you. I cut a deal. For you, Maddy. So you could stay with us. I can guarantee your safety. Amnesty with the Angels. The unsanctioned save forgotten."

Maddy was stunned. It took her a moment before she could find herself, but her response was sharp. "No one asked you to do that!"

"I knew you wouldn't. So I had to do it myself, I . . ." Jacks trailed off, leaning forward and putting his hand on the guardrail. Maddy came closer to Jacks. His energy, which she always felt so clearly, and which was normally so calm to her, was abrupt, scattered. She reached a light hand toward his muscular shoulder to calm the pain.

He turned at her touch, and before they knew it they were kissing, his lips smashing against hers in the overwhelming moment. Jacks locked Maddy in his strong arms and she pulled up against him, running her hand behind his neck.

She pulled back. "No, Jacks, I . . ."

Jacks looked at her incredulously. "What's wrong, Maddy?"

"Nothing's wrong." She ran the back of her hand across her lips. "Nothing's wrong, Jacks. I just need to think. It's hard to when we're doing . . . that."

"Maddy, I'm offering you a chance to be saved. To be safe with us. You have no idea what could happen," Jackson said darkly. "This is your chance."

She looked at the Angel she had loved for a year, his perfect features contorted with anguish as he looked down on her.

"A line has been drawn in the sand, Maddy. You belong on our side," he said. "There have been problems, but we can fix them. Together, Maddy. The Council and the Archangels are willing to do that. But humans are greedy, impatient, jealous. You belong on the side of good. On the side of Angels."

"But, Jacks . . . I don't know what side I'm on," Maddy said with doubt.

"Maddy, you swore to uphold the ideals of being a Guardian. You made an oath. Don't forget that!"

"But am I really an Angel? Or just an 'abomination'?"

She turned away, watching as a calico cat surreptitiously dashed across the empty street, its paws barely touching the asphalt.

Jacks walked toward Maddy, tiny pebbles crunching under his feet. He took her face in his hands. "Maddy, you are the best Angel I've ever seen. I watched the footage of your save. The skill there. There's no doubt in my mind: you have more Angel skill than they could ever imagine.

"Don't you see? Doesn't the Angel in you see? We can bring Angels to a new era—there must be reforms. But you're an Angel. They'll turn against you, the humans. You're too much of an Angel now."

"How do you know you're right, Jacks?" Maddy pulled away again, studying the grooves in the asphalt at her feet. "I finally realized what becoming a Guardian made me. What I had become. You tried to warn me, but I couldn't hear you. The whole time I thought I was somehow keeping true to my purpose, but I was getting further away. And I would have let her die for a fashion line and the cover of *Angels Weekly*." Maddy turned her face up to Jacks. It was a bitter mask of anger and regret.

"I don't love you because you're an Angel!" Jacks said. "I love you because you're Maddy. But you *are* an Angel now. It's no longer a choice. It's a fact."

He took Maddy's hands in his, and she felt the jolt of electricity, the same she had felt the first night they met, in the back of the diner.

"What would I have to do?" Maddy asked.

"Come over to our side, in support of the Angels." Jackson squeezed her hands in his. "I know it's difficult, almost unthinkable. But you have to make a decision: Do you stand with us or the mortals?"

Jackson was so close as he looked down at her, their hands clasped, that she could feel his intoxicating breath on her. His face was expectant. Waiting for an answer.

"I don't know, Jacks," Maddy finally said, breaking away. "I need to think . . . it's just . . . I need to think."

"We have only days, maybe only hours."

Maddy knew it was true. She nodded.

"I need until tomorrow morning. Can you give me until then?"

After sneaking back home—this time through the back door of the diner—Maddy went directly upstairs and shut herself in her room. She saw she had a missed call from Tom, but she just had to ignore it for the time being. Maybe forever.

The room was stuffy, almost confining. She threw open the window to let a breeze in as night began falling on the Immortal City, the street-lights slowly flickering on along the thousands of streets, one-by-one. Maddy took off her shoes and lay down on her bed, toes pointing to the ceiling. Her mind moved back and forth, back and forth, over the choice that Jacks had set before her. And she knew there was no sidestepping it. She had to make the decision. Whether right or wrong. She had to make it. Across Angel City, law enforcement and military were prepar-ing to do anything to stop Angels from breaking the law. And that could very well include her.

Raising her arm straight up above her, and then bending her wrist so her hand was parallel to the bed, she looked at the Divine Ring on her finger. As if it had its own energy source, it glowed. She pulled her father's Divine Ring from the hollow of her neck, where it hung on her mother's beautiful necklace that she now wore all the time. The two Divine Rings seemed to glow more strongly as they neared each other. Maddy had never noticed it before. She played with moving the rings back and forth, watching the glows change. Her father. What would he want her to do?

Maddy reached down, fishing for the Hermès bag that seemed to have replaced her old Jansport for a lot of things, including carrying books around. She found it and pulled out her father's old leather note-book Uncle Kevin had given her. She hadn't looked at it since she passed recommendation for Guardianship.

She flipped through the pages, marveling at the wide range of her father's knowledge, his passions, and his wittiness. For maybe the mil-lionth time, she wished to herself that somehow she could have gotten to know him. That they could have spent time together. Maddy had a strange feeling they'd have gotten along just fine.

Throughout the notebook were peppered little sayings or riddles

315

her father had inscribed. Just as she was about to put the notebook away, she came across one that caught her eye.

*Neither Angel nor Man Can Escape Their Destiny. That Is Both Their Gift and Their Curse.*

Closing the notebook, Maddy placed it on the side table and then looked for her phone.

# CHAPTER THIRTY-FIVE

The first light of day began creeping across the top of the hills, filtering onto Angel City, a purple glow that slowly grew, piercing the darkness in the still-sleeping metropolis. Fingers of red began peering over the ridges, casting Angel City in a luminous dawn light as the city slowly began to stir at its corners.

Maddy's Audi threaded its way along the still-dark Mulholland Drive, her headlights slashing around the dark corners as the rosy morning light began filtering from above. She had been up all night, her eyes red and weary as she drove along the windy road. She swerved to miss a jackrabbit that dashed in front of her wheels, and then was back on course. Maddy knew the way, almost by heart, although she hadn't driven it too many times. She and Jacks had needed a place they could go where they could be alone. There were too many eager eyes and photographers out there. They needed privacy.

Gravel crunched under her wheels as she pulled off to the side of the road. Maddy turned off the engine, and all was silent. Crickets still were chirping in the sparse underbrush, although a chorus of noisy birds was signaling the coming morning.

Jacks was there already. His Ferrari was parked on the other side of the road, the side that dropped steeply off down into the lower foothills and ravines. The Angel was standing outside his car, his hands thrust in the pockets of his jacket as he waited for Maddy. He turned toward Maddy as he heard her drive up, then turned back to gazing at the view as the lights twinkling in Angel City slowly gave way to dawn.

They were at the lookout where Jacks had taken her on their first date, just before they'd gone flying. A lifetime ago. The dawn light continued stretching further across the Angel City basin, although the imposing hill behind her was still blocking the early sun. It was still quite dark. She could see Jacks standing next to the Ferrari. She could also see the bench they'd been sitting on when Jacks put his coat around her that night. Maddy crossed the dark road and approached the Angel.

"Hi," Maddy said quietly.

"You're late," Jackson said.

"Not too late, Jacks," Maddy said softly. "I'm sorry. I didn't sleep much last night."

"Me neither." Jacks's body seemed tense, coiled, waiting for Maddy to speak. He kicked a stone, and it tumbled off the precipice into the dark void that plummeted below.

Maddy stood next to the Angel at the edge of the lookout. Pockets of mist in the ravines were illuminated by the emerging rays of the dawn, and Angel City lay just beyond. An Angel City on the brink of battle.

"Who would have thought that all of this could have happened since we were first here, Jacks?"

Jackson remained silent, his neck tense, his cheekbones taut.

"I didn't mean for things to happen this way," Maddy said. "I really didn't, Jacks.

"I never asked to be this, Jackson. I could have just stayed Maddy Montgomery, waitress at the diner. I never knew what was in me. You helped show me. You showed me until I believed in myself. And then, in the process, I found things I never knew I had, both good and bad. It's true, I found my inner Angel.

"But someone very important to me once said that the strength of a hero isn't in her weapons or abilities, but is in an idea. The idea of the right, triumphing, no matter what. He also said that in defense of this idea, she's willing to put herself in mortal danger. After what happened two days ago, I know now more than ever what that idea was and always should be.

"I've always been more human than Angel. I will always be a half-human, half-Angel. The Angels will never fully welcome me into your world. You know it as much as I do. I could never betray my uncle Kevin or Gwen or my mother's memory," Maddy said, tears starting to well up in her eyes. "I love you, Jacks, but you have to understand—I have to choose the mortals."

Jacks's tense face shifted imperceptibly as Maddy's words fell upon his ears. He closed his eyes for a moment, slowly, as if physically taking the blow.

Silence hung like a deadly snake in the space between them.

Cautiously, deliberately, Jackson's eyelids opened. There was something newly dead and dangerous in those blue eyes. His strong hands curled into fists at his sides.

"It's *him*, isn't it?" Jacks said. His voice dripped with pain and bitterness.

"Jacks, you're not understanding. This isn't about Tom—"

"I understand pretty clearly, Maddy," he threw back at her. "You've made your choice."

Maddy felt her body ripple with sadness as she looked at the figure next to her, his nostrils flaring. "Something's happened to you over the past few months, Jacks. You were never so . . . hard."

"Something did happen to me, Maddy, remember?" Jacks spit back.

"I'm sorry," Maddy said, fighting back the overwhelming emotion that just wanted her to break down, fall on her knees, beg for Jacks to forgive her. "I'm sorry for . . . everything."

Jacks didn't respond. By now the sun had fully risen over the ragged tops of the hills, bathing all of Angel City in the golden morning light. Buildings glinted in the sun. Jackson took one last look out at the Immortal City before walking to his car. Maddy stood rooted to her spot.

Jacks stopped just before opening his car door and turned back to Maddy.

"Do you want to know why it's different?" Jackson asked.

"Why what's different?"

"You asked me in the diner. Our unsanctioned saves. The difference between when I saved you, and when you saved the girl. What's different?"

"I don't know, Jacks."

Jackson's eyes were unblinking as he looked at Maddy.

"It was different because I loved you," Jacks said.

The car door closed with a hollow thud as Jacks got in. Snarling to life, the sports car screeched its way down Mulholland, throwing dust and gravel high in the air as Jackson disappeared.

The neon sign for Kevin's Diner had been shut off, and the placard in the window read "CLOSED." The diner wouldn't be opening today. Barely even registering the crowd of paparazzi and news vans across the street, Maddy slipped her key in the steel lock and opened the glass door. The bell chimed. Maddy stepped into the restaurant.

Tom got up and gave her a tentative hug. As their bodies touched for a bittersweet, painful moment, she just wanted to cry. She was think-ing about the Angel at the outlook, and what she had done to him.

Kevin stood up from the booth where he and the pilot had been sit-ting over two steaming mugs of coffee, waiting for his niece.

"It's . . . it's done," Maddy said, burying her face in Tom's shoulder.

"You did the right thing, Maddy," Tom said, lowering his eyes to her with gentle concern. "You did the right thing."

Jackson's footsteps echoed in the great hall as the near-translucent young woman in the fine gold-threaded robe led the young Angel into the chamber. The Council of Twelve rose from their seats as he walked in. His stepfather, Mark, was already there.

"Jacks," Mark said, embracing his stepson.

Jackson's face remained strangely neutral.

The enormous televisions mounted on the front walls of the chapel played incessant coverage of the standoff between the U.S. government and the Angels, showing military and police units preparing to occupy NAS offices throughout Angel City and the country. The problem was, they had no clue where the Council was.

"We heard the good news about your wings, young Godspeed," Uriah said, nodding in his golden robe. "We had nothing but hope for this new technology. And now it has come just in time."

Gabriel stepped forward, his perfect, ageless features looking at Jackson.

"And so you are sure?" Gabriel asked. "This would be of greatest service to us and your fellow Angels. The act of a true hero, befitting your father."

Jackson nodded.

The image of Maddy leaning her head against Tom's shoulder flared again angrily in his mind. She was doing it for *him*. For Tom. She had left Jackson for the human pilot. Jacks's mind became murky and deadly, pulsing with quick anger and pain whenever he thought about it. He shook his head slightly to get rid of the sensation.

The ADC agent standing to the side handed Jackson one piece of armor at a time. Jacks put each section on deliberately, coldly. Making sure each joint was snapping together, all the seams correctly aligned.

When he was finished, Jackson stepped back and looked at himself in the full-length mirror. His broad shoulders were pronounced, his muscles defined by the contours of the sleek shell. He looked formidable. He was dressed in the sleek, black, modern armor of a Battle Angel.

"It fits you perfectly," the agent said.

Jacks looked at Gabriel and the Council. A bead of sweat emerged on his forehead. He trembled for a moment, the muscles straining in his neck. Concentrating.

Suddenly, razor-sharp, Jackson's new wings ripped forth from underneath the battle armor, a full eight feet of them, with an enormous *whoosh*. They were bigger than ever. The famous wings glowed blue once again, but this time they were built out partially with titanium, and golden threads of circuitry ran and glowed throughout. The part-Angel, part-robotic circuitry was visible just underneath the strange, translucent skin. They grew brighter and dimmer with each breath he took in and let out. Hot to the touch, the wings were bristling with strength, their metal steaming. They were stunning, utterly intimidating.

"Your Angelic perfection had been sullied, broken," Gabriel said, admiring the wings. "And you now might be different with these wings on your back. Not entirely Angel. But they might make you better than perfect, my son."

Jackson turned to Gabriel, cold anger in his voice. "We all have to make sacrifices. As one of the Godspeed class, I am now ready to make mine. We must win. There is no other option. They'll take away our way of life, if given a chance. We can't let them do that."

To Jackson's side, Mark nodded slowly. Knowingly. "It's true. We all must fight for what we want to keep."

Jackson's shocking blue eyes were distant, bitter.

"I will do it. I will lead us against the humans."

# CHAPTER THIRTY-SIX

It was dark and cold in the concrete pit known as the Angel City River. What had once been an actual river was now nothing more than a filthy cement gutter running through the overpopulated sprawl of the Angel City basin. Mist hung heavy in the air, forming ghostly halos around the streetlamps that lit the river's graffiti-covered banks. Clusters of insects circled around the lights in the restless night.

Tonight, like most of the year, the river was almost entirely dry, causing the sound of Detective Sylvester's and Sergeant Garcia's footsteps to echo eerily in the emptiness as they clambered down the gently sloping concrete. The two carefully made their way down the concrete ravine. The leather of Sylvester's shoe sole slipped as he descended further toward the bottom, but he steadied himself on a faded and mangled Big Wheel.

*Gerald Maze.* The name Minx had given him, weeks ago. It had been a dead end. The detective and Sergeant Garcia had run the name through all the databases, but the most recent data that came up was from eight years ago, and that was out in Imperial County, not Angel City. Maze was likely just one in a sea of nameless nomads, pitching tents at night in the squalid alleys of downtown Angel City, living day-by-day, bottle-by-bottle. They'd put out an all-points bulletin on him in the database. And nothing. Then, miraculously, on a stop-and-search by a uniformed cop downtown, he'd popped up. Disturbing the peace: he'd been hollering at passersby while drinking beer out of a Styrofoam cup. He had been prophesying mankind's doom. He said he'd seen it. Looked into the eyes of doom and lived to tell the tale. ACPD had him drying out in a cell downtown in the Twin Towers jail. Sylvester and Garcia were there in twenty minutes.

The man was borderline delusional, a drunk, and a crackpot. A few days in jail would probably improve his situation. Or at least the shower, complimentary from the county, would improve his smell a bit. He may have been antisocial and slightly crazed. But there was something in his eyes that told Sylvester to believe him.

At first, Gerald was suspicious of Sylvester, his eyes rolling wildly in his head. But once he realized the detective might take him seriously—and that he could maybe shave a few days off his jail time—he began talking.

Gerald told them a story. A story about how he'd been down in the dry ravine of the Los Angeles River, looking for something he hid. A bottle, if you must know. He'd hidden it a week ago. Or maybe a month. He couldn't remember. But he was looking for it.

And that was when he saw *them*.

And smelled them.

The doom. Fire and smoke. He'd heard the men's screams. Their pleas. Begging to just kill them. He'd seen it all with his own two eyes.

He hadn't stopped running until he'd reached Santa Fe and Third.

When Sylvester asked him exactly where this happened, Gerald was able to give them specific directions by landmarks. The detective wrote them down. On his way out, he put in a good word for Gerald with the duty officer. "See that he's out tonight."

Now Sylvester and Garcia found themselves following Gerald's path. They were close—Sylvester could somehow sense it. He just needed to see it for himself. He recalled his infuriating meeting with the Council. Gabriel's flippant attitude. He didn't know what he was going to do, but he just needed to be doing *something*. He just couldn't sit and wait for it.

Rats large enough to be small cats scattered as Sylvester and Garcia made their way along the river's left bank, their shoes squishing and crunching over God-knew-what. The hazy blue light of one of the men's cell phones glowed in his hand as GPS showed a map of where they were.

The men navigated around myriad bizarre items dumped down the river's banks and forgotten. A baby carriage. A couch. A mannequin. A boat full of old tires.

"There's the boat he mentioned, detective," Garcia said, motioning.

Sylvester nodded. It was here. Somewhere near.

"Let's cover this ground here; we'll move in squares. Something's got to turn up."

The two began inspecting the concrete ground in front of them. They moved methodically back and forth across the dry riverbed. Nothing was coming up.

Suddenly, near the bank, Garcia stopped: "Jesus." The sound of crickets hung in the night. "You better come here, David."

Detective Sylvester walked near the bank. There, on the concrete, was a deep, dark stain. Maybe twenty feet across. It was blood. The stain was deep, not fresh. It extended to the bank. To a circular opening, one of hundreds that lined the river's shore.

The cement tunnel was about eight feet high, overgrown with algae and mold, and absolutely filthy. Putrid sewer air wafted out at him as Sylvester peered into the tunnel's gaping mouth.

Garcia's eyes grew wide as he saw the tunnel. "Are we going in there?"

Sylvester nodded. He wiped his glasses with his shirt. "I am. You don't have to come, Bill. I'd understand."

Sergeant Garcia put a hand on the detective's shoulder. "If you think I'm letting you go in there alone, you're crazy." He drew his service revolver.

Sylvester put his hand in the pocket of his overcoat and gripped for comfort the King James Bible he had. Then he, too, drew his pistol.

He turned on a small flashlight, cutting the darkness with a delicate white beam, and, trembling with anticipation, stepped carefully into the tunnel.

Water sloshed around their feet, and the smell that drifted up to his nose nearly made him gag. Still, they pressed on. The splashing of the water echoed in the tunnel.

Something was different about this tunnel. Something unusual. As he made his way deeper into its stinking blackness, he realized the air was getting . . . *warmer.* The cold, dark air of the river was quickly becoming hot—startlingly hot—and muggy. Beads of sweat jumped out on Sylvester's forehead and he wiped his face with the sleeve of his jacket. His glasses were becoming fogged, difficult to see through. Steam thickened in the air with each step until it was nearly too painful to breathe. Finally, just as Sylvester was thinking about turning back, he saw that the tunnel opened up into a larger, cavernous space, like a large concrete box.

Sylvester put his arm across Garcia's chest. "Stay here, Bill."

One step, then another. Sylvester crept toward the open cavern just ahead. He held his breath and stepped forward.

He shone his light into the cavern. The stark beam revealed a steaming charnel house. Sylvester gagged. All around were the filthy rags of the homeless men, their grisly, rotting carcasses somehow stacked into the walls and ceiling, dripping. Half-eaten skulls, rotting limbs, a severed foot still in a shoe. There were dozens upon dozens. A mass grave.

*They'd been feeding.*

Garcia had approached behind Sylvester. He looked at the scene. The sergeant quickly retreated, stumbling backward away from the shocking, gory sight. The detective could hear him retching down the tunnel. After finishing, the sergeant walked back to Sylvester.

"They're not fresh. Couple days, at least," Sylvester said.

Punctuating the walls were smaller tunnels, all draining their contents into a shallow pool at the bottom of the room. Although the heat remained, there was no sign of the demons. And something in Sylvester's gut told him they were gone. Had been called. For something else.

"They're gone?" Garcia said.

"Yes, they're gone."

"Maybe they went away for good?" Garcia said.

Detective Sylvester shook his head slowly. Before turning to leave the tunnel, he crossed himself. "May God help us all."

# CHAPTER THIRTY-SEVEN

All across the Immortal City, the streets were nearly deserted as both humans and Angels stayed inside. It was only a matter of time before the war would begin. A war no one would have imagined in Angel City even a month before. A war between humans and Angelkind.

A few stalwart tourist shops on Angel Boulevard remained open, selling "I WAS SAVED IN ANGEL CITY!" T-shirts to the occasional tourist who braved the eerily empty famous streets. Word was that the mayor was going to call a curfew at dusk, and that ACPD and National Guard units would be patrolling throughout the night. Up in the Angel City Hills, Angel families hid quietly behind their gated luxury homes, watching their best and brightest prepare for the unthinkable and join forces against the very humans they had once sworn to protect.

On the networks, normal programming had been preempted, and the news was running nonstop. In the diner, as Tom turned the channel to a local Angel City affiliate, the female anchor was serious and grave. He walked closer to the TV.

*"Reports are coming in this morning of elite Angel forces maneuvering in the desert outside Angel City. And word has come to us through confidential sources that if war breaks out, none other than Jackson Godspeed will be leading the Angel powers on the ground and in the air. It looks inevitable, with neither side willing to back down. Across the country, police and military are on full alert, with all active National Guard units called up and readying to enforce the international ban on Angel activities. Experts are unsure of what an Angel-versus-human battle could even look like, but some are saying the Immortals possess supernatural weapons that humans have never seen. President Linden is taking no chances."*

In a sight that seemed out of some surreal nightmare, the screen showed footage of tanks rolling down Wilshire Boulevard in Beverly Hills, palm trees waving above them. The tanks settled outside the NAS headquarters, which the military had isolated and surrounded with weaponry and troops.

*"And just an hour ago, Madison Montgomery Godright, the half-Angel, half-human who sparked the final stage of the human-Angel crisis and who has become a symbolic leader of this movement against Angel corruption, finally made a brief statement on the front lawn of her uncle's house. In addition, Tom Cooper, U.S. Navy pilot, was with Godright during her statement."*

"Maddy, here you are," Tom said, watching the TV. She stood up from the booth and looked at the screen.

At first, it showed stock footage of Maddy on the red carpet at her Commissioning, Jacks at her side. A knife of ambiguous pain plunged into Maddy's heart. But the footage quickly cut to video of her statement an hour earlier.

The screen showed Maddy walking to a makeshift podium in Kevin's front yard, under the morning sun. The podium teetered under an improbable number of microphones as news agencies around the world eagerly awaited word from America's sweetheart. Behind her stood

Uncle Kevin. And just off to the side, Tom stood stoically in his service dress uniform.

Maddy looked around at the sea of reporters on the street, all waiting for word from her.

"*As you all know, I have roots in both the human and the Angel world. Any violence on either side would sadden me deeply. That being said, I support the abolition of Protection for Pay and a return to the Angelic ideals that preceded the National Angel Services. Angels once stood for an idea of good and justice, and they can do it again. I ask the Angels to compromise and meet with President Linden and the GAC to come to a peaceful conclusion. No blood needs to be spilled. There is time to avert catastrophe. Thank you.*"

On screen, Maddy stepped away from the podium, flanked by Uncle Kevin and Tom. The reporters began shouting rabid questions at her, but Maddy paid them no mind as she reentered the house.

Tom turned the volume down.

"What's going to happen now?" Maddy asked uncertainly.

"No one knows," Tom said. "We wait."

The pilot turned to Maddy. He seemed taller and even more striking in his service dress uniform, his wings gleaming, pinned above the breast pocket of his shirt. Stepping closer, he was against Maddy. In this swirling series of events, somehow he seemed the only thing that was remaining real. Something she could count on.

"I have to go now," Tom said. "I only had a few hours off; we're on standby. According to my commander, the situation is expected to escalate within hours."

"Be careful, Tom," Maddy said.

He squeezed Maddy tightly for one brief second, and, needing the comfort, she let him.

"Mr. Montgomery," he said, nodding to Kevin as he left. The uniform made him strangely more formal.

Maddy watched him get in his pickup and leave the parking lot. Her heart sagged as she watched him depart, knowing the danger he might be heading into. And yet she also felt deeply sad for Jackson. She had known he was going to be angry, bitter, disappointed, but she had never imagined that he would volunteer to lead the Angels against the humans. He and she were now enemies. Maddy suddenly felt very tired.

"I'm going to go upstairs and rest for a bit," Maddy said to her uncle.

"Okay, Mads, let me know if you need anything," Kevin said with concern.

Maddy made her way past the oak, almost bare of its leaves now, up the back path to Kevin's house. The stairs creaked in a familiar way as she ascended them; she hadn't realized how much she had missed the old house.

Lying on her bed, Maddy was asleep within minutes.

The window rattling woke Maddy from her slumber. First a pen, then her bottle of water, then an old framed photo of Maddy and Gwen from sophomore year slowly shook and tumbled off her desk and onto the floor with a clatter.

Maddy's eyes opened in confusion. One, then the other. What was happening, and where was she? What time was it? Suddenly her eyes focused, and she realized she was in her old room at Kevin's. Her entire bed was shaking. She jumped up in a panic before realizing it was a small earthquake. It slowly faded.

She'd been taking a nap. How long had she been out? It had been a strangely dreamless sleep. Clear and endless. She could've been asleep for hours. She checked the clock and saw it had only been a full two hours.

*BZZZZ. BZZZZ.*
*BZZZZ. BZZZZ.*

Her phone was on the bedside table, dancing and rotating as it vibrated. She fumbled for it and looked at the caller ID: TOM.

"Hello?"

Tom's voice was quick and sharp. "Are you by a TV?"

"No . . . I mean, yes, just wait a second," Maddy said, pushing her hair behind her ear and walking downstairs. "What's happening?"

"I . . . I don't know," Tom said. "It seems so incredible."

"Have the Angels attacked?" she asked, breathless. "Are we at war?"

Tom took a breath. "There is no Angel war anymore," he said.

She bolted up. "What?"

There was a crackle on the line. "Maddy, I think it may be worse. Something worse than we could have ever imagined. Get to a TV."

Maddy scrambled downstairs, still on the phone with Tom.

"Did you feel that earthquake, Kevin?" Maddy asked. "*Kevin?* What's going on?"

Uncle Kevin was standing in the living room in his jeans and tucked-in polo shirt, frozen, openmouthed, looking at the TV.

On-screen it looked like a giant whirlpool in the middle of the ocean. It was grim and terrifying, spinning slowly, like the eye of some dread hurricane. Its dimensions were enormous—a helicopter flying near it seemed like just a speck. It must have been over half a mile across. The water was frothy and almost black as it slowly turned counterclockwise. And Maddy could swear she was seeing *smoke* and steam rise from its dark center. The walls of the hole were steep, and it seemed to extend forever downward into the churning depths. The news helicopter was directly above the hole but could not see to the bottom of its pit. It seemed to reach forever.

"Tom, what is it?!" Maddy brought the phone up to her ear and asked in panic, her hand fumbling for and finally finding the remote to turn up the volume on the television.

Tom's voice was strangely detached. "I can't say for sure. The people on TV know more than I do. It's close to Angel City, though. Too close."

Kevin moved closer and embraced Maddy as they watched the horrifying footage unfold on screen. The cameraman in the helicopter was talking.

*"Within recent hours, this enormous sinkhole has appeared just thirty miles off the coast of Angel City, swallowing everything in its sight. It was discovered in the past hour, when a freighter bound for the Oregon port of Astoria was suddenly drawn into the pull of the hole and has since disappeared. Scientific assessment of the atmosphere shows that incredible heat and sulfuric gases are escaping from the hole, and it is expanding at an astonishing rate. And moving directly toward Angel City. For you viewers at home, I cannot explain the scope and terror of this sight. Although there has been no official confirmation, many believe this is indeed the coming of the often-doubted revelations from the ending chapters of* The Book of Angels. *And I, for one, am not about to doubt it."*

On screen another helicopter dipped closer down into the swirling sinkhole. The rotating water walls became blacker and blacker as it dropped below sea level. The aircraft seemed like a mere toy against the massive swirling walls of the cone. Black brine and foam began splashing toward the helicopter's blades.

*"And it looks like they are trying to get a closer read on what is happening down there, and—oh my God, get out of there! Get out of there!"*

Suddenly it seemed as if the swirling black watery walls of the sinkhole bulged and grew, drawing the observation helicopter into its grasp. The helicopter teetered slightly and then suddenly was pulled into the foaming, glistening black water. It crumpled and twisted in on itself, instantly bursting into hot flames as the waters drew it into the bottomless pit that had opened.

Kevin pulled Maddy closely, drawing her face against his chest as she hid her eyes.

*"And we are back in the studio after shocking footage of what, well, of what appears to be some kind of portal. Questions of the Angel-human war have immediately disappeared as humanity turns to this great threat from the ocean."*

Behind the anchor, TV-station workers were running around in pandemonium.

"President Linden, the GAC, and military are reallocating all resources to fight the demons. No one's even talking about the Angel-human war anymore," Kevin said. "But where are the Angels? Shouldn't they be helping?"

Maddy dashed outside and looked at the skies. Off toward the ocean, aircraft were converging toward the sinkhole. No Angels flying, though. Neighbors were coming out onto the street, watching the skies as strange clouds seemed to be rolling off the coast. The clouds shimmered gray with the slightest hint of portentous red. The weather was becoming humid, sticky. Strange for Angel City. Suddenly, what looked like a compact fireball emerged on the horizon, sailing east. Maddy remembered the terror of last year and knew in her gut it must be a demon. The neighbor's dog began barking incessantly. For once it was barking at real danger.

The fiery demon ball sailed over the hill, barely clearing the Angel City sign before heading into Burbank. Panicked, Maddy looked out in the distance toward the ocean, where it had come from. But it was the only one she saw. An early scout?

Maddy ran back inside, where Kevin was still watching reports.

"Are they saying anything about the clouds or . . . any demon sightings in the city?" Maddy asked.

"Not yet."

*"Now, we cannot say for certain that this is what is happening, but we*

*have the world's foremost Angel expert and philosopher from Harvard University, Professor Paul Kemper, with us via satellite. Professor Kemper, what do you have to say about this sinkhole?"*

The man on screen was wearing a tweedy jacket with elbow patches and a white button-up without a tie. He seemed calm, almost unnaturally so. As if resigned to his fate. He began speaking.

*"Susan, we are undoubtedly witnessing the somewhat unexpected fulfillment of one of the most terrible of prophecies we have, that of the coming of the 'Darkness.' Although many in the fringe communities have been monitoring world events and predicting this for months, it was ignored by the mainstream media. It all seems so clear in hindsight now.*

*"As many know, it states in* The Book of Angels, *'And then when the seven burn across the earth, evil will rise upon humanity from the West. The Darkness will come from a pit in the Great Ocean, out of which no light has ever been seen, straight from the depths of the other world. Death will surely find a home with you, and mercy shall be driven out by the hordes of doom. And you will beg for the end.'*

*"Given the early scientific evidence of what we are seeing, and its clear connection with the prophecy, it seems that we may be experiencing it at this very moment."*

The woman in the studio looked in disbelief at the professor. The bedlam was still occurring on screen behind her in the studio.

*"What does it mean, the 'Darkness'?"*

The professor cleared his throat.

*"That has been debated for some time among scholars. But after last year's incidents with the demon in Angel City, it has been considered almost conclusive that it would be some kind of Dark Angel contingent. And from my confidential sources in both the Angels organization and the ACPD, we are almost certain it is demons. I just spoke with President Linden and urged him to focus all our available military resources, and those of all our allies, on meeting this*

*threat. But conventional weapons will have limited effect on our supernatural enemies. Given the rapid growth of the hole, I would say we have twenty-four hours at most before the full attack begins. And we still have no idea what its form will take, or who or what is leading it."*

The anchor posed a question: *"What would you have viewers do?"*

The professor almost laughed, but then just shook his head slowly, sadly. *"Do? I would say it is an important time to be with your loved ones. That's what I will be doing."*

Maddy heard a small voice, distant. She realized it was Tom on the phone still.

"Maddy? Maddy?"

She slowly lifted the phone back to her ear. "I'm here, Tom."

"We just got the order from Linden." His voice was tense, focused. "I'm on my way to the carrier. We're deploying within the hour, Maddy."

"But the professor just said that conventional weapons won't do anything against the demons. You don't know what you're up against!" Maddy protested, her voice quaking with emotion as she remembered once again the terrible sight of that demon careening along the freeway, and then atop the library tower. Smoke, fire, and the emissary of hellishness. She imagined an army of them and shuddered.

After the destruction last year in Angel City with just one demon, what was an army of thousands upon thousands of demons going to do?

"We have to, Maddy. The war on Angels is over. Now we're just fighting for our survival," Tom said. "I'm doing my duty."

"Tom," she said, tears streaming down her face. "I'll come see you. Before you leave. To say goodbye."

"I would"—she could hear the fighter pilot's voice quavering slightly—"I would love that. I will see you there, then. I need to go now, Maddy. I'll be at Dock 2."

The phone went silent. "Tom's going to fight them, Kevin."

"Sit down for one minute, Maddy," Uncle Kevin said, putting a kind hand on her shoulder as she sank down to the couch. He came back shortly with two cups of tea. The warm smell of the tea filled the living room, a stark contrast to the darkness they were feeling.

"There are still the Angels," he said. "They can fight. For earth."

Maddy looked up at her uncle with uncertain eyes.

"Well, they can't just stand by. How could they?" Kevin said.

"The demons, they're here for the mortals. Not the Angels," Maddy said. "The Angels know that. According to the prophecy, this coming of the demons has one purpose: to overtake the world and enslave mankind. Now, after we were at the brink of war, the Angels . . . they'll be too proud to help us now."

Maddy's mind cast back to her final meeting with Jackson. His bitterness. Her heart ached.

Suddenly, from the kitchen, they heard the faint tinkling of glasses in the cupboard. The pictures on the mantle started to shift slightly under the vibrations. The windows rolled under the trembling. Maddy steadied herself by putting a hand on the side of a chair. It was another small earthquake, and it quickly faded. But Maddy could only assume that it wouldn't be the last.

Maddy and Kevin faced each other.

"Tom's waiting for me," she said.

Squeezing Kevin's hand, she stood up. Here, in this incredible time of uncertainty, doubt, and darkness, she was sure of one thing, at least: she had somewhere to be, someone to see.

The last tremors of the quake had faded by the time Archangel William Holyoake recorded the brief video statement to be released to President Linden, the GAC, and the worldwide media. Simple, to the point, and brutal: *"We regret to inform you that we will not intercede on the humans' behalf in this conflict with the demons."*

Just behind the Archangel, to his left, stood Jackson Godspeed, wearing his advanced, matte-black battle armor. His daunting wings remained sheathed for now. Jackson's eyes remained neutrally focused forward toward the camera as Holyoake spoke. Emotionless. Other Guardians were also collected near the podium, including Mitch, Steven Churchson, and Emily Brightchurch, in a show of strength and solidarity. Emily stood just beside Jackson in black leggings and a loose, low-cut tank top, and, on her right wrist, a ton of bracelets that matched her Divine Ring.

The statement was being recorded and transmitted from what looked like little more than a glass cube perched in a grove of trees in the middle of the Angel City Hills. The glass cube was simple: it had a marble floor and an elevator. An elevator that led down to a complex underground system that humans had never laid eyes on. A contingency plan for something exactly like this.

Archangel Holyoake finished his statement and began walking away from the podium. The low buzz of conversation filled the glass room as Guardians began speaking to each other.

Jackson felt his hand getting squeezed. He looked down and saw it was Emily. She smiled at him.

"I'm with you, Jacks. I've always believed in you. No matter what state your wings were in. You aren't weak. We Angels aren't weak."

"Oh," Jacks said without too much enthusiasm. "Thanks, Emily."

"Now that Maddy's not in your life, if you ever need anyone to talk to . . . to keep you company, let me know," Emily said. "I'm strong. Like you."

"Okay," said Jacks, but his mind seemed elsewhere, and his stare remained distant.

Suddenly a few Guardians shouted and pointed to the horizon. It was another demon scout, sent to Angel City from the growing sinkhole.

The demon, curled tightly into a ball, an emissary of smoke, fire, and death, roared overhead, leaving a contrail of ash to float down in the sky. It smashed into the hillside closer to the Angel City sign. The fireball exploded in a maelstrom of flame, and in the distance one could see the limbs of the demon expanding out from the ball. Fire started spreading up the hill with the wind. The demon screamed, and its screech echoed down across the Angel City basin.

Emily jumped and clutched Jacks's arm. In the distance, the *thing* began to fly, moving toward the glass cube the Guardians were in. It drew closer and closer, until the terrible shifting shape of fire and smoke hovered above the building, its eyes a window into hell.

The Dark Angel screamed, the glass of the cube shivering under the sound waves.

Emily began whimpering. All her talk of being courageous seemed to be an act. Other Guardians began slowly backing up.

Jackson alone was unmoved at the spectacle of the demon. He had already faced his worst fears on the library tower. Not fighting a demon: losing Maddy. Now he had nothing to fear. He walked toward the demon and looked in its eyes.

"Not now. Get out of here."

The demon, still hovering, snarled and beat its wings once, twice, and was gone, out across the Angel City basin.

Emily was crying in the corner. Jacks turned back to his fellow Guardians, who had retreated in the face of the demon.

"The scouts are getting more frequent," he said flatly. "Don't worry, they won't be bothering us. They have humans to concern themselves with."

Guardians began speaking over each other.

"The humans will be massacred."

"It's saving us a war."

"I don't know. I just don't know."

"They signed their own death warrant with the Immortals Bill. They can't expect us to help them now."

"But how do we know the Dark Ones won't ultimately come for us?"

"We don't, for sure. *The Book* seems clear, but we can't be positive. We'll be ready regardless."

"The humans would never be ready."

Mitch was shaking his head as he heard the fragments of conversation. He stepped up to Jacks and gripped his forearm. He spoke under his breath. "You've seen what those things can do, Jacks. What it's done to Angels. If we're prepared, we can handle our own. But the humans, Jacks."

Jacks nodded distantly. Mitch squeezed his arm.

"Are you listening to me?" Mitch asked. "The humans don't stand a chance."

A pained expression crossed Jackson's face. Just for a split second. "Oftentimes difficult decisions must be made."

"I know you're hurt. In pain. I can only imagine, man. But she's not a decision," Mitch said. "She's a person, Jacks."

Mitch let go of Jackson's arm and began walking across the marble floor toward the elevator. Jackson watched as he went, his pale eyes flickering.

# CHAPTER THIRTY-EIGHT

The door to the dark old bar swung open as someone left, letting bright daylight pour into the dusty establishment. Two men in a dim corner yelled in anger as the light invaded. It momentarily illuminated dusty photos of Angels, the worn dark wood of the proud old tables, the empty glasses in front of the two drunks. Once the glamorous meeting place for the Angels in the last century, the bar was now a musty Angel City dive, trading on nostalgia, cheap bottom-shelf liquor, and not too many questions.

Propped on a stool, hunched over the bar, Detective Sylvester peered up at the dusty TV. There was going to be a statement from the president. He brought the glass of whiskey rocks to his lips and took a long drink.

The bar was almost empty at this time of the day, everyone at home, riveted by the terrifying footage of the sinkhole in the Pacific. The coming of the prophecy in *The Book of Angels*. No one could have seen it coming—except for the detective, of course. Everyone was waiting to hear if the Angels would join the fight, despite their conflict with the humans. The boulevards of Angel City were ghostly, empty, the billboards of the perfect Angels leering over empty sidewalks and bare streets. The Walk of Angels an abandoned corridor, a brutal reminder of how far things had fallen, and were continuing to fall.

The TV squawked, and Sylvester looked up at it again. President Linden walked to the podium. He seemed to have already aged a couple of years in the past week: a few more strands of gray in his presidential hair, his face drawn and tired, his Brooks Brothers suit slightly rumpled. But he still appeared strong for the people.

*"My fellow Americans. I speak to you in a dark hour, perhaps the darkest hour we have yet seen. We have had confirmation from numerous theologians and scientists that the sinkhole many of you have seen in the Pacific Ocean is indeed an opened portal for demons, a fulfilling of the prophetic revelations of* The Book of Angels. *It saddens me to say that mankind will have to face this terrible threat alone. After sending emergency ambassadors to the Archangels of the NAS, to plead with them about the necessity of joining forces and repelling the demon invasion together, I am sad to say that we have made no headway. The Angels refuse our plea for aid in the inevitable battle against the common threat we are now facing. The battle of all time, between good and evil.*

*"I have said that this may, in fact, be our darkest hour. But I also hope it may ultimately prove to be our brightest, as well. Our military heroes across the globe are preparing to meet this challenge head-on and are ready to make the ultimate sacrifice as we make a stand.*

*"May God bless you all, and God bless America."*

The screen immediately cut back to live footage of the sinkhole.

Sylvester tilted his glass back, draining the glass of the amber liquid. Sylvester wasn't one for daytime drinking, but he was damn well going to try to change that on a day like this.

"Excuse me, can I get another one?" Sylvester asked.

The bartender was just standing there, slack-jawed, as the TV turned back to footage of the sinkhole in the ocean. A graphic read: DEMON SINKHOLE GROWS—ANGELS TO STAY ON SIDELINES.

Without even really drawing his gaze from the TV, the bartender dropped two new cubes in the glass and filled it to the brim with liquor.

"That one's on me," he said.

Sylvester just nodded and looked back at the screen.

*He had failed.*

That's all Sylvester could think of. Despite everything, despite even getting into the inner chambers of the Council to petition Gabriel himself, he had failed. He had been too late. It had been for nothing.

The humans didn't stand a chance.

And if the Angels thought the Dark Ones would stop with just conquering humanity . . .

The door swung open again, drawing another bout of noisy complaint from the back corner, before it closed. Sylvester didn't pay it any mind, still looking at the TV.

The person who entered sat on a stool next to him. Sylvester instantly stiffened. *It was an Angel.* Although many years had passed since he had his wings removed, he could still instantly feel the presence, the energy, of one of the Immortals.

"Get you something?" the bartender asked, before suddenly being drawn up short by the perfect Immortal in front of him. How long had it been since an Angel had graced the bar?

"No, I'm fine, thank you," a woman's voice said. "We'll be leaving shortly."

"An Angel doesn't need a drink for the apocalypse?" Sylvester said, his voice dripping with bitterness. He lifted up his glass and took a sip, still only looking at the TV.

"Your partner said I could find you here," the voice next to him said.

The detective shook his head. "Bill," he said.

"You shouldn't be here at a time like this," the voice said.

Sylvester finally turned his head. He was met by the face of Archangel Susan Archson.

"Susan?" His brow furrowed in puzzlement.

"How long has it been? Fifteen years? Too long," she said.

The detective's face darkened. "What are you doing here? Shouldn't you be with the rest of the Angels, getting some popcorn and a front row seat?" He motioned to the sinkhole on TV.

"I'm here to get you, David," she said. Maddy's former instructor almost glowed in the dark bar, her red lipstick set against her light skin. "We have work to do. It's not too late."

"What do you mean?"

Susan studied the detective's face for a moment. Her eyes suddenly sparkled. "The girl."

Adrenaline pumped in Sylvester's veins. "Maddy?"

Susan nodded.

"You think she has a part to play?"

"I'm positive," Susan said.

"And what about him?"

"We can't say," Maddy's professor said. She looked toward the door. "They don't know I'm here. A car is waiting outside. Louis is there."

"Kreuz?"

"Yes. There are . . . some who do not agree with the Council, David."

A look of comprehension suddenly came across Sylvester's face. "It wasn't DeWitt or Minx who sent me the anonymous emails about the demon attacks . . . it was you."

Susan's silence was all the confirmation he needed.

"We need to go. Now," Susan said.

Sylvester pushed the almost untouched drink away from him on the bar. Susan put a hundred-dollar bill on the bar, but the detective put his hand over hers and forced her to pick it back up.

"I can buy my own drinks," he said, slapping a twenty down and moving to leave.

In astonishment at the Angel who had just come in, the bartender spoke: "What should I do?"

Both Sylvester and Susan stopped at the threshold, the door half-open. The detective was silhouetted by the plentiful sunshine outside, hands buried in the pockets of his overcoat.

"I would recommend praying," Sylvester said.

# CHAPTER THIRTY-NINE

Maddy's car squeaked to a stop in the parking lot along the pier. She had made it quickly—the freeways were nearly empty. Residents were advised to stay inside until further notice. Fires had already started burning in the hills. Outside Maddy's windshield, the aircraft carrier loomed heavy on the grim gray-red horizon, a juggernaut preparing for war. Yet at the moment it floated calmly on the glassy aquamarine water of the bay.

The palm trees drifted lazily along the shore, against a sky darkening from the west. They didn't seem to pay heed to the fact that those just below were in the moment of saying goodbye to each other, perhaps forever.

Stepping out of her car, Maddy put on her sunglasses and started walking quickly to the mass of sailors, pilots, and families congregating along the dock. The unmistakable salty presence of the ocean invaded her nostrils as she made her way toward the pier, through the crowd of families trying to say goodbye. Stunned, teary-eyed farewells were happening all around her, as sailors were being ripped from their families and sent on what many experts were already calling a suicide mission against the demon horde arising in the Pacific. The coming of the prophecy. Heading directly toward Angel City.

Maddy's head craned around the groups of people, trying to find Tom in the mass of people. With a panic, she realized some sailors were already starting to climb the long metal staircase to the deck of the aircraft carrier. They waved regretfully down at their loved ones as they reached the flight deck and stood along the rails. A small girl holding a teddy bear wept as she saw her father disappear onto the vessel of war.

Was Maddy too late? She moved faster and faster through the people, looking for Tom.

"Tom!" she cried out, scanning the crowd. What if he'd already had to board? She wouldn't have a chance to see him. "Tom!"

Suddenly she was in his arms, their bodies against each other, arms wrapping, faces touching. "Maddy," he said, embracing her.

She looked up at him, suddenly embarrassed. "I'm sorry, I just . . . I thought maybe you'd already left."

Tom gazed down upon Maddy, a smile in his eyes. "I'm here. I wouldn't have left without saying goodbye to you."

Maddy pressed the side of her face against the side of Tom's smooth uniform. What was happening? Where was her heart taking her?

"Why do you have to go?" she asked. She knew the question was foolish, something a little girl would ask. But she asked it anyway.

"We have to, Maddy," Tom said. "Is it better to just sit here and wait for the demons to come slaughter us in our homes? We have to at least try. We've sworn a duty to protect this country. And we will do it. Even if we die trying."

Maddy knew he was right.

"The Angels are refusing to help," she said. "Archangel Holyoake just released the official statement."

"Are you surprised?" Tom said, his expression darkening, cheeks tensing. "They were about to go to war with us over the Immortals Bill. We already knew they'd give us no aid."

Maddy looked at him. "No," she said. "Actually, I . . . I don't know." A pang crossed her heart as she thought of Jacks, alone and bitter in his jealousy, having offered to lead the Angels against them. How had everything gone so wrong so quickly?

With a panic, Maddy realized that the sailors and aviators on the dock were starting to thin out, embarking on the ship, leaving only the civilians on the dock.

A junior officer approached Tom and saluted. "Captain, we need you to board, sir."

"Thank you, ensign," he said. "I'll only be a moment longer."

Tom turned back to Maddy.

"Maddy, when you came out in public as a half-blood, and then I met you, I felt something. I felt I didn't have to be alone anymore. I didn't have anything to prove. I could be what I was. Not feel different. Maybe even be proud."

"No goodbyes, Tom" Maddy sputtered out, trying to hold back tears.

"You gave me courage, everything you've done in so short a time. You may not see it, your incredible courage, but I do. And so does the rest of the world. You gave courage to us all with your training, your save of the girl. Maddy, you are what I would want to be."

Emotion flooded Maddy, threatening to overtake her as she held the pilot's hands in hers. The impending war; her love for Jacks, who was now her enemy; what she now recognized as a conflicting love for Tom—it all threatened to break through the defenses around her heart and leave her surrendered, overwhelmed. She bit her lip hard as she looked up at Tom, tears rimming her eyes.

"All my achievements, my flight status—none of it matters when I think about the past couple of months with you," Tom said. He took a breath. "I love you, Maddy."

"Tom, we'll have time to talk about all this when you get back."

His voice began to waver, only slightly. "Maddy, if I don't come back again, I want you to—"

"You're going to be back again," she cut him off, the renegade tears starting to come. "You'd better."

The brilliant sun glinted off the insignia of Tom's crisp, navy blue uniform. A pair of gulls wheeled above in the flawless blue sky, lighter than air. Navy personnel crowded the rails of the towering aircraft carrier, looking down on the dock at those they were leaving behind.

"My grandfather always told me not to get caught up and instead to search for the one girl I wanted to spend the rest of my life with," Tom said, his voice quavering. He moved in closer and looked at her with his deep green eyes. "I'm sure now that it's you."

The world seemed to pitch under Maddy's feet, as if she were at sea. "Tom . . ."

"Maddy Montgomery Godright, I want to know if you'll be here for me if—I mean, when—I get back."

Her face turned down, tears streaming. "Tom, don't talk like that. Of course I'll be here."

Suddenly a shadow crossed over her and Tom, as if a giant bird had flown across the sun. In surprise, Maddy looked up.

An Angel with enormous wings outstretched floated to the ground in front of them, silhouetted black against the sun. Golden rays bled around the edges of the black figure as it touched down.

With a shock, Maddy realized it was Jacks. But not a Jacks she fully knew. Futuristic black Angel armor clung to his muscular body, a new generation of Battle Angel protection she'd never seen before. His half-

Angel, half-cyborg wings were awe-inspiring in their breadth. Jackson also looked somehow older. His jaw stronger. The lines along his cheekbones more defined and immutable.

Tom's muscles grew taut as he realized who it was, and Maddy unconsciously withdrew from the pilot, taking a few steps away.

"What are you doing here?" Tom asked sharply, standing up straight, his shoulders broad. Jackson's impressive new wings didn't daunt him. "This is no place for you. You and your Angels have made your choice. You've abandoned Maddy."

"Jacks . . . your wings," Maddy said softly. "But why did you come? How did you find me?" Pain twisted her face. She thought she had already faced the agony of this choice.

"I had to come. To give you a chance," Jacks said. "And I know your frequency better than any, Maddy. You should know that by now."

Maddy searched his pale blue eyes. They seemed deeper, flecked with more gray than she had ever seen. They seemed almost haunted.

On the deck of the ship, some sailors noticed the Angel down on the pier. They began shouting and drawing their sidearms, pointing them at Jacks.

"You! Angel! Down on the ground! NOW!"

Jackson paid them not the slightest attention.

He motioned toward the ocean horizon, where the demon sinkhole was just miles off shore.

"Maddy, I'm offering you a choice," Jacks said. "To survive. To choose your Angel side once and for all. It's your destiny. Don't tell me you can't feel that, honestly, in your bones."

The words were blunt against her ears. Maddy could feel her Immortal Marks warming under her shirt. Stirrings of her beautiful wings, which she'd come to think of as an indispensable part of her.

Jacks continued. "The humans may be right about some things. But they are also confused, and weak, about many others. The Immortals Bill is wrong, and you know it. We can work together to change things for the Angels."

Jackson stretched his hands out toward Maddy and took a few steps forward. "I'm giving you the chance to come with me. Be with me. It's what I want. And I know it's what you truly want, deep down." The biotechnology circuits in Jackson's wings glowed deeply orange as he took a breath in, then let it out.

"Lies," Tom said, voice dripping with anger. His finger pointed accusatorily at Jackson's impressive figure. "More Angel lies. Maddy, they're deserting humanity in our hour of greatest need. They'd let us be exterminated by whatever *things* are out there, coming for us. Because we wanted to end their dishonesty—their entitlement—and democratize Protection for Pay. And you can trust what they say?" Tom snorted and looked at Jackson. "She's smarter than that, Godspeed."

Jacks took a threatening step toward Tom.

"DO NOT MOVE TOWARD THE LIEUTENANT!" a marine sharpshooter from the deck of the aircraft carrier screamed down at Jackson. Jacks looked up irritatedly at him, as you would at a persistent gnat.

"You need to forget him, Maddy," Tom said. "It's as much for you as for me. He'll destroy you in the end. The Angels will never change. They're too corrupted. I'm offering you something more. Something real. Something human. Something honest." Tom looked into Maddy's confused eyes, the windows into her conflicted soul. "You know that that's what's important in your life. What you truly want."

The pilot's gazed directly at her, unblinking. He reached out his hand.

All the bystanders on the dock had given them a wide berth, and sailors stood along the bridge, guns trained on Jackson. Maddy was now standing between the two young men, Tom in his olive green flight suit on one side, and Jackson in his indomitable black armor on the other, his fearsome wings curling slightly in as he waited for Maddy's decision.

Maddy's mind flashed to Jackson and the lookout: the site of both their first date and their last meeting. She looked at the man who had been so much a part of her life and who had driven away in heartbreak and bitterness. The pain on his face. And the pain in her heart. But also her feelings for Tom, which had swept upon her—swept upon both of them—unaware. What she felt when she was with him. And how he represented everything human about her.

And now she had to make a choice.

Between Jackson and Tom. Between Angels and humanity.

The aircraft carrier towered behind the Battle Angel and the pilot, somehow cruelly beautiful against the red-tinged clouds, as Maddy drew in a breath.

# Acknowledgments

*Immortal City* and its sequel *Natural Born Angel* have been more than books; they have been an amazing journey with amazing people. I'd like to thank my incredible team: Brian, Claudia, and my editor Laura, as well as my film agents and managers Simon, Allen, Brian, and Susan. To my family and friends, thank you for your unwavering support and your patience. When the going gets tough, the tough get going.